P9-DCO-591

DISCARDED
Rye Public Library

RYE PUBLIC LIBRARY
581 WASHINGTON ROAD
RYE NH 03870-2318

Shut Your Eyes Tight

Also by John Verdon

Think of a Number

John Verdon

Shut your eyes Tight

A novel

Crown Publishers
NEW YORK

This is a work of fiction. Names, characters, places, and incidents either are the product of the author's imagination or are used fictitiously. Any resemblance to actual persons, living or dead, events, or locales is entirely coincidental.

Copyright © 2011 by John Verdon

All rights reserved.
Published in the United States by Crown Publishers,
an imprint of the Crown Publishing Group,
a division of Random House, Inc., New York.
www.crownpublishing.com

CROWN and the Crown colophon are
registered trademarks of Random House, Inc.

Library of Congress Cataloging-in-Publication Data
Verdon, John.
Shut your eyes tight / by John Verdon.—1st ed.
p.   cm.
1. Detectives—New York (State)—New York—Fiction.   I. Title.
PS3622.E736S57 2011
813'.6—dc22   2010053589

ISBN 978-0-307-71789-4
eISBN 978-0-307-71791-7

Printed in the United States of America

Book design by Lynne Amft
Jacket design by Superfantastic

10 9 8 7 6 5 4 3 2 1

First Edition

For Naomi

Shut Your Eyes Tight

Prologue

The perfect solution

He stood in front of the mirror and smiled with deep satisfaction at his own smiling reflection. He could not at that moment have been more pleased with himself, with his life, with his intelligence—no, it was more than that, more than mere intelligence. His mental status could more accurately be described as a profound understanding of everything. That was precisely what it was—a profound understanding of everything, an understanding that went far beyond the normal range of human wisdom. He watched the smile on his face in the mirror stretching wider at the aptness of the phrase, which he had italicized in his mind as he thought it. Internally he could feel—literally feel— the power of his insight into all things human. Externally, the course of events was proof of it.

First of all, to put it in the simplest terms, he had not been caught. Almost twenty-four hours had passed, almost to the minute now, and in that nearly complete revolution of the earth he had only grown safer. But that was predictable; he had taken care to ensure that there would be no trail to follow, no logic that could lead anyone to him. And in fact no one had come. No one had found him out. Therefore it was reasonable to conclude that his elimination of the presumptuous bitch had been a success in every way.

Everything had gone according to plan, smoothly, conclusively— yes, conclusively *was an excellent word for it. Everything occurred as anticipated, no stumbles, no surprises ... except for that sound. Cartilage? Must have been. What else?*

Such a minor thing, it made no sense that it would create such a lasting sensory impression. But perhaps the strength, the durability of the impression was simply the natural product of his preternatural sensitivity. Acuteness had its price.

Surely that snickety little crunch would one day be as faint in his memory as the image of all that blood, which was already beginning to fade. It was important to keep things in perspective, to remember that all things pass. Every ripple in the pond eventually subsides.

Part One

The Mexican
Gardener

Chapter 1

Life in the country

There was a stillness in the September-morning air that was like the stillness in the heart of a gliding submarine, engines extinguished to elude the enemy's listening devices. The whole landscape was held motionless in the invisible grip of a vast calm, the calm before a storm, a calm as deep and unpredictable as the ocean.

It had been a strangely subdued summer, the semi-drought slowly draining the life out of the grass and trees. Now the leaves were fading from green to tan and had already begun to drop silently from the branches of the maples and beeches, offering little prospect of a colorful autumn.

Dave Gurney stood just inside the French doors of his farm-style kitchen, looking out over the garden and the mowed lawn that separated the big house from the overgrown pasture that sloped down to the pond and the old red barn. He was vaguely uncomfortable and unfocused, his attention drifting between the asparagus patch at the end of the garden and the small yellow bulldozer beside the barn. He sipped sourly at his morning coffee, which was losing its warmth in the dry air.

To manure or not to manure—that was the asparagus question. Or at least it was the first question. If the answer turned out to be yes, that would raise a second question: bulk or bagged? Fertilizer, he had been informed by various websites to which he'd been directed by Madeleine, was the key to success with asparagus, but whether he needed to supplement last spring's application with a fresh load now was not entirely clear.

He'd been trying, at least halfheartedly, for their two years in the Catskills to immerse himself in these house-and-garden issues that Madeleine had taken up with instant enthusiasm, but always nibbling at his efforts were the disturbing termites of buyer's remorse—remorse not so much at the purchase of that specific house on its fifty scenic acres, which he continued to view as a good investment, but at the underlying life-changing decision to leave the NYPD and take his pension at the age of forty-six. The nagging question was, had he traded in his first-class detective's shield for the horticultural duties of a would-be country squire too soon?

Certain ominous events suggested that he had. Since relocating to their pastoral paradise, he had developed a transient tic in his left eyelid. To his chagrin and Madeleine's distress, he had started smoking again sporadically after fifteen years of abstinence. And, of course, there was the elephant in the room—his decision to involve himself the previous autumn, a year into his supposed retirement, in the horrific Mellery murder case.

He'd barely survived that experience, had even endangered Madeleine in the process, and in the moment of clarity that a close encounter with death often provides, he had for a while felt motivated to devote himself fully to the simple pleasures of their new rural life. But there's a funny thing about a crystal-clear image of the way you ought to live. If you don't actively hang on to it every day, the vision rapidly fades. A moment of grace is only a moment of grace. Unembraced, it soon becomes a kind of ghost, a pale retinal image receding out of reach like the memory of a dream, receding until it becomes eventually no more than a discordant note in the undertone of your life.

Understanding this process, Gurney discovered, does not provide a magic key to reversing it—with the result that a kind of halfheartedness was the best attitude toward the bucolic life that he could muster. It was an attitude that put him out of sync with his wife. It also made him wonder whether anyone could ever really change or, more to the point, whether *he* could ever change. In his darker moments, he was disheartened by the arthritic rigidity of his own way of thinking, his own way of *being*.

The bulldozer situation was a good example. He'd bought a small, old, used one six months earlier, describing it to Madeleine as a practical tool appropriate to their proprietorship of fifty acres of woods and meadows and a quarter-mile-long dirt driveway. He saw it as a means of making necessary landscaping repairs and positive improvements—a good and useful thing. She seemed to see it from the beginning, however, not as a vehicle promising his greater involvement in their new life but as a noisy, diesel-stinking symbol of his discontent—his dissatisfaction with their environment, his unhappiness with their move from the city to the mountains, his control freak's mania for bulldozing an unacceptable new world into the shape of his own brain. She'd articulated her objection only once, and briefly at that: "Why can't you just accept all this around us as a gift, an incredibly beautiful gift, and stop trying to *fix* it?"

As he stood at the glass doors, uncomfortably recalling her comment, hearing its gently exasperated tone in his mind's ear, her actual voice intruded from somewhere behind him.

"Any chance you'll get to my bike brakes before tomorrow?"

"I said I would." He took another sip of his coffee and winced. It was unpleasantly cold. He glanced at the old regulator clock over the pine sideboard. He had nearly an hour free before he had to leave to deliver one of his occasional guest lectures at the state police academy in Albany.

"You should come with me one of these days," she said, as though the idea had just occurred to her.

"I will," he said—his usual reply to her periodic suggestions that he join her on one of her bike rides through the rolling farmland and forest that constituted most of the western Catskills. He turned toward her. She was standing in the doorway of the dining area in worn tights, a baggy sweatshirt, and a paint-stained baseball hat. Suddenly he couldn't help smiling.

"What?" she said, cocking her head.

"Nothing." Sometimes her presence was so instantly charming that it emptied his mind of every tangled, negative thought. She was that rare creature: a very beautiful woman who seemed to care very little about how she looked. She came over and stood next to him, surveying the outdoors.

"The deer have been at the birdseed," she said, sounding more amused than annoyed.

Across the lawn three shepherd's-crook finch feeders had been tugged far out of plumb. Gazing at them, he realized that he shared, at least to some extent, Madeleine's benign feelings toward the deer and whatever minor damage they caused—which seemed peculiar, since his feelings were entirely different from hers concerning the depredations of the squirrels who even now were consuming the seed the deer had been unable to extract from the bottoms of the feeders. Twitchy, quick, aggressive in their movements, they seemed motivated by an obsessive rodent hunger, an avariciously concentrated desire to consume every available speck of food.

His smile evaporating, Gurney watched them with a low-level edginess that in his more objective moments he suspected was becoming his reflexive reaction to too many things—an edginess that arose from and highlighted the fault lines in his marriage. Madeleine would describe the squirrels as fascinating, clever, resourceful, awe-inspiring in their energy and determination. She seemed to love them as she loved most things in life. He, on the other hand, wanted to shoot them.

Well, not *shoot* them, exactly, not actually kill or maim them, but maybe thwack them with an air pistol hard enough to knock them off the finch feeders and send them fleeing into the woods where they belonged. Killing was not a solution that ever appealed to him. In all his years in the NYPD, in all his years as a homicide detective, in twenty-five years of dealing with violent men in a violent city, he had never drawn his gun, had hardly touched it outside a firing range, and he had no desire to start now. Whatever it was that had drawn him to police work, that had wed him to the job for so many years, it surely wasn't the appeal of a gun or the deceptively simple solution it offers.

He became aware that Madeleine was watching him with that curious, appraising look of hers—probably guessing from the tightness in his jaw his thoughts about the squirrels. In response to her apparent clairvoyance, he wanted to say something that would justify his hostility to the fluffy-tailed rats, but the ringing of the phone intervened—in fact, the ringing of two phones intervened simultaneously, the wired phone in the den and his own cell phone on the kitchen sideboard. Madeleine headed for the den. Gurney picked up the cell.

Chapter 2

The butchered bride

Jack Hardwick was a nasty, abrasive, watery-eyed cynic who drank too much and viewed just about everything in life as a sour joke. He had few enthusiastic admirers and did not readily inspire trust. Gurney was convinced that if all of Hardwick's questionable motives were removed, he wouldn't have any motives left.

But Gurney also considered him one of the smartest, most insightful detectives he'd ever worked with. So when he put the phone to his ear and heard that unmistakable sandpaper voice, it generated some mixed feelings.

"Davey boy!"

Gurney winced. He was not a Davey-boyish kind of guy, never would be, which he assumed was the precise reason Hardwick had chosen that particular sobriquet.

"What can I do for you, Jack?"

The man's braying laugh was as annoying and irrelevant as ever. "When we were working on the Mellery case, you used to brag about getting up with the chickens. Just thought I'd call and see if it was true."

There was a certain amount of banter one always had to endure before Hardwick would deign to get to the issue at hand.

"What do you want, Jack?"

"You got any actual live chickens on that farm of yours, running around clucking and shitting, or is that 'up with the chickens' just some kind of folksy saying?"

"What do you want, Jack?"

"Why the hell would I want anything? Can't one old buddy just call another old buddy for old times' sake?"

"Shove the 'old buddy' crap, Jack, and tell me why you're calling."

Again the braying laugh. "That's so cold, Gurney, so cold."

"Look. I haven't had my second cup of coffee yet. You don't get to the point in the next five seconds, I hang up. Five . . . four . . . three . . . two . . . one . . ."

"Debutante bride got whacked at her own wedding. Thought you might be interested."

"Why would I be interested in that?"

"Shit, how could an ace homicide detective not be interested? Did I say she got 'whacked'? Should've said 'hacked.' Murder weapon was a machete."

"The ace is retired."

There was a loud, prolonged bray.

"No joke, Jack. I'm really retired."

"Like you were when you leaped in to solve the Mellery case?"

"That was a temporary detour."

"Is that a fact?"

"Look, Jack . . ." Gurney was losing patience.

"Okay. You're retired. I got it. Now give me two minutes to explain the opportunity here."

"Jack, for the love of Christ . . ."

"Two lousy minutes. Two. You're so fucking busy massaging your retirement golf balls you can't spare your old partner two minutes?"

The image triggered the tiny tic in Gurney's eyelid. "We were never partners."

"How the hell can you say that?"

"We worked on a couple of cases together. We weren't *partners.*"

If he were to be completely honest about it, Gurney would have to admit that he and Hardwick did have, in at least one respect, a unique relationship. Ten years earlier, working in jurisdictions a hundred miles apart on different aspects of the same murder case, they had individually discovered separate halves of the victim's severed body. That sort of serendipity in detection can forge a strong, if bizarre, bond.

Hardwick lowered his voice into the sincere-pathetic register. "Do I get two minutes or don't I?"

Gurney gave up. "Go ahead."

Hardwick jumped back into his characteristic carnival-barker-with-throat-cancer oratorical style. "You're obviously a busy guy, so let me get right to it. I want to do you a giant favor." He paused. "You still there?"

"Talk faster."

"Ungrateful bastard! All right, here's what I got for you. Sensational murder committed four months ago. Spoiled little rich girl marries hotshot celebrity psychiatrist. An hour later at the wedding reception on the psychiatrist's fancy estate, his demented gardener decapitates her with a machete and escapes."

Gurney had a slight recollection of seeing a couple of tabloid headlines at that time that were probably related to the affair: BLISS TO BLOODBATH and NEW BRIDE BUTCHERED. He waited for Hardwick to go on. Instead the man coughed so disgustingly that Gurney had to hold the phone away from his ear.

Eventually Hardwick asked again, "You still there?"

"Yep."

"Quiet as a corpse. You ought to make little beeping sounds every ten seconds, let people know you're still alive."

"Jack, why the hell are you calling me?"

"I'm handing you the case of a lifetime."

"I'm not a cop anymore. You're not making any sense."

"Maybe your hearing is failing in your old age. What are you, forty-eight or eighty-eight? Listen up. Here's the meat of the story. The daughter of one of the richest neurosurgeons in the world marries a controversial hotshot psychiatrist, a psychiatrist who's appeared on *Oprah*, for Godsake. An hour later, in the midst of two hundred guests, she steps into the gardener's cottage. She's had a few drinks, wants the gardener to join in the wedding toast. When she doesn't come out, her new husband sends someone to get her, but the cottage door is locked and she doesn't answer. Then the husband, the renowned Dr. Scott Ashton, goes and bangs on the door and calls to her. No response. He gets a key, opens the door, and finds her sitting there in her wedding dress with her head chopped off—back window of the cottage open, no gardener in sight. Pretty soon every cop in the county is at the scene. In case you didn't get the message yet, these are very important people. Case ends up in our lap at BCI, specifically in my lap. Starts out simple—find the crazy gardener. Then it starts getting complicated. This was not your average gardener. The renowned Dr. Ashton had sort of taken him under his wing. Hector Flores—that's the gardener—was an undocumented Mexican laborer. Ashton hires him, soon realizes that the man is smart, very smart, so he starts testing him, pushing him, educating him. Over a period of two to three years, Hector becomes more like the doctor's protégé than his leaf raker. Almost a member of the family. Seems that with his new status, he even had an affair with the wife of one of Ashton's neighbors. Interesting character, Señor Flores. After the murder he disappears off the face of the earth, along with the neighbor's wife. Last concrete trace of Hector is the bloody machete he left a hundred and fifty yards away in the woods."

"So where did all this end up?"

"Nowhere."

"What do you mean?"

"My brilliant captain had a certain view of the case—you might recall Rod Rodriguez?"

Gurney recalled him with a shudder. Ten months earlier—six months before the murder Hardwick was describing—Gurney had been involved semiofficially in an investigation controlled by a unit of the State Police Bureau of Criminal Investigation that the rigid, ambitious Rodriguez commanded.

"His view was that we should bring in for questioning every Mexican within twenty miles of the crime and threaten them with all kinds of crap until one of them led us to Hector Flores, and if that didn't work, we should extend the radius to fifty miles. That's where he wanted all the resources—one hundred percent."

"You didn't agree with that?"

"There were other avenues worth exploring. It's possible Hector was not what he appeared to be. The whole thing had a funny feel to it."

"So what happened?"

"I told Rodriguez he was full of shit."

"Really?" Gurney smiled for the first time.

"Yeah, really. So I was taken off the case. And it was given to Blatt."

"Blatt!?" The name tasted like a mouthful of food gone bad. He remembered Investigator Arlo Blatt as the only BCI detective more irritating than Rodriguez. Blatt embodied an attitude Gurney's favorite college professor long ago had described as "ignorance armed and ready for battle."

Hardwick went on. "So Blatt did exactly what Rodriguez told him to do, and he got nowhere. Four months have passed, and we know less today than when we started. But I can tell you're wondering, what's all this got to do with Dave Gurney?"

"The question did cross my mind."

"The mother of the bride is not satisfied. She suspects that the investigation's been botched. She has no confidence in Rodriguez, she thinks Blatt's an idiot. But she thinks you're a genius."

"She thinks what?"

"She came to me last week—four months to the day after the murder, wondering if I could get back on the case or, if I couldn't do that, could I work on it without anybody knowing. I told her that wouldn't be a practical approach, my hands were tied, I was already on pretty thin ice with the bureau—however, I did happen to have personal access to the most highly decorated detective in the history of the NYPD, recently retired, still full of vim and vigor, a man who would be more than happy to provide her with an alternative to the Rodriguez-Blatt approach. To put the icing on the cake, I just happened to have a copy of that adoring little piece that *New York* magazine did on you after you cracked the Satanic Santa case. What was it they called you—Supercop? She was impressed."

Gurney grimaced. Several possible responses collided in his head, all canceling each other out.

Hardwick seemed encouraged by his silence. "She'd love to meet you. Oh, did I mention? She's drop-dead gorgeous, early forties but looks about thirty-two. And she made it clear that money wasn't an issue. You could pretty much name your price. Seriously—two hundred dollars an hour would not be a problem. Not that you'd be motivated by anything as common as money."

"Speaking of motives, what's in it for you?"

Hardwick's effort to sound innocent instead sounded comical. "Seeing justice done? Helping out a family that's been through hell? I mean, losing a child's got to be the worst thing in the world, right?"

Gurney froze. The mention of losing a child still had the power to send a tremor through his heart. It was more than fifteen years since Danny, barely four at the time, had stepped into the street when Gurney wasn't looking, but grief, he'd discovered, was not an experience you went through once and then "moved on" (as the idiotic popular phrase would have it). The truth was that it came over you in successive waves—waves separated by periods of numbness, periods of forgetfulness, periods of ordinary living.

"You still there?"

Gurney grunted.

Hardwick went on. "I want to do what I can for these people. Besides—"

"Besides," Gurney broke in, speaking fast, forcing his debilitating emotion aside, "if I did get involved, which I have no intention of doing, it would drive Rodriguez batshit, wouldn't it? And if I managed to come up with something, something new, something significant, it would make him and Blatt look really bad, wouldn't it? Might that be one of your perfectly good reasons?"

Hardwick cleared his throat again. "That's a fucked-up way of looking at it. Fact is, we got a tragically bereaved mother here who isn't satisfied with the progress of the police investigation—which I can understand, since the incompetent Arlo Blatt and his crew have rousted every Mexican in the county and haven't come up with so much as a taco fart. She's desperate for a real detective. So I'm laying this golden egg in your lap."

"That's great, Jack, but I'm not in the PI business."

"For the love of God, Davey, just talk to her. That's all I'm asking you to do. Just talk to her. She's lonely, vulnerable, beautiful, with big bucks to burn. And deep down inside, Davey boy, deep down inside there's something wild in that woman. I guarantee it. Cross my heart and hope to die!"

"Jack, the last thing I need right now——"

"Yeah, yeah, yeah, you're happily married, in love with your wife, yadda, yadda, yadda. All right. Fine. And maybe you don't care about a chance to reveal Rod Rodriguez finally and absolutely as the total asshole he really is. Okay. But this case is *complex.*" He gave the word a depth of meaning, made it sound like the most precious of all characteristics. "It's got *layers* to it, Davey. It's a fucking onion."

"So?"

"You're a natural-born onion peeler—the best that ever was."

Chapter 3

Elliptical orbits

When Gurney finally noticed Madeleine at the den door, he wasn't sure how long she'd been standing there, nor even how long he himself had been at the den window facing the back pasture that ran up toward the wooded ridge behind the house. To save his life, he could not have described the pasture's current pattern of blazing goldenrod, browning grasses, and wild blue asters at which he had appeared to be gazing, but he could have come very close to reciting Hardwick's telephone narrative word for word.

"So?" said Madeleine.

"So?" he repeated, as though he hadn't understood the question.

She smiled impatiently.

"That was Jack Hardwick." He was about to ask if she remembered Jack Hardwick, chief investigator on the Mellery case, when the look in her eyes told him he didn't need to ask. It was the look she got whenever a name came up that was associated with that terrible chain of murders.

She stared at him, waiting, unblinking.

"He wants my advice."

Still she waited.

"He wants me to speak to the mother of a girl who was killed. She was killed on her wedding day." He was about to say how she was killed, describe the peculiar details, but realized that would be a mistake.

Madeleine nodded almost imperceptibly.

"You all right?" he asked.

"I'd been wondering how long it would take."

"How long . . . ?"

"For you to find another . . . situation that required your attention."

"All I'm going to do is talk to her."

"Right. And then, after a nice long talk, you'll conclude that there's nothing especially interesting about a woman being killed on her wedding day, and you'll yawn and walk away. Is that the way you see it?"

His voice tightened reflexively. "I don't know enough yet to see it in any particular way."

She gave him her patented skeptical smile. "I have to go," she said. Then, seeming to notice the question in his eyes, she added, "The clinic, remember? See you back here tonight." And she was gone.

At first he just stared at the empty doorway. Then he thought he should go after her, started to do so, got as far as the middle of the kitchen, stopped, and wondered what he would say, had no idea, thought he should go after her anyway, went out the side door by the garden. But by the time he got around to the front of the house, her car was halfway down the rough little farm lane that bisected the low pasture. He wondered if she saw him in her rearview mirror, wondered if it made a difference that he'd come out after her.

In recent months he'd imagined that things were going pretty well. The raw emotion at the end of the Mellery nightmare had evolved into an imperfect peace. He and Madeleine had slipped smoothly, gradually, mostly unconsciously into affectionate or at least tolerant patterns of behavior that resembled separate elliptical orbits. While he gave his occasional lectures at the state police academy, she had accepted a part-time position in the local mental-health clinic, doing intakes and assessments. It was a function for which her LCSW credentials and experience clearly overqualified her, but it seemed to have provided a sense of balance in their marriage, a relief from the pressure of their unrealistic expectations of each other. Or was that just wishful thinking?

Wishful thinking. The universal anodyne.

He stood in the matted, drought-wilted grass and watched her car disappear behind the barn onto the narrow town road. His feet were cold. He looked down and discovered he had come outside in his socks, which were now absorbing the morning dew. As he turned to go back into the house, a movement by the barn caught his eye.

A lone coyote had emerged from the woods and was loping across the clearing between the barn and the pond. Partway across, the animal stopped, turning its head toward Gurney, and studied him for a long ten seconds. It was an intelligent look, thought Gurney. A look of pure, unemotional calculation.

Chapter 4

The art of deception

"What goal is common to every undercover assignment?" Gurney's question was greeted by various expressions of interest and confusion on the thirty-nine faces in the academy classroom. Most guest instructors started their lectures by introducing themselves and giving their résumé highlights, then presented an outline of the subjects to be covered, content and objectives, blah, blah, blah—a general overview to which no one paid much attention. Gurney preferred a cut-to-the-chase approach, particularly for a seminar group like this, made up of experienced officers. And they'd know who he was, anyway. He had a definite reputation in law-enforcement circles. Professionally, the reputation was about as good as it gets in that world, and since his retirement from the NYPD two years earlier, it had only gotten better—if being regarded with increasing levels of respect, awe, envy, and resentment could be considered "better." Personally, he wished he had no reputation at all, no image to live up to. Or fall short of.

"Think about it," he said with quiet intensity, making eye contact with as many people in the room as he could. "What's the one thing you need to achieve in every undercover situation? This is an important question. I'd like to get a response from each of you."

A hand went up in the front row. The face, set atop a hulking offensive lineman's body, was young and baffled. "Wouldn't the goal be different in every case?"

"The *situation* would be different," said Gurney, nodding agreeably. "The people would be different. The risks and rewards would be different. The depth and duration of your immersion in the environment would be different. The persona you project, your cover story, could be very different. The nature of the intelligence or evidence to be acquired would vary from case to case. There are definitely lots of differences. But"—he paused, again making as much eye contact as possible before continuing with rising emphasis—"there's one goal common to every assignment. It's your primary goal as an undercover officer. Your success in achieving every other goal of an operation hangs on your success in achieving this primary goal. Your life depends on it. Tell me what you think it is."

For nearly half a minute, there was absolute silence, the only movement the formation of thoughtful frowns. Waiting for the replies he knew would eventually come, Gurney glanced around at his physical surroundings—the concrete-block walls with their matte beige paint; the vinyl-tile floor whose brown-and-tan pattern was indistinguishable from the scuff marks that obscured it; the rows of long, speckled-gray Formica tables, shabby with age, serving as shared desks; the stark orange plastic chairs with tubular chrome legs, too small for their large and muscular occupants, their brightness oddly depressing. A time capsule of mid-seventies architectural awfulness, the room created a bleak echo of his last city precinct.

"Gathering accurate information?" offered a questioning face in the second row.

"A reasonable guess," said Gurney encouragingly. "Anyone have any other ideas?"

Half a dozen suggestions followed rapidly, mostly from the front of the room, mostly variations on the accurate-information theme.

"Any other ideas?" Gurney prodded.

"Goal is to get the bad guys off the street," came a comment in a weary growl from the back row.

"Prevent crime," said another.

"Get the truth, the whole truth, the facts, names, find out what's going down, who's doing what to who, what the plan is, who's the man, who sits on top of the food chain, follow the money, shit like that. Basically, you want to know everything there is to be known— it's that simple." The dark, wiry man who rattled off this litany of goals with his arms folded across his chest was sitting directly in front of where Gurney was standing. His smirk announced that there was no more to be said on the subject. The name on the tent card nearest him on the long table read "Det. Falcone."

"Any other ideas?" asked Gurney blandly, scanning the far corners of the room. The wiry man looked disgusted.

After a long pause, one of the three women attendees spoke up in a low but confident Hispanic-accented voice. "Establish and maintain trust."

"What was that?" The question came from three different directions at once.

"Establish and maintain trust," she repeated, a bit louder.

"Interesting," said Gurney. "What makes that the most important goal?"

She gave a little shrug as though the answer were the most obvious thing on earth. "Because if you don't have their trust, you have nothing."

Gurney smiled. " 'If you don't have their trust, you have nothing.' Very good. Anybody disagree with that?"

Nobody did.

"Of course we want the truth," said Gurney. "The whole truth, with all the incriminating details, just like Detective Falcone here said."

The man eyed him coldly.

Gurney went on, "But as this other officer said—without trust what do you have? You have nothing. Maybe worse than nothing. So trust comes first—always. Put trust first, you've got a good chance of getting the truth. Put getting the truth first, you've got a good chance of getting a bullet in the back of the head."

That got some nods, plus some increased attention.

"Which brings us to the second big question for today. *How do you do it?* How do you go about establishing the level of trust that will not only keep you alive but also make your undercover work pay off?" Gurney felt himself warming to the subject. As his energy level rose, he could see it starting to spread out into his audience.

"Remember, in this game you're dealing with naturally suspicious people. Some of these guys are very impulsive. Not only might they shoot you on the spot, but they'd also be proud of it. They like looking bad. They like looking sharp, quick, decisive. How do you get guys like that to trust you? How do you survive long enough to make the operation worthwhile?"

This time the responses came quicker.

"By acting and behaving like they do."

"By acting exactly like whoever you're supposed to be."

"Consistency. Stick to your cover identity, no matter what."

"Believe the identity. Believe that you really are who you say you are."

"Stay cool, always cool, no sweat. Show no fear."

"Courage."

"Brass balls."

"Believe your own truth, baby. I am who I am. I am invincible. Untouchable. Do not fuck with me."

"Yeah, make believe you're Al Pacino," said Falcone, looking for a laugh, not getting it, just creating a hiccup in the group momentum.

Gurney ignored him, glanced inquiringly at the Hispanic woman.

She hesitated. "You have to show them some passion."

This triggered a few wiseass laughs around the room and a leering grin from Falcone.

"Grow up, assholes," she said calmly. "What I mean is, you have to let them see something *real* in you. Something they can feel, that they know in their gut is true. It can't all be bullshit."

Gurney felt a pleasant rush of excitement—his reaction whenever he recognized a star student in one of his classes. It was an experience that reinforced his decision to participate as a guest lecturer in these seminars.

" 'It can't all be bullshit,' " he repeated, in a voice loud enough for everyone to hear. "Absolutely true. *Authentic emotion—credible passion—is essential to effective deception.* Your undercover persona must be based on a real emotional piece of yourself. Otherwise it's all posing, all imitation, all fake, all bullshit. And superficial bullshit rarely works. Superficial bullshit gets undercover people killed."

He did a quick survey of the thirty-nine faces and found he now had the positive attention of at least thirty-five. "So it's all about trust. Credibility. The more your target believes in you, the more you'll get out of him. And a big part of his belief in you depends on your ability to channel real emotion into your artificial role, to use a real piece of yourself to bring your cover personality to life—real anger, rage, greed, lust, disgust—whatever the moment calls for."

He turned away from them, ostensibly to insert an old VHS videotape into a player beneath a large monitor set against the front wall and to check that everything was plugged in. When he turned back, however, his expression—in fact, the whole attitude of his body, the way he moved, the impression he gave of a man struggling to stifle a volcano of rage—sent a shock wave of tension through the classroom.

"You gonna get some crazy motherfucker to buy your act, you better find a sick place in you, then you talk to him from that place, you let that crazy motherfucker know that deep down inside you there's an even crazier motherfucker who someday is gonna tear some motherfucker's heart out, chew it up, and spit it in his fucking face. But for now, just for now, you're keeping that rabid dog in your gut under control. Just barely under control." He took a sudden step toward the first row and noted with satisfaction that everyone, including Falcone—especially Falcone—jerked back into a position of defensive readiness.

"Okay," said Gurney with a reassuring smile, resuming his normal demeanor, "that's just a quick example of the emotional side. Credible passion. Most of you had a gut-level reaction to that anger, that lunacy. Your first thought was that it was real, that this Gurney guy's got a screw loose, right?"

There were some nods, a few nervous laughs, as the body language in the room relaxed about halfway.

"So what are you saying?" asked Falcone edgily. "That somewhere inside you there's a fucking lunatic?"

"I'll leave that question open for now."

There were a few more laughs, friendlier.

"But the fact is, there's more shit, nasty shit, inside each of us—all of us—than we realize. Don't let it go to waste. Find it and use it. In the undercover life, the shit you normally don't want to look at in yourself could be your biggest asset. The buried treasure that saves your life."

There were personal examples he could have given them, situations in which he had taken a dark tile from the mosaic of his childhood and magnified it into a hellish mural that fooled some very perceptive antagonists. In fact, the single most compelling example of the process had occurred at the end of the Mellery case, less than a year earlier. But he wasn't about to go into that now. It was attached to some unresolved issues in his life he didn't feel like stirring up, not now, not for a seminar. Besides, it wasn't necessary. He had the feeling his students were already with him. Their minds were more open. They'd stopped debating. They were thinking, wondering, receptive.

"Okay, like I said, that was the emotional part. Now I want to take you to the next level—the level where your brains and emotions come together and make you the best undercover operative you can be, not just a guy with a stupid hat and baggy pants falling off his ass trying to look like a crack addict."

A few smiles, shrugs, maybe a defensive frown here and there.

"Now—I want you to ask yourselves a strange question. I want you to ask yourself why you believe the things you believe. *Why do I believe anything?*"

Before they had time to get lost in, or put off by, the abstract depths of this line of inquiry, he punched the "play" button on the videotape machine. As the first image appeared, he said, "While you're watching the video clip, keep that question in the back of your mind: *Why do I believe anything?*"

Chapter 5

The eureka fallacy

It was a famous scene from a famous movie, but as Gurney scanned the faces in the room, he saw no sign that anyone recognized it. In the scene, an older man is interrogating a younger man.

The young man is eager to work for the Irgun, a radical organization fighting to establish a Jewish homeland in Palestine at the end of World War II. He presents himself boastfully as a demolitions expert, seasoned in combat, who acquired his expertise with dynamite by fighting the Nazis in the Warsaw Ghetto. He claims that after killing many Nazis he was captured and imprisoned in the Auschwitz concentration camp, where he was assigned to a routine cleaning job.

The older man wants to know more. He asks him several specific questions about his story, the camp, his duties.

The young man's version of events begins to fall apart when the interrogator reveals that there was no dynamite available in the Warsaw Ghetto. As his heroic narrative crumbles, he's forced to admit that he learned what he knows about dynamite from his real job in the camp, which was blasting holes in the ground big enough to hold the thousands of bodies of his fellow prisoners, being killed each day in the gas chambers. Beyond that, the older man makes him admit, even more degradingly, that his other job was picking the gold fillings out of the mouths of the corpses. And finally, collapsing in tears of rage and shame, the young man admits that his captors repeatedly raped him.

The raw truth is exposed—along with his desperation to redeem himself. The scene concludes with his induction into the Irgun.

Gurney switched off the tape player.

"So," he said, turning to the thirty-nine faces, "what was that all about?"

"Every interview should be that simple," said Falcone dismissively.

"And that fast," someone chimed in from the back row.

Gurney nodded. "Things in movies always seem simpler and faster than real life. But something happens in that scene that's very interesting. When you remember it a week or a month from now, what aspect do you think will stick with you?"

"The kid getting raped," said a broad-shouldered guy next to Falcone.

Murmurs of agreement spread around the room, encouraging other people to speak up.

"His breakdown in the interrogation."

"Yeah, the whole macho thing evaporating."

"It's funny," said the only black woman. "He starts out by telling lies about himself to get what he wants, but he ends up getting it—getting into the Irgun—by finally telling the truth. By the way, what the hell is the Irgun?"

That got the biggest laugh of the day.

"Okay," said Gurney. "Let's stop there and take a closer look. The naïve young guy wants to get into the organization. He tells a lot of lies to make himself look good. The smart old guy sees through it, calls him on his bullshit, drags the truth out of him. And it just so happens that the awfulness of the truth makes the kid an ideal psychological candidate for the fanatical Irgun. So they let him join. Is that a fair summary of what we just saw?"

There were various nods and grunts of agreement, some more cautious than others.

"Anyone think that's not what we saw?"

Gurney's Hispanic star looked troubled, which made him grin, which seemed to give her the nudge she needed. "I'm not saying that's not what I saw. It's a movie, I know, and in the movie what you said is probably true. But if that was real—you know, a real inter-view video—it might not be true."

"The fuck is that supposed to mean?" someone whispered, not quite softly enough.

"I'll tell you what the fuck it's supposed to mean," she said, sparking to the challenge. "It means there's no proof at all that the old guy actually got to the truth. So the young guy breaks down and cries and says he got fucked in the ass, excuse my language. 'Boo-hoo, boo-hoo, I'm no big hero after all, just a pathetic little pussycat that gave the Nazis blow jobs.' So how do we know *that* story isn't just *more* bullshit? Maybe the pussycat is smarter than he looks."

Christ, thought Gurney, *she did it again.* He decided to step into the speculative silence that followed her impressive exposition. "Which brings us to the question we started with," he said. *"Why do we believe what we believe?* As this perceptive officer here just pointed out, the interrogator in that scene may not have gotten to the truth at all. The question is, what made him think that he did?"

This new twist produced a number of reactions.

"Sometimes your gut tells you what's what, you know?"

"Maybe the breakdown the kid had looked legit to him. Maybe you had to be there, catch the attitude."

"Real world, the interrogator would know more stuff than he's putting on the table. Could be the kid's confession squares with some of that stuff, confirms it."

Other officers offered variations on these themes. Others said nothing but listened intently to every word. A few, like Falcone, looked as if the question was making their heads hurt.

When the flow of replies seemed to be stopping, Gurney stepped in with another question. "Do you think a tough-minded interroga-tor could be misled once in a while by his own wishful thinking?"

A few nods, a few affirmative grunts, a few expressions of pained indecision or maybe plain indigestion.

A guy at the far end of the second row, with a fire-hydrant neck emerging from a black T-shirt, along with densely tattooed Popeye forearms, a shaved head, and tiny eyes—eyes that looked like they were being forced shut by the muscles in his cheeks—raised his hand. The fingers were curled almost into a fist. The voice was slow, deliberate, thoughtful. "You asking, do we sometimes believe what we want to believe?"

"That's pretty much what I'm asking," said Gurney. "What do you think?"

The squinty eyes opened a little. "I think that's . . . right. That's human nature." He cleared his throat. "I'll speak for myself. I've made mistakes because of that . . . factor. Not because I so much want to believe good things about people. I've been on the job awhile, don't have a lot of illusions about people's motives, what they're willing to do." He bared his teeth in apparent revulsion at some passing image. "I've seen my share of hideous shit. Lot of people in this room have seen the same shit. What I'm saying, though, is that sometimes I get an idea about the way something is, and I may not even know how much I want that idea to be right. Like, *I know what went down*, or *I know* exactly how some scumbag thinks. *I know* why he did what he did. Except sometimes—not often, but definitely sometimes—I don't know shit, I just think I do. In fact, I'm positive I do. It's like an occupational hazard." He fell silent, gave the impression that he was considering the bleak implications of what he'd said.

Once again, for perhaps the thousandth time in his life, Gurney was reminded that his first impressions were not especially reliable.

"Thank you, Detective Beltzer," he said to the big man, glancing at his ID tag. "That was very good." He scanned the faces along the rows of tables and saw no signs of disagreement. Even Falcone seemed subdued.

Gurney took a minute to extract a mint from a little tin box and pop it into his mouth. Mostly he was stalling to let Beltzer's comments resonate before going on.

"In the scene we watched," said Gurney with new animation, "that interrogator might *want* to believe in the validity of the young man's breakdown for a number of reasons. Name one." He pointed randomly at an officer who hadn't yet spoken.

The man blinked, looked embarrassed. Gurney waited.

"I guess . . . I guess he might like the idea that he broke the kid's story . . . you know, that he succeeded in the interrogation."

"Absolutely," said Gurney. He caught the eye of another previously silent attendee. "Name one more."

The very Irish face beneath a carroty crew cut grinned. "Thought he'd win a few points, maybe. Must report to somebody. Enjoy walking into the boss's office. 'Look at what I did.' Get some props. Maybe a boost for a promotion."

"Sure, I can see that," said Gurney. "Can anyone name another reason he might want to believe the kid's story?"

"Power," said the young Hispanic woman disdainfully.

"How so?"

"He'd like the idea that he forced the truth out of the subject, forced him to admit painful things, forced him to give up what he was trying to hide, forced him to expose his shame, made him crawl, even made him cry." She looked like she was smelling garbage. "He'd get a rush out of it, feel like Superman, the all-powerful genius detective. Like God."

"Big emotional benefit," said Gurney. "Could warp a man's vision."

"Oh, yeah," she agreed. "Big time."

Gurney saw a hand go up in the back of the room, a brown-faced man with short, wavy hair who hadn't yet spoken. "Excuse me, sir, I'm confused. There's an interrogation-techniques seminar here in this building and an undercover seminar. Two separate seminars, right? I signed up for undercover. Am I in the right place? This, what I'm hearing, it's all about interrogation."

"You're in the right place," said Gurney. "We're here to talk about undercover, but there's a link between the two activities. If you understand how an interrogator can fool himself because of what he wants to believe, you can use the same principle to get the target of your undercover operation to believe in you. It's all about maneuvering the target into 'discovering' the facts about you that you want him to believe. It's about giving him a powerful motive to swallow your bullshit. It's about making him *want* to believe you—just like the guy in the movie *wants* to believe the confession. There's tremendous believability to facts a person thinks he's discovered. When your target believes that he knows things about you *that you didn't want him to know,* those things will seem doubly true to him. When he thinks he's penetrated below your surface layer, what he uncovers in that deeper layer he'll see as the *real* truth. That's what I call the eureka fallacy. It's that peculiar trick of the mind that gives total credibility to what you think you've discovered on your own."

"The *what* fallacy?" The question came from multiple directions.

"The *eureka* fallacy. It's a Greek word roughly translated as 'I found it' or, in the context in which I'm using it, 'I've discovered the truth.' The point is . . ." Gurney slowed down to emphasize his next statement. *"The stories people tell you about themselves seem to retain the possibility of being false. But what you discover about them by yourself seems to be the truth.* So what I'm saying is this: Let your target think he's discovering something about you. Then he'll feel that he really knows you. That's the place at which you will have established Trust. You will have established Trust, with a capital *T,* the trust that makes everything else possible. We're going to spend the rest of the day showing you how to make that happen—how to make the thing you want your target to believe about you the very thing he thinks he's discovering on his own. But right now let's take a break."

Saying this, Gurney realized that he'd grown up in an era when "a break" automatically meant a cigarette break. Now, for virtually everyone, it meant a cell-phoning or texting break. As if to illustrate the thought, most of the officers getting to their feet and heading for the door were reaching for their BlackBerrys.

Gurney took a deep breath, extended his arms above his head, and stretched his back slowly from side to side. His introductory segment had created more muscle tension than he'd realized.

The female Hispanic officer waited for the tide of cell phoners to pass, then approached Gurney as he was removing the videotape from the machine. Her hair was thick and framed her face in a mass of soft, kinky curls. Her full figure was packed into a pair of tight black jeans and a tight gray sweater with a swooping neckline. Her lips glistened. "I just wanted to thank you," she said with a serious-student frown. "That was really good."

"The tape, you mean?"

"No, I mean you. I mean . . . what I mean is"—she was incongruously blushing under her serious demeanor—"your whole presentation, your explanation of why people believe things, why they believe some things more strongly, all of that. Like that *eureka fallacy* thing—that really made me think. The whole presentation was really good."

"Your own contributions helped make it good."

She smiled. "I guess we're just on the same wavelength."

Chapter 6

Home

B y the time Gurney was nearing the end of his two-hour drive from the academy in Albany to his farmhouse in Walnut Crossing, dusk was settling stealthily into the winding valleys of the western Catskills.

As he turned off the county road onto the dirt-and-gravel lane that led up to his hilltop property, the jazzed illusion of energy he'd received from two large containers of strong coffee during the afternoon seminar break was now sinking deep into its inversion phase. The fading day generated an overwrought image that he assumed was the product of caffeine withdrawal: summer sidling off the stage like an aging actor while autumn, the undertaker, waited in the wings.

Christ, my brain is turning to mush.

He parked the car as usual on the worn patch of weedy grass at the top of the pasture, parallel to the house, facing a deep rose-and-purple swath of sunset clouds beyond the far ridge.

He entered the house through the side door, kicked off his shoes in the room that served as a laundry and pantry, and continued into the kitchen. Madeleine was on her knees in front of the sink, brushing shards of a broken wineglass into a dustpan. He stood watching her for several seconds before speaking. "What happened?"

"What does it look like?"

He let a few more seconds pass. "How are things at the clinic?"

"Okay, I guess." She stood, smiled gamely, walked over to the pantry, and emptied the dustpan noisily into the plastic trash barrel. He walked to the French doors and stared out at the monochrome landscape, at the large pile of logs by the woodshed waiting to be split and stacked, the grass that needed its final mowing of the season, the ferny asparagus ready to be cut down for the winter—cut and then burned to avoid the risk of asparagus beetles.

Madeleine came back into the kitchen, switched on the recessed lights in the ceiling over the sideboard, replaced the dustpan under the sink. The increased illumination in the room had the effect of further darkening the outside world, turning the glass doors into reflectors.

"I left some salmon on the stove," she said, "and some rice."

"Thank you." He watched her in the glass pane. She seemed to be gazing into the dishwater in the sink. He remembered her saying something about going out that night, and he decided to risk a guess. "Book-club night."

She smiled. He wasn't sure whether it was because he'd gotten it right or wrong.

"How was the academy?" she asked.

"Not bad. A mixed bag of attendees—all the basic types. There's always the cautious group—the ones who wait and watch, who believe in saying as little as possible. The utilitarians, the ones who want to know exactly how they can *use* every fact you give them. The minimizers who want to know as little as possible, get involved as little as possible, do as little as possible. The cynics who want to prove that any idea that didn't occur first to them is bullshit. And, of course, the 'positives'—probably the best name for them—the ones who want to learn as much as they can, see more clearly, become better cops." He felt comfortable talking, wanted to go on, but she was studying the dishwater again. "So . . . yeah," he concluded, "it was an okay day. The 'positives' made it . . . interesting."

"Men or women?"

"What?"

She lifted the spatula out of the water, frowning at it as though noticing for the first time how dull and scratched it was. "The 'positives'—were they men or women?"

It was curious how guilty he could feel when, really, there was nothing to feel guilty about. "Men *and* women," he replied.

She held the spatula up closer to the light, wrinkled her nose in disapproval, and tossed it into the garbage receptacle under the sink.

"Look," he said. "About this morning. This business with Jack Hardwick. I think we need to start that discussion over again."

"You're meeting with the victim's mother. What is there to discuss?"

"There are good reasons to meet with her," he pressed on blindly. "And there may be some good reasons not to."

"A very intelligent way of looking at it." She seemed coolly amused. Or, at least, in an ironical mood. "Can't talk about it right now, though. Don't want to be late. For my book club."

He heard a subtle emphasis on that last phrase—just enough, perhaps, to let him know she knew that he'd guessed. A remarkable woman, he thought. And despite his anxiety and exhaustion, he couldn't help smiling.

Chapter 7

Val Perry

As usual, Madeleine was first up the next morning.

Gurney awoke to the hiss and gurgle of the coffee-maker—along with the sinking realization that he'd forgotten to fix her bicycle brakes.

Hard upon that pang came a sense of uneasiness about his plan to meet later that morning with Val Perry. Although he'd emphasized to Jack Hardwick that his willingness to talk to her did not imply any further commitment—that the meeting was primarily a gesture of courtesy and condolence to someone who'd suffered a dreadful loss—a cloud of second thoughts was descending on him. Pushing them aside as best he could, he showered, dressed, and strode purposefully out through the kitchen to the pantry, mumbling good morning to Madeleine, who was sitting in her customary position at the breakfast table with a slice of toast in her hand and a book propped open in front of her. Slipping into his canvas barn jacket that he removed from its hook in the pantry, he went out the side door and headed for the tractor shed that housed their bicycles and kayaks. The sun had not yet appeared, and the morning was surprisingly raw for early September.

He rolled Madeleine's bicycle out from behind the tractor into the light at the front of the open shed. The aluminum frame was shockingly cold. The two small wrenches he chose from the set on the shed wall were just as cold.

Cursing, twice banging his knuckles against the sharp edges of the front forks, the second time drawing blood, he adjusted the cables that controlled the position of the brake pads. Creating the proper clearance—allowing the wheel to move freely when the brake was disengaged, yet providing adequate pressure against the rim when the brake was applied—was a trial-and-error process that he had to repeat four times to get right. Finally, with more relief than satisfaction, he declared the job done, replaced the wrenches, and headed back to the house, one hand numb and the other aching.

Passing the woodshed and the adjacent pile of logs made him wonder for the tenth time in as many days, should he rent a wood-splitter or buy one? There were disadvantages either way. The sun was still not up, but the squirrels were already engaged in their morning attack on the bird feeders, raising another question that seemed to have no happy answer. And, of course, there was the matter of the manure for the asparagus.

He went into the kitchen and ran warm water over his hands.

As the stinging subsided, he announced, "Your brakes are fixed."

"Thank you," said Madeleine cheerily without looking up from her book.

Half an hour later—resembling a paint-by-numbers sunset in her lavender fleece pants, pink Windbreaker, red gloves, and an orange wool hat pulled down over her ears—she went out to the shed, mounted her bike, rode slowly and bumpily down the pasture path, and disappeared onto the town road beyond the barn.

Gurney spent the next hour on a mental review of the facts of the crime as they had been related to him by Hardwick. Each time he went over the scenario, he was increasingly troubled by its theatricality, its almost-operatic excess.

At 9:00 A.M. exactly, the time appointed for his meeting with Val Perry, he went to the window to see if she might be coming up the road.

Think of the devil and the devil arrives. In this case at the wheel of a Turbo Porsche in racing green—a model Gurney thought sold for around $160,000. The sleek vehicle crept past the barn, past the pond, slowly up the pasture hillside, to the small parking area next to the house, its hugely powerful engine purring softly. With a mixture of cautious curiosity and a bit more excitement than he'd want to admit, Gurney went out to greet his guest.

The woman who emerged from the car was tall and curvaceously slim, wearing a satiny cream blouse and satiny black pants. Her shoulder-length black hair was cut in a straight bob across her fore-head like Uma Thurman's in *Pulp Fiction*. She was, as Hardwick had promised, "drop-dead gorgeous." But there was something more—a tension in her as striking as her looks.

She took in her surroundings with a few appraising glances that seemed to absorb everything and reveal nothing. *An ingrained habit of circumspection*, thought Gurney.

She walked toward him with the hint of a grimace—or was it the customary set of her mouth?

"Mr. Gurney, Val Perry. I appreciate your making time for me," she said, extending her hand. "Or should I call you Detective Gurney?"

"I left the title in the city when I retired. Call me Dave." They shook hands. The intensity of her gaze and strength of her grip sur-prised him. "Would you like to come inside?"

She hesitated, glancing around the garden and the small blue-stone patio. "Can we sit out here?"

The question surprised him. Even though the sun was now well above the eastern ridge in a cloudless sky and most of the dew was gone from the grass, the morning was still chilly.

"Seasonal affective disorder," she said with an explanatory smile. "Do you know what that is?"

"Yes." He returned her smile. "I think I have a mild case of it myself."

"I have more than a mild case. From this time of year on, I need as much light, preferably sun, as possible. Or I really do want to kill myself. So if you don't mind, Dave, perhaps we could sit out here?" It wasn't really a question.

The detective part of his brain, dominant and hardwired, un-affected by the technicality of retirement, wondered about her seasonal-disorder story, wondered if there was another reason. *An eccentric control need, a desire to make others conform to her whims? A desire, for whatever reason, to keep him off balance? Neurotic claus-trophobia? An effort to minimize the risk of being recorded? And if being recorded was a worry, did it have a practical or paranoid basis?*

He led her to the patio that separated the French doors from the asparagus bed. He indicated a couple of folding chairs on either side of a small café table Madeleine had purchased at an auction. "Is this all right?"

"It's fine," she said, pulling one of the chairs out from the table and sitting on it without bothering to brush off the seat.

No concern about ruining her obviously pricey slacks. Ditto the ecru leather handbag she tossed on the still-damp tabletop.

She studied his face with interest. "How much information has Investigator Hardwick already given you?"

Hard edge on the voice, hard look in the almond eyes.

"He gave me the basic facts surrounding the events leading up to and following the . . . the murder of your daughter. Mrs. Perry, if I may stop for a moment. I need to tell you before we go on how terribly sorry I am for your loss."

At first she didn't react at all. Then she nodded, but the movement was so slight it could have been nothing more than a tremor.

"Thank you," she said abruptly. "I appreciate that."

Clearly she didn't.

"But my loss is not the issue. The issue is Hector Flores." She articulated the name with tightened lips as though biting down defiantly on a bad tooth. "What did Hardwick tell you about him?"

"He said there was clear and convincing evidence of his guilt . . . that he was a strange, controversial character . . . that his background is still undetermined and his motivation uncertain. Current location unknown."

"Current location unknown!" She repeated the phrase with a kind of ferocity, leaning toward him over the little table, placing her palms on the moist metal surface. Her wedding ring was a simple platinum band, but her engagement ring was crowned with the largest diamond he'd ever seen. "You summed it up perfectly," she went on, her eyes as wildly bright as the stone. " 'Current location unknown.' That's not acceptable. Not endurable. I'm hiring you to put an end to it."

He sighed softly. "I think we may be getting a little ahead of ourselves."

"What's that supposed to mean?" The pressure of her hands on the tabletop had turned her knuckles white.

He answered almost sleepily, an inverted reaction he'd always had to displays of emotion. "I don't know yet if it makes any sense for me to get involved in a situation that's the subject of an active police investigation."

Her lips twitched into an ugly smile. "How much do you want?"

He shook his head slowly. "Didn't you hear what I said?"

"What do you want? Name it."

"I have no idea what I want, Mrs. Perry. There are a lot of things I don't know."

She took her hands off the table and placed them in her lap, interlacing the fingers as though it were a technique to maintain self-control. "I'll keep it simple. You find Hector Flores. You arrest him or kill him. Whichever you do, I'll give you whatever you want. *Whatever you want.*"

Gurney leaned back from the table, letting his gaze drift to the asparagus patch. At the far end of it, a red hummingbird feeder hung from a shepherd's crook. He could hear the rising and falling pitch of the buzzing wings as two of the tiny birds swooped viciously at each other—each claiming sole right to the sugar water, or so it seemed. On the other hand, it might be some strange remnant of a spring mating dance, and what looked like a killer instinct might be another instinct altogether.

He made an effort to focus his attention on Val Perry's eyes, trying to discern the reality behind the beauty—the actual contents of this perfect vessel. There was rage in her, no doubt of that. Desperation. A difficult past—he would bet on that. Regret. Loneliness, though she would not admit to the vulnerability that word implied. Intelligence. Impulsiveness and stubbornness—the impulsiveness to grab hold of something without thinking, the stubbornness to never let it go. And something darker. A hatred of her own life?

Enough, he said to himself. Too easy to confuse speculation with insight. Too easy to fall in love with a wild guess and follow it over a cliff.

"Tell me about your daughter," he said.

Something in her expression shifted, as if she, too, were putting aside a certain train of thought.

"Jillian was difficult." Her announcement had the dramatic

tone of the opening sentence of a story read aloud. He suspected that whatever followed would be something she'd said many times before. "More than difficult," she continued. "Jillian was dependent on medication to remain merely *difficult* and not utterly impossible. She was wild, narcissistic, promiscuous, conniving, vicious. Addicted to oxies, roxies, Ecstasy, and crack cocaine. A world-class liar. Dangerously precocious. Horribly attuned to the weaknesses of other people. Unpredictably violent. With an unhealthy passion for unhealthy men. And that's with the benefit of the finest therapy money could buy." Oddly excited by this litany of abuse, she sounded more like a sadist hacking at a stranger with a razor than a mother describing the emotional disorders of her child. "Did Hardwick tell you what I'm telling you about Jillian?" she asked.

"I don't recall those specific details."

"What *did* he tell you?"

"He mentioned that she came from a family with a lot of money."

She made a loud, grating sound—a sound he was surprised to hear coming from so delicate a mouth. He was even more surprised to realize that it was a burst of laughter.

"Oh, yes!" she cried, the harshness of the laugh still in her voice. "We're definitely a family with a lot of money. You might say we have a *shitload* of it." She articulated the vulgarity with a contemptuous relish. "Does it shock you that I don't sound the way a bereaved parent is supposed to sound?"

The chilling specter of his own loss limited his response, making speech difficult. He finally said, "I've seen stranger reactions to death than yours, Mrs. Perry. I'm not sure how we're . . . how someone in your circumstances . . . is supposed to sound."

She seemed to be considering this. "You say you've seen stranger *reactions* to death, but have you ever seen a stranger death? A stranger death than Jillian's?"

He didn't answer. The question sounded histrionic. The more Gurney looked into those intense eyes, the harder it became to assemble what he saw into one personality. Had she always been so fragmented, or was there something about her daughter's murder that broke her into these incompatible pieces?

"Tell me more about Jillian," he said.

"Like what?"

"Apart from the personal characteristics you mentioned, do you know anything about your daughter's life that might have given this Flores a motive for killing her?"

"You're asking me why Hector Flores did what he did? I have no idea. Neither do the police. They've spent the past four months bouncing back and forth between two theories, both idiotic. One is that Hector was gay, secretly in love with Scott Ashton, resentful of Jillian's relationship with him, and driven by jealousy to kill her. And the opportunity to kill her in her wedding dress would be irresistible to his drama-queen sensibility. Makes a nice story. Their other theory contradicts the first. A marine engineer and his wife lived next door to Scott. The engineer was away a lot on ships. The wife disappeared the same time Hector did. So the police geniuses conclude that they were having an affair, which Jillian found out about and threatened to reveal to get back at Hector, with whom she was also having an affair, and one thing led to another, and—"

"And he cut off her head at the wedding reception to keep her quiet?" Gurney broke in, incredulous. Hearing himself, he immediately regretted the brutality of the comment and was about to apologize.

But Val Perry showed no reaction to it. "I told you, they're morons. According to them, Hector Flores was either a closeted homosexual pining madly for the love of his employer or a macho Latino screwing every woman in sight and using his machete on anyone who objected. Maybe they'll flip a coin to decide which fairy tale they believe."

"How much contact did you personally have with Flores?"

"None. I never had the pleasure of meeting him. Unfortunately, I have a very vivid picture of him in my mind. He lives there in my mind, with no other address. As you said, 'current location unknown.' I have a feeling he'll live there until he's captured or dead. With your help I look forward to solving that problem."

"Mrs. Perry, you used the word 'dead' a few times, so I need to make something clear, so there's no misunderstanding. I'm not a hit man. If that's part of the assignment, spoken or unspoken, you need to look elsewhere—starting now."

She studied his face. "The assignment is to find Hector Flores . . . and bring him to justice. That's it. That's the assignment."

"Then I need to ask you . . ." he began, then stopped as a grayish brown movement in the pasture caught his attention. A coyote—likely the one he'd seen the day before—was crossing the field. He followed its progress until it disappeared into the maple copse on the far side of the pond.

"What is it?" she asked, turning in her chair.

"Maybe a loose dog. Sorry for the distraction. What I want to know is, why me? If the money supply is as unlimited as you say, you could hire a small army. Or you could hire people who would be, shall we say, less careful about the fugitive's availability for trial. So why me?"

"Jack Hardwick recommended you. He said you were the best. The very best. He said if anyone could get to the bottom of it—resolve it, end it—you could."

"And you believed him?"

"Shouldn't I have?"

"Why did you?"

She considered this for a while, as though a great deal depended on the answer. "He was the initial officer on the case. The chief investigator. I found him rude, obscene, cynical, jabbing people with the sharp end of a stick whenever he could. Horrible. But almost always right. This may not make much sense to you, but I understand dreadful people like Jack Hardwick. I even trust them. So here we are, Detective Gurney."

He stared at the asparagus ferns, calculating, for no reason he was aware of, the compass point to which they were leaning en masse. Presumably, it would be 180 degrees away from the prevailing winds on the mountain, into the lee of the storms. Val Perry seemed content with his silence. He could still hear the modulated buzzing of the hummingbirds' wings as they continued their ritual combat—if that's what it was. It sometimes went on for an hour or more. It was hard to understand how such a prolonged confrontation, or seduction, could be an efficient use of energy.

"You mentioned a few minutes ago that Jillian had an unhealthy interest in unhealthy men. Were you including Scott Ashton in that description?"

"God, no, of course not. Scott was the best thing that ever happened to Jillian."

"You approved of their marriage decision?"

"*Approved?* How quaint!"

"I'll put it another way. Were you pleased?"

Her mouth smiled while her eyes regarded him coolly. "Jillian had certain significant… *deficits,* shall we say? Deficits that demanded professional intervention for the foreseeable future. Being married to a psychiatrist, one of the best in the field, could certainly be an advantage. I know that sounds … wrong, somehow. Exploitative, perhaps? But Jillian was unique in many ways. And uniquely in need of help."

Gurney raised a quizzical eyebrow.

She sighed. "Are you aware that Dr. Ashton is the director of the special high school Jillian attended?"

"Wouldn't that create a conflict of—"

"No," she interrupted, sounding like she was accustomed to arguing the point. "He's a psychiatrist, but when she was enrolled at the school, he was never *her* psychiatrist. So there was no ethical issue, no doctor-patient thing. Naturally, people talked. Gossip-gossip-gossip. 'He's a doctor, she was a patient, blah, blah, blah.' But the legal, ethical reality was more like a former student marrying the president of her college. She left that place when she was seventeen. She and Scott didn't become personally involved for another year and a half. End of story. Of course, it wasn't the end of the gossip." Defiance flashed in her eyes.

"Seems like skating close to the edge," commented Gurney, as much to himself as to Val Perry.

Again she burst into her shocking laugh. "If Jillian thought they were skating close to the edge, for her that would have been the best thing about it. The edge was where she always wanted to be."

Interesting, thought Gurney. Interesting, too, was the glitter in Val Perry's eyes. Maybe Jillian wasn't the only one in love with life on the edge.

"And Dr. Ashton?" he asked mildly.

"Scott doesn't care what anyone thinks about anything." It was a trait she clearly admired.

"So when Jillian was eighteen, maybe nineteen, he proposed marriage?"

"Nineteen. She did the proposing, he accepted."

As he considered this, he watched the strange excitement in her subsiding.

"So he accepted her proposal. How did you feel about that?"

At first he thought she hadn't heard him. Then, in a small hoarse voice, looking away, she said, "Relieved." She stared at Gurney's asparagus ferns as though somewhere among them she might locate an appropriate explanation for her rapidly shifting feelings. A mild breeze had materialized while they'd been speaking, and the tops of the ferns were waving gently.

He waited, saying nothing.

She blinked, her jaw muscles clenching and relaxing. When she spoke, it was with apparent effort, forcing the individual words out as though each were as heavy as something in a dream. "I was relieved to have the responsibility taken off my hands." She opened her mouth as though she were about to say more, then closed it with only a slight shake of her head. A gesture of disapproval, thought Gurney. Disapproval of herself. Was that the root of her desire to see Hector Flores dead? To pay her guilty debt to her daughter?

Whoa. Slow down. Stay in touch with the facts.

"I didn't intend . . ." She let her voice trail off, leaving it unclear what was unintended.

"What do you think of Scott Ashton?" Gurney asked in a brisk tone, as far from her dark and complex mood as he could get.

She responded instantly, as though the question were a lifesaving escape hatch. "Scott Ashton is brilliant, ambitious, decisive . . ." She paused.

"And?"

"And cool to the touch."

"Why do you think he would want to marry a—"

"A woman as crazy as Jillian?" She shrugged unconvincingly. "Possibly because she was breathtakingly beautiful?"

He nodded, unconvinced.

"I know this sounds incredibly trite, but Jillian was special, really *special.*" She gave the word an almost lurid depth and color. "Did you know her IQ was 168?"

"That's remarkable."

"Yes. It was the highest score the testing service had ever measured. They tested her three times, just to make sure."

"So in addition to everything else, Jillian was a genius?"

"Oh, yes, a genius," she agreed, a brittle animation returning to her voice. "And, of course, a nymphomaniac. Did I forget to mention that?"

She searched his face for a reaction.

He looked off into the distance, out over the treetops beyond the barn. "And all you want me to do is look for Hector Flores."

"Not look for him. *Find* him."

Gurney had a fondness for puzzles, but this one was starting to feel more like a nightmare. Besides, Madeleine would never . . .

Jesus, think of her name and . . .

Amazingly, there she was, in her explosion of red and orange attire, making her way gradually up through the pasture, pushing her bicycle along the rutted incline of the path.

Val Perry turned anxiously in her chair to follow his gaze. "Are you expecting someone?"

"My wife."

They said nothing more until Madeleine arrived at the edge of the patio on her way to the shed. The women exchanged blandly polite gazes. Gurney introduced them, saying only—to maintain the appearance of confidentiality—that Val was "a friend of a friend" who had dropped by for some professional advice.

"It's so *restful* here," said Val Perry, her emphasis making it sound like a foreign word whose pronunciation she was practicing. "You must *love* it."

"I do," said Madeleine. She gave the woman a brief smile and rolled her bicycle on toward the shed.

"Well," said Val Perry uneasily, after Madeleine had passed out of sight behind the rhododendrons at the back of the garden, "is there anything else I can tell you?"

"Were you bothered at all by the nineteen versus thirty-eight difference in ages?"

"No," she snapped, confirming his suspicion that she was.

"How does your husband feel about your intention to engage a private detective?"

"He's supportive," she said.

"Meaning what, exactly?"

"He supports what I want to do."

Gurney waited.

"Are you asking me how much he's willing to pay?" Anger twisted some of the beauty out of her face.

Gurney shook his head. "It's not that."

She seemed not to hear him. "I *told* you money was not an issue. I told you we have a shitload of money—a *shitload*, Mr. Gurney, a *SHITLOAD*—and I'll spend whatever it takes to get done what I want to get done!"

Cherry splotches were appearing on her vanilla skin, the words rushing out contemptuously. "My husband is the fucking highest-paid fucking neurosurgeon in the fucking world! He makes over forty fucking million dollars a year! We live in a fucking twelve-million-dollar house! You see this fucking thing on my finger?" She glared furiously at her ring, as though it were a tumor on her hand. "This shiny lump of shit is worth two million fucking dollars! For fucking Christ's sake, don't ask me about money!"

Gurney was sitting back, his fingers steepled under his chin. Madeleine had returned and was standing quietly at the edge of the patio. She came over to the table.

"You all right?" she asked, as though the meltdown she'd just witnessed had no more significance than a bad fit of sneezing.

"Sorry," said Val Perry vaguely.

"You want some water?"

"No, I'm fine, I'm perfectly . . . I'm . . . No, actually, yes, water would be good. Thank you."

Madeleine smiled, nodded pleasantly, and went into the house through the French doors.

"My point," said Val Perry, nervously straightening her blouse, "my point, which I . . . overstated . . . My point is simply that money is not an issue. The goal is the important thing. Whatever resources are needed to reach the goal . . . the resources are available. That's all I was trying to say." She pressed her lips together as if to ensure no further outburst.

Madeleine returned with a glass of water and laid it on the table. The woman picked it up, drank half, and put it down carefully. "Thank you."

"Well," said Madeleine, with a malicious twinkle in her eye as she went back into the house, "if you need anything else, just holler."

Val Perry sat erect and motionless. She seemed to be reassembling her composure through an act of will. After a minute she took a deep breath.

"I'm not sure what to say next. Maybe there's nothing to say, other than to ask for your help." She swallowed. "Will you help me?"

Interesting. She could have said, "Will you take the case?" Did she consider that way of saying it and realize that this was a better way, a way that would be harder to reject?

However she asked, he knew he'd be crazy to say yes.

He said, "I'm sorry. I don't think I can."

She didn't react, just sat there, holding on to the edge of the table, looking into his eyes. He wondered if she'd heard him.

"Why not?" she asked in a tiny voice.

He considered what to say.

For one thing, Mrs. Perry, you seem a bit too much like your descriptions of your daughter. My inevitable collision with the official investigating agency could turn into a major train wreck. And Madeleine's potential reaction to my immersion in another murder case could redefine marital trouble.

What he actually said was, "My involvement could disrupt the ongoing police efforts, and that would be bad for everyone involved."

"I see."

He saw in her expression no real understanding or acceptance of his decision. He watched her, waiting for her next move.

"I understand your reluctance," she said. "I'd feel the same way in your place. All I ask is that you keep an open mind until you see the video."

"The video?"

"Didn't Jack Hardwick mention it?"

"I'm afraid not."

"Well, it's all there, the whole . . . event."

"You don't mean a video of the reception where the murder took place?"

"That's exactly what I mean. The whole thing was recorded. Every minute of it. It's all on a neat little DVD."

Chapter 8

The murder movie

In the Gurneys' spacious farmhouse kitchen, there were two tables for meals—the cherrywood Shaker trestle table used mainly for guest dinners, when it would be dusted off and bedecked by Madeleine with candles and bright flowers from their garden, and the so-called breakfast table, with a round pine top on a cream-painted pedestal base, where, singly or together, they ate most of their meals. This smaller table stood just inside the south-facing French doors. On a clear day, it was touched by sunlight from early morning till sunset, making it one of their favorite places to read.

At two-thirty that afternoon, they were sitting in their usual chairs when Madeleine looked up from her book, a biography of John Adams. Adams was her favorite president—largely, it seemed, because his solution to most emotional and physical problems was to take long, curative walks in the woods. She frowned attentively. "I hear a car."

Gurney cupped his hand to his ear, but even then it was a good ten seconds before he heard it, too. "It's Jack Hardwick. Apparently there's a complete video record of the party where the Perry girl was killed. He said he'd bring it over. I said I'd take a look."

She closed her book, letting her gaze drift into the middle distance beyond the glass doors. "Has it occurred to you that your prospective client is . . . not exactly sane?"

"All I'm doing is looking at the video. No promises to anyone. You're welcome to watch it with me."

Madeleine's quick flash of a smile seemed to brush aside the invitation. She went on. "I'd be willing to go a little further and say that she's a poisonous psycho who probably fits at least half a dozen diagnostic codes from the DSM-IV. And whatever she's told you? I'll bet it's not the whole truth, not even close."

As she was speaking, she was picking unconsciously at the cuticle of her thumb with one of her fingernails, an intermittent new habit that Gurney regarded with alarm as a kind of tremor in her otherwise stable constitution.

Minor and short-lived as these moments were, they shook him, interrupted his fantasy of her infinite resilience, left him temporarily without that secure point of reference, the night-light that warded off gloom and monsters. Absurdly, this tiny nervous gesture had the power to arouse the feeling of sickness and constriction he'd had as a child when his mother started smoking. His mother puffing anxiously on her cigarette, sucking the mouthfuls of smoke into her lungs. *Get hold of yourself, Gurney. Grow up, for Godsake.*

"But I'm sure you know all that already, right?"

He stared at her for a moment, searching for the conversational thread he'd lost.

She shook her head in mock despair. "I'll be in my sewing room for a while. Then I have to run up to the stores in Oneonta. If there's anything you want, add it to the list on the sideboard."

Hardwick arrived with a gust of wind and a growling muffler. He parked his vintage gas guzzler—a red GTO half restored, with epoxy patches yet to be primed—next to Gurney's green Subaru Outback. The wind channeled an eddy of fallen leaves around the cars. The first thing Hardwick did when he got out was to cough violently, hack up phlegm, and spit it on the ground.

"Never could stand the stink of dead leaves! Always reminded me of horse manure."

"Nicely put, Jack," said Gurney as they shook hands. "You have a delicate way with words."

They faced each other like badly matched bookends. Hardwick's messy crew cut, florid skin, spider-veined nose, and watery blue malamute eyes gave him the appearance of a badly aging man with a perennial hangover. By contrast, Gurney's salt-and-pepper hair was neatly combed—too neatly, Madeleine often told him—and at forty-eight he was still trim, kept his stomach firm with a regimen of sit-ups before his morning shower, and looked barely forty.

As Gurney ushered him into the house, Hardwick grinned. "She got to you, eh?"

"Not sure what you mean, Jack."

"What was it got your attention? Love of truth and justice? Chance to kick Rodriguez in the balls? Or was it her fantastic ass?"

"Hard to say, Jack." He found himself articulating the man's name with a peculiar emphasis, as though it were a quick left jab. "Right now I'm just curious about the video."

"That so? Not bored to death yet by retirement? Not desperate to get back in the game? Not hot to help the hot lady?"

"Just like to see the video. You bring it?"

"The murder movie? You've never seen anything like it, Davey boy. High-def DVD taken at the crime scene with the crime in progress."

Hardwick was standing in the middle of the big room that served as kitchen, dining room, and sitting room, with an old country stove at one end and a fieldstone fireplace forty feet away at the other end. His gaze covered it all in a few seconds. "Shit, it's a fucking feature spread in *Mother Earth News*."

"The DVD player is in the den," said Gurney, leading the way.

The video began arrestingly with an aerial shot of the countryside, the camera's position slowly moving down at a steep angle until it was sweeping over green treetops, the bright green of springtime, following the course of a narrow road and a rushing stream—parallel ribbons of black asphalt and glittering water that linked a series of well-kept homes amid sprawling lawns and picturesque outbuildings.

An estate somewhat larger and grander than any of the others came into view, and the progress of the airborne camera slowed. When it reached a position directly above a vast emerald lawn with daffodil borders, its forward movement ceased entirely, and it descended smoothly to ground level.

"Jesus," said Gurney. "They rented a helicopter to shoot their wedding video?"

"Doesn't everyone?" rasped Hardwick. "Actually, the helicopter was just for the intro. From this point on, the video was recorded by four fixed cameras that were set up on the lawn in a way that covered the whole property. So there's a complete sound-and-image file of everything that happened outdoors."

The cream-colored stone house with its surrounding stone patios and free-form flower beds looked like a transplant from the Cotswolds—springtime in the bucolic English countryside.

"Where is this place?" asked Gurney as he and Hardwick settled down on the den couch in front of the DVD monitor.

Hardwick feigned surprise. "You don't recognize the exclusive little hamlet of Tambury?"

"Why should I?"

"Tambury is a hotbed of important people, and you're an important guy. Anyone who's anybody knows somebody who lives in Tambury."

"Guess I haven't made the grade. You going to tell me where it is?"

"Hour northeast of here, halfway to Albany. I'll give you directions."

"I won't be needing—" Gurney began, then stopped with a quizzical frown. "Wait a second. That wouldn't by any chance be within Sheridan Kline's—"

Hardwick cut him off. "Kline's county? You bet it would. So you'll have a chance to work with your old friends. The DA has a soft spot in his heart for you."

"Jesus," muttered Gurney.

"Man thinks you're a fucking genius. Course, he did take the credit for your Mellery triumph, being the suck-ass politician he is, but deep down inside he knows he owes you."

Gurney shook his head, looking back at the screen as he spoke. "Deep down inside Sheridan Kline there is nothing but a black hole."

"Davey, Davey, Davey, you have such cruel opinions of God's children." Then, without waiting for a response, he turned to the screen and began narrating the video.

"Caterers," he said as a team of spikily coiffed young men and women in black pants and crisp white tunics set up a serving bar and half a dozen hot tables.

"The host," he said, pointing at the screen as a smiling man in a midnight blue suit with a red flower on the lapel emerged from an arched doorway in the back of the house and walked out onto the lawn. "Fiancé, groom, husband, widower—all true on the same day, so call him whatever you want."

"Scott Ashton?"

"The man himself."

The man made his way purposefully along the edge of a flower bed toward the right side of the screen, but just before he disappeared, the angle of the scene switched, showing him walking toward what appeared to be a small guest cottage situated at the edge of the lawn where it abutted the woods, perhaps a hundred feet from the main house.

"How many cameras did you say this was shot with?" asked Gurney.

"Four on tripods—plus the one in the helicopter."

"Who did the editing?"

"Video department at the bureau."

Gurney watched Scott Ashton knocking on the cottage door—watched and heard, although the sound was not as sharp as the picture. The front of the door and Ashton's back were about forty-five degrees to the camera. Ashton knocked again, calling out, "Hector."

Gurney then heard what sounded to him like a Spanish-accented voice, too faint for the words to be recognizable. He glanced questioningly at Hardwick.

"We did an audio enhancement in the lab. 'Está abierta.' Translation: 'It's open.' Confirms what Ashton thought he remembered Hector saying."

Ashton opened the door, went inside, closed it behind him.

Hardwick picked up the remote, pressed the "fast-forward" button, explaining, "He's in there five or six minutes. Then he opens the door, and you can hear Ashton saying, 'If you change your mind . . .' Then he comes out, closes the door behind him, walks away." Hardwick let go of the "fast-forward" button as Ashton was emerging from the cottage, looking less happy than when he went in.

"Is that the way they spoke to each other?" asked Gurney. "Ashton speaking English, Flores speaking Spanish?"

"I asked about that myself. Ashton told me it was a recent development, that up till a month or two earlier they'd both been speaking English. Said he believed it was a form of hostile regression, that going back to his native Spanish was Hector's way of rejecting Ashton—by rejecting the language he'd taught him. Or some kind of psychobabble bullshit like that."

On the screen, as Ashton was about to exit the frame, the view switched to another camera to reveal him walking toward a Greek-columned garden pavilion—the kind of miniature Parthenon-like structure popularized by Victorian landscape designers—where four tuxedoed men were arranging their music stands and folding chairs. Ashton spoke briefly with the tuxedoed men, but none of the voices were audible.

"String quartet instead of your basic DJ?" asked Gurney.

"This is Tambury—nothing basic about it." Hardwick fast-forwarded through the rest of Ashton's conversation with the musicians, through panning shots of the baronial grounds and main house, the catering staff arranging dinner plates and silverware on white linen tablecloths, a pair of willowy female bartenders setting up bottles and glasses, close-ups of red and white petunias cascading from carved stone urns.

"This was exactly four months ago?" asked Gurney.

Hardwick nodded. "Second Sunday in May. Perfect time for a wedding. Glories of spring, balmy breezes, nest-building time, doves cooing."

The relentlessly sardonic tone was rubbing Gurney's nerves raw.

When Hardwick stopped fast-forwarding and returned the DVD to "play" mode, the camera was focused on an elaborate ivied trellis that served as an entryway to the main expanse of the lawn. A loose line of wedding guests was strolling through it. There was music in the background, something cheerily baroque.

As each couple passed under the arched bower, Hardwick identified them, referring to a wrinkled list he'd pulled from his pants pocket. "Tambury chief of police Burt Luntz and his wife . . . President of Dartwell College and her husband . . . Ashton's literary agent and her husband . . . President of the Tambury British Heritage Society and his wife . . . Congresswoman Liz Laughton and her husband . . . Philanthropist Angus Boyd and his young male whatever-he-is, calls him his 'assistant' . . . Editor of the *International Journal of Clinical Psychology* and his wife . . . Lieutenant governor and his wife . . . Dean of the medical—"

Gurney interrupted. "Are they all like that?"

"Do they all reek of money, power, connections? Yes. CEOs, major politicians, newspaper publishers, even a goddamn bishop."

For the next ten minutes, the stream of privileged overachievers flowed into Scott Ashton's backyard botanical garden. None appeared out of place in the rarefied environment. But none appeared particularly thrilled to be there.

"We're getting to the end of the line," said Hardwick. "Next we have the bride's parents: Dr. Withrow Perry, world-famous neurosurgeon, and Val Perry, his trophy wife."

The doctor looked to be in his early sixties. He had a fleshy, contemptuous mouth, the double chin of a gourmand, and sharp eyes. He moved with a surprising quickness and grace—like a former fencing instructor, thought Gurney, remembering the lessons he and Madeleine had taken together in the second or third year of their marriage, when they were still actively searching for things they might enjoy doing together.

The Val Perry standing beside the doctor on the screen like a film fantasy of Cleopatra radiated a satisfaction missing from the Val Perry who'd visited Gurney that morning.

"And now," said Hardwick, "the groom and his soon-to-be-headless bride."

"Jesus," murmured Gurney. There were times when Hardwick's lack of feeling seemed to go far enough beyond routine cop cynicism to qualify him as a marginal sociopath. But this was neither the time nor the place to . . . to what? To tell the man he was a sick prick?

Gurney took a deep breath and refocused his attention on the video—on Dr. Scott Ashton and Jillian Perry Ashton walking together toward the camera, smiling—a smattering of applause, a few shouts of "Bravo!" and a joyful baroque crescendo in the background.

Gurney was staring in amazement at the bride.

"The hell is wrong?" asked Hardwick.

"She's not quite what I imagined."

"The hell did you expect?"

"From what her mother told me, I wasn't expecting her to look like a cover shot on *Brides* magazine."

Hardwick studied the image of the beaming young beauty in a floor-length white satin gown, the modest neckline dotted with tiny sequins, her white-gloved hands holding a bouquet of pink tea roses, her golden hair swept up in a tight swirl topped by a glittering tiara, her almond eyes accented with a touch of eyeliner, her perfect mouth enlivened with a lipstick that matched the pink of the tea roses.

Hardwick shrugged. "Don't they all want to look like that?"

Gurney frowned, troubled by the conventionality of Jillian's appearance.

"It's in their goddamn genes," Hardwick insisted.

"Yeah, maybe," said Gurney, unconvinced.

Hardwick fast-forwarded through scenes of bride and groom moving through the crowd, the string quartet attacking their instruments with great gusto, the catering staff gliding among the sipping and munching throng. "We're going to cut to the chase," he said, "straight to the segment where everything happens."

"You mean the actual murder?"

"Plus some interesting stuff just before and just after."

After a few seconds of digital artifacts, the screen was filled with a medium shot of three people conversing in a triangle. Some words were more audible than others, partly buried in the buzz of other conversations, partly overwhelmed by the exuberance of Vivaldi.

Hardwick pulled another folded sheet of paper from his pocket, opened it, and handed it to Gurney, who recognized the familiar format: the typed transcript of a recorded conversation.

"Watch the video and listen to the sound track," said Hardwick. "I'll tell you when you can start following it on the transcript, in case you can't make out the audio. The three speakers are Chief Luntz and his wife, Carol, both facing you, and Ashton, with his back to you." The Luntzes were holding tall drinks topped with lime wedges. The chief was balancing a couple of canapés on the

palm of his free hand. Whatever Ashton was drinking he was holding in front of him, out of the fixed camera's line of sight. The
audible snippets of dialogue seemed thoroughly trite and came entirely from Mrs. Luntz.

"Yes, yes . . . day for it . . . fortunate that the forecast, which
was very . . . flowers . . . the time of year that makes living in the
Catskills worthwhile . . . music, very different, perfect for the occasion . . . mosquito, not a single . . . altitude makes it impossible, thank
God, because mosquitoes down on Long Island . . . ticks, no ticks at
all, thank God . . . had Lyme disease, absolutely horrible . . . wrong
diagnosis . . . nauseous, aching, absolutely in despair, wanted to kill
herself, the pain . . ."

As Gurney glanced sideways at Hardwick on the couch, a raised
eyebrow questioning the point of all this, he heard the chief's louder
voice for the first time. "Carol, it's no time to be talking about ticks.
It's a happy day—right, Doctor?"

Hardwick pointed a forefinger at the top line of the typed page
on Gurney's lap.

Gurney looked down at it, finding it a useful supplement to the
hubbub on the sound track.

SCOTT ASHTON:	Very happy, indeed, Chief.
CAROL LUNTZ:	I was just trying to say how perfect everything is today—no bugs, no rain, no problems at all. And what a lovely affair, the music, handsome men everywhere . . .
CHIEF LUNTZ:	How you doing with your Mexican genius?
SCOTT ASHTON:	I wish I knew, Chief. Sometimes . . .
CAROL LUNTZ:	I heard there were some . . . strange . . . I don't know, I don't like repeating . . .
SCOTT ASHTON:	Hector is going through some sort of emotional dif- ficulty. His behavior has been different lately. I guess it's been noticed. I'd be very interested in anything you've witnessed, anything that caught your attention.
CAROL LUNTZ:	Well, not witnessed by me, not directly, I only . . . ru- mors, but I try not to listen to rumors.

SCOTT ASHTON: Oh. Oh, just one second. Excuse me just one minute. Jillian seems to be waving at me.

Hardwick pushed the "pause" button. "See?" he said. "On the far left side of the picture?" Frozen in the pause frame was Jillian, looking in Ashton's direction, holding up the gold watch on her left wrist and pointing to it. Hardwick pushed "play" again, and the action resumed. As Ashton made his way across the lawn through a scattering of guests to Jillian, the Luntzes continued their conversation without him, most of which was clear enough to Gurney with only an occasional glance at the transcript.

CHIEF LUNTZ: You planning to tell him about that business with Kiki Muller?

CAROL LUNTZ: Don't you think he has a right to know?

CHIEF LUNTZ: You don't even know how that rumor started.

CAROL LUNTZ: I think it's more than a rumor.

CHIEF LUNTZ: Yeah, yeah, you think. You don't know. You think.

CAROL LUNTZ: If you had someone living in your house, eating your food, who was secretly screwing your neighbor's wife, wouldn't you want to know?

CHIEF LUNTZ: What I'm saying is, you don't know.

CAROL LUNTZ: What do I need, pictures?

CHIEF LUNTZ: Pictures would help.

CAROL LUNTZ: Burt, you can be ridiculous all you want, but if some weirdo Mexican was living in our house and screwing Charley Maxon's wife, what would you do then, wait for pictures?

CHIEF LUNTZ: Jesus fucking Christ, Carol . . .

CAROL LUNTZ: Burt, that's blasphemy. I told you, Burt, don't talk that way.

CHIEF LUNTZ: Got it. No blasphemy. Listen—here's the point. You heard something from somebody who heard something from somebody who heard something from somebody—

CAROL LUNTZ: All right, Burt, we can do without the sarcasm!

They fell silent. After a minute or so, the chief tried to get one of the canapés resting on his left hand into his mouth, finally succeeding by employing the base of his glass like a tiny shovel. His wife made a face, looked away, drained her drink, began tapping her foot to the rhythms emanating from the mini-Parthenon. Her expression became festive, bordering on manic, and her gaze darted around the crowd as though searching for a promised celebrity. When one of the servers approached with a tray of drinks, she traded in her empty glass for a full one. The chief was now observing her with lips compressed into a hard line.

CHIEF LUNTZ: You might want to slow down a bit.
CAROL LUNTZ: I beg your pardon?
CHIEF LUNTZ: You heard me.
CAROL LUNTZ: Someone's got to tell the truth.
CHIEF LUNTZ: What truth?
CAROL LUNTZ: The truth about Scott's slimy Mexican.
CHIEF LUNTZ: The truth? Or is it just a rotten little rumor embellished by one of your idiot friends—total, slanderous, actionable bullcrap!

While the tempers of the Luntzes flared, Ashton and Jillian were visible in the left background of the scene, their distance from the fixed camera position putting their conversation out of audio range. It ended with Jillian turning and walking in the direction of the cottage, which was set with its rear against the bordering woodland on the opposite side of the lawn, and Ashton heading back toward the Luntzes with a troubled frown.

When Carol Luntz saw Ashton approaching, she downed her margarita in a couple of fast swallows. Her husband reacted to this with an inaudible word hissed through clenched teeth. (Gurney glanced down at the audio transcript, but it offered no interpretation.)

Switching expressions as Ashton rejoined them, the chief asked, "So, Scott, everything okay? Everything fine?"

"I hope so," said Ashton. "I mean, I wish Jillian would just . . ." He shook his head, his voice trailing off.

"Oh, God," exclaimed Carol Luntz, rather too hopefully, "there's nothing wrong, is there?"

Ashton shook his head. "Jillian wants Hector to join us for the wedding toast. He told us earlier he doesn't want to, and ... well, that's about it." He smiled awkwardly, gazing down at the grass.

"What's his problem, anyway?" asked Carol, leaning in toward Ashton.

Hardwick pushed "pause," freezing Carol in a conspiratorial pose. He turned to Gurney with the fire of a man sharing a revelation. "This bitch is one of those bitches that gets off on trouble, wants to savor every detail, pretends she's bursting with empathy. Cries for your pain and hopes you die so she can cry harder and show the world how much she cares."

Gurney sensed truth in the diagnosis but found Hardwick's excess hard to take. "What's next?" he asked, turning impatiently toward the screen.

"Relax. It gets better." Hardwick pushed "play," reanimating the exchange between Carol Luntz and Scott Ashton.

Ashton was saying, "It's all rather silly; I don't want to bore you with it."

"But what's *wrong* with that man?" Carol persisted, turning *wrong* into a wail.

Ashton shrugged, looked too exhausted to keep the matter private any longer. "Hector has a negative attitude toward Jillian. Jillian, on the other hand, is determined to solve whatever undefined issue has come between them. For that reason she insisted that I invite him to our reception, which I attempted to do on two occasions—a week ago and again this morning. On both occasions he declined. Just a moment ago Jillian called me over to inform me that she intends to pry him out of his little cottage over there for the wedding toast. In my opinion it's a waste of time, and I told her so."

"Why would she want to bother with ... with ... *him*?" She stumbled at the end, as though grabbing for a nasty epithet and finding none within reach.

"Good question, Carol, but not one I can answer."

His comment was followed by a cut to the view from another

camera, a camera positioned to cover a quadrant of the property that included the cottage, the rose garden, and half of the main house. Jillian, the picture-book bride, was knocking on the cottage door.

Again Hardwick stopped the video, causing the three figures to break down into a mosaic pattern on the screen. "All right," he said. "Here we are. Starting now. The critical fourteen minutes. The fourteen minutes during which Hector Flores kills Jillian Perry Ashton. The fourteen minutes during which he cuts her head off with a machete, slips out the back window, and escapes without a trace. Those fourteen minutes start when she steps inside and closes the door."

Hardwick released the "pause" button, and the action resumed. Jillian opened the cottage door, stepped inside, and closed it behind her.

"That's it," said Hardwick, pointing at the screen, "the last sight of her alive."

The camera remained on the cottage while Gurney imagined the murder about to occur behind the floral-curtained windows.

"You said Flores 'slips out the back window and escapes without a trace' after killing her. You mean that literally?"

"Well," said Hardwick, pausing dramatically, "I'd have to say . . . yes and no."

Gurney sighed and waited.

"The thing is," said Hardwick, "Flores's disappearance has a familiar echo about it." Another pause, accented by a sly smile. "There was a trail from the back window of the cottage that went out into the woods."

"What's your point, Jack?"

"That trail out into the woods? It just stopped dead a hundred and fifty yards from the house."

"What are you saying?"

"It doesn't remind you of anything?"

Gurney stared at him incredulously. "You mean the Mellery case?"

"Don't know of a whole lot of other murder cases with trails stopping in the middle of the woods with no obvious explanation."

"So you're saying . . . what?"

"Nothing definite. Just wondering if you might have missed a loose end when you wrapped up the Mellery lunacy."

"What kind of loose end?"

"Possibility of an accomplice?"

"*Accomplice?* Are you nuts? You know as well as I do there was nothing about the Mellery case that suggested even the remote possibility of more than one perp."

"You a little touchy on that subject?"

"*Touchy?* I'm touchy about time-wasting suggestions based on nothing more than your demented sense of humor."

"So it's all a coincidence?" Hardwick was striking the precise supercilious note that went through Gurney like nails on a blackboard.

"*All what,* Jack?"

"The MO similarities."

"You better tell me pretty damn quick what you're talking about."

Hardwick's mouth stretched sideways—maybe a grin, maybe a grimace. "Watch the movie," he said. "Only a few minutes to go."

A few minutes passed. Nothing of significance was happening on the screen. Several guests wandered over to the flower beds that bordered the cottage, and one of the women in the group, the one Hardwick had earlier identified as the lieutenant governor's wife, seemed to be conducting a kind of botanical tour, speaking energetically as she pointed at various blooms. Her group moved gradually out of the frame as though attached by invisible threads to its leader. The camera remained focused on the cottage. The curtained windows revealed nothing.

Just as Gurney was about to question the purpose of this segment of the video, the view switched back to one showing Scott Ashton and the Luntzes in the foreground and the cottage in the background.

"Time for the toast," Ashton was saying. All three were looking toward the cottage. Ashton glanced at his watch, raised his hand in a summoning gesture, and called to a member of the serving staff. She hurried over with an accommodating smile.

"Yes, sir?"

He pointed toward the cottage. "Let my wife know it's past four o'clock."

"She's in that cute little house over there by the trees?"

"Yes, please tell her it's time for the wedding toast."

As she headed off on her assignment, Ashton turned to the Luntzes. "Jillian tends to lose track of time, especially when she's trying to get someone to do what she wants."

The video showed the young woman crossing the lawn, arriving at the cottage door, and knocking. After a few seconds, she knocked again, then tried the knob with no success. She looked back across the lawn toward Ashton, turning her palms up in a gesture of bafflement. In reply he mimed a more energetic knock. She frowned but made the repeat effort, anyway. (This time the sound was loud enough to register on the sound track of the camera, which Gurney reckoned must have been around fifty feet from the cottage.) When there was no reply to her final attempt, she turned up her palms again and shook her head.

Ashton muttered something, seemingly more to himself than to the Luntzes, and strode off toward the cottage. He went straight to the door, knocked loudly, then yanked and pushed roughly at the knob, at the same time calling, "Jilli! Jilli, the door is locked! Jillian!" He stood scowling at the door, his body language conveying frustration and confusion, then turned and walked briskly to the back door of the main house.

Perched on the arm of Gurney's couch, Hardwick explained, "He went to get a key. Told us he always kept an extra in the pantry."

A moment later the video showed Ashton emerging from the main house. He went back to the cottage door, knocked again, apparently got no response, inserted a key, opened the door inward. From the perspective of the camera recording all this, about forty-five degrees to the cottage, very little of the building's interior was visible and only Ashton's back, but there was an abrupt stiffening in his body. After a momentary hesitation, he stepped inside. Several seconds later there was an awful sound, a howl of shock and anguish—the word "HELP" screamed desperately once, twice, three times, and then, seconds later, Scott Ashton came staggering out the door, tripping over his own feet, falling sideways into a flower bed, screaming "HELP" so primally and repeatedly that it ceased being a word at all.

Chapter 9

The view from the doorway

The wedding videographer's stationary cameras, positioned at their four key viewpoints on the lawn, continued to run for another twelve minutes after Ashton's collapse, creating a comprehensive video record of the ensuing chaos—at which point they were switched off and impounded by Chief Luntz for their evidentiary value.

The full twelve minutes of hyperactivity were included on the edited DVD that Gurney was watching with Hardwick—twelve minutes of shouted orders and questions, horrified shrieks, guests running to Ashton, into the cottage, backing out, a woman falling, another tripping over her, falling on top of her, guests helping Ashton up from the flower bed, guiding him to the back door of the main house, Luntz blocking the door of the cottage and frantically working his cell phone, guests turning this way and that with crazed looks, the four musicians entering the scene, one violinist with his instrument still in his hand, another with just his bow, three uniformed Tambury cops running up to Luntz as he guarded the doorway, the president of the British Heritage Society vomiting on the grass.

At the end of the recording, after a final digital jitter, Gurney sat back slowly on his couch and looked over at Hardwick.

"Jesus."

"So what do you think?"

"I think I'd like to know a little more."

"For instance?"

"When did BCI arrive at the scene, and what did you find in the cottage?"

"Uniformed troopers arrived three minutes after Luntz shut down the cameras, which would be fifteen minutes after Ashton discovered the body. While Luntz was calling in his own uniforms, guests were calling 911—which got passed along to the trooper barracks and the sheriff's department. As soon as the uniforms took a peek in the cottage, they called BCI, call got routed to me, and I got to the scene maybe twenty-five minutes later. So the customary clusterfuck was in high gear in no time at all."

"And?"

"And the prevailing wisdom was that the whole deal should get dumped ASAP into BCI's lap—which meant Senior Investigator Jack Hardwick's lap. Where it remained for approximately one week, until I had the urge to inform our beloved captain that his approach to the case—the approach he insisted I follow—had certain logical flaws."

Gurney smiled. "You told him he was a fucking idiot?"

"Words to that effect."

"And he reassigned the case to Arlo Blatt?"

"He did exactly that, and there it has remained stuck for nearly four months now in a dust storm of wheel spinning, without a centimeter of real progress. Hence the beautiful mother of the beautiful bride's interest in exploring another avenue of resolution."

An exploration likely to replace the dust storm of wheel spinning with a shit storm of territorial defense, thought Gurney.

Back away now, before it's too late, the small voice of wisdom whispered.

Then another voice spoke with a carefree confidence. *You should at least find out what they discovered in the cottage. More knowledge is always a good thing.*

"So you arrived at the scene and someone directed you to the body?" asked Gurney.

A twitch in Hardwick's mouth signaled the arrival of the memory. "Yes. I was directed to the body. I was conscious of how the fuckers were watching me as they brought me to the doorway. I remember thinking, 'They're expecting a major reaction, which means that there's something awful in there.' " He paused. His lips drew back from his teeth for a second or two, and then he went on. "Well, I was right about that. One hundred percent right." He seemed authentically disturbed.

"The body was visible from the doorway?" asked Gurney.

"Oh, yeah, it was visible all right."

Chapter 10

The only way it could have been done

Hardwick heaved himself up from the couch, rubbed his face roughly with both hands like a man trying to get himself fully awake after a night of bad dreams.

"Any chance you might have a cold bottle of beer in the house?"

"Not at the moment," said Gurney.

"Not at the moment? Fuck does that mean? Not at the moment, but maybe in a minute or two an icy Heineken might materialize in front of me?"

Gurney noted that whatever fleeting vulnerability the man had just experienced at his recollection of what he'd seen four months ago was now gone.

"So," Gurney went on, ignoring the beer diversion, "the body was observable from the doorway?"

Hardwick walked over to the den window that looked out on the back pasture. The northern sky was dusky gray. As he spoke, he gazed out in the direction of the high ridge that led to the old bluestone quarry.

"The body was sitting in a chair at a small square table in the front room, six feet from the entry door." He grimaced, as one might at the smell of a skunk. "As I said, the *body* was sitting at the table. But the head was not on the body. The head was on the table in a pool of blood. On the table, facing the body, still wearing the tiara you saw in the video."

He paused, as if to ensure the accurate ordering of details. "The cottage had three rooms—the front room and, behind it, a small kitchen and a small bedroom—plus a tiny bathroom and a closet off the bedroom. Wood floors, no rugs, nothing on the walls. Apart from the substantial amount of blood on and around the body, there were a few drops of blood toward the back of the room near the bedroom doorway and a few more drops near the bedroom window, which was wide open."

"Escape route?" asked Gurney.

"No doubt about that. Partial footprint in the soil outside the window." Hardwick turned from the den window and gave Gurney one of his obnoxiously sly looks. "That's where it gets interesting."

"The facts, Jack, just the facts. Spare me the coy bullshit."

"Luntz had called the sheriff's department because they had the nearest K-9 team, and they got to Ashton's estate about five minutes after I did. The dog picks up a scent from a pair of Flores's boots and races straight out through the woods like the trail is red hot. But he stops all of a sudden a hundred and fifty yards from the cottage—sniffing, sniffing, sniffing around in a pretty tight circle, and he stops and barks right on top of the weapon, which turned out to be a razor-sharp machete. But here's the thing—after he found the machete, he couldn't pick up any scent leading away from it. Handler led him around in a small circle, then a wider circle—kept at it for half an hour—but it was no good. The only trail the dog could find led from the back window of the cottage to the machete, nowhere else."

"This machete was just lying out there on the ground?" asked Gurney.

"It had some leaves and loose dirt kicked over the blade, like a half-assed attempt had been made to conceal it."

Gurney pondered this for a few seconds. "No doubt about it being the murder weapon?"

Hardwick looked surprised by the question. "Zero doubt. Victim's blood still on it. Perfect DNA match. Also supported by the ME's report." Hardwick's tone switched to one of rote repetition of something he'd said many times before. "Death caused by the severing of both carotid arteries and the spinal column between the cervical vertebrae C1 and C2 as the result of a chopping blow by a sharp, heavy blade, delivered with great force. Damage to neck tissues and vertebrae consistent with the machete discovered in the wooded area adjacent to the crime scene. So," said Hardwick, switching back to his normal tone, "zero doubt. DNA is DNA."

Gurney nodded slowly, absorbing this.

Hardwick continued, adding a familiar touch of provocation. "The only open question about that particular spot in the woods is why the trail stopped there, kind of like the trail at the Mellery crime scene that just—"

"Hold on a second, Jack. There's a big difference between the visible boot prints we found at Mellery's place and an invisible scent trail."

"Fact is, they both ended in the middle of nowhere with no explanation."

"No, Jack," Gurney snapped, "the fact is, there was a perfectly good explanation for the boot prints—just as there will be a perfectly good, but entirely different, explanation for your scent problem."

"Ah, Davey boy, that's what always impressed me about you: your omniscience."

"You know, I always believed you were smarter than you pretended to be. Now I'm not so sure."

Hardwick's smirk conveyed a sense of satisfaction with Gurney's irritation. He switched to a new tone, all innocence and earnest curiosity. "So what do you think happened? How could Flores's scent trail just end like that?"

Gurney shrugged. "Changed his shoes? Put plastic bags over his feet?"

"Why the hell would he do that?"

"Maybe to create the problem the dog ended up having? Make it impossible to track him wherever he went next, wherever he went to hide out?"

"Like Kiki Muller's house?"

"I heard that name on the tape. Isn't she the one who—"

"Who Flores was supposedly screwing. Right. Lived next door to Ashton. Wife of Carl Muller, marine engineer who was away on a ship half the time. Kiki was never seen after the day Flores disappeared, presumably not a coincidence."

Gurney leaned back on the couch, mulling this over, having trouble with a piece of it. "I can understand why Flores might take precautions to keep from being tracked to a neighbor's house or wherever he was actually going, but why wouldn't he do that before he left the cottage? Why in the woods? Why after he went out and hid the machete and not before?"

"Maybe he wanted to get out of the cottage ASAP?"

"Maybe. Or maybe he wanted us to find the machete?"

"Then why bury it?"

"You mean half bury it. Didn't you say that only the blade was covered with dirt?"

Hardwick smiled. "Interesting questions. Definitely worth pursuing."

"And one other thing," said Gurney. "Has anyone verified where either of the Mullers was at the time of the murder?"

"We know that Carl was chief engineer on a commercial fishing boat about fifty miles off Montauk that whole week. But we couldn't find anyone who'd seen Kiki the day of the murder, or the day before for that matter."

"That mean anything to you?"

"Not a damn thing. Very private kind of community—at least at Ashton's end of the road. Minimum property size is ten acres, private kind of people, not likely to hang out at the back fence and shoot the shit, probably be considered rude up there to say hello without an invitation."

"Do we know if anyone saw her anytime after her husband left for Montauk?"

"Seems nobody did, but . . ." Hardwick shrugged, reiterating that not being seen by your neighbors in Tambury was the rule, not the exception.

"And the guests at the reception, their locations were all accounted for during 'the critical fourteen minutes' you referred to?"

"Yep. Day after the murder, I went thorough the video personally, accounted for the whereabouts of every guest for every minute the victim was in that cottage—with our encouraging captain telling me I was wasting time that I should be spending searching the woods for Hector Flores. Who the hell knows, maybe numbnuts was right for once. Of course, if I'd ignored the video and it later turned out . . . well, you know what the little *shithead* is like." He hissed the obscenity through tightened lips. "What are you looking at me like that for?"

"Like what?"

"Like I'm crazy."

"You *are* crazy," said Gurney lightly. He was also thinking that during the ten months since they'd been involved in the Mellery case, Hardwick's attitude toward Captain Rod Rodriguez had for some reason progressed from contemptuous to venomous.

"Maybe I am," said Hardwick, as much to himself as to Gurney. "Seems to be the general consensus." He turned and stared out the den window again. It was darker now, the northern ridge nearly black against a slate sky.

Gurney wondered: Was Hardwick, uncharacteristically, inviting a personal discussion? Did he have a problem that he might actually be willing to talk about?

Whatever personal door might have been ajar was quickly closed. Hardwick pivoted on his heel, the sardonic spark back in his eye. "There's a question about the fourteen minutes. Might not be exactly fourteen. I'd like to get your omniscient perspective." He came away from the window, sat on the arm of the couch farthest from Gurney, spoke to the coffee table as though it were a communications channel between them. "No doubt about the point when the clock starts running. When Jillian walked into the cottage, she was alive. Nineteen minutes later, when Ashton opened the door, she was sitting at the table in two pieces." He wrinkled his nose and added, "Each piece in its own private puddle of blood."

"Nineteen? Not fourteen?"

"Fourteen takes it back to the point when the catering girl knocked and got no answer. Reasonable assumption would be that the victim didn't answer because the victim was already dead."

"But not necessarily?"

"Not necessarily, because at that point she might have been taking orders from Flores with a machete in his hand, telling her to keep her mouth shut."

Gurney thought about it, pictured it.

"You got a preference?" asked Hardwick.

"Preference?"

"You think she got the big slice before or after the fourteen-minute mark?"

The big slice? Gurney sighed, knowing the routine: Hardwick being outrageous, his audience wincing. Probably been going on all his life, the shock-jock clown—a style reinforced by the prevailing cynicism in the world of law enforcement, deepening and souring as he aged, concentrated by career problems and bad chemistry with his boss.

"So?" Hardwick prodded. "Which is it?"

"Almost certainly before the first knock on the door. Probably quite a bit before. Most likely within a minute or two of her entering the cottage."

"Why?"

"The sooner he did it, the more time he'd have to escape before her body was discovered. The more time he'd have to get rid of the machete, to do whatever he did to keep the dogs from following the trail any farther, to get to where he was going before the neighborhood was flooded with cops."

Hardwick looked skeptical, but not more so than usual—it had become the natural set of his features. "You're assuming this was all conducted according to plan, all premeditated?"

"That would be my take on it. You see it differently?"

"There are problems either way."

"For instance?"

Hardwick shook his head. "First, give me your argument for premeditation."

"The position of the head."

Hardwick's mouth twitched. "What about it?"

"The way you described it—facing the body, tiara in place. It sounds like a deliberate arrangement that meant something to the killer or was intended to mean something to someone else. Not a spur-of-the-moment thing."

Hardwick looked like he had a touch of acid reflux. "Problem with premeditation is that going into the cottage was the victim's idea. How would Flores know she was going to do that?"

"How do you know she hadn't discussed it with him beforehand?"

"She told Ashton she just wanted to talk Flores into joining the wedding toast."

Gurney smiled, waited for Hardwick to think about what he was saying.

Hardwick cleared his throat uncomfortably. "You think that was bullshit? That she had some other reason for going into the cottage? That Flores had set her up earlier with some line of shit and she was lying to Ashton about the wedding-toast thing? Those are big assumptions, based on nothing."

"If the murder was premeditated, something along those lines must have happened."

"But if it wasn't premeditated?"

"Nonsense, Jack. This wasn't an impulse. It was a message. I don't know who the recipient was or what it meant. But it was definitely a message."

Hardwick made another acid-reflux face but didn't argue. "Speaking of messages, we found an odd one on the victim's cell phone—a text message sent to her an hour before she was killed. It said, 'For all the reasons I have written.' According to the phone company, the message came from Flores's phone, but it was signed 'Edward Vallory.' That name mean anything to you?"

"Not a thing." The room had grown dark, and they could hardly see each other at opposite ends of the couch. Gurney switched on the end-table lamp beside him.

Hardwick rubbed his face again, hard, with the palms of both hands. "Before I forget, I wanted to mention a small oddity I observed at the scene and was reminded of in the ME's report. Might not mean anything, but . . . the blood on the body itself, the torso, it was all on the far side."

"Far side?"

"Yeah, the side away from where Flores would have been standing when he swung the machete."

"Your point being?"

"Well, you know . . . you know how you just kind of absorb what you're seeing at a homicide scene? And you start to picture what it was that someone did that would account for things being the way they are?"

Gurney shrugged. "Sure. It's automatic. That's what we do."

"Well, I'm looking at how the blood from the carotids all went down the far side of her body, despite the fact that the torso was sitting up straight, kind of supported by the chair arms, and I'm wondering *why*. I mean, there's an artery on each side, so how come all the blood went one way?"

"And what did you picture happening?"

Hardwick bared his teeth in a quick flinch of distaste. "I pictured Flores grabbing her by the hair with one hand and swinging that machete full force with the other right through her neck—which is pretty much what the ME says must have happened."

"And?"

"And then . . . then he holds the severed head at an angle against the pulsing neck. In other words, he uses the head to deflect the blood. To keep it from getting on him."

Gurney began to nod slowly. "The ultimate sociopathic moment . . ."

Hardwick offered a small grimace of agreement. "Not that hacking her head off had left much doubt about the killer's mental status. But . . . there's something about the . . . the *practicality* of the gesture that's kind of disturbing. Talk about having ice water in your veins . . ."

Gurney continued to nod. He could see and feel what Hardwick was getting at.

The two men were silent for several long, thoughtful seconds.

"There's a small oddity that's been bothering me, too," said Gurney. "Nothing macabre, just a bit perplexing."

"What?"

"The wedding reception's guest list."

"You mean the hot-shit who's who of upstate New York?"

"When you were at the scene, do you recall seeing anybody under the age of thirty-five? Because watching that video just now, I didn't."

Hardwick blinked, scowled, looked like he was flipping through files in his head. "Probably not. So what?"

"Definitely no one in their twenties?"

"Apart from the catering staff, definitely no one in their twenties. So what?"

"Just wondering why the bride didn't have any friends at her own wedding."

Chapter 11

The evidence on
the table

When Hardwick left just before sunset, turning down a halfhearted offer to stay for dinner, he entrusted his copy of the DVD to Gurney, along with a copy of the case file containing records of the initial days when he was chief investigating officer and of the subsequent months during which Arlo Blatt was in charge. It was everything Gurney could have asked for, which he found unsettling. Hardwick was taking a major risk in copying police file material, removing it from headquarters, and giving it to an individual with no authorization to have it.

Why would he do that?

The simple answer—that any substantial progress Gurney might make would embarrass a senior BCI officer for whom Hardwick had no respect—didn't quite justify the level of risk the man was subjecting himself to. Perhaps the full answer could be discovered in the file material itself. Gurney had spread it out on the main dining table under the chandelier—which, as the light from the windows faded, would be the brightest place in the house.

He'd divided the voluminous reports and other documents into piles according to the type of information they contained. Within each pile he placed the items in chronological order as best he could.

Altogether it was a daunting aggregation of data: incident reports, field notes, investigative progress reports, sixty-two interview summaries and transcripts (from one to fourteen pages each), landline and cell-phone records, crime-scene photos taken by BCI personnel, additional still photos culled from the wedding videographer's cameras, the minutely detailed thirty-six-page ViCAP crime-description form, the stolen-object report form, the serial-number database form, an identikit portrait of Hector Flores, the autopsy report, evidence-collection forms, forensic lab reports, DNA blood-sample analyses, the K-9 team report, a master list of wedding guests with contact info and nature of their relationship with the victim and/ or Scott Ashton, sketches and aerial photos of the Ashton estate, interior sketches of the cottage with measurements of the front room, biographical data sheets, and, of course, the DVD that Gurney had viewed.

By the time he'd sorted it all into some kind of workable order, it was nearly 7:00 P.M. At first the lateness of the hour surprised him, and then it didn't. Time always accelerated when his mind was fully engaged, and it seemed to be fully engaged only when, he realized a little ruefully, a puzzle had been placed before him. Madeleine had once told him that his life had narrowed down to one obsessive pursuit: unraveling the mysteries of other people's deaths. Nothing more, nothing less, nothing else.

He reached for the file folder nearest him on the table. It was the set of scene-of-crime reports created by the evidence techs. The top form described the cottage's immediate surroundings. The next form recorded their initial visual inventory of the interior. It was striking in its brevity. The cottage contained none of the normal objects and materials that a crime lab would subject to analysis for trace evidence. No furniture beyond the table on which the victim's head was found, the narrow chair with wooden arms in which the body was propped up, and one similar chair across from it. There were no lounging chairs, couches, beds, blankets, or rugs. Equally strange, there were no clothes in the closet, no clothes or footwear of any kind anywhere in the cottage—with one peculiar exception: a pair of light rubber boots, the kind normally worn over regular shoes. These boots were found in the bedroom next to the window through which the killer had evidently exited. No doubt they were the boots the dog got the scent from to follow the trail.

He turned in his chair toward the French doors and gazed out over the pasture, his eyes alive with speculation. The peculiarities and complications of the case—what Sherlock Holmes would have called "its unique features"—were multiplying, generating like an electrical current the magnetic field that drew Gurney to problems that would naturally repel most men.

His thoughts were interrupted by the loud squeak of the side door opening—a squeak that for the past year he'd been meaning to eliminate with a drop of oil.

"Madeleine?"

"Yes." She came into the kitchen with three straining plastic bags from the supermarket in each hand, hefted all six of them up onto the sideboard, and headed back out.

"Can I help?" he said.

There was no answer, just the sound of the side door opening and closing. A minute later the sound was repeated, followed by her return to the kitchen with a second load of bags, which she also placed on the sideboard. Only then did she take off the quirky purple, green, and pink Peruvian hat with the dangling ear flaps that always seemed to add an antic dimension to whatever her underlying mood might be.

He felt the transient tic in his left eyelid, a twitch in the nerve so distinct it had taken several trips to the mirror in recent months to convince him that it wasn't visible. He wanted to ask where she'd been, apart from the supermarket, but he had the feeling she might have mentioned the rest of her plan to him earlier, and his failure to remember it would not be a good thing. Madeleine equated forgetting, as she equated poor hearing, with lack of interest. Maybe she was right. In twenty-five years in the NYPD, he'd never forgotten to show up for a witness interview, never forgotten a court date, never forgotten what a suspect said or how he sounded, never forgotten a single thing of significance to his job.

Had anything else ever come close in importance to his job? Even made it into the same ballpark? Parents? Wives? Children?

When his mother died, he'd felt almost nothing. No, it was worse than that. Colder and more self-centered than that. He'd felt a sense of relief, the removal of a burden, a simplification of his life. When his first wife left him, another complication was removed. Another impediment out of the way, relief from the pressure of having to respond to the needs of a difficult person. Freedom.

Madeleine went to the refrigerator, started taking out glass containers of food left over from the night before and from the night before that. She laid them in a row on the countertop next to the microwave, five of them, removed the tops. He watched her from the other side of the sink island.

"Have you eaten yet?" she asked.

"No, I was waiting for you to come home," he replied, not quite truthfully.

She glanced past him at the papers spread out on the dining table, raised an eyebrow.

"Bunch of stuff from Jack Hardwick," he said, too casually. "He asked me to look it over." He imagined her level gaze examining his thoughts. He added, "It's stuff from the Jillian Perry case file." He paused. "I'm not sure exactly what I'm supposed to do, or why anyone thinks my observations would be helpful under the existing circumstances, but . . . I'll take a look at what's here and give him my reactions."

"And her?"

"Her?"

"Val Perry. Will you be giving her your reactions, too?" Madeleine's voice had taken on a light, airy quality that communicated rather than concealed her concern.

Gurney stared down into the fruit bowl on the granite top of the sink island, resting his hands on the cold surface. Several fruit flies, disturbed by his presence, rose from a bunch of bananas, flew in asymmetric zigzags above the bowl, then settled again on the fruit, becoming invisible against the speckled skin.

He tried to speak softly, but the effect was condescending. "I think you're disturbed by the assumptions you're making, not by what's actually happening."

"You mean my assumption that you've already decided to jump on the roller coaster?"

"Maddie, how many times do I have to say it? I haven't made any commitment to anyone to do anything. I've made absolutely no decision to get involved in any way beyond reading the case file."

She gave him a look he couldn't quite understand, a look that went *into* him—a look that was knowing and gentle and strangely sad.

She began placing the tops back on the glass storage containers. He watched her without comment until she started putting the containers back into the refrigerator.

"Aren't you going to eat anything?" he asked.

"I'm not that hungry right now. I think I'll take a shower. If it wakes me up, then I'll eat. If it makes me drowsy, I'll go to bed early." As she passed the table with its burden of paperwork, she said, "Before our guests arrive tomorrow, you'll put all that away where we won't have to look at it, right?" She left the room, and half a minute later he heard the bathroom door closing.

Guests? Tomorrow? Christ!

A dim recollection, something Madeleine had mentioned to him about someone coming for dinner—the shadow of a memory, stored in an inaccessible storage bin, a bin containing objects of little importance.

What the hell is going on with you? Isn't there any room left in your head for ordinary life? For a simple life, shared in good and simple ways, with ordinary people? Or maybe there was never any room for that. Maybe you always were the way you are right now. Maybe life here on a secluded mountaintop—cut loose from the demands of the job, deprived of convenient excuses for never being present in the lives of people you claim to love—is making the truth harder to hide. Could the simple truth be that you don't really care about anybody?

He walked around to the far side of the sink island and switched on the coffeemaker. Like Madeleine, he'd lost his appetite for dinner. But the idea of coffee was appealing. It was going to be a long night.

Chapter 12

Peculiar facts

It made sense to begin at the beginning by examining the identikit portrait of Hector Flores.

Gurney had mixed feelings about computer-generated facial composites. Constructed from the input of eyewitnesses, they
mirrored the strengths and weaknesses of all eyewitness testimony.

In the case of Hector Flores, however, there was good reason to
trust the likeness. The descriptive details had been provided by a
man with the observational skills of a psychiatrist and who was said
to have been in daily contact with the subject for nearly three years.
A computer rendering with input of that quality could rival a good
photograph.

The image was of a man, probably in his mid-thirties, good-
looking in an unremarkable way. The facial bone structure was regular, with no feature predominating. The skin was relatively free of
lines, the eyes dark and emotionless. The hair was black, fairly neat,
casually parted. There was only one distinguishing mark Gurney
could discern, oddly shocking in the midst of such an otherwise ordinary appearance: The man's right earlobe was missing.

Appended to the composite portrait was the inventory of physical statistics. (Again Gurney's assumption was that these would
have been provided primarily by Ashton and would therefore have
a high likelihood of accuracy.) Hector Flores's height was listed as
five feet nine inches; weight 140–150; race/nationality Hispanic;
eyes dark brown; hair black, straight; complexion tan, clear; teeth
uneven, with one gold incisor, upper left. In the "Scars and Other

Identifying Marks" section, there were two entries: the missing ear-lobe and severe scarring on the right knee.

Gurney looked again at the picture, searched for some spark of madness, a glimpse of the mind of the ice man who beheaded a woman, used the head to deflect the body's spurting blood away from himself, then placed her head on the table, facing the body from which it came. In the eyes of some killers—Charlie Manson, for instance—there was a demonic intensity, urgent and uncon-cealed, but most of the murderers Gurney had brought to justice during his career as a homicide detective were driven by a less ob-vious madness. Hector Flores's bland, uncommunicative face—in which Gurney could see no hint of the hideous violence of the crime itself—put him in this category.

Stapled to the physical-statistics form was a typed page with the heading "Supplementary Statement Provided by Dr. Scott Ashton on May 11, 2009." It was signed by Ashton and witnessed by Hard-wick, as chief investigating officer. The statement was brief, consid-ering the time period and events it covered.

> *My first meeting with Hector Flores was in late April of 2006, when he came to my home as a day laborer looking for employment. Starting then, I began giving him work around the yard—mowing, raking, mulching, fertilizing, etc. He spoke al-most no English at first but learned quickly, impressing me with his energy and intelligence. In the following weeks, seeing that he was a skilled carpenter, I came to rely on him for a broad range of outdoor and indoor maintenance and repair projects. By mid-July he was working in and around the house seven days a week—adding routine housecleaning to his list of chores. He was becoming the perfect domestic employee, showing great initiative and common sense. In late August he asked if, in lieu of some of the money I was paying him, he might be allowed to occupy the small unfurnished cottage behind the house on the days he was here. With some misgivings I agreed, and shortly thereafter he began living in it, approximately four days a week. He got himself a small table and two chairs at a thrift store, and later an*

inexpensive computer. He said that was all he wanted. He slept in a sleeping bag, insisted that was the way he was most comfortable. As time passed, he began exploring various educational opportunities on the Internet. Meanwhile his appetite for work only seemed to grow, and he began evolving into a kind of personal assistant. By the end of the year, I was trusting him with reasonable amounts of cash, and he was handling occasional grocery shopping and other errands with great efficiency. His English had become grammatically flawless, although it was still heavily accented, and his manner was charming. He frequently answered my phone, took cogent messages, even provided me with subtle shadings of information about the tone or mood of certain callers. (In retrospect this seems bizarre—that I would be relying in this way on a man who had not long before been looking for a job spreading mulch—but the arrangement worked well, without a single problem I was aware of, for almost two years.) Things began to change in the fall of 2008, when Jillian Perry came into my life. Flores soon became moody and reclusive, always finding reasons to be away from the house when Jillian was present. The changes became more disturbing in early 2009, when we announced our wedding plans. He disappeared for several days. When he returned, he claimed to have discovered terrible things about Jillian and that I would be risking my life by marrying her, but he refused to provide details. He said that he couldn't tell me anything more without revealing the source of his information, which he couldn't do. He begged me to reconsider my decision to marry. When it became clear that I was not going to reconsider anything without knowing exactly what he was talking about, and that I would not tolerate unsupported accusations, he seemed to accept the situation, although he continued to avoid Jillian. In retrospect, of course, I should have fired him at these indications of his instability, but with the arrogance of my profession, I assumed that I would be able to discover the nature of the problem and solve it. I saw myself conducting a grand experiment in education, never fully accepting the fact that I was dealing with a dangerously complex personality and that everything might spin out of control. I must also admit that he had made my

*life easier and more convenient in so many ways that I was re-
luctant to let him go. I cannot overemphasize the degree to which
his intelligence, rapid self-education, and range of talents had
impressed me—all of which now sounds delusional in the light
of what has happened. My final encounter with Hector Flores occurred the morning of the wedding. Jillian, who was well aware
that Hector despised her, was obsessed with getting him to accept
the reality of our marriage, and she prevailed upon me to make
one last effort to persuade him to attend the ceremony. I went to
the cottage that morning, found him sitting like a block of stone
at the table. I went through the motions of extending one more
invitation, which he refused. He was dressed entirely in black—
black T-shirt, black jeans, black belt, black shoes. Perhaps that
should have meant something to me. That was the last I saw
of him.*

At that point in the transcript, Hardwick had inserted a handwritten marginal notation: "Upon submission and review of the
above written statement by Scott Ashton, it was supplemented by
the following questions and answers."

J.H.: Do I understand correctly that you knew little or nothing
about this man's background?

S.A.: That's correct.

J.H.: He provided virtually no information about himself?

S.A.: Correct.

J.H.: Yet you came to trust him enough to let him live on your property, have access to your home, answer your phone?

S.A.: I'm aware that it sounds idiotic, but I regarded his refusal
to talk about his past as a form of honesty. I mean, if he'd
wanted to conceal something, it would have been more persuasive to construct a fictitious past. But he didn't do that. In
an upside-down way, that impressed me. So yes, I trusted him
even though he refused to discuss his past.

Gurney read the entire statement a second time, more slowly,
and then a third time. He found the narrative as extraordinary for

what was left out as for what was put in. Among the missing elements was a singular lack of fury. And a striking absence of the visceral horror that on the day prior to making this statement had sent the man reeling out of the cottage seconds after he'd entered it, screaming and collapsing.

Was the change simply the result of medication? A psychiatrist would have easy access to appropriate sedatives. Or was it something more than that? Impossible to tell from just words on paper. It would be interesting to meet the man, look into his eyes, hear his voice.

At least the portion of the statement referring to the unfurnished state of the cottage and Flores's insistence on keeping it that way answered part of the mystery of its bareness in the evidence report—part, but not all. It didn't explain why there were no clothes or shoes or bathroom items. It didn't explain what had happened to the computer. Or why, if he removed all his personal items, Flores had chosen to leave behind a pair of boots.

Gurney's gaze wandered over the piles of documents arrayed in front of him. He remembered earlier seeing two incident reports, not just the one he would have expected, covering the murder, and wondering why. He reached across the table, extracted the second from under the first.

It had been generated by the Tambury Village PD in response to a call received at 4:15 P.M. on May 17, 2009—exactly one week after the murder. Complainant was listed as Dr. Scott Ashton of 42 Badger Lane, Tambury, New York. The report was filed by Sergeant Keith Garbelly. It was noted that a copy had been forwarded to the Bureau of Criminal Investigation at State Police Regional Headquarters, to the attention of Senior Investigator J. Hardwick. Gurney assumed that it was a copy of that copy he was now reading.

Complainant was sitting at patio table on south side of residence, facing main lawn area, with cup of tea on table. His habit in good weather. Heard single gunshot, simultaneously witnessed teacup shatter. Ran into house through back (patio) door, called Tambury PD. When I arrived on scene (with backup following) complainant appeared tense, anxious. Initial interview conducted in living room. Complainant could not pinpoint source of gunshot, guessed "long range, from that general direction" (gestured out the rear window toward wooded hillside at least 300 yards away). Complainant had no additional understanding of the event, other than "possibly connected to the murder of my wife." Claimed no actual knowledge of what the connection might be. Speculated that Hector Flores might want to kill him, too, but could provide no reason or motive.

A copy of a BCI investigatory follow-up form was clipped to the initial incident report, indicating that a quick handoff of the matter had occurred, consistent with BCI's primary responsibility for the case. The follow-up form had three short entries and one long one, all initialed "JH."

Search of Ashton property, woods, hills: negative. Area interviews: negative.

Reconstruction of cup shows impact point at exact top-to-bottom, left-to-right center. Lends support to the hypothesis that cup, not Ashton, may have been shooter's target.

Bullet fragments recovered from patio area too small for conclusive ballistics. Best guess: small to med caliber high-powered rifle, equipped with sophisticated scope, in the hands of an experienced shooter.

Weapon estimate and cup-as-target conclusion shared with Scott Ashton to ascertain whether he knew anyone with that kind of equipment and shooting skills. Subject appeared troubled. When pressed, he named two people with similar rifle and scope: himself and Jillian's father, Dr. Withrow Perry. Perry, he said, liked to go on exotic hunting trips and was an expert marksman. Ashton claimed to have purchased his own rifle (high-end Weatherby .257) at Perry's suggestion. When I asked to see it, he discovered that it was missing from the wooden case in which he kept it locked in his den closet. He could not date the last time he had seen the gun but said that it might have been two or three months earlier. Asked whether Hector Flores knew of its existence and

location, he replied that Flores had accompanied him to Kingston
the day he purchased it and that Flores had built the oak box in
which it was stored.

Gurney turned the form over, looked for a backup sheet, riffled
through the pile from which it came, but could find no follow-up
entry on the interview that must have been conducted subsequently
with Withrow Perry. Or maybe it wasn't. Maybe it had fallen into
the crack that sometimes swallowed critical issues during the
transfer of a case from one CIO to another—in this case from the
wild-swinging Hardwick to the clumsy Blatt. It wouldn't be hard to
imagine that happening.

It was time for a second cup of coffee.

Chapter 13

Weirder and twistier

It could have been any number of things—the fresh rush of caffeine, a natural restlessness arising from sitting in the same chair too long, the oppressive prospect of navigating his solitary way in the middle of the night through that landscape of unprioritized documents, the seemingly unpursued questions concerning the whereabouts of Withrow Perry and his rifle on the afternoon of May 17. Perhaps it was all those forces together that drove him to pick up his cell phone and call Jack Hardwick. All those forces, plus an idea that had occurred to him about the shattered teacup.

The phone was answered after five rings, just as Gurney was thinking about the message he'd leave.

"Yeah?"

"Lot of charm in that greeting, Jack."

"If I knew it was just you, I wouldn't have tried so hard. What's up?"

"That's a big file you gave me."

"You got a question?"

"I'm looking at five hundred sheets of paper here. Just wondering if you wanted to point me in any particular direction."

Hardwick erupted in one of his harsh laughs that sounded more like a sandblasting tool than a human emotion. "Shit, Gurney, Holmes isn't supposed to ask Watson to point him in the right direction."

"Let me put it another way," said Gurney, remembering what a pain it always was to get a simple answer out of Hardwick. "Are there any documents in this mountain of crap that you think I'd find especially interesting?"

"Like pictures of naked women?"

These games with Hardwick could go on way too long. Gurney decided to change the rules, change the subject, catch him off balance.

"Jillian Perry was beheaded at 4:13 P.M.," he announced. "Give or take thirty seconds."

There was a brief silence. "How the fuck . . . ?"

Gurney pictured Hardwick's mind caroming over the case terrain—around the cottage, the woods, the lawn—trying to pick up the clue he'd missed. After allowing what he imagined to be the man's amazement and frustration to blossom fully, Gurney whispered, "The answer is in the tea leaves." Then he broke the connection.

Hardwick called back ten minutes later, faster than Gurney had expected. The surprising truth about Hardwick: Lurking at the center of that exasperating personality was a very sharp mind. How far might the man have gone, Gurney often wondered, and how much happier might he be were he not so encumbered by his own attitudes? Of course, that was a question that applied to a lot of people, himself not the least.

Gurney didn't bother saying hello. "You agree with me, Jack?"

"It's not a sure thing."

"Nothing is. But you understand the logic, right?"

"Sure," said Hardwick, managing to convey that he understood it without being impressed by it. "The time Tambury PD got the call from Ashton about the teacup was four-fifteen. And Ashton said he ran into the house as soon as he realized what had happened. Making some assumptions about the time it would take him to get from the patio table to the nearest phone inside the house, maybe looking out the window a few times to check for any sign of the shooter, dialing the actual local PD number rather than just 911, allowing for a couple of rings before it was answered—all that would put the actual gunshot back to about four-thirteen. But that's just the gunshot. To connect it the way you're connecting it to the exact time of the murder the week before, you gotta make three giant leaps. One, the teacup shooter is the same guy who killed the bride. Two, he knew the precise minute he killed her. Three, he wanted to send a message by blasting the teacup at the same minute of the same hour of the same day of the week. That's what you're saying?"

"Close enough."

"It's not impossible." Hardwick's voice conjured the habitually skeptical expression that had etched permanent lines into his face. "But so what? What the hell difference does it make whether it's true or not?"

"I don't know yet. But there's something about the echo effect . . ."

"One severed head and one smashed teacup, each in the middle of a table, one week apart?"

"Something like that," said Gurney, suddenly doubtful. Hardwick's tone had a way of making other people's ideas sound absurd. "But getting back to the mountain of crap you dumped in my lap, is there anyplace you'd like me to start?"

"Start anywhere, ace. You won't be disappointed. Just about every sheet of paper there has at least one weird twist. Never seen a weirder, twistier case. Or a weirder, twistier bunch of people. The message from my gut? Whatever the fuck's going on ain't what it seems to be."

"One more question, Jack. How come there's no record of a follow-up interview with Withrow Perry regarding the teacup incident?"

After a moment's silence, Hardwick emitted a raspy bray, hardly a laugh at all. "Sharp, Davey, very sharp. Zeroed in on that super quick. There wasn't any official interview because I was officially removed from the case the same day we discovered that the good doctor happened to own the perfect gun for putting a bullet through a teacup at three hundred yards. I'd call the failure to follow up on that fact a fucking stupid oversight on the part of the new CIO, wouldn't you?"

"I gather you didn't go out of your way to remind him?"

"Not allowed anywhere near the active investigation. I was warned off by no less than our revered captain."

"And you were taken off the case because . . . ?"

"I already told you. I spoke inappropriately to my superior. I informed him of the limitations of his approach. I may also have alluded to the limitations of his intelligence and general unsuitability for command."

A long ten seconds passed without either man speaking.

"You sound like you hate him, Jack."

"Hate? Nah. I don't hate him. I don't hate anybody. I love the whole fucking world."

Chapter 14

The lay of the land

Having cleared just enough space for his laptop between a couple of document piles on the long table, Gurney went to the Google Earth website and entered Ashton's Tambury address. He centered the image over the cottage and the thicket behind it, enlarging it to the maximum resolution available. With the help of the scale data attached to the image and the directional and distance information from the rear of the cottage shown in the case file, Gurney was able to narrow the location of the murder weapon's discovery to a fairly small area in the thicket about a hundred feet from Badger Lane. So after leaving the cottage through the back window, Flores walked or ran out there, partially covered the blade of the still-bloody weapon with some dirt and leaves, and then . . . what? Managed to get to the road without leaving any further scent for the dogs to follow? Headed down the hill to Kiki Muller's house? Or was she right there on the road in her car—waiting to help him escape, waiting to run off with him to a new life they'd been planning together?

Or did Flores simply walk back to the cottage? Is that why the scent trail went no farther than the machete? Is it conceivable that Flores concealed himself in or around the cottage itself—concealed himself so effectively that a swarm of troopers, detectives, and crime-scene techs failed to discover him? That seemed unlikely.

As Gurney looked up from his laptop screen, he was startled to see Madeleine sitting at the end of the table, watching him—so startled that he jumped in his seat.

"Jesus! How long have you been there?"

She shrugged, made no effort to answer.

"What time is it?" he asked, and immediately saw the inanity of the question. The clock over the sideboard was in his line of sight, not hers. The time, 10:55 P.M., was also displayed on the computer screen in front of him.

"What are you doing?" she asked. It sounded less a question than a challenge.

He hesitated. "Just trying to make sense out of this . . . material."

"Hmm." It was like one syllable of a humorless laugh.

He tried to return her steady gaze, found it difficult.

"What are you thinking?" he said.

She smiled and frowned, almost at the same time.

"I'm thinking life is short," she said finally, in the way of someone who has come face-to-face with a sad truth.

"And therefore . . . ?"

Just as he concluded she wasn't going to answer him, she did. "Therefore we're running out of time." She cocked her head— or maybe it was a tiny, involuntary spasm—and regarded him curiously.

"Time for what?" he was tempted to ask, feeling an urge to turn this untethered exchange into a more manageable argument, but something in her eyes stopped him. Instead he asked, "Do you want to talk about it?"

She shook her head. "Life is short. That's all. It's something to consider."

Chapter 15

Black and white

Several times during the hour following Madeleine's visit to the kitchen, Gurney was on the verge of going into the bedroom to pursue the significance of her comment.

Madeleine did, from time to time, for brief periods, seem to view things through a bleak lens. It was as though the focus of her vision shifted to a barren spot in the landscape and saw in it a paradigm of the whole earth. But the shift had always been temporary; her focus widened again, her joy and pragmatism returned. It had happened that way before, so no doubt it would happen that way again. But for the moment her attitude disconcerted him, creating an anxious hollowness in his stomach—a feeling that he wanted to escape from. He went to the coatrack in the pantry, slipped on a light jacket, and stepped out through the side door into the starless night.

Somewhere above the thick overcast, a partial moon made the darkness less than total. As soon as he could discern the outline of the path through the overgrown weeds, he followed it down the gentle pasture slope to the weathered bench that faced the pond. He sat, watching and listening, and his eyes slowly distinguished a few dim shapes, edges of objects, perhaps parts of trees, but nothing clearly enough to be identified for sure. Then, across the pond, maybe twenty degrees off his line of sight, he sensed a slight movement. When he looked directly at the spot, the dark shapes, indistinct at best—large bramble bushes, drooping branches, cattails growing up in tangled clumps at the edge of the water, and whatever else might be there—blended formlessly together. But when he looked away, just off to the side of where he thought the movement had been, he saw it again—almost certainly an animal of some kind, perhaps the size of a small deer or a large dog. His eyes darted back, and once again it disappeared.

He understood the retinal-sensitivity phenomenon involved. It was the reason that one could often see a dim star by looking not directly at it but to the side of it. And the animal, if that's what he'd seen, if he'd seen anything at all, was surely harmless. Even if it was a small bear, bears in the Catskills were no danger to anyone, much less to someone sitting quietly a hundred yards away. And yet at some primal level of perception, there was something eerie about an unidentifiable movement in the dark.

The night was windless, soundless, had a dead stillness about it, but to Gurney it felt far from peaceful. He realized that this deficit resided more likely in his own mind than in the atmosphere around him, was attributable more to the tension in his marriage than to shadows in the woods.

The tension in his marriage. His marriage was not perfect. It had twice been on the brink of fracturing. Fifteen years earlier, when their four-year-old son was killed in an accident for which Gurney held himself responsible, he had become an emotionally frozen mess, almost impossible to live with. And just ten months ago, his obsessive immersion in the Mellery case came close to ending not only his marriage but his life.

However, he liked to think that the difficulty between him and Madeleine was simple, or at least that he understood it. To begin with, they occupied radically different boxes on the Myers-Briggs personality grid. His instinctive route to understanding was primarily through thinking, hers was through feeling. He was fascinated by connecting the dots, she by the dots themselves. He was energized by solitude, drained by social engagement, and for her the reverse was true. For him, observing was just one tool to enable clearer judging; for her, judging was just one tool to enable clearer observing.

Within the framework of traditional psychological testing, they had very little in common. Yet there was an electricity that often ran with a shocking joy through their shared perceptions of people or events, a shared sense of irony, a shared sense of what was touching, what was funny, what was precious, what was honest, and what was dishonest. A shared sense that the other was unique and more important than anyone else. An electricity that Gurney, in his warmer and fuzzier moments, believed to be the essence of love.

So there it was—the contradiction that described their relationship. They were seriously, contentiously, sometimes miserably different in their hardwired inclinations, yet joined by powerful moments of common insight and affection. The problem was . . . since their move to Walnut Crossing, those moments had been few and far between. It had been a long time since they'd hugged each other, really hugged each other, as if each were holding the most precious object in the universe.

Sitting there in the dark, lost in these thoughts, he had drifted inward, away from his surroundings. The yipping of coyotes brought him back.

It was hard to pinpoint the location of the sharp, feral cries or the number of animals. He guessed it was a pack of three or four or five somewhere on the next ridge, a mile or so east of the pond. When the yipping stopped suddenly, it deepened the silence. Gurney pulled up his jacket zipper a few more inches.

His mind was soon filling the sensory void with more ideas about his marriage. But he was aware that generalizations, as much as he was addicted to them, did little to solve problems on the ground. And the pressing problem on the ground right now was the need to make a decision, a decision about which he and Madeleine were obviously at odds: to accept the Perry case or not.

He had a vivid sense of how Madeleine felt about it, not only from her latest comments but also from the low drumbeat of concern she'd been expressing at any police-related activity he'd gotten close to since retiring two years earlier. He assumed she would see the Perry case as a black-and-white issue. His acceptance of the case would prove that his obsession with solving murders, even in retirement, was intractable and that their future together would be clouded. His rejection of the case, on the other hand, would signal a change, the first step in his transformation from a workaholic detective into a bird-watching, kayak-paddling nature enthusiast. But, he argued in his imagination, as though she were present, black-and-white options are unrealistic and lead to lousy decisions, because by definition they exclude so many solutions. In this instance the most tenable course would surely lie in a middle ground between black and white.

Following this general principle, he realized how the ideal compromise could be defined. He would accept the case, but with a strict time limitation—say, one week. Two weeks maximum. Within that circumscribed time period, he would delve into the evidence, pursue loose ends, perhaps reinterview some key people, follow the facts, find out what he could, offer his conclusions and recommendations, and . . .

At that point the yipping of the coyotes started again as abruptly as it had ceased, seeming closer now, perhaps halfway down the wooded slope descending toward the barn. The sounds were jagged, shrill, excited. Gurney wasn't sure whether they were actually drawing closer or just getting louder. Then nothing. Not the tiniest sound. A piercing silence. Ten slow seconds passed. Then, one by one, they began to howl. Gooseflesh spread up Gurney's back and along the outside of his arms to the backs of his hands. Once more he thought he saw from the corner of his eye some hint of motion in the dark.

There was the sound of a car door slamming. Then there were headlights coming down through the pasture, the beams waving erratically over the scrubby vegetation, the car traveling too fast for the uneven surface. It jounced and came to a halt at the end of a short sideways skid about ten feet from the bench.

From the open driver's window came Madeleine's voice, uncharacteristically loud, even panicky. "David!" And again, even as he rose from the bench, moving toward the car in the peripheral glare of the headlights, her voice nearly screeching, "David!"

Not until he was in the car and she was closing her window did he notice that the chorus of ghastly howling had stopped. She pressed the button that locked the doors and put her hands on the wheel. His eyes were now sufficiently adjusted to the darkness that he could see—perhaps partly see, partly imagine—the rigidity of her arms and grip, the tightness of the skin over her knuckles.

"Didn't . . . didn't you hear them getting closer?" she asked, sounding out of breath.

"I heard them. I assumed they were chasing something—a rabbit, maybe."

"A rabbit?" Her voice was hoarse, incredulous.

Surely he could not have seen so much detail, but her face seemed to tremble with barely restrained emotion. Eventually she took a long, shaky breath, then another, opened her hands on the steering wheel, flexed the fingers.

"What were you doing down here?" she asked.

"I don't know. Just . . . thinking about things, trying to . . . figure out what to do."

After another long breath, a steadier one, she turned the ignition key, unaware that the engine was still running, producing a grating shriek of protest from the starter mechanism and an echoing burst of irritation from her own throat.

She turned around in front of the barn and drove back up through the pasture to the house. She parked the car closer than usual to the side door.

"And what was it you figured out?" she asked as he was about to get out.

"Sorry?" He'd heard the question, wanted to postpone answering it.

She seemed aware of all this, just turned her head partly toward him and waited.

"I was just trying to figure a way . . . a way of approaching things reasonably."

"Reasonably." She articulated the word in a tone that seemed to strip it of its meaning.

"Maybe we could talk about it in the house," he said, opening his door, wanting to escape, if only for a minute. As he started to step out, his foot caught on something like a bar or a pole on the car floor. He looked down and saw in the yellowish wash of the dome light the heavy wooden handle of the ax they normally kept in the wood bin by the side door.

"What's this?" he said.

"An ax."

"I mean, what's it doing in the car?"

"It was the first thing I saw."

"You know, coyotes are not really—"

"How the hell do you know that?" she interrupted furiously. "How the hell do you know that?" She jerked away as though he had reached for her arm. She got out of the car in a clumsy rush, slammed the door, ran into the house.

Chapter 16

A sense of order and purpose

D uring the wee hours of the morning, the heavy overcast had been blown away by a fast-moving cold front of dry, autumnal air. At dawn the sky was a pale blue and by nine a deep azure. The day promised to be crisp and lucid, as bright and reassuring as the night before had been bleak and unnerving.

Gurney sat at the breakfast table in a slanting rectangle of sunlight, gazing out through the French doors at the yellowish green asparagus ferns swaying in the breeze. As he raised his warm coffee mug to his lips, the world appeared to be a place of defined edges, of definable problems and appropriate responses—a world in which his planned two-week approach to the Perry matter made perfect sense.

The fact that Madeleine an hour earlier had greeted his presentation of the idea with a less-than-happy stare was not surprising. He hadn't expected her to be thrilled. A black-and-white frame of mind naturally resists compromise, he told himself. But reality was on his side, and in time she would recognize the reasonableness of his approach. He was sure of it.

In the meantime he wasn't going to allow her doubts to paralyze him.

When Madeleine went out to her garden to bring in the season's final harvest of string beans, he went to the center drawer of the sideboard to get a yellow legal pad on which to start a list of priorities.

Call Val Perry, discuss two-week commitment.
Set hourly rate. Other fees, costs. E-mail follow-up.

Inform Hardwick.
Interview Scott Ashton—ask VP to expedite.
Ashton background, associates, friends, enemies.
Jillian background, associates, friends, enemies.

It occurred to Gurney that agreeing with Val Perry on the terms of their arrangement took priority over extending his list of things to do. He put down his pen and picked up his cell phone. He was routed directly into her voice mail. He left his number and a brief message referring to "possible next steps."

She called back less than two minutes later. There was a childish elation in her voice, plus the kind of intimacy that sometimes results from the lifting of a great burden. "Dave! It was so good to hear your voice just now! I was afraid you wouldn't want anything to do with me after the way I behaved yesterday. I'm sorry about that. I hope I didn't scare you off. I didn't, did I?"

"Don't worry about it. I just wanted to get back to you and let you know what I'd be willing to do."

"I see." Apprehension had taken her elation down a notch.

"I'm still not sure how helpful I can be."

"I'm positive you could be *very* helpful."

"I appreciate your confidence, but the fact is—"

"Excuse me a second," she broke in, then spoke away from the phone. "Could you wait just a minute? I'm on the phone . . . What? . . . Oh, shit! All right. I'll look at it. Where is it? Show it to me . . . That's it? . . . Fine! . . . Yes, it's fine. Yes!" Then, back on the phone, to Gurney, "God! You hire someone to do something and it turns into a full-time job for you, too. Don't people realize that you're hiring them in order to have *them* do the job?" She let out an exasperated sigh. "I'm sorry. I shouldn't be wasting your time with this. I just had the kitchen redone, with special tiles that were custom-made in Provence, and there doesn't seem to be any end to the problems between the installer and the interior designer, but this is not what you're calling about. I'm sorry, I really am. Wait. I'm closing the door. Maybe they can understand a closed door. Okay, you were starting to say what you'd be willing to do. Please go on."

"Two weeks," he said. "I'll work on it for two weeks. I'll look into the case, do what I can, make whatever progress I can in that period of time."

"Why only two weeks?" Her voice was strained, as though she were consciously trying to practice the alien virtue of patience.

Why indeed? Until she asked this obvious question, he had not recognized the difficulty of articulating a sensible answer. The real answer, of course, involved his desire to mitigate Madeleine's reaction to his involvement in the case, not the nature of the case itself.

"Because . . . in two weeks I'll either have made significant progress or . . . I'll have demonstrated that I'm not the right guy for the job."

"I see."

"I'll maintain a daily log and bill you weekly at the rate of a hundred dollars an hour, plus out-of-pocket expenses."

"Fine."

"I'll clear any major expenses with you beforehand: air travel, anything that—"

She interrupted. "What do you need to start? A retainer? You want me to sign something?"

"I'll draft an agreement and e-mail it. Just print it out, sign it, scan it, and e-mail it back. I don't have a PI license, so officially you'll be retaining me not as a detective but as a consultant to review the evidence and evaluate the status of the investigation. No need for money up front. I'll send you an invoice a week from today."

"Fine. What else?"

"A question—out of left field, maybe, but it's been on my mind since I watched the video."

"What?" There was a touch of alarm in her voice.

"Why weren't there any friends of Jillian's at the wedding?"

She emitted a sharp little laugh. "Jillian had no friends at the wedding because Jillian had no friends."

"None at all?"

"I described my daughter to you yesterday. Are you shocked that she would have no friends? Let me make something perfectly clear. My daughter, Jillian Perry, was a sociopath. *A sociopath.*" She repeated the term as though she were teaching it to an ESL student. "The concept of friendship did not fit in her brain."

Gurney hesitated before going on. "Mrs. Perry, I'm having trouble—"

"Val."

"All right. Val, I'm having trouble putting a couple of things together here. I'm wondering—"

She cut him off again. "You're wondering why the hell I'm so determined to . . . to bring to justice . . . the killer of a daughter I obviously couldn't stand?"

"Close enough."

"Two answers. That's the way I am. And it's none of your fucking business!" She paused. "And maybe there's a third answer. I was a lousy mother, *really* lousy, when Jilli was a kid. And now . . . Shit . . . never mind. Let's go back to it being none of your fucking business."

Chapter 17

In the shadow
of the bitch

*In the past four months, he'd hardly thought of the other one at all—
the one just before the Perry bitch, the one of little importance by comparison, the overshadowed one, the one no one had discovered yet, the
one whose fame was yet to come—the one whose elimination was, in
part, a matter of convenience. Some might say entirely a matter of convenience, but they would be wrong. Her end was well deserved, for all
the reasons that damned her kind:*

> *the stain of Eve,*
> *rotten heart,*
> *rutting heart,*
> *heart of a slut,*
> *a slut at heart,*
> *sweat on the upper lip,*
> *grunts of a pig,*
> *horrid gasps,*
> *lips parting,*
> *lascivious lips,*
> *devouring lips,*
> *wet tongue,*
> *slithering serpent,*
> *enveloping legs,*
> *slippery skin,*
> *vile fluids,*
> *slime of a snail.*
> *Wiped clean by death,*

evaporated by death,
damp limbs dried by death,
purification by desiccation,
dry as dust.
Harmless as a mummy.
Vaya con Dios!

He smiled. He must remember to think of her more often—to keep her death alive.

Chapter 18

Ashton's neighbors

By 10:00 A.M., Gurney had e-mailed Val Perry a memo of agreement and called three numbers she'd given him for Scott Ashton—his home number, personal cell number, and the Mapleshade Residential Academy number—in an effort to arrange a meeting. He'd left voice-mail messages at the first two and a live message at the third, with an assistant who identified herself only as Ms. Liston.

At 10:30 Ashton called him back, said he'd gotten all three messages, plus one from Val Perry explaining Gurney's role. "She said you'd want to speak to me."

Ashton's voice was familiar from the video, but richer and softer on the phone, impersonally warm, like an advertising voice for an expensive product—quite suitable for a top-shelf psychiatrist, thought Gurney.

"That's right, sir," he said. "As soon as it's convenient for you."

"Today?"

"Today would be ideal."

"The academy at noon or my home at two. Your choice."

Gurney chose the latter. If he started out for Tambury immediately, he'd have time to drive around, get a sense of the area, Ashton's road in particular, maybe talk to a neighbor or two. He went to the table, got the BCI interview list that Hardwick had provided, and made a pencil dot next to each name with a Badger Lane address. From the same pile, he chose the folder marked "Interview Summaries" and headed for his car.

* * *

The village of Tambury owed its sleepy, secluded quality in part to having grown up around an intersection of two nineteenth-century roads that had been bypassed by newer routes, a circumstance that usually produces an economic decline. However, Tambury's location in a high open valley on the northern edge of the mountains with postcard views in every direction saved it. The combination of out-of-the-way peace and great beauty made it an attractive location for wealthy retirees and second-home owners.

But not all the population fit that description. Calvin Harlen's weed-choked shambles of a former dairy farm sat at the corner of Higgles Road and Badger Lane. It was just past noon when the crisp librarian's voice of Gurney's GPS delivered him to this final segment of his hour-and-a-quarter drive from Walnut Crossing. He pulled over onto the northbound shoulder of Higgles Road and eyed the dilapidated property, whose most striking feature was a ten-foot-high mountain of manure, overgrown with monstrous weeds, next to a barn that was leaning precipitously toward it. On the far side of the barn, sinking into a field of waist-high scrub, a haphazard line of rusting cars was punctuated by a yellow school-bus carcass with no wheels.

Gurney opened his folder of interview summaries and pulled the appropriate one to the top. He read:

> *Calvin Harlen. Age 39. Divorced. Self-employed, odd jobs (home repair, lawn mowing, snowplowing, seasonal deer cutting, taxidermy). General maintenance work for Scott Ashton until arrival of Hector Flores, who took over his jobs. Claims he had "unwritten contract" with Ashton that Ashton broke. Claims (without supporting facts) that Flores was illegal alien, gay, HIV-positive, crack addict. Referred to Flores as a "filthy spic," Ashton as a "lying piece of shit," Jillian Perry as a "snotty little cunt," and Kiki Muller as a "spic-fucking whore." No knowledge of the homicide, related events, location of the suspect. Claims he was working alone in his barn the afternoon of the homicide.*

Subject has low credibility. Unstable. Record of multiple arrests over 20-year period, for bad checks, domestic violence, drunk and disorderly, harassment, menacing, assault. (See Unified Criminal Record form attached.)

Gurney closed the folder, put it on the passenger seat. Apparently Calvin Harlen's life had been a prolonged audition for White-Trash Poster Boy.

He got out of the car, locked it, and walked across the trafficless road to a rutted expanse of dirt that served as a kind of driveway onto the property. It forked into two loosely defined directions, separated by a triangle of stunted grass: one toward the manure pile and barn on the right, the other on the left toward a ramshackle two-story farmhouse whose last paint job was so many decades in the past that the patches of paint on the rotting wood no longer had a definable color. The porch overhang was supported by a few four-by-four posts of more recent vintage than the house but far from new. On one of the posts was a plywood sign advertising DEER CUTING in red, dripping, hand-painted letters.

From inside the house came an eruption of the frantic barking of at least two large-sounding dogs. Gurney waited to see if the commotion would bring someone to the door.

It brought someone out of the barn, or at least out from someplace behind the manure pile—a thin, weathered man with a shaved head, holding what appeared to be either a very fine screwdriver or an ice pick.

"You lose something?" He was smirking as though the question were a clever joke.

"You asking me if I lost something?" said Gurney.

"You say you're lost?"

Whatever the game was, the thin man seemed to be enjoying it.

Gurney wanted to knock him off balance, make *him* wonder what the game was.

"I know some people with dogs," said Gurney. "Right kind of dog, you can make a lot of money. Wrong kind, you're out of luck."

"Shut the fuck up!"

It took Gurney a second or two—and the sudden end of the barking in the house—to realize whom the thin man had shouted at.

The situation had the potential for becoming unsafe. Gurney knew he still had the option of walking away, but he wanted to stay, had a lunatic urge to spar with the lunatic. He began studying the ground around him. After a while he picked up a small oval stone about the size of a robin's egg. He massaged it slowly between his palms as if to warm it, flipped it in the air like a coin, caught and enclosed it in his right fist.

"Fuck are you doing?" the man asked, taking a short step closer.

"Shhh," said Gurney softly. Finger by finger, he slowly opened his fist, examined the stone closely, grinned, and tossed it over his shoulder.

"What the fuck . . . ?"

"Sorry, Calvin, didn't mean to ignore you. But that's the way I make my decisions, and it takes a lot of concentration."

The man's eyes widened. "How'd you know my name?"

"Everybody knows you, Calvin. Or do you prefer being called Mr. Hard-On?"

"What?"

"Calvin, then. Simpler. Nicer."

"The fuck are you? What do you want?"

"I want to know where I can find Hector Flores."

"Hec . . . What?"

"I'm looking for him, Calvin. I'm going to find him. Thought maybe you could help me."

"How the hell . . . ? Who . . . ? You ain't no cop, right?"

Gurney said nothing, just let his expression fade into his best imitation of a dead-eyed killer. The ice-man look seemed to rivet Harlen, widen his eyes a little more.

"Flores the spic, that's who you're after?"

"Can you help me, Calvin?"

"I don't know. How?"

"Maybe you just could tell me everything you know—about our mutual friend." Gurney inflected the last three words with such ironic menace that he was afraid for a second he'd overdone it. But

Harlen's inane grin removed the fear that anything with this guy could be overdone.

"Yeah, sure, why not? Like what do you want to know?"

"To start with, do you know where he came from?"

"Bus stop in the village where these spic workers come, hang around. They *loiter*," he said, making it sound like a legal term for masturbating in public.

"How about before that? You know where he came from originally?"

"Some Mexican dump, wherever the fuck they all come from."

"He never told you?"

Harlen shook his head.

"Did he ever tell you anything?"

"Like what?"

"Anything at all. Did you ever actually speak to him?"

"Once. On the phone. Which is another reason I know he's full of shit. Last—I don't know—October, November? I called Dr. Ashton about the snowplowing, but the spic answered the phone, wanted to know what I wanted. Told him I wanted to talk to the doctor, why the fuck should I talk to him? Tells me I got to tell him what it's about and he'll tell the doctor. I tell him I didn't call to talk to him—go fuck himself! Who the fuck's he think he is? These fucking Mexican scumbags, they come up here, bring their fucking swine-flu AIDS leprosy shit, go on fucking welfare, steal fucking jobs, don't pay taxes, nothing, fucking stupid diseased bastards. I ever see the slimy little fuck again, I'll shoot him in the fucking head. First I'll shoot his fucking balls off."

In the middle of Harlen's rant, one of the dogs in the house started barking again. Harlen turned to the side, spit on the ground, shook his head, shouted, "Shut the fuck up!" The barking stopped.

"You said that was another reason you knew he was full of shit?"

"What?"

"You said that speaking to Flores on the phone was another reason you knew he was full of shit."

"Right."

"Full of shit how?"

"Fuckhead came here, couldn't speak a fucking word of English. Year later he's talking like a fucking—I don't know, a fucking . . . like he knows everything."

"Right, so you figure . . . what, Calvin?"

"I figure maybe it was all bullshit, you know what I mean?"

"Tell me."

"Nobody learns English that fucking fast."

"You're thinking he wasn't really a Mexican?"

"I'm saying he was full of shit, pulling some kind of deal."

"What are you saying?"

"It's obvious, man. He's that fucking smart, why the fuck did he show up at the doctor's house asking if he could rake leaves? He had a fucking *agenda*, man."

"Interesting, Calvin. You're a bright guy. I like the way you think."

Harlen nodded, then spit on the ground again as if to emphasize his agreement with the compliment. "And there's another thing." He lowered his voice conspiratorially. "Guilty spic would never let you see his face. Always had one of them rodeo hats on, brim pulled down in front, sunglasses. You know what I think? I think he was afraid to be seen, always hiding in the big house or in that fucking dollhouse. Just like the cunt."

"Which cunt would that be?"

"The cunt that got whacked. Drive past you on the road, she'd look away like you was some kind of dirt. Like you was roadkill, fucking stupid cunt. So I'm thinking maybe they had something on the side, right, her and Mr. Fucking Greaseball? Both too fucking guilty to look anybody in the eye. Then I'm thinking, hey, wait a minute, maybe it's more than that. Maybe the spic is afraid of being identified. You ever think of that?"

When Gurney finally concluded the interview, thanking Harlen and telling him he'd be in touch, he wasn't sure how much he'd learned or what it might be worth. If Ashton had started using Flores instead of Harlen for jobs around the property, Harlen would no doubt have a huge resentment, and all the rest, all the bile that Harlen had been spewing, might have arisen directly from the blow to his wallet and his pride. Or maybe there was more to it. Maybe, as Hardwick had claimed, the whole situation had hidden layers, wasn't what it seemed to be at all.

Gurney returned to his car on the shoulder of Higgles Road and wrote three short notes to himself in a little spiral pad.

Flores not who he said he was? Not Mexican?

Flores afraid of Harlen recognizing him from past? Or afraid of Harlen being able to ID him in the future? Why, if Ashton could ID him?

Any evidence of an affair between Flores and Jillian? Any prior connection between them? Any pre-Tambury motive for the murder?

He looked skeptically at his own questions, doubtful that any of them would lead to a useful discovery. Calvin Harlen, angry and seemingly paranoid, was hardly a reliable source.

He checked the clock on the dashboard: 1:00 P.M. If he skipped lunch, he'd have time for one more interview before his appointment with Ashton.

The Muller property was next to the last at the high end of Badger Lane, the last being Ashton's manicured paradise. It was a world apart from Harlen's dump at the corner of Higgles Road.

Gurney pulled over just past a mailbox bearing the address listed for Carl Muller on his interview master sheet. The house was a very large white Colonial with classic black trim and shutters, set well back from the road. Unlike the meticulously tended houses preceding it, it had a subtle aura of neglect—a shutter a little askew, a broken-off branch lying on the front lawn, grass shaggy, fallen leaves matted on the driveway, a blown-over lawn chair upside down on a brick path by the side door.

Standing at the paneled front door, Gurney could hear music playing faintly somewhere inside. There was no doorbell, just an antique brass knocker, which he used several times with increasing impact before the door was finally opened.

The man facing him did not look well. Gurney figured that his age could be anywhere from forty-five to sixty, depending on how much of his appearance was attributable to sickness. His limp hair matched the grayish beige of his drooping cardigan.

"Hello," he said, with no hint of greeting or curiosity.

It struck Gurney as an odd way for the man to speak to a stranger at his door. "Mr. Muller?"

The man blinked, looked like he was listening to a taped replay of the question. "I'm Carl Muller." His voice had the pallid, toneless quality of his skin.

"My name is Dave Gurney, sir. I'm involved in the search for Hector Flores. I was wondering if I might have a minute or two of your time."

The taped replay took longer this time. "Now?"

"If that's possible, sir. It would be very helpful."

Muller nodded slowly. He stepped back, making a vague gesture with his hand.

Gurney stepped into the dark center hall of a well-preserved nineteenth-century home with wide floorboards and abundant original woodwork. The music he'd dimly heard before entering he now heard more identifiably. It was, strangely out of season, "Adeste Fideles," and it seemed to be coming from the basement. There was another sound as well, a kind of low, rhythmic buzzing, also coming from somewhere below them. To Gurney's left, a double doorway opened into a formal dining room with a massive fireplace. In front of him, the broad hallway extended to the rear of the house, where there was a glass-paneled door to what appeared to be an endless lawn. On the side of the hallway, a wide staircase with an elaborate balustrade led to the second floor. To his right was an old-fashioned parlor furnished with overstuffed couches and armchairs and antique tables and sideboards over which hung Winslow-style seascapes. Gurney's impression was that the inside of the house was better cared for than the outside. Muller smiled vacuously, as though waiting to be told what to do next.

"Lovely house," said Gurney pleasantly. "Looks very comfortable. Perhaps we could sit for a moment and talk?"

Again the tape delay. "All right."

When he didn't move, Gurney gestured inquiringly toward the parlor.

"Of course," said Muller, blinking as though he were just waking up. "What did you say your name was?" Without waiting for an answer, he led the way to a pair of armchairs that faced each other in front of the fireplace. "So," he said casually when they were both seated, "what's this all about?"

The tone of the question was, like everything else about Carl Muller, roughly twenty degrees off center. Unless the man had some organic tendency toward confusion—unlikely in the rigorous profession of marine engineering—the explanation had to be some form of medication, perhaps understandable in the aftermath of his wife's disappearing with a murderer.

Maybe because of the position of the heating vents, Gurney noted that the strains of "Adeste Fideles" and the faint rising and falling buzz were more audible in this room than in the hall. He was tempted to ask about it but thought it better to stay focused on what he really wanted to know.

"You're a detective," said Muller—a statement, not a question.

Gurney smiled. "I won't keep you long, sir. There are just a few things I need to ask you."

"Carl."

"I beg your pardon?"

"Carl." He was gazing into the fireplace, speaking as though the ashy remnants of the last fire had jogged his memory. "My name is Carl."

"Okay, Carl. First question," said Gurney. "Before the day she disappeared, did Mrs. Muller have any contact with Hector Flores that you were aware of?"

"Kiki," he said—another revelation from the ashes.

Gurney repeated his question, changing the name.

"She would have, wouldn't she? Under the circumstances?"

"The circumstances being . . . ?"

Muller's eyes closed and opened, too lethargic a process to be described as a blink. "Her therapy sessions."

"Therapy sessions? With whom?"

Muller looked at Gurney for the first time since they'd entered the room, blinking more quickly now. "Dr. Ashton."

"The doctor has an office in his home? Next door?"

"Yes."

"How long had she been seeing him?"

"Six months. A year. Less? More? I don't remember."

"When was her last session?"

"Tuesday. They were always on Tuesday."

For a moment Gurney was bewildered. "You mean the Tuesday before she disappeared?"

"That's right, Tuesday."

"And you're assuming that Mrs. Muller—Kiki—would have had contact with Flores when she went to Ashton's office?"

Muller didn't answer. His gaze had returned to the fireplace.

"Did she ever talk about him?"

"Who?"

"Hector Flores?"

"He wasn't the sort of person we'd discuss."

"What sort of person was he?"

Muller uttered a humorless little laugh and shook his head. "That would be obvious, wouldn't it?"

"Obvious?"

"From his name," said Muller with sudden, intense disdain. He was still staring into the fireplace.

"A Spanish name?"

"They're all the same, you know. So bloody obvious. Our country is being stabbed in the back."

"By Mexicans?"

"Mexicans are just the tip of the knife."

"That's the kind of person Hector was?"

"Have you ever been to those countries?"

"Latin countries?"

"Countries with hot climates."

"Can't say that I have, Carl."

"Filthy places, every one of them. Mexico, Nicaragua, Colombia, Brazil, Puerto Rico—every one of them, filthy!"

"Like Hector?"

"Filthy!"

Muller glared at the ash-covered iron grate as though it were displaying infuriating images of that filth.

Gurney sat silently for a minute, waiting for the storm to

subside. He watched the man's shoulders slowly relaxing, his grip on the arms of the chair loosening, his eyes closing.

"Carl?"

"Yes?" Muller's eyes reopened. His expression had become shockingly bland.

Gurney spoke softly. "Did you ever have evidence that anything inappropriate might be going on between your wife and Hector Flores?"

Muller looked perplexed. "What did you say your name was?"

"My name? Dave. Dave Gurney."

"Dave? What a remarkable coincidence! Did you know that was my middle name?"

"No, Carl, I didn't."

"Carl David Muller." He stared into the middle distance. " 'Carl David,' my mother used to say, 'Carl David Muller, you go straight to your room. Carl David Muller, you better behave or Santa may lose your Christmas list. You mind what I say, Carl David.' "

He stood up from his chair, straightened his back, and chanted the words in the voice of a woman—"Carl David Muller"—as though the name and voice had the power to break down the wall to another world. Then he walked out of the room.

Gurney heard the front door opening.

He found Muller holding it ajar.

"It was nice of you to drop by," said Muller blandly. "You have to leave now. Sometimes I forget. I'm not supposed to let people into the house."

"Thank you, Carl, I appreciate your time." Taken aback by what looked like some form of psychotic decompensation, Gurney was inclined to comply with Muller's request in order to avoid creating any additional stress, then make some calls from his car and wait for help to arrive.

By the time he was halfway to his car, he had second thoughts. It might be better to keep an eye on the man. He returned to the front door, hoping he wouldn't have a problem persuading Muller to admit him a second time, but the door wasn't fully closed. He knocked on it, anyway. There was no response. He eased it open and looked inside. Muller wasn't there, but a door in the hallway that Gurney was sure had been shut before was now ajar. Stepping into the center hall, he called out as mildly and pleasantly as he could, "Mr. Muller? Carl? It's Dave. You there, Carl?"

No answer. But one thing was certain. The buzzing sound— more of a metallic whooshing sound, now that he could hear it more clearly—and the "Adeste Fideles" Christmas hymn were coming from someplace behind that barely open hall door. He went to it, nudged it wide open with his toe. Dimly lit stairs led down to the basement.

Cautiously, Gurney started down. After a few steps, he called out again, "Mr. Muller? Are you down there?"

A boy-soprano choir began to reprise the hymn in English: "O come, all ye faithful / Joyful and triumphant / O come ye, O come ye to Bethlehem."

The stairs were enclosed on both sides all the way down, so only a small slice of the basement was visible to Gurney as he gradually descended the steps. The part he could see seemed to be "finished" with the traditional vinyl tiles and pine paneling of millions of other American basements. For a brief moment, the commonness of it was oddly reassuring. That feeling disappeared when he stepped out of the stairwell and turned to the source of the light.

In the far corner of the room was a very large Christmas tree, its top bent over against the nine-foot-high ceiling. Its hundreds of tiny lights were the room's source of illumination. There were colored garlands and foil icicles and scores of glass ornaments in every traditional Christmas shape from simple orbs to handblown glass angels—all hanging from silver hooks. The room was filled with a piney fragrance.

Beside the tree, standing transfixed behind a huge platform the size of two Ping-Pong tables set end to end, was Carl Muller. His hands were on two control levers attached to a black metal box. A model train buzzed around the perimeter of the platform, made figure eights across the middle, climbed and descended gentle grades, roared through mountain tunnels, passed through tiny villages and farms, crossed rivers, traversed forests . . . around and around . . . again . . . again.

Muller's eyes—glimmering spots in the sagging pallor of his face—glowed with all the colors of the tree lights. He reminded Gurney of a person afflicted with progeria, the weird accelerated-aging disease that makes a child look like an old man.

After a while Gurney went back upstairs. He decided to go on to Scott Ashton's house and see what the doctor knew about Muller's condition. The trains and the tree provided reasonable evidence that it was an ongoing situation, not an acute breakdown requiring intervention.

Without setting the lock, he closed the heavy front door behind him with a solid thump. As he started back along the brick path to the lane where his car was parked, an elderly woman was getting out of a vintage Land Rover that was parked directly behind his Outback.

She opened the rear door, spoke a few stern, clipped words, and out stepped a very large dog, an Airedale.

The woman, like her imposing dog, had something about her that was both patrician and wiry. Her complexion was as outdoorsy as Muller's was sickly. She came toward Gurney with the determined stride of a hiker, leading the dog on a short leash, carrying a walking stick more like a cudgel than a cane. Halfway up the path, she stopped with feet apart, stick planted firmly to one side and the dog on the other, blocking his way.

"I'm Marian Eliot," she announced—as one might announce, "I am your judge and jury."

The name was familiar to Gurney. It had appeared on the list of Ashton's neighbors interviewed by the BCI team.

"Who are you?" she demanded.

"My name is Gurney. Why do you ask?"

She tightened her grip on her long, gnarled stick: scepter and potential weapon. This was a woman accustomed to being answered, not questioned, but it would be a mistake to be bullied by her. It would make it impossible to gain her respect.

Her eyes narrowed. "What are you doing here?"

"I'd be tempted to say it's none of your business, if your concern for Mr. Muller weren't so obvious."

He wasn't sure whether he'd hit the right note of assertiveness and sensitivity until, at the conclusion of a piercing stare, she asked, "Is he all right?"

"Depends on what you mean by all right."

There was a flicker of something in her expression suggesting that she understood his equivocation.

"He's in the basement," Gurney added.

She made a scrunched-up face, nodded, seemed to be picturing something. "With the trains?" Her imperious voice had softened.

"Yes. A regular thing with him?"

She studied the top end of her big stick as though it might be a source of useful information or next steps. She exhibited no interest in answering Gurney's question.

He decided to nudge the conversation forward from a different angle. "I'm involved in the Perry murder investigation. I remember your name from the list of people who were interviewed back in May."

She made a contemptuous little sound. "It wasn't really an interview. I was initially contacted by . . . I'll remember the name in a moment . . . Senior Investigator Hardpan, Hardscrabble, Hardsomething . . . a rough-edged man, but far from stupid. Fascinating in a way—rather like a smart rhinoceros. Unfortunately, he disappeared from the case and was replaced by someone called Blatt, or Splat, or something like that. Blatt-Splat was marginally less rude and far less intelligent. We spoke only briefly, but the brevity was a blessing, believe me. Whenever I meet a man like that, my heart goes out to the teachers who once had to endure him from September to June."

The comment brought forth a recollection of the words next to the name Marian Eliot on the interview file's cover sheet: *Professor of Philosophy, retired (Princeton).*

"In a way that's why I'm here," said Gurney. "I've been asked to follow up on some of the interviews, get some more detail into the picture, maybe develop a better understanding of what really happened."

Her eyebrows shot up. *"What really happened?* You have doubts about that?"

Gurney shrugged. "Some pieces of the puzzle are still missing."

"I thought the only things missing were the Mexican ax murderer and Carl's wife." She seemed both intrigued and annoyed that
the situation might not be as she had assumed. The Airedale's sharp,
querying eyes seemed to be taking it all in.

Gurney suggested, "Perhaps we could speak somewhere other
than right here?"

Chapter 19

Frankenstein

Marian Eliot's suggested location for carrying on their conversation was her own home, which happened to be across the lane and a hundred yards back down the hill from Carl Muller's. The actual location turned out to be not so much her home as her driveway, where she enlisted Gurney's help unloading bags of peat moss and mulch from the back of her Land Rover.

She'd traded her cudgel for a hoe and stood by the edge of a rose garden about thirty feet from the vehicle. As Gurney hefted the bags into a wheelbarrow, she asked him about his precise role in the investigation and his position in the state police chain of command.

His explanation that he was an "evidence consultant" who'd been retained by the victim's mother outside the official BCI process was greeted with a skeptical eye and tightened lips.

"What on earth is that supposed to mean?"

He decided to take a chance and reply bluntly. "I'll tell you what it means if you can keep it to yourself. The fact is, it's a job description that lets me carry on an investigation without waiting for the state to issue an official PI license. If you want to check on my background as an NYPD homicide detective, call the smart rhinoceros—whose name, by the way, is Jack Hardwick."

"Hah! Good luck with the state! Do you think you might be able to push that wheelbarrow over here?"

Gurney took that as her way of accepting him and how things were. He made three more trips from the back of the Land Rover to the rose garden. After the third she invited him to sit with her on a white-enameled cast-iron bench under an overgrown apple tree.

She turned so she could look at him squarely. "What's all this about missing pieces?"

"We'll come to the missing pieces, but I need to ask a few questions first to help me get oriented." He was feeling his way toward the right balance of assertiveness and accommodation, watching her body language for signs of needed course corrections. "First question: How would you describe Dr. Ashton in a sentence or two?"

"I wouldn't try. He's not the sort of man to be captured in a sentence or two."

"A complex man?"

"Very."

"Any predominant personality trait?"

"I wouldn't know how to answer that."

Gurney suspected that the quickest means of getting something from Marian Eliot was to stop tugging on it. He sat back and studied the shapes of the apple tree's branches, twisty from a series of long-ago prunings.

He was right. After a minute she began speaking. "I'll tell you something about Scott, something he did, but you'll have to make up your own mind about what it means, whether it would add up to a 'personality trait.' " She articulated the phrase distastefully, as though she found it too simplistic a concept to apply to human beings.

"When Scott was still in medical school, he wrote the book that made him famous—well, famous in certain academic circles. It was called *The Empathy Trap*. It argued quite cogently—with biological and psychological data to back up his hypothesis—that empathy is essentially a boundary defect, that the empathic feelings human beings have for one another are really a form of confusion. His point was that we care about each other because at some location in the brain we fail to distinguish between *self* and *other*. He conducted one elegantly simple experiment in which the subjects watched a man peeling an apple. In the course of peeling it, the man's hand seemed to slip and the knife jabbed his finger. The subjects were being videotaped for later analysis of their reactions to the jabbing. Virtually all the subjects reflexively flinched. Only two out of the hundred tested failed to have any reaction, and when those two were later given psychological tests, they revealed the mental and emotional characteristics common to sociopaths. Scott's contention was that we flinch when someone else is cut because for a split second we fail to distinguish between that person and ourselves. In other words, the normal human being's boundary is imperfect in a way that the sociopath's is perfect. The sociopath never confuses himself and his needs with anyone else's and therefore has no feelings related to the welfare of others."

Gurney smiled. "Sounds like an idea that could stir up a reaction."

"Oh, indeed it did. Of course, a lot of the reaction had to do with Scott's choice of words: *perfect* and *imperfect.* His language was interpreted by some of his peers as a glorification of the sociopath." Marian Eliot's eyes were gleaming with excitement. "But all that was part of his plan. Bottom line, he got the attention he wanted. At the age of twenty-three he was the hottest topic in the field."

"So he's smart, and he knows how to—"

"Wait," she interrupted, "that's not the end of the story. A few months after his book stirred up that hornet's nest of controversy, another book was published that was in essence a broadside attack on Scott's theory of empathy. The title of the competing book was *Heart and Soul.* It was rigorous and well argued, but its tone was entirely different. Its message was that love is all that matters, and 'boundary porosity'—as Scott had described empathy—was in fact an evolutionary leap forward and the very essence of human relationships. People in the field were dividing into opposing camps. Journal articles were generated by the score. Impassioned letters were written." She sat back against the arm of the bench, watching his expression.

"I have a feeling," said Gurney, "that there's more."

"More indeed. A year later it was discovered that Scott Ashton had written both books." She paused. "What do you think of that?"

"I'm not sure what I think of it. How was it received in his field?"

"Total rage. Felt like they'd all been had. Some truth in that. But the books themselves were unimpeachable. Both perfectly legitimate contributions."

"And you think all that was to draw attention to himself?"

"No!" she snapped. "Of course not! The *tone* was attention-getting. Posing as two writers in conflict with each other was attention-getting. But there was a deeper purpose, a deeper message to each reader: *You need to make up your own mind, find your own truth.*"

"So you'd say Ashton was a pretty smart guy?"

"Brilliant, actually. Unconventional and unpredictable. A supremely good listener and a fast learner. And a strangely tragic figure."

Gurney was getting the impression that despite being in her late sixties, Marian Eliot was afflicted with something she would surely never acknowledge: a consuming crush on a man who was nearly three decades her junior.

"You mean 'tragic' in the sense of what happened on his wedding day?"

"It goes well beyond that. The murder, of course, ended up being part of it. But consider the mythic archetypes embedded in the story from start to finish." She paused, allowing him time for such consideration.

"Not sure I follow that."

"Cinderella . . . Pygmalion . . . Frankenstein."

"You're taking about the evolution of Scott Ashton's relationship with Hector Flores?"

"Precisely." She gave him a smile of approval befitting a good student. "The story has a classic beginning: A stranger wanders into the village, hungry, looking for work. A local landowner, a man of substance, hires him, takes him to his home, tries him at various tasks, sees great potential in him, gives him increasing responsibility, gives him entry into a new life. The poor scullery worker, in effect, is magically elevated to a rich new life. Not the Cinderella story in its gender details, but certainly in its essence. Yet in the larger scheme of the Ashton-Flores saga, the Cinderella story is only act one. Then a new paradigm becomes operative, as Dr. Ashton grows enthralled by the opportunity to mold his student into something greater, to lead him to his highest potential, to sculpt the statue into a kind of perfection—to bring Hector Flores to life in the fullest possible sense. He buys him books, a computer, online courses—spends hours each day supervising his education, pushing him toward a kind of perfection. Not the Pygmalion myth in its specific Greek details, but close enough. That was act two. Act three, of course, became the Frankenstein story. Intended to be the best of human creatures, Flores turns out to harbor the worst of human flaws, bringing havoc and horror into the life of the genius who created him."

Nodding slowly, appreciatively, Gurney took all of this in— fascinated not only by the fairy-tale parallels to the real-life events but also by Marian Eliot's insistence on their huge significance. Her eyes burned with conviction and something that resembled triumph. The question in Gurney's mind: Was the triumph in some way related to the tragedy, or did it simply reflect an academic's satisfaction with the profundity of her own understanding?

After a brief silence during which her excitement subsided, she asked, "What were you hoping to find out from Carl?"

"I don't know. Maybe why the inside of his house is so much neater than the outside." He wasn't entirely serious, but she replied in a businesslike tone.

"I look in on Carl fairly regularly. He hasn't been himself since Kiki disappeared. Understandable. While I'm there, I put things where they seem to belong. It's nothing, really." She gazed over Gurney's shoulder in the direction of Muller's house, hidden behind a couple of acres of trees. "He takes better care of himself than you might think."

"You've heard his opinion of Latinos?"

She uttered a short, exasperated sigh. "Carl's position on that issue isn't much different from the campaign speeches of certain public figures."

Gurney gave her a curious look.

"Yes, I know, he's a bit intense about it, but considering . . . well, considering the situation with his wife . . ." Her voice trailed off.

"And the Christmas tree in September? And the Christmas carols?"

"He likes them. Finds them soothing." She stood, took her hoe with a firm hand from where it was leaning against the trunk of the apple tree, and gave Gurney a quick little nod that communicated the end of their conversation. Discussing Carl's craziness was clearly not her favorite activity. "I have work to do. Good luck with your inquiries, Mr. Gurney."

Either she had forgotten or she had consciously chosen not to pursue her earlier interest in the missing puzzle pieces. Gurney wondered which it was.

The big Airedale, seemingly sensing a change in the emotional atmosphere, appeared out of nowhere at her side.

"Thank you for your time. And your insight," Gurney said. "I hope you'll give me an opportunity to speak with you again."

"We'll see. Despite retirement, I lead a busy life."

She turned to the rose garden with her hoe and began hacking fiercely into the crusty soil, as if disciplining an unruly element of her own nature.

Chapter 20

Ashton's manor

Many of the houses on Badger Lane, especially those up toward Ashton's end of the road, were old and large and had been maintained or restored with costly attention to detail. The result was a casual elegance toward which Gurney felt a resentment he would have resisted identifying as envy. Even measured by the elevated standards of Badger Lane, the Ashton property was striking: an impeccable two-story farmhouse of pale yellow stone surrounded by wild roses, huge free-form flower beds with herbaceous borders, and trellises of English ivy serving as passageways among the various areas of a gently sloping lawn. Gurney parked in a Belgian-block driveway that led to the kind of garage a real-estate agent would call a carriage house. Across the lawn stood the classical pavilion where the wedding musicians had played.

Gurney got out of his car and was immediately struck by a scent in the air. As he struggled to name it, a man came around from the rear of the main house carrying a pruning saw. Scott Ashton looked familiar but different, less vivid in person than on video. He was dressed in casually expensive country attire: Donegal tweed pants and a tailored flannel shirt. He noted Gurney's presence without apparent pleasure or displeasure.

"You're on time," he said. His voice was even, mellow, impersonal.

"I appreciate your willingness to see me, Dr. Ashton."

"Would you like to come inside?" It was purely a question, not an invitation.

"It would be helpful if I could see the area behind the house first—the location of the garden cottage. Also the patio table where you were sitting when the bullet hit the teacup."

Ashton responded with a movement of his hand indicating that Gurney should follow him. As they passed through the trellis linking the garage and driveway area beside the house to the main lawn behind it—the trellis through which the wedding guests had entered the reception—Gurney experienced a feeling of combined recognition and dislocation. The pavilion, the cottage, the rear of the main house, the stone patio, the flower beds, the enclosing woods were recognizable but jarringly altered by the change of season, the emptiness, the silence. The odd scent in the air, exotically herbal, was stronger here. Gurney asked about it.

Ashton motioned vaguely toward the planting beds bordering the patio. "Chamomile, windflower, mallow, bergamot, tansy, boxwood. The relative strength of each component changes with the direction of the breeze."

"Do you have a new gardener?"

Ashton's features tightened. "In place of Hector Flores?"

"I understood he handled most of the work around the house."

"No, he hasn't been replaced." Ashton noted the pruning saw he was carrying and smiled without warmth. "Unless by myself." He turned toward the patio. "There's that table you wanted to see." He led Gurney through an opening in the low stone wall to an iron table with a pair of matching chairs near the back door of the house.

"Did you want to sit here?" Once again it was a question, not an invitation.

Gurney had settled into the chair that gave him the best view of the areas he remembered from the video when a slight movement drew his attention to the far side of the patio. There, on a small bench against the sunny back wall of the house, sat an elderly man in a brown cardigan with a twig in his hand. He was rocking his hand from side to side, making the twig resemble a metronome. The man had thinning gray hair, sallow skin, and a dazed look.

"My father," said Ashton, sitting in the chair opposite Gurney.

"Here for a visit?"

Ashton paused. "Yes, a visit."

Gurney responded with a curious look.

"He's been in a private nursing home for about two years as the result of progressive dementia and aphasia."

"He can't speak?"

"Hasn't been able to for at least a year now."

"You brought him here for a visit?"

Ashton's eyes narrowed as though he might be about to tell Gurney it was none of his business, but then his expression softened. "Jillian's . . . death created . . . a kind of *loneliness.*" He seemed confused by the word and hesitated. "I think it was a week or two after her death that I decided to bring my father here for a while. I thought that being with him, taking care of him . . ." Again he fell silent.

"How do you manage that, going to Mapleshade every day?"

"He comes with me. Surprisingly, it's not a problem. Physically, he's fine. No difficulty walking. No difficulty with stairs. No difficulty eating. He can tend to his . . . hygiene requirements. In addition to the speech issue, the deficit is mainly in orientation. He's generally confused about where he is, thinks he's back in the Park Avenue apartment where we lived when I was a child."

"Nice neighborhood." Gurney glanced across the patio at the old man on the bench.

"Nice enough. He was a bit of a financial genius. Hobart Ashton. Trusted member of a social class in which all the men's names sounded like boys' prep schools."

It was an old witticism and sounded stale. Gurney smiled politely.

Ashton cleared his throat. "You didn't come here to talk about my father. And I don't have much time. So what can I do for you?"

Gurney put his hands on the table. "Is this where you were sitting the day of the gunshot?"

"Yes."

"It doesn't make you nervous to be in the same spot?"

"A lot of things make me nervous."

"I'd never know it, looking at you."

There was a long silence, broken by Gurney. "Did you think the shooter hit what he was aiming at?"

"Yes."

"What makes you so sure he wasn't aiming at you and missed?"

"Did you see *Schindler's List*? There is a scene in which Schindler attempts to talk the camp commandant into sparing the lives of Jews whom he would normally shoot for minor offenses. Schindler tells him that being *able* to shoot them, having a perfect right to shoot them, and then choosing in a godlike way to spare them, would be the greatest proof of his power over them."

"That's what you think Flores was doing? Proving, by sparing you and smashing the teacup, that he has the power to kill you?"

"It's a reasonable hypothesis."

"Assuming that the shooter was Flores."

Ashton held Gurney's gaze. "Who else did you have in mind?"

"You told the original investigating officer that Withrow Perry had a rifle of the same caliber as the bullet fragments gathered from this patio."

"Have you ever met him or spoken to him?"

"Not yet."

"Once you do, I think you'll find the notion of Dr. Withrow Perry crawling around in those woods with a sniperscope utterly ridiculous."

"But not so ridiculous for Hector Flores?"

"Hector has proven himself capable of anything."

"That scene you mentioned from *Schindler's List*? As I think about it, I seem to remember that the commandant doesn't take the advice for very long. He doesn't have the patience for it, and he very quickly goes back to shooting Jews who aren't behaving the way he wants them to."

Ashton did not reply. His gaze drifted toward the wooded hillside behind the pavilion and rested there.

Most of Gurney's decisions were conscious and well calculated, with one conspicuous exception: deciding when it was time to switch the tone of an interview. That was a gut call, and right then it felt like the right time. He leaned back in his iron chair and said, "Marian Eliot is quite a fan of yours."

The signs were subtle; maybe Gurney was imagining them, but he got the impression from the odd look Ashton gave him that for the first time in their conversation he'd been thrown off stride. He recovered quickly.

"Marian is easy to charm," he said in his smooth psychiatrist's voice, "as long as you don't try to be charming."

Gurney realized that that had been his own perception, precisely. "She thinks you're a genius."

"She has her enthusiasms."

Gurney tried another twist. "What did Kiki Muller think of you?"

"I have no idea."

"You were her psychiatrist?"

"Very briefly."

"A year doesn't seem that brief."

"A year? More like two months, not even two months."

"When did the two months end?"

"I can't tell you that. Confidentiality restrictions. I shouldn't even have said two months."

"Her husband told me that she had an appointment with you every Tuesday up until the week she disappeared."

Ashton offered only an incredulous frown and shook his head.

"Let me ask you something, Dr. Ashton. Without improperly divulging anything Kiki Muller might have told you during the time she was seeing you, can you tell me why her treatment period ended so quickly?"

He considered this, seemed uncomfortable answering. "I discontinued it."

"Can you tell me why you did that?"

He closed his eyes for a few seconds, then seemed to make a decision. "I discontinued her therapy because in my opinion she wasn't interested in therapy. She was only interested in being here."

"Here? On your property?"

"She'd show up half an hour early for her appointments, then linger afterward, supposedly fascinated by the landscaping, the flowers, whatever. The fact is, wherever Hector was, that's where her attention was. But she wouldn't admit it. Which made her communications with me dishonest and pointless. So I stopped seeing her after six or seven sessions. I'm taking a risk in telling you this, but it seems an important fact if she was lying about the duration of her treatment. The truth is, she ceased being my patient at least nine months prior to her disappearance."

"Might she have been seeing Hector secretly all that time, telling her husband she was coming here for her appointments with you?"

Ashton took a deep breath and let it out slowly. "I'd hate to think something so blatant was going on under my nose, right there in that damned cottage. But it's consistent with the two of them running off together . . . afterward."

"This Hector Flores character," said Gurney abruptly, "what kind of person were you imagining he was?"

Ashton winced. "You mean, as a psychiatrist, how could I have been so miserably wrong about someone I was observing daily for three years? The answer is embarrassingly simple: blindness in pursuit of a goal that had become far too important to me."

"What goal was that?"

"The education and blossoming of Hector Flores." Ashton looked like he was tasting something bitter. "His remarkable growth from gardener to polymath was going to be the subject of my next book—an exposition of the power of nurture over nature."

"And after that," said Gurney with more sarcasm than he'd intended, "a second book under another name demolishing the argument in your first book?"

Ashton's lips stretched in a cold, slow-motion smile. "That was an informative conversation you had with Marian."

"Which reminds me of something else I wanted to ask you. About Carl Muller. Are you aware of his emotional condition?"

"Not through any professional contact."

"As a neighbor, then?"

"What is it you want to know?"

"Put simply, I'd like to know how nuts he really is."

Again Ashton presented his humorless smile. "Basing my opinion on hearsay, I'd guess he's in full retreat from reality. Specifically, from grown-up reality. Sexual reality."

"You get all that from the fact that he plays with model trains?"

"There's a key question one must always ask about inappropriate behavior: Is there an age at which that behavior would have been appropriate?"

"Not sure I understand."

"Carl's behavior appears appropriate for a prepubescent boy. Which suggests it may be a form of regression in which the individual returns to the last secure and happy time in his life. I'd say that Carl has regressed to a time in his life before women and sex entered the equation, before he experienced the pain of having a woman deceive him."

"You're saying that somehow he discovered his wife's affair with Flores and it drove him off the deep end?"

"It's possible, if he were fragile to begin with. It's consistent with his current behavior."

A bank of clouds, which had materialized out of nowhere in the blue sky, drifted gradually in front of the sun, dropping the temperature on the patio at least ten degrees. Ashton seemed not to notice. Gurney stuffed his hands into his pockets.

"Could a discovery like that be enough to make him kill her? Or kill Flores?"

Ashton frowned. "You have reason to believe that Kiki and Hector are dead?"

"None, apart from the fact that neither one of them has been seen for the past four months. But I have no evidence that they're alive, either."

Ashton looked at his watch, a softly burnished antique Cartier. "You're painting a complicated picture, Detective."

Gurney shrugged. *"Too* complicated?"

"Not for me to say. I'm not a forensic psychologist."

"What are you?"

Ashton blinked, perhaps at the abruptness of the question. "I beg pardon?"

"Your field of expertise . . . ?"

"Destructive sexual behavior, particularly sexual abuse."

It was Gurney's turn to blink. "I had the impression you were director of a school for troubled kids."

"Yes. Mapleshade."

"Mapleshade is for kids who've been sexually abused?"

"Sorry, Detective. You're opening a subject that cannot be discussed briefly without the risk of misunderstanding, and I don't have the time now to discuss it in detail. Perhaps another day."

He glanced again at his watch. "The fact is, I have two appointments this afternoon I need to prepare for. Do you have any simpler questions?"

"Two. Is it possible that you were mistaken about Hector Flores being Mexican?"

"Mistaken?"

Gurney waited.

Ashton appeared agitated, moved to the edge of his chair. "Yes, I may have been mistaken about that, along with everything else I thought I knew about him. Second question?"

"Does the name Edward Vallory mean anything to you?"

"You mean the text message on Jillian's phone?"

"Yes. 'For all the reasons I have written. Edward Vallory.' "

"No. The first officer on the case asked me about that. I said it wasn't a familiar name then, and that hasn't changed. I was told that the phone company traced the message back to Hector's cell phone."

"But you have no idea why he would use the name Edward Vallory?"

"None. I'm sorry, Detective, but I do need to prepare for my appointments."

"Can I see you tomorrow?"

"I'll be at Mapleshade all day—with a full schedule."

"What time do you leave in the morning?"

"Here? Nine-thirty."

"How about eight-thirty, then?"

Ashton's expression flickered between consternation and concern. "All right. Eight-thirty tomorrow morning."

On the way to his car, Gurney glanced back into the far corner of the patio. The sun was gone now, but Hobart Ashton's metronomic twig was still rocking back and forth to a slow, monotonous beat.

Chapter 21

A word to the wise

As Gurney drove down Badger Lane under gathering clouds, the homes that had looked picturesque when bathed in sunlight now looked grim and guarded. He was eager to reach the openness of Higgles Road and the pastoral valleys that lay between Tambury and Walnut Crossing.

Ashton's decision to end the interview, necessitating a return trip, didn't bother Gurney at all. It would give him time to digest his first live impressions of the man, along with the opinions offered by his extraordinary neighbors. Having an opportunity to organize it all in his mind would help him start to make connections and put together the right questions for tomorrow. He decided he'd head straight for the Quick-Mart on Route 10, get the biggest container of coffee they offered, and make some notes.

As he came within sight of the intersection at Calvin Harlen's tumbledown farm, he could see that a black car was blocking the road, angled directly across it. Two muscular young men with matching buzz cuts, sunglasses, dark jeans, and shiny Windbreakers were leaning against the side of the car, watching Gurney's approach. The fact that the car was an unmarked Ford Crown Victoria—as obvious a law-enforcement vehicle as a cruiser with its siren blaring—made the state police ID tags pinned to their jackets no surprise.

They ambled over to where Gurney had stopped, one on each side of his car.

"License and registration," said the one at Gurney's window in none too friendly a tone.

Gurney already had his wallet out, but now he hesitated. "Blatt?"

The man's mouth twitched as if a fly had landed on it. He slowly removed his glasses, managing to inject menace into the action. His eyes were small and mean. "Where do I know you from?"

"The Mellery case."

He smiled. The wider the smile got, the nastier it got. "Gurney, right? The genius from shit city. The hell you doing here?"

"Visiting."

"Visiting who?"

"When it's appropriate to share that information with you, I will."

"Appropriate? *Appropriate?* Get out of the car."

Gurney complied calmly with the order. The other officer had circled around to the back of the car.

"Now, like I said, license and registration."

Gurney opened his wallet, handed the two items to Blatt, who studied them with great care. Blatt went back to the Crown Victoria, got in, and started punching keys on his in-car computer. The officer in back of the car was watching Gurney as if he might be about to sprint across Higgles Road into the thornbushes. Gurney smiled wearily and tried to read the man's ID, but the plastic holder was reflecting the light. He gave up and introduced himself instead. "I'm Dave Gurney, NYPD Homicide, retired."

The officer nodded slightly. Several minutes passed. Then several more. Gurney leaned back against his car door, folded his arms, and closed his eyes. He had little appetite for pointless delays, and the complexity of the day was wearing him down. His fabled patience was fraying. Blatt returned and handed him back his items as though he were sick of holding them.

"What's your business here?"

"You asked me that already."

"All right, Gurney, let me make something clear to you. There's a murder investigation in progress here. You understand what I'm saying? Murder investigation. Big mistake for you to get in the way. Obstruction of justice. Impeding the investigation of a felony. Get the message? So I'll ask you one more time. What are you doing on Badger Lane?"

"Sorry, Blatt, private matter."

"You saying you're not here about the Perry case?"

"I'm not saying anything."

Blatt turned to the other officer, spit on the ground, and pointed his thumb back at Gurney. "This is the guy that almost got everyone killed at the end of the Mellery case."

The stupid accusation was dangerously close to pushing a button in Gurney that most people didn't know existed.

Maybe the other officer sensed ominous vibrations, or maybe he'd gotten jammed up by Blatt's animosities before, or maybe a little light finally went on. "Gurney?" he asked. "Isn't that the guy with all the NYPD commendations?"

Blatt didn't answer. But something about the question changed the dynamic of the situation just enough to restrain further escalation. He stared dully at Gurney.

"A word to the wise: Get out of here. Get out of here right this fucking minute. You even breathe on this case, I guarantee you'll get banged for obstruction." He raised his hand, pointed his forefinger between Gurney's eyes, and dropped his thumb like a hammer.

Gurney nodded. "I hear you, but . . . I have a question. Suppose I discover that all your assumptions about this murder are bullshit. Who should I tell?"

Chapter 22

Spider man

The coffee on the drive home was a mistake. The cigarette was a bigger mistake.

The gas-station brew had been concentrated by time and evaporation into a caffeine-packed, tar-colored liquid that didn't taste much like coffee at all. Gurney drank it anyway: a comforting ritual. Not so comforting was the impact of the caffeine on his nerves as the first rush of stimulation gave way to a vibrating anxiety that demanded a cigarette. But that, too, came with pluses and minuses: a brief feeling of ease and freedom, followed by thoughts as bleak as the dispiriting overcast. The memory of something a therapist had said fifteen years earlier: *David, you behave like two different people. In your professional life, you have drive, determination, direction. In your personal life, you're a ship without a rudder.* Sometimes he had the illusion of making progress—giving up smoking, living more of his life outdoors and less of it in his head, focusing on the here and now and Madeleine. But inevitably he slipped back from what he'd hoped to be into the shape of the person he'd always been.

His new Subaru had no ashtray, and he was making do with the rinsed-out sardine tin he kept in the car for that purpose. As he ground his butt into it, it suddenly brought to mind another acute instance of failure in his personal life, another jabbing reminder of a mind adrift: He'd forgotten about dinner.

His call to Madeleine—omitting his memory lapse, asking only if she wanted him to pick up anything on his way home—did not leave him feeling any better. He had the sense that she knew he'd forgotten, knew he was trying to cover it up. It was a short call with long silences. Their final exchange:

"You'll clear your murder files off the dinner table when you get home?"

"Yes. I said I would."

"Good."

For the balance of the drive, Gurney's restless mind skittered around a set of bothersome questions: Why was Arlo Blatt waiting at the bottom of Badger Lane? There was no surveillance car there earlier. Had he been tipped that someone was asking questions? That Gurney in particular was asking questions? But who would care enough to call Blatt? Why was Blatt so eager to keep him off the case? Which reminded Gurney of another unresolved question: Why was Jack Hardwick so eager to have him on it?

At exactly 5:00 P.M. under a glowering sky, Gurney turned onto the dirt-and-gravel road that ran up into the hills to his farmhouse. A mile or so along the way, he caught sight of a car ahead of him, a grayish green Prius. As they proceeded up the dusty road, it became increasingly certain that the people in the car were the mystery dinner guests.

The Prius slowed to a cautious crawl on the rutted farm track through the pasture to the informal parking area of matted-down grass next to the house. A second before they emerged, Gurney remembered: George and Peggy Meeker. George, retired professor of entomology in his early sixties, a gangling praying mantis of a man; and Peggy, bubbly social worker in her early fifties who'd talked Madeleine into her current part-time job. As Gurney parked, the Meekers removed from their backseat a platter and a bowl covered with aluminum foil.

"Salad and dessert!" cried Peggy. "Sorry we're late. George lost the car keys!" She seemed to find this both exasperating and entertaining.

George raised his hand in a gesture of greeting, accompanied by a sour glance at his wife. Gurney managed only a small smile of welcome. The George-and-Peggy dynamic was too close for comfort to what had gone on between his parents.

Madeleine came to the door, her smile directed at the Meekers.

"Salad and dessert," explained Peggy, handing the covered dishes to Madeleine, who made appreciative noises and led the way into the big farmhouse kitchen.

"I love it!" said Peggy with wide-eyed appreciation, the same reaction she'd had on their two previous visits, adding as she always did, "It's the perfect house for you two. Don't you think it fits their personalities perfectly, George?"

George nodded agreeably, eyeing the case files on the table, tilting his head to read the abbreviated content descriptions on the covers. "I thought you were retired," he said to Gurney.

"I am. This is just a brief consulting assignment."

"An invitation to a beheading," said Madeleine.

"What sort of consulting assignment?" asked Peggy with real interest.

"I've been asked to review the evidence in a murder case and suggest alternative directions for the investigation if they seem warranted."

"Sounds fascinating," said Peggy. "Is it a case that's been in the news?"

He hesitated a moment before answering, "Yes, a few months ago. The tabloids referred to it as the case of the butchered bride."

"No! Why, that's incredible! You're investigating that horrible murder? The young woman who was killed in her wedding dress? What exactly—"

Madeleine broke in, her voice's volume a little high for the proximity of the company. "What can I get you folks to drink?"

Peggy kept her eyes on Gurney.

Madeleine went on, loud and cheery. "We have a California pinot grigio, an Italian Barolo, and a Finger Lakes something-or-other with a cute name."

"Barolo for me," said George.

"I want to hear the inside story of this murder," declared Peggy, adding as an afterthought, "Any wine is fine for me. Except the cute one."

"I'll have a Barolo like George," said Gurney.

"Could you clear the table now?" asked Madeleine.

"Absolutely," said Gurney. He turned to the task and began consolidating the many piles of papers into a few. "I should have done it this morning. Can't remember a damn thing anymore."

Madeleine smiled dangerously, got a couple of bottles from the pantry, and went about the business of extracting corks.

"So . . . ?" said Peggy, still staring expectantly at Gurney.

"How much do you remember from the news stories?" he asked.

"Gorgeous young woman, murdered by a crazy Mexican gardener about ten minutes after marrying none other than Scott Ashton."

"Sounds like you know who he is."

"Know who he is? Jeez, everybody in the world— Wait, let me take that back. Everybody in the world of *social sciences* knows Scott Ashton—or at least his reputation, his books, his journal articles. He's the hottest sexual-abuse therapist out there."

"*Hottest?*" said Madeleine, approaching with two glasses of red wine.

George guffawed, an oddly hearty sound from his sticklike frame.

Peggy winced. "Poor word choice. Should have said *most famous*. Lots of cutting-edge therapies. I'm sure Dave can tell us a heck of a lot more than that." She accepted the glass Madeleine offered her, took a small sip, and smiled. "Lovely. Thanks."

"So tomorrow's the big day, right?" said Madeleine.

Peggy blinked confusedly at the change of subject.

"Big day," echoed George.

"Not every day your son goes off to Harvard," said Madeleine. "And didn't you tell us he was going to major in biology?"

"That's the *plan*," said George, ever the cautious scientist.

Neither parent showed much appetite for the subject, perhaps because this was the third of their sons to take this path and everything that could be said had been said.

"Are you still teaching?" Peggy addressed the question to Gurney.

"You mean at the academy?"

"Guest lecturer, wasn't it?"

"Yes, I do it from time to time. A special seminar on undercover work."

"He teaches a course in lying," said Madeleine.

The Meekers laughed uneasily. George polished off his Barolo.

"I teach the good guys how to lie to the bad guys so the bad guys tell the good guys what we need to know."

"That's a way of putting it," said Madeleine.

"You must have some great stories," said Peggy.

"George," said Madeleine, stepping between Peggy and Gurney, "let me refill your glass." He handed it to her, and she retreated to the sink island. "It must be a very nice feeling to have your sons following in your footsteps."

"Well . . . not entirely in my footsteps. Biology, yes, in a general way, but so far no interest expressed by any of them in entomology, much less my own specialty of arachnology. On the contrary—"

"Now, if I remember rightly," Peggy interrupted, "you folks have a son?"

"David has a son," said Madeleine, stepping back to the sink island, pouring herself a pinot grigio.

"Ah. Yes. His name's on the tip of my tongue—something with an *L*, or was it a *K*?"

"Kyle," said Gurney, as though it were a word he rarely pronounced.

"He's on Wall Street, right?"

"*Was* on Wall Street. Now he's in law school."

"Casualty of the bursting bubble?" asked George.

"More or less."

"Classic disaster," intoned George with intellectual disdain. "House of cards. Million-dollar mortgages being handed out like lollipops to three-year-olds. Moguls and bigwigs leaping from the towers of high finance. Bloody big bankers dug their own graves. Only bad thing is that our government in its infinite wisdom decided to resurrect the idiot bastards—bring them back to life with our tax money. Should have let the scum-of-the-earth CEOs rot in hell!"

"Bravo, George!" said Madeleine, raising her glass.

Peggy shot him an icy glance. "I'm sure he's not including your son among the evildoers."

Madeleine smiled at George. "You were starting to say something about your sons' careers in biology?"

"Oh, yes. Well, no, actually, I was about to say that the oldest not only has no interest in arachnology, he claims to suffer from arachnophobia." He said this as though it were the equivalent of apple pie–phobia. "And that's not all, he even——"

"For Godsake, don't get George talking about spiders," said Peggy, interrupting him for the second time. "I realize that they're the most fascinating creatures on earth, endlessly beneficial, and so forth and so on. But right now I would much rather hear about Dave's murder case than the Peruvian orb weaver."

"My lonely little vote would be for the orb weaver. But I guess that can wait," said Madeleine, taking a long sip of her wine. "Why don't you folks all sit by the fireplace and exhaust the subject of beheadings while I put a few finishing touches on dinner. It'll just be a few minutes."

"Can I help?" Peggy asked. She looked liked she was trying to assess Madeleine's tone.

"No, everything is just about ready. Thanks, anyway."

"You sure?"

"Sure."

After another querying look, she retreated with the two men to three overstuffed chairs at the other end of the room. "Okay," she said to Gurney as soon as they were settled, "tell us the story."

By the time Madeleine called them to the table for dinner, it was getting close to six o'clock and Gurney had related a reasonably complete history of the case to date, including its twists and open ends. His narrative had been dramatic without being gory, suggestive of possible sexual entanglements without implying that they were the essence of the case, and as coherent as the facts permitted. The Meekers had been attentive, listening with care and saying nothing.

At the table—halfway into the spinach, walnut, and Stilton salad—the comments and questions started coming, mostly from Peggy.

"So if Flores was gay, the motive for killing the bride would be jealousy. But the method sounds psychotic. Is it believable that one of the top psychiatrists in the world wouldn't have noticed that the man living on his property was stark raving mad—capable of chopping someone's head off?"

"And if Flores was straight," said Gurney, "the jealousy motive would disappear, but we'd still have the 'stark raving mad' part and the problem of Ashton's not noticing it."

Peggy leaned forward in her chair, gesturing with her fork. "Of course, his being straight works with the scenario that he was having an affair with the Muller woman, and their running off together, but then we're left with the 'stark raving mad' thing as the only explanation for killing the bride."

"Plus," said Gurney, "you'd have both Scott Ashton and Kiki Muller both failing to notice that Flores is bonkers. And there's another problem. What woman would willingly run off with a man who'd just cut off another woman's head?"

Peggy gave a little shudder. "I can't imagine that."

Madeleine spoke with a bored sigh. "Didn't seem to bother the wives of Henry VIII."

There was a momentary silence, broken by another of George's guffaws.

"I guess there might be a difference," ventured Peggy, "between the king of England and a Mexican gardener."

Madeleine, studying one of the walnuts in her salad, didn't reply.

George stepped into the open space in the conversation. "What about the fellow you were telling us about with the toy trains, 'Adeste Fideles,' and so on? Suppose he killed them all."

Peggy screwed up her face. "What are you talking about, George? All who?"

"It's a possibility, isn't it? Suppose his wife was a bit of a slut and jumped into bed with the Mexican. And maybe the bride was a bit of a slut, and she'd jumped in bed with the Mexican, too. Maybe Mr. Muller just decided to kill them all—good riddance to bad rubbish, two sluts and their cheap little Romeo."

"My God, George!" cried Peggy. "You sound pleased with what happened to the victims."

"All victims are not necessarily innocent."

"George——"

"Why did he leave the machete in the woods?" Madeleine cut in.

After a pause during which everyone looked at her, Gurney asked, "Is it the trail that bothers you? The scent trail going only so far, then stopping?"

"It bothers me that the machete was left in the woods for no apparent reason. It doesn't make any sense."

"Actually," said Gurney, "that's a hell of a good point. Let's look closer at that."

"Actually, let's not." Madeleine's voice was controlled but rising. "I'm sorry I even mentioned it. In fact, this whole discussion is giving me indigestion. Can we please talk about something else?" There was an awkward silence around the table. "George, tell us about your favorite spider. I bet you have a favorite."

"Oh . . . I couldn't say." He looked a bit disoriented, not quite here or there.

"Come on, George."

"You heard—I've been warned off that subject."

Peggy glanced around nervously. "Go ahead, George. It's perfectly all right."

Now everyone was looking at George. The attention seemed to please him. It was easy to imagine the man at the front of a college lecture hall—Professor Meeker, respected entomologist, font of wisdom and pertinent anecdotes.

Careful, Gurney, any judgment of him may apply to you. What are you doing at that police academy, anyway?

George raised his chin proudly. "Jumpers," he said.

Madeleine's eyes widened. "Jumping . . . spiders?"

"Yes."

"Do they really *jump?*"

"Indeed they do. They can jump fifty times their body length. That's the same as a six-foot man jumping the length of a football field, and the amazing thing is, they have practically no leg muscles. So how, you may ask, do they manage so prodigious a leap? With hydraulic pumps! Valves in their legs release spurts of pressurized blood, causing the legs to extend and propel them into the air. Imagine a deadly predator dropping out of nowhere onto its prey without warning. No hope of escape." Meeker's eyes sparkled. Not unlike a proud parent.

The parent thought made Gurney queasy.

"And then, of course," Meeker went on excitedly, "there's the black widow—a truly elegant killing machine. A creature lethal to adversaries a thousand times its size."

"A creature," said Peggy, coming to life, "that fits Scott Ashton's definition of perfection."

Madeleine gave her a quizzical look.

"I'm referring to Scott Ashton's infamous book that treats empathy—concern for the welfare and feelings of others—as a defect, an imperfection in the human boundary system. The black widow spider, with its nasty habit of killing and eating its mate after intercourse, would probably be his idea of perfection. The perfection of the sociopath."

"But since he wrote a second book attacking his first book," said Gurney, "it's hard to know what he really thinks of sociopaths or black widows—or anything, for that matter."

Madeleine's quizzical look at Peggy sharpened. "This is the man you said is a big authority on treating sexual-abuse victims?"

"Yes, but . . . not exactly. He doesn't treat the victims. He treats the abusers."

Madeleine's expression shifted, as though she considered this bit of information of great significance.

For Gurney all it did was add to the list of questions he wanted to ask Ashton in the morning. And that reminded him of another open question, one he decided to ask his guests: "Does the name Edward Vallory ring a bell with either of you?"

At 10:45 P.M., just as Gurney finally dozed off, his cell phone rang on the night table on Madeleine's side of the bed. He heard it ring, heard her answering it, heard her say, "I'll see if he's awake." Then she tapped him on the arm and held the phone toward him until he sat up and took it.

It was Ashton's smooth baritone, tightened slightly by anxiety. "Sorry to bother you, but this may be important. I received a text message a little while ago. The caller ID number indicates it came from Hector's phone—one of those prepaid things. He got it about a year ago and gave me the number. But this text message—I believe it's exactly the same as the one Jillian received on our wedding day: 'For all the reasons I have written. Edward Vallory.' I called the BCI office and reported it, and I wanted you to know about it as well." He paused, cleared his throat nervously. "Do you think it means that Hector might be coming back?"

Gurney was not a man who revered the mystique of coincidence. In this case, however, the intrusion of the name Edward Vallory so soon after his bringing it up himself gave him an unpleasant chill.

It took over an hour for him to get back to sleep.

Chapter 23

Leverage

"Just two weeks," said Gurney as he brought his coffee to the breakfast table.

"Hmm." Madeleine was very articulate with her little sounds. This one conveyed that she understood what he was saying but had no desire to discuss the subject at the moment. In the early-morning light, she was somehow managing to read *Crime and Punishment* for an upcoming meeting of her book club.

"Just two weeks. That's what I'm giving it."

"That's what you've decided?" she asked, without looking up.

"I don't see why it should be such a huge problem."

She partially closed the book, leaving her finger between the pages she was reading, tilted her head a little to the side, and gazed at him. "Exactly how *huge* a problem do you think it is?"

"Jesus, I'm not a mind reader. Forget it, erase that, that was a stupid comment. What I'm saying is, I'm limiting my involvement in this Perry business to a two-week window. No matter what happens, that's it." He put his coffee cup on the table, sat down across from her. "Look, I'm probably not making much sense here. But I really do understand your concern. I know what you went through last year."

"Do you?"

He closed his eyes. "I think so. I really do. And it won't happen again."

The fact was, he'd almost been killed at the end of the last investigation he'd volunteered his way into. A full year into his retirement, he'd come closer to his own death than he ever had in over twenty years as an NYPD homicide detective. He thought it was probably that aspect of it that had hit Madeleine the hardest—not just the danger, but that it had actually increased at the very point in their lives when she'd imagined that it would go away.

A long silence passed between them.

She finally sighed, withdrew the finger she was using as a book-mark, and pushed the book away from her. "You know, Dave, what I want is not all that complicated. Or maybe it is. I'd thought when we left our careers behind we'd discover a different kind of life together."

He smiled weakly. "All that damn asparagus is pretty different."

"And your bulldozer is different. And my flower garden is different. But we seem to have trouble with the 'life *together*' part."

"Don't you think we're together more now than when we were in the city?"

"I think we're in the same house at the same time more often. But it's obvious now that I was more willing to leave that other life behind us than you were. So that's my mistake, thinking we were on the same page. My mistake," she repeated, speaking softly with anger and sadness in her eyes.

He sat back in his chair, looked up at the ceiling. "A therapist once told me that an expectation is nothing but a resentment wait-ing to be born." As soon as he said this, he wished he hadn't. Jesus, he thought, if he'd been as clumsy in his undercover work as he was in speaking to his own wife, he'd have been sliced and diced a decade ago.

"Nothing but a resentment waiting to be born? Cute," snapped Madeleine. "Very cute. What about hope? Did he have something equally clever and dismissive to say about hope?" The anger was moving from her eyes into her voice. "What about progress? Did he have anything to say about progress? Or closeness? What did he say about that?"

"Sorry," Gurney said. "Just another stupid comment on my part. I seem to be full of them. Let me start over. All I wanted to say was that—"

She cut in, "That you've decided to sign on for a two-week tour of duty, working for a crazy woman, searching for a psychotic murderer?" She stared at him, apparently daring him to try restating the proposition in milder terms. "Okay, David. Fine. Two weeks. What can I say? You're going to do what you're going to do. And by the way, I know that what you do takes great strength, great courage, great honesty, and a superb mind. I really do know what a remarkable man you are. You truly are one in a million. I'm in awe of you, David. But you know what? I'd like to be a little less in awe of you and a little more *with* you. Do you think that would be possible? That's all I want to know. Do you think we could be a little bit closer?"

His mind went nearly blank.

Then he muttered softly, "God, Maddie, I hope so."

It started to rain on the way to Tambury. An intermittent-wiper sort of rain, more like a light drizzle. Gurney stopped along the way in Dillweed for a second cup of coffee—not at a gas station but at Abelard's organic-produce market, where the coffee was freshly ground, freshly made, and very good.

He sat with the coffee in his parked car in front of the market, thumbing through the case notes, finding the page he wanted: a record supplied by the phone company of the dates and times of text-message exchanges between the cell phones of Jillian Perry and Hector Flores during the three weeks leading up to the murder—thirteen from Flores to Perry, twelve from Perry to Flores. On a separate sheet, stapled to the record, was a report from the state police computer lab, indicating that all messages had been deleted from Jillian Perry's phone, with the exception of the final "Edward Vallory" message, received approximately one hour prior to the fourteen-minute window within which the murder was committed. The report also noted the fact that the phone company retains date, duration, originating and receiving cell numbers, and transmitting-cell-tower data on all calls, but no content data. So once those texts had been erased from Jillian's phone, there was no method of retrieval, unless Hector had saved the message strings on *his* phone and its memory could be accessed in the future—not possibilities to be optimistic about.

Gurney put the sheets back into their folder, finished his coffee, and continued on through the gray, wet morning to his eight-thirty appointment with Scott Ashton.

The door swung open before Gurney had a chance to knock. Ashton was dressed as before in expensively casual clothes, the sort he might have ordered from a catalog with a Cotswold stone house on the cover.

"Come in, let's get to it," he said with a perfunctory smile. "We don't have a great deal of time." He led the way through a large center hall into a sitting room on the right that seemed to have been furnished in an earlier century. The upholstered chairs and settees were mostly Queen Anne. The tables, the mantel above the fireplace, the chair legs, and other wood surfaces had an ancient, softly lustrous patina.

Among the predictable grace notes one might expect to find in an upper-class English-style country home, there was one startling discordance. On the wall above the dark chestnut mantel hung a very large framed photograph in the horizontal orientation and the approximate size of a two-page spread in the magazine section of the Sunday *Times*.

Then Gurney realized why that particular size comparison came readily to mind: The photograph was one he'd actually seen in that very publication. It fit into that overpriced-fashion-ad genre in which the models gaze at each other or at the world in general with an arrogant, druggy sensuality. Even among its kind, however, this example was striking in its communication of something profoundly unwell. The composition consisted of two very young women, surely not yet out of their teens, sprawled on what appeared to be a bedroom floor, eyeing each other's body with a combination of exhaustion and insatiable sexual hunger. They were naked except for a couple of adroitly placed silk scarves, presumably the products of the fashion house sponsoring the ad.

When Gurney looked closer, he saw that it was a manipulated photograph—in fact, two differently posed photographs of the same model positioned and retouched in a way that made them appear to be gazing at each other, adding a dimension of narcissism to the already ample pathology of the scene. It was, in a way, an impressive work of art—a depiction of pure decadence worthy of illustrating Dante's *Inferno*. Gurney turned toward Ashton, his curiosity evident in his expression.

"Jillian," said Ashton flatly. "My late wife."

Gurney was speechless.

The picture raised so many questions that he didn't know which to ask first.

He had the feeling that Ashton was not only observing but enjoying his confusion. Which raised more questions. Finally he thought of something to say, something he'd completely forgotten about during their first meeting. "I'm terribly sorry for your tragic loss. And I'm sorry for not saying so yesterday."

A heaviness, a cloud of depression and weariness, seemed to draw all of Ashton's features downward. "Thank you."

"I'm surprised you've been able to stay in this house—seeing that cottage out in back every day, knowing what happened there."

"It will be torn down," said Ashton, almost brutally. "Torn down, crushed, burned. As soon as the police give their permission. They still have some lingering jurisdiction over it as a crime scene. But the day will come. The cottage will cease to exist."

Ashton took a deep breath, and the display of emotion slowly faded. "So where shall be begin?" He gestured toward a pair of burgundy velvet wing chairs with a small, square table between them. The tabletop consisted of a hand-carved intarsia chessboard, but there were no chess pieces in sight.

Gurney decided to address the elephant in the room, the sensationally tawdry picture of Jillian, head-on. "I'd never have guessed that the girl in that photo on the wall was the bride I saw in the video."

"The flowing white gown, demure makeup, et cetera?" Ashton looked almost amused.

"None of that seems consistent with this," said Gurney, staring at the photo.

"Would it make more sense if you knew that her traditional bridal getup was Jillian's idea of a joke?"

"A joke?"

"This may strike you as crude and unfeeling, Detective, but we haven't much time, so let me tell you quickly about Jillian. Some of this you might have heard from her mother and some not. Jillian's personality was irritable, intensely moody, easily bored, self-centered, intolerant, impatient, and volatile."

"Quite a profile."

"That was her brighter side—the relatively harmless Jillian, spoiled and bipolar. Her darker side was something else entirely." Ashton paused, gazed fixedly at the picture on the wall as if to check the accuracy of his words.

Gurney waited, wondered where this extraordinary commentary was going.

"Jillian . . ." Ashton began, still looking at the picture, speaking softly now and more slowly. "Jillian was in her childhood a sexual predator, an abuser of other children. That was the chief symptom of the central pathology that brought her to Mapleshade at the age of thirteen. Her more obvious affective and behavioral problems were ripples on the surface."

He moistened his lips with the tip of his tongue, then rubbed them with his thumb and forefinger as if to dry them again. His gaze shifted from the picture to Gurney's face. "Now, do you want to ask your questions, or shall I ask them for you?"

Gurney was happy to let Ashton keep talking. "What do you think my first question would be?"

"If your mind weren't spinning with a dozen of them? I think your first question, at least to yourself, would be: Is Ashton crazy? Because, if so, that would explain a lot. But if not, then your second question would be: Why on earth would he want to marry a woman with such a disordered background? To the first question, I have no credible answer. No man is a trustworthy guarantor of his own sanity. To the second question, I would say that it's unfairly slanted, since Jillian had another quality I failed to mention. Brilliance. Brilliance beyond the normal scope of the term. She had the fastest, most facile mind I've ever encountered. I am an exceptionally intelligent man, Detective. I am not being immodest, just truthful. You see the chessboard built into this table? There are no chessmen. I play without them. I find it a stimulating mental challenge to play the game in my mind, imagining and remembering the positions of the pieces. Sometimes I play against myself, visualizing the board alternately from the white side and the black side, back and forth. Most people are impressed by that ability. But believe me when I tell you that Jillian's mind was more formidable than my own. I find intelligence like that in a woman very attractive—attractive in both the companionable and erotic senses."

The more Gurney heard, the more questions came to mind. "I've heard that sexual abusers are often victims of abuse themselves. Is that true?"

"Yes."

"True in the case of Jillian?"

"Yes."

"Who was the abuser?"

"It wasn't just one person."

"Who were *they*, then?"

"According to an unverified account, they were Val Perry's crack-addict friends, and the abuse, by numerous perpetrators, occurred repeatedly between the ages of three and seven."

"Jesus. Are there any legal intervention records, social-service case files?"

"None of it was reported at the time."

"But when she was finally sent to Mapleshade, it all came out? What about the records of the treatment she was given, statements she made to her therapists?"

"There are none. I should explain something about Mapleshade. First of all, it's a school, not a medical facility. A private school for young women with special problems. In recent years we have admitted a growing percentage of students whose problems center on sexual issues, especially abuse."

"I was told that your treatment emphasis is on abusers rather than the abused."

"Yes—although *treatment* is not the right word, since we are not, as I said, a medical facility. And the line between abuser and abused is not always as clear as you might think. The point I'm making is that Mapleshade is effective because it is discreet. We accept no court or social-service referrals, no insurance, no state aid, provide no medical or psychiatric diagnoses or treatment, and—this is vitally important—we keep no 'patient' records."

"Yet the school apparently has a reputation for offering state-of-the-art treatment, or whatever you choose to call it, directed by the renowned Dr. Scott Ashton." Gurney's voice had taken on a sharper edge, to which Ashton showed no reaction.

"A greater stigma attaches to these disorders than to any other. Knowing that everything here is absolutely confidential, that there are no case files or insurance forms or therapy notes that can be purloined or subpoenaed, is a priceless benefit to our clientele. Legally we're just a private secondary school with a knowledgeable staff available for informal chats on a variety of sensitive issues."

Gurney sat back, pondering Mapleshade's unusual structure and the implications of that structure. Perhaps sensing his uneasiness, Ashton added, "Consider this: The feeling of security that our system offers makes it possible for our students and their families to tell us things that they would never dream of divulging if the information were going into a file. There's no source of guilt and shame and fear deeper than the disorders we deal with here."

"Why didn't you reveal Jillian's horrendous background to the investigation team?"

"There was no reason to."

"No reason?"

"My wife was killed by my psychotic gardener, who then escaped. The task of the police is to track him down. What should I have said? Oh, by the way, when my wife was three years old, she was raped by her mother's crazed crackhead friends? How would that help them apprehend Hector Flores?"

"How old was she when she made the transition from victim to abuser?"

"Five."

"*Five?*"

"This area of dysfunction always shocks people outside the field. The behavior is so inconsistent with what we like to think of as the innocence of childhood. Unfortunately, five-year-old abusers of even younger children are not as rare as you might think."

"Jesus." Gurney looked with growing concern at the picture on the wall. "Who were her victims?"

"I don't know."

"Val Perry is aware of all this?"

"Yes. She's still not comfortable talking about it in any detail, in case you're wondering why she didn't tell you. But it's why she came to you."

"I don't follow you."

Ashton took a deep breath. "Val is driven by guilt. To make a complicated story simple, in her twenties she was part of a drug scene and not much of a mother. She surrounded herself with addicts even crazier than she was, which led to the abuse situation I described, which led to Jillian's ensuing sexual aggression and other behavior disorders, which Val was unable to deal with. Her guilt tore her apart—a colorful cliché, but accurate. She felt responsible for every problem in her daughter's life, and now she feels responsible for her death. She's frustrated by the official police investigation—no leads, no progress, no closure. I believe she came to you in one final attempt to do something right for Jillian. Certainly too little too late, but it's the only thing she could think of doing. She heard about you from one of the officers at BCI, about your reputation as a homicide detective in the city, read some article about you in *New York* magazine, and decided you represented her best and last chance to make up for being a terrible mother. It's pathetic, but there it is."

"How do you know all this?"

"After Jillian's murder, Val was close to a breakdown, and she still is. Talking about these things was one way of holding herself together."

"And you?"

"Me?"

"How have you held yourself together?"

"Is that curiosity or sarcasm?"

"Your discussion of the most horrible event of your life, and the people involved in it, seems remarkably detached. I don't know what to make of that."

"Don't you? That's hard to believe."

"Meaning what?"

"My impression, Detective, is that you would respond the same way to the death of someone close to you." He regarded Gurney with the neutrality of the classic therapist. "I suggest the parallel as a way of helping you understand my position. You're asking yourself, 'Is he concealing his emotion at the death of his wife, or is there no emotion to conceal?' Before I give you the answer, think about what you saw on the video."

"You mean your reaction to what you saw in the cottage?"

Ashton's voice hardened, and he spoke with a rigidity that seemed to vibrate with the power of a barely contained fury. "I believe that part of Hector's motive was to inflict pain on me. He succeeded. My pain was recorded on that video. It's a fact I can't change. However, I did make a resolution never to show that pain again. Not to anyone. Not ever."

Gurney's eyes rested on the chessboard's delicate intarsia inlay. "You have no doubt at all about the murderer's identity?"

Ashton blinked, looked like he was having trouble understanding the question. "I beg your pardon?"

"You have no doubt that Hector Flores is the person who killed your wife?"

"No doubt at all. I gave some thought to the suggestion you made yesterday that Carl Muller might be involved, but frankly I don't see it."

"Is it possible that Hector was gay, that the motive for the killing—"

"That's absurd."

"It's a theory the police were considering."

"I know something about sexuality. Trust me. Hector was not gay." He looked deliberately at his watch.

Gurney sat back, waited for Ashton to make eye contact with him. "It must take a special kind of person—the field you're in."

"Meaning?"

"It must be depressing. I've heard that sex offenders are almost impossible to cure."

Ashton sat back like Gurney, held his gaze, steepled his fingers under his chin. "That's a media generalization. Half true, half nonsense."

"Still, it must be a difficult kind of work."

"What sort of difficulty are you imagining?"

"All the stress. So much at stake. The consequences of failure."

"Like police work. Like life in general." Again Ashton looked at his watch.

"So what's the glue?" asked Gurney.

"The glue?"

"The thing that attaches you to the sexual-abuse field."

"This is relevant to finding Flores?"

"It may be."

Ashton closed his eyes and bowed his head so that his steepled fingers assumed a prayerful attitude. "You're right about the high stakes. Sexual energy in general has tremendous power, the power to concentrate one's attention like nothing else, to become the sole reality, to warp judgment, to obliterate pain and the perception of risk. The power to make all other considerations irrelevant. There is no force on earth that comes close to it in its power to blind and drive the individual in its grip. When this energy within a person is focused on an inappropriate object—specifically, another person of less-than-equal strength and understanding—the potential for damage is truly endless. Because in the intensity of its power and primitive excitement, its ability to twist reality, inappropriate sexual behavior can be as contagious as the bite of a vampire. In pursuit of the magic power of the abuser, the abused may become an abuser herself. There are simple evolutionary, neurological, and psychological roots for the overwhelming strength of the sex drive. Its diversions into destructive channels can be analyzed, described, diagrammed. But altering those diversions is another matter entirely. To understand the genesis of a tidal wave is one thing; to change its direction is something else." He opened his eyes, lowered his steepled hands from his face.

"It's the challenge in it that attracts you?"

"It's the *leverage* in it."

"You mean the ability to make a difference?"

"Yes!" Some inner rheostat turned up the light in Ashton's eyes. "The ability to intervene in what otherwise would be an everlasting chain of misery spreading out from the abuser into everyone he or she touched, and from those to others, and down through future generations. This is not like the removal of a tumor, which may save one life. Success rates in the field are debatable, but even one success can prevent the destruction of a hundred lives."

Gurney smiled, looked impressed. "So that's the mission of Mapleshade?"

Ashton mirrored the smile. "Exactly." Another glance at his watch. "And now I really do need to leave. You can stay if you wish, have a look around the grounds, a look at the cottage. The key is under the black rock to the right of the doorstep. If you want to see the spot where the machete was found, go around to the rear of the cottage as far as the middle window, then walk straight out into the woods about a hundred and fifty yards, and you'll find a tall stake in the ground. There was originally a yellow police ribbon tied around the top, but that may be gone by now. Good luck, Detective."

He showed Gurney out, left him standing on the brick-paved driveway, and drove off in a vintage Jaguar sedan, as evocatively English as the chamomile scent in the damp air.

Chapter 24

A patient spider

Gurney felt an urgent need to sort and review, to take the mass of data and possibilities crowding his mind and arrange them in a manageable order. Although the drizzle had finally stopped, there was no place outside Ashton's house dry enough to sit, so he retreated to his car. He took out the spiral pad with his notes on Calvin Harlen, turned to a new page, closed his eyes, and began rerunning the mental tapes of his meeting with Ashton.

He soon found this disciplined process hopeless. However hard he tried to go over the details in their actual chronology, weigh them, match them like puzzle pieces with similar pieces, one huge fact kept elbowing its way in front of all the others: *Jillian Perry had sexually abused other children. It was not uncommon for a victim of that offense, or a member of a victim's family, to seek revenge. It was not unheard-of for that revenge to take the form of murder.*

The impact of this possibility filled his mind. It fit the contours of his thinking in a way no other aspect of the case had so far. Finally there was a motive that made sense, that didn't bring with it an immediate surge of doubt, that didn't create more problems than it solved. And along with it came certain implications. For example: *The key questions about Hector Flores might not be where did he disappear to and how, but where did he come from and why?* The focus needed to shift from what might have happened in Tambury that drove Flores to commit murder to what might have happened in the past that drove him to Tambury.

Gurney was now too restless to sit still. He got back out of his car, looked around at the house, the slate-roofed garage, the arched trellis entrance to the rear lawn. Was this the first view Hector Flores had had of Ashton's manorial property three and a half years earlier? Or had he been looking it over for some time, watching Ashton come and go? When he knocked on the door for the first time, how far along were his plans? Was Jillian his target from the beginning? Was Ashton, director of the school she'd attended, a route to her? Or were his plans more general—perhaps a violent assault on one or more of the offenders that Mapleshade harbored? Or for that matter, might the original target have been Ashton himself—the harborer, the doctor who helped abusers? Might Jillian's murder have offered a double benefit: her death and Ashton's pain?

Whatever the specifics, the questions were the same: Who was Hector Flores, really? What awful transgression had brought so determined a killer to Ashton's doorstep? A killer of such deception and foresight that he'd inveigled an invitation to live in a cottage in his eventual victim's backyard. A web in which he'd waited. Waited for the ideal moment.

Hector Flores. A patient spider.

Gurney went to the cottage, unlocked the door.

Inside, the place had the bare look of an apartment for rent. No furniture, no possessions, nothing but a faint odor of detergent or disinfectant. The simplest of floor plans: a wide all-purpose room in front and two smaller rooms behind it—a bedroom and a kitchen, with a tiny bathroom and closet sandwiched between them. He stood in the middle of the front room and let his gaze travel slowly over the floor, walls, ceiling. His brain was not wired to accommodate the notion of a place having an aura, but every homicide scene he'd visited over the years affected him in a way that was both strange and familiar.

Responding to a call from the uniformed 911 responders, stepping into a violent crime scene with its blood and gristle, splintered bones and splattered brains, never failed to ignite in him a certain set of feelings: revulsion, pity, anger. But visiting the site at a later date—after the inevitable scouring, all tangible evidence of butchery removed—was just as deeply affecting, but in a different way. A blood-soaked room would slam him in the face. Later, stripped and sanitized, the same room would lay a cold hand on his heart, reminding him that at the center of the universe there was a boundless emptiness. A vacuum with a temperature of absolute zero.

He cleared his throat loudly, as if relying on the noise to transport him from these morbid musings to a more practical frame of mind. He went into the little kitchen, examined the empty drawers and cabinets. Then he went into the bedroom, straight to the window through which the killer had exited. He opened it, looked out, then climbed out through it.

The ground outside was only about a foot lower than the floor inside. He stood with his back to the cottage, peering out into the dreary copse. The atmosphere was humid, silent, the herbal redolence of the gardens yielding here to a woodsier scent. He made his way forward with long, deliberate steps, counting his paces. At 140 he caught sight of a yellow ribbon atop a plastic stake driven like a thin broomstick into the ground.

He went to the spot, looking around in all directions. His route was circumscribed on his right by a steep-sided ravine. The cottage behind him was hidden by the intervening foliage, as was the road that he knew from the Google satellite photos to lie fifty yards ahead. He examined the ground, the area of leafy soil where the machete had been partly concealed, wondering what might explain the inability of the K-9 team to follow the trail any farther. The idea that Flores had changed his shoes at this point, or covered them with plastic, and proceeded on through the woods to the road, or through the woods to another house on the lane (Kiki Muller's?) seemed unlikely. The question that had bothered Gurney before still had no answer: What would the point be of leaving half a trail, a trail to the weapon? And if the goal was for the weapon to be found, why half bury it? And then there was the little mystery of the boots—the one personal item Flores had left behind, the boots that the scent-tracking dog had keyed on. How did they fit into Flores's escape scenario?

Since the boots were found in the house, did that suggest that the trail to the machete could have been one leg of a round trip?

Might Flores have come out here from the cottage, disposed of the machete, and returned the way he came—back through the window? That solved part of the scent-trail conundrum. But it created a new and greater difficulty: It put Flores back in the cottage at the point when the body was discovered, with no way of leaving it again unobserved prior to the arrival of the police. On top of that, the out-and-back hypothesis didn't answer the other question: Why would Flores leave a trail out to the machete to begin with? Unless the whole idea was to create the impression that he'd left the area, when really he hadn't . . . to create the impression that he'd run off through the woods, hurriedly hiding the machete on his way, when he was actually back in the cottage. But back in the cottage where? Where could a man hide in such a tiny building—a building fine-combed for six hours by a team of evidence techs whose whole expertise lay in missing nothing?

Gurney made his way back through the woods, climbed through the cottage window, and reexplored the three rooms, looking for access points to spaces above the ceiling or below the floor. The roof pitch was low, likely a truss structure that would have a limited area toward the middle where a man could sit or crouch. However, as with most such useless spaces, there was no entry point. The floor also appeared seamless, with no way down into whatever space might exist beneath it. He went from room to room, checking the position of each wall from each side of it to make sure there were no unaccounted-for interior spaces.

The notion that Flores had returned from the woods in those boots and secreted himself and remained undetected in this little twenty-four-by-twenty-four building was unraveling as rapidly as it had been conceived. Gurney locked the door, put the key back under the black rock, and returned to his car. He rummaged through his case folder and located Scott Ashton's cell number.

The soft baritone recording, the essence of tranquillity, invited him to leave a message that would be returned as soon as possible, conveying through its chocolate tone the feeling that all the troubles in a person's life were ultimately manageable. Gurney identified himself and said he had a few more questions about Flores.

He checked the dashboard clock. It was 10:31. Might be a good time to check in with Val Perry, share his initial thoughts on the case, see if she was still eager for him to pursue it. As he was about to place the call, the phone rang in his hand.

"Gurney." It was a hard habit to break, having answered his phone that way for so many years at the NYPD.

"This is Scott Ashton. I got your message."

"I was wondering . . . did you take Flores in your car with you from time to time?"

"Occasionally. When there was heavy shopping to do. Plant nurseries, lumberyards, that sort of thing. Why?"

"Did you ever notice him trying to avoid being seen by your neighbors? Hiding his face, anything like that?"

"Well . . . I don't know. It's hard to say. He tended to slouch. Wore a hat with a brim that curved down in front. Sunglasses. I suppose that might have been a way of hiding. Or not. How would I know? I mean, I did from time to time employ other day laborers on Hector's days off, and they may have behaved in a similar way. It's not something that I keyed in on."

"Did you ever take Flores to Mapleshade?"

"To Mapleshade? Yes, quite a few times. He had volunteered to install a little flower garden behind my office. As other projects came up, he offered to help with them as well."

"Did he have any contact with the students?"

"What are you getting at?"

"I have no idea," said Gurney.

"He may have spoken to a few of the girls, or they may have spoken to him. I didn't witness it, but it's possible."

"When was this?"

"He volunteered to help with the work at Mapleshade shortly after he arrived here. So about three years ago, give or take a month."

"And that continued how long?"

"His trips to the school? Until . . . the end. Is there some significance I'm missing?"

Gurney ignored the question, asked another of his own. "Three years ago. At that time Jillian would still have been a student there, is that right?"

"Yes, but . . . Where are you going with this?"

"I wish I knew, Doctor. Just one more question. Did Jillian ever tell you about people she might have reason to be afraid of?"

After a pause long enough to make Gurney think the connection had been broken, Ashton replied, "Jillian wasn't afraid of anyone. That may have been what killed her."

Gurney sat in his car in Ashton's driveway, gazing out past the ivied trellis at the site of the fatal wedding reception, trying to make sense of the bride and groom as a couple. Fellow geniuses they may have been, if Ashton were to be believed, but matching IQs were hardly a sufficient motive for marriage. Gurney remembered Val claiming that her daughter had an unhealthy interest in unhealthy men. Could that include Ashton, seemingly a paragon of rational stability? Not likely. Could Ashton be so much of a caretaker that he would be attracted to someone as patently troubled as Jillian? He didn't appear to be. True, his professional specialty lay in that direction, but there was no evidence in the man himself of that nosy, parental protectiveness that characterized caretaker personalities. Or was Jillian just another material girl selling her young body to the highest bidder—in this case Ashton? Nothing about it felt that way.

So what the hell was the mystery factor that made that marriage seem like a good idea? Gurney concluded that he wasn't going to figure it out sitting in the driveway.

He backed out, stopping just long enough to enter the number for the call he'd intended to make to Val Perry, then headed slowly down the long, shaded lane.

He was surprised and pleased when she answered on the second ring. Her voice had a subtle sexiness, even when all she was saying was, "Hello?"

"It's Dave Gurney, Mrs. Perry. I'd like to fill you in on where I am and what I'm doing."

"I told you to call me Val."

"Val. Sorry. Do you have a couple of minutes?"

"If you're making progress, you can have as much of my time as you want."

"I don't know how much progress I'm making, but I want you to know what's on my mind. I don't think the arrival of Hector Flores in Tambury three years ago was an accident, and I don't think what he did to your daughter was a sudden decision. I'd bet that his name isn't Flores, and I doubt that he's Mexican. Whoever he is, I believe he had a purpose and a plan. I believe he came here because of something that happened in the past involving your daughter or Scott Ashton."

"What sort of thing in the past?" She sounded like she was struggling to remain calm.

"It may have to do with why you sent Jillian to Mapleshade to begin with. Do you know of anything Jillian ever did that might make someone want to kill her?"

"You mean did she fuck up the lives of some little children? Did she give them nightmares and doubts they'll have the rest of their lives? Did she make them frightened and guilty and crazy? Maybe crazy enough to do to someone else what she did to them? Maybe crazy enough to kill themselves? And might someone want to see her rot in hell for that? Is that what you mean?"

He was silent.

When she spoke again, she sounded weary. "Yes, she did things that might make someone want to kill her. There were times I could have killed her myself. Of course, that's . . . that's exactly what I ended up doing, isn't it?"

A platitude about self-forgiveness passed through Gurney's mind. Instead he said, "If you want to whip yourself to death, you'll have to do it another time. Right now I'm working on an assignment you gave me. I called to let you know what I'm thinking and that it's the opposite of the official police position. That collision may create problems. I need to know how far you're willing to take this."

"Follow the trail wherever it goes, whatever it costs. I want to get to the bottom of this. I want to get to the *end* of it. Is that clear?"

"One last question. You may find it in bad taste, but I have to ask it. Is it conceivable that Jillian was having an affair with Flores?"

"If he was male, good-looking, and dangerous, I'd say it was a lot more than conceivable."

* * *

Gurney's mood, along with his concept of the case, shifted more than once on the drive home.

The idea that Jillian's murder was related to her chaotic past, a past to which Hector Flores might be connected, gave Gurney a sense of solid footing and a promising direction in which to press his inquiries. The ritualistic presentation of the corpse—with the severed head placed in the center of the table facing the body—was making a warped statement that went beyond simple homicide. It even occurred to him that the murder scene created an ironic echo of the photograph over Ashton's fireplace, the two shots of Jillian manipulated into one scene: Jillian gazing hungrily at Jillian.

Jesus. Was it a joke? Was it possible that the arrangement of the body in the cottage was a subtle parody of Jillian Perry's pose in a fashion ad? The thought made him nauseous, a rare reaction for a man whose years as a homicide cop had exposed him to just about everything people could do to other people.

He pulled over on the shoulder in front of a farm-equipment dealership, rooted through the papers on the seat next to him, found Jack Hardwick's cell number. As it rang, his gaze wandered over the hillside behind the dealership offices, dotted with tractors large and small, balers, brush cutters, rotary rakes. Then he noted something moving. A dog? No, a coyote. A coyote loping across the hillside, traveling in a straight line, purposefully—almost, it struck Gurney, thoughtfully.

Hardwick picked up on the fifth ring, just as the call was going into voice mail.

"Davey boy, what's up?"

Gurney grimaced—his usual reaction to the sardonic rasp of Hardwick's voice. The tone reminded him of his father. Not the sandpapery sound itself, but the sharp cynicism shaping it.

"I have a question for you, Jack. When you pulled me into this Perry business, what did you think it was all about?"

"I didn't pull you into it, just offered you an opportunity."

"Right, fine. So what did you think this 'opportunity' was about?"

"Never got far enough into it to form a solid opinion."

"Bullshit."

"Anything I'd say would be pure speculation, so I'm not saying."

"I don't like games, Jack. Why did you want me involved? While you're figuring out how not to answer that one, here's another one: Why is Blatt bent out of shape? I ran into him yesterday, and he was beyond unpleasant."

"No relevance."

"What?"

"No relevance. Look, we had a little shake-up here. Like I told you, some static between me and Rodriguez re the direction of the investigation. So I'm off it, and Blatt's on it. Ambitious little prick, no ability, just like Captain Rod. I call him Junior Shithead. This is his chance, prove himself, show he can handle a big case. But deep down he knows he's a useless little turd. Now you come along—big star from the big city, genius who solved the Mellery murder case, et cetera. Course he hates you. The fuck you expect? But there's no relevance. The fuck's he gonna do? Keep doing what you're doing, Sherlock, and don't lose any sleep over Blatt."

"Is that why you got me involved? To make Junior Shithead look bad?"

"To see that justice is done—by peeling the layers of a very interesting onion."

"That's what you think it is?"

"Don't you?"

"Could be. Would you be surprised if we found out that Flores came to Tambury with a plan to kill someone?"

"I'd be surprised if he didn't."

"So tell me again why you got kicked off the case."

"I told you—" Hardwick began with exaggerated impatience, but Gurney cut him off.

"Yeah, yeah, you were rude to Captain Rod. Why am I thinking it was more than that?"

"Because that's what you think about everything. You don't trust anybody. You're not a trusting person, Davey. Look, I've got to take a wicked piss. Talk to you later."

Nothing the man liked better, thought Gurney, than to make a wiseass exit. He put down the phone and restarted his car. A thin overcast still hung over the valley, but the white sun-disk behind it was brightening and the telephone poles were starting to cast faint shadows across the deserted road. The array of blue tractors for sale, still wet from the morning rain, began to gleam on the green hillside.

D uring the final half of the trip home, odd bits and pieces of the affair occupied his mind: Madeleine's comment that the placement of the machete made no sense, the decision by a super-rational man to marry a profoundly disturbed woman, Carl's train going around and around under the tree, the *Schindler's List* interpretation of the bullet through the teacup, the morass of sexual disorder in which everything seemed mired.

By the time he'd left the county highway and was following the dirt road that meandered up from the river valley into the hills, his thoughts had exhausted him. There was a CD protruding from the dashboard player. Craving distraction, he pushed it in. The voice that emerged from the speakers, accompanied by some bleak chords on an acoustic guitar, had the whiny singsong rhythm of Leonard Cohen at his bleakest. The performer was a sad-eyed middle-aged folkie by the unlikely name of Leighton Lake whom he and Madeleine had gone to see at a local music venue to which she'd acquired a season subscription. During intermission she'd purchased one of Lake's CDs. Of all the songs on it, Gurney found the one he was listening to now, "At the End of My Time," by far the most depressing.

> *There once was a time*
> *When I had all the time*
> *In the world. What a time*
> *I had then, when I had*
> *All the time in the world.*
>
> *Lied to my lovers,*
> *Chased all the others,*
> *Left all my lovers behind,*

When I had all the time
In the world.

Took what I wanted.
Never thought twice.
Had the time of my life
When I had all the time
In the world.

Lied to my lovers,
Chased all the others,
Left all my lovers behind,
When I had all the time
In the world.

No one's left to lie to,
No one's left to leave,
In this time of my life
At the end of my time
In this world.

Lied to my lovers,
Chased all the others,
Left all my lovers behind,
When I had all the time
In the world.

When I had all the time
In the world.

While Lake was crooning the final maudlin refrain, Gurney was passing between his barn and pond, with the old farmhouse just in sight beyond the patch of goldenrod at the top of the pasture. As he hit the player's "off" button, wishing he'd done so sooner, his cell phone rang.

The caller ID displayed the words REYNOLDS GALLERY.

Jesus. What the hell did she want?

"Gurney here." His voice was all business with an edge of suspicion.

"Dave! It's Sonya Reynolds." Her voice, as usual, radiated a level of animal magnetism that could get her stoned to death in some countries. "I have fabulous news for you," she purred. "And I don't mean a little fabulous. I mean change-your-life-forever fabulous! We have to get together ASAP."

"Hello, Sonya."

"*Hello?* I'm calling to give you the biggest gift you've ever been given, and that's all you can say?"

"It's good to hear from you. What are we talking about?"

Her answer was a rich, musical laugh, a sound as disturbingly sensual as everything else about her. "Oh, that's my Dave! Detective Dave with the piercing blue eyes. Suspicious of everything. As though I were— What do you call it? A 'perp' like on TV? As though I were a *perp*—that's what you call the bad guy, right? As though I were a *perp* giving you a fishy story." She had a slight accent that reminded him of the alternate universe he'd discovered in the French and Italian movies of his college years.

"Never mind 'fishy.' So far you haven't given me *any* story."

Again that laugh, bringing to mind her luminous green eyes. "And I'm not going to, not until I see you. Tomorrow. It must be tomorrow. But you don't have to come to me in Ithaca. I'll come to you. Breakfast, lunch, dinner—anytime tomorrow you want. Just tell me what time, and we'll pick a place. I guarantee you won't be sorry."

Chapter 25

Enter Salome, dancing

He still had no final name for the experience. Dream *missed all the power of it. It was true that the first time it happened he was in the process of falling asleep, his senses disconnected from all the shabby demands of a disgusting world, his mind's eye free to see what it would see, but there the superficial resemblance to common dreaming ended.*

Vision was a larger, better word for it, but it, too, failed to convey even a fraction of the impact.

Guiding light captured a certain facet of it, an important facet, but the soap-opera association polluted the meaning hopelessly.

A guided meditation, then? No. That sounded trite and unexciting—the opposite of the experience itself.

A living fable?

Ah, yes. That was getting closer. It was, after all, the story of his salvation, the new pattern of his life's purpose. The master allegory for his crusade.

His inspiration.

All he had to do was turn out the lights, close his eyes, put himself in the infinite potential of the darkness.

And summon the dancer.

In the embrace of the experience, the living fable, he knew who he was—so much more clearly than he did when his eyes and heart were distracted by the glittering trash and slimy cunts of the world, by noise, by seduction and filth.

In the embrace of the experience, in its absolute clarity and purity, he knew exactly who he was. Even if he was now, technically, a fugitive, that fact—like his name in the world, the name by which ordinary people knew him—was secondary to his true identity.

His true identity was John the Baptist.

Just thinking of it gave him gooseflesh.

He was John the Baptist.

And the dancer was Salome.

Ever since the first time he'd had the experience, the story had been all his, his to live and his to change. It didn't have to end the stupid way it ended in the Bible. Far from it. That was the beauty of it. And the thrill of it.

Part Two

Salome's Executioner

Chapter 26

The verisimilitude
of incongruity

"After I ice the stupid fuck, I see he's only wearing one shoe. I think, what the fuck? Closer look, I see there's no sock on the foot that's got the shoe on it. On the bottom of the shoe, I see this little slanted *M*, the Marconi logo, so this is like a two-thousand-dollar shoe. The other foot that's got no shoe—that one's got a sock on it. Cashmere. I think, who the fuck does that? Who the fuck puts on one cashmere sock and one two-thousand-dollar shoe—on different feet? I'll tell you who does that—a fucking juicehead with bucks, a rich fucking drunk."

That was the way Gurney opened his presentation that morning. Ultimate cut-to-the-chase approach. And it worked. He had the attention of every set of eyes in the bleak, concrete-walled police-academy lecture hall.

"The other day we talked about the eureka fallacy—the tendency of people to put a lot more faith in things they've *discovered* about someone than in things that person has *told* them. We're wired to believe that the hidden truth is the real truth. Undercover, you can take advantage of that tendency by letting your target 'discover' the things about you that you most want him to believe. It's not an easy technique, but it's very powerful. Today we'll look at another factor that creates credibility, another way of making your undercover line of bullshit sound true: layers of unusual, striking, incongruous detail."

All the people in the room appeared to be in the same seats they were in two days earlier, with the exception of the attractive Hispanic cop with the lip gloss who had moved into the front row, displacing the dyspeptic Detective Falcone, who was now in the second row—a pleasant switch from Gurney's point of view.

"The story I just started telling you about whacking the guy with the Marconi logo on the sole of his shoe, that's a story I actually told in an undercover situation. The odd little facts are all there for specific reasons. Can anyone tell me what they might be?"

A hand went up in the middle of the room. "Make you sound cold and hard."

Other opinions were offered without raised hands:

"Make you sound like you got a little problem with drunks."

"Like maybe you're a little crazy."

"Like Joe Pesci in *Goodfellas.*"

"Distraction," said a thin, colorless female in the back row.

"Tell me about that," said Gurney.

"You get somebody focused on a lot of weird shit, trying to figure out why the guy you shot is only wearing one shoe, they don't focus so much on the main question, which is whether or not you shot anybody to begin with."

"Bury 'em in bullshit!" another female voice chimed in.

"That's the idea," said Gurney. "Now, there's one more thing—"

The pretty cop with the glistening lips broke in, "The little *M* on the sole of his shoe?"

Gurney couldn't help grinning. "Right. The little *M*. What's that all about?"

"It makes the hit more credible?"

Falcone, behind her, rolled his eyes. Gurney felt like tossing him out of the class but doubted he had the authority to make it stick and didn't want to get tangled up in an academy pissing contest. He concentrated on his Hispanic star pupil, a much easier task.

"How does it do that?"

"By the way you picture it in your mind. The victim is down, shot, on the floor. That's how the sole of his shoe would be visible. So when I'm picturing that, wondering about that little logo, I'm already believing the guy has been shot. You know what I mean? Once I'm seeing his feet in that position, I'm already past the question of whether you shot him. It's kind of like the other little detail you tossed in—that the sock on the other foot was cashmere. The only way to know something is cashmere is to feel it. So I'm picturing this killer, curious about the sock, feeling the dead guy's foot. Very icy. Scary guy. Believable."

The restaurant where Gurney had agreed to meet Sonya Reynolds was in a hamlet outside Bainbridge, halfway between the police academy in Albany and her gallery in Ithaca. He'd finished his lecture at eleven and got to the Galloping Duck—her choice— at a quarter to one.

There was a curious disconnect between the country-cutesy name of the place with its cockeyed cutout of a giant duck on the front lawn and the plain, almost Shaker-like decor inside—like the crossed wires of a bad marriage.

He arrived first and was shown to a table for two next to a window overlooking a pond, the possible home of the eponymous fowl if ever it had existed. A chubby, cheerful teenage waitress with pink spiked hair and an indescribable mélange of neon clothes brought two menus and two glasses of ice water.

Gurney counted a total of nine tables in the small dining room, only two of which were occupied, both silently—one by a youngish couple staring intently at their BlackBerry screens, the other by a middle-aged man and woman from the pre-electronic era staring stolidly into their own thoughts.

Gurney's gaze drifted out to the pond. He sipped his water and thought about Sonya. Looking back on their relationship—not a "relationship" in the romantic sense, just a business association with a fair amount of suppressed lust on his part—it struck him as one of the stranger interludes in his life. Inspired by an art-appreciation course Sonya was teaching, which he and Madeleine attended shortly after moving upstate, he'd begun creating art prints from the mug shots of murderers—illuminating their violent personalities through the subtle manipulation of the stark official photographs taken at the time of their arrests. Sonya's great enthusiasm for the project and her sale of eight of the prints (at two thousand dollars apiece through her Ithaca gallery) kept Gurney involved for several months, despite Madeleine's discomfort with the morbid subject matter and with his eagerness to please Sonya. The tension in that conflict came back to him now, along with an uneasy recollection of the near disaster that ended it.

In addition to almost getting him killed, the Mellery murder case had brought him face-to-face with his acute failures as a husband and father. In the humbling clarity of the experience, it had occurred to him that love is the only thing on earth that matters. Seeing the mug-shot art endeavor and his contact with Sonya as disrupters of his relationship with the only person he really loved, he turned away from them toward Madeleine.

Now, however, a scant year later, the white light of his realization had dimmed. He still knew there was truth in it—that love, in a sense, was the most important thing—but he no longer saw it as the only true light in the universe. The gradual fading of its priority happened quietly and did not announce itself as a loss. It felt more like the growth of a more realistic perspective, surely not a bad thing. After all, one could not function long in the state of emotional intensity created by the Mellery affair, lest one forget to mow the lawn and buy food—or make the money one needed to buy food and lawn mowers. Wasn't it in the very nature of intense experiences to settle down, permitting the ordinary rhythms of life to resume? So Gurney wasn't especially concerned that now, from time to time, the "love is all that matters" idea seemed to have the ring of a sentimental shibboleth, a country-music title.

Which is not to say that his guard was completely down. There was an electricity in Sonya Reynolds that only a very foolish man would consider harmless. And when the pink-haired girl ushered the shapely, elegant Sonya into the dining room, that electricity was radiating like the hum of a power plant.

"David, my love, you look . . . exactly the same!" she cried, gliding toward him as if to music, offering him her cheek to kiss. "But of course you do! How else would you look? You're such a rock! Such *stability*!" This last word she pronounced with an exotic delight, as though it were the perfect Italian term for something the English language was inadequate to express.

She was wearing very tight designer jeans and a silky T-shirt under a linen jacket so casually unconstructed it couldn't have cost less than a thousand dollars. There was neither jewelry nor makeup to distract from her perfect olive skin.

"What are you looking at?" Her voice was playful, her eyes sparkling.

"You. You look . . . great."

"I should be mad at you, you know that?"

"Because I stopped producing pictures?"

"Of course because you stopped producing pictures. Wonderful pictures. Pictures I loved. Pictures my customers loved. Pictures I could sell for you. Pictures I *did* sell for you. But with no warning you call me and you tell me you can't do it anymore. You have personal reasons. Can't make any more pictures, can't talk about it. End of story. Don't you think I should be mad at you?"

She didn't sound mad at all, so he didn't answer, just watched her, amazed at how much bright energy she managed to channel into every word. It was the first thing that had seized his attention in her art-appreciation class. That and those wide-set green eyes.

"But I forgive you. Because you're going to make pictures again. Don't shake your head at me. Believe me, when I explain what's happening, you won't shake your head." She stopped, looked around the little dining room for the first time. "I'm thirsty. Let's have a drink."

When the pink-haired girl reappeared, Sonya ordered a vodka with grapefruit juice. Against his better judgment, so did Gurney.

"So, Mr. Retired Policeman," she said after their drinks had arrived and been sampled, "before I tell you how your life is going to change, tell me about the way it is now."

"My life?"

"You do have a life, yes?"

He had the disconcerting feeling that she already knew all about his life, complete with its reservations, doubts, conflicts. But there was no way she *could* know. Even when he was involved with her gallery, he'd never talked about those things. "My life is good."

"Ah, but you say this in a way that makes it not true, like it's something you're supposed to say."

"Is that the way it sounds?"

She took another sip of her drink. "You don't want to tell me the truth?"

"What do you think the truth is?"

She cocked her head a little to the side, studied his face, shrugged. "It's none of my business, right?" She looked out at the pond.

He consumed half his drink in two swallows. "I suppose it's like everyone's life—some of this and some of that."

"You make this-and-that sound like a pretty grim combination."

He laughed, not happily, and for a while they were both silent. He was the first to speak.

"I find that I'm not so much of a nature lover as I hoped I might be."

"But your wife is?"

He nodded. "It's not that I don't find it beautiful up here, the mountains and all, but . . ."

She gave him a shrewd look. "But it gets you tangled up in double negatives when you try to explain it?"

"What? Oh. I see what you mean. Are my problems that obvious?"

"Discontent is always obvious, no? What's the matter? You don't like that word?"

"Discontent? It's more like . . . what I'm good at, the way my mind works, isn't very useful up here. I mean . . . I analyze situations, unravel the elements of a problem, focus on discrepancies, solve puzzles. None of which . . ." His voice trailed off.

"And, of course, your wife thinks you should be loving the daisies, not analyzing them. You should be saying 'How beautiful!' and not 'What are they doing here?' Am I right?"

"That's one way of putting it."

"So," she said, changing the subject with sudden enthusiasm, "there's a man you must meet. As soon as possible."

"Why is that?"

"He wants to make you rich and famous."

Gurney made a face.

"I know, I know, you're not very interested in getting rich, and famous you're not interested in at all. I'm sure you have good theoretical objections. But suppose I were to tell you something very specific." She glanced around the dining room. The older couple were standing slowly, as though getting up from the table were a project to be undertaken with care. The BlackBerry couple were still at whatever it was they were at, texting away rapidly with the edges of their thumbs. The antic idea that they might be texting each other across the table popped into Gurney's mind. Sonya's voice dropped to a dramatic whisper. "Suppose I were to tell you he wants to buy one of your portrait prints for a hundred thousand dollars. What would you say to that?"

"I'd say he was crazy."

"You think so?"

"How could he not be?"

"Last year at an auction in the city, Yves Saint-Laurent's office chair sold for twenty-eight million dollars. That might be a little bit crazy. But a hundred thousand for one of your amazing serial-killer portraits? I don't think that's crazy at all. Wonderful, yes. Crazy, no. In fact, from what I know of this man and the way he operates, the price of your portraits is only going to go up."

"You know him?"

"I just met him face-to-face for the first time. But I know *of* him. He's a recluse, an eccentric who every so often emerges, shakes up the art world with some purchase or other, then disappears again. Dutch-sounding name, but no one knows where he lives. Switzerland? South America? Seems to like being a man of mystery. Very secretive, but more money than God. When Jykynstyl shows interest in an artist, the financial impact is huge. *Huge.*"

Cute little Pink Hair had added a chartreuse scarf to her eclectic ensemble and was clearing dessert plates and coffee cups from the vacated table across from them. Sonya caught her eye. "Darling, could I have another vodka grapefruit? And, I think, for my friend here, too?"

Chapter 27

A lot to think about

Gurney didn't know what to make of it. On the drive home that afternoon, he was having a hell of a time staying focused on anything.

The "art world" was not a place he knew anything about, other than suspecting that it was populated by people as different from policemen as parrots were from rottweilers. The brief dip of his toe into the water a year earlier with his mug-shot portraits had not exposed him to much of that world beyond the university-town gallery scene—not exactly the playground of eccentric billionaire collectors. Not the sort of place where a dress designer's chair would sell for twenty-eight million dollars. Or where a mystery celebrity by the unlikely name of Jay Jykynstyl would offer to buy a computer-manipulated picture of a serial killer for a hundred thousand dollars.

On top of that—the rather fantastical business deal she was placing in his lap—the lubricious Sonya herself had never seemed more available. She'd even hinted that she might rent a room at the Galloping Duck, which was also an inn, if she ended up drinking too much at lunch to drive legally. Walking away from that not-especially-subtle invitation had demanded a level of integrity he wasn't sure at first that he had. But maybe *integrity* was too big a word for it. The simple truth was that he'd never lied to Madeleine, and he wasn't comfortable with the idea of starting now.

Then he wondered if he were honestly walking away from Sonya's invitation or simply postponing his acceptance. He had agreed to meet the wealthy and weird Mr. Jykynstyl over dinner that coming

Saturday in Manhattan and listen to the full details of his offer—
which, if legitimate, would be hard to refuse—with Sonya acting as
a broker between them for whatever sales might follow. So it wasn't
as though he were barring her from his life. Quite the opposite.

The whole thing was bouncing around in his head with an unpleasant sort of energy. He tried to focus his mind on the Perry case,
instead, recognizing as he did so the irony of trying to calm himself
by sorting through that monstrous can of worms.

His racing mind eventually reached the stage of natural collapse, and the result was that he came close to killing himself by
falling asleep at the wheel and was saved only by a series of small
potholes on the highway shoulder that jolted him back into full consciousness. A few miles farther along, he pulled off at a gas station,
bought a container of muddy coffee whose bitter edge he attempted
to soften with an excess of milk and sugar. The taste still made him
grimace.

Back in his car, he took out a master list of names and phone
numbers he'd compiled from the Perry case file and placed calls first
to Scott Ashton and then to Withrow Perry, getting voice mail each
time. His message to Ashton was a request for a return call to discuss
a new line of inquiry. His message to Perry was a request for a meeting at the busy neurosurgeon's earliest convenience, with a small
hook at the end: "Remind me to ask about your Weatherby rifle."

As soon as he broke the connection, the phone rang.

"Dave, it's Val. I want you to go to a meeting."

"What meeting?"

She explained that she'd called Sheridan Kline, the county DA,
and told him everything Gurney had told her.

"Like what, for example?"

"Like the fact that the whole thing is a lot deeper than the cops
think it is, that it's got *roots,* maybe some kind of twisted revenge,
that Hector Flores probably isn't Hector Flores at all, and if they're
searching for some kind of illegal Mexican—which they are—
they're never going to find him. I told him they're wasting everybody's time, and they're a pack of fucking idiots."

"That's the term you used? *Fucking idiots*?"

"In four months they haven't caught on to half of what you saw in two days. So yeah, I called them fucking idiots. Which is what they are."

"You sure do know how to toss a brick into a hornet's nest."

"If that's what it takes, so be it."

"What did Kline say?"

"Kline? Kline's a politician. My husband—let me correct that, my husband's money—has some influence in New York State politics. So DA Kline expressed interest in hearing about any alternative approaches to the case. He also seems to know you pretty well, asked how come you were involved. I said you were *consulting*. Stupid word, but it satisfied him."

"You said something about a meeting."

"His office tomorrow at three P.M. You, him, and someone from the state police—he didn't say who. You'll be there, right?"

"I'll be there."

He got out of the car to toss his coffee container into a trash barrel by the gas pumps. An ancient orange Farmall tractor was chugging past pulling an overflowing hay wagon. Smells of hay, manure, and diesel oil blended in the air. When he returned to the car, his phone was ringing again.

It was Ashton. "What new line of inquiry?" he asked, quoting Gurney's message.

"I need some names from you: classmates of Jillian, going back to when she first came to Mapleshade; also, her counselors, therapists, anyone who dealt with her on a regular basis. It would also be helpful to have a list of possible enemies—anyone who might have wanted to harm you or Jillian."

"I'm afraid you're marching into a blind alley. I can't give you any of the things you're asking for."

"Not even a list of classmates? Names of staff members she may have spoken to?"

"Perhaps I haven't adequately explained Mapleshade's policy of absolute privacy. We maintain only the minimum academic records the state requires, and we maintain them for not one day longer than the regulations stipulate. We are not legally mandated, for example, to retain the names and addresses of former staff beyond the periods specified for tax purposes, and therefore we do not. We maintain no records of 'diagnoses' or 'treatments,' because officially we provide neither. Our policy is to disclose nothing to anyone, and we will allow Mapleshade to be shut down by the state before we will violate that policy. Our students and their families trust us in a way few other facilities are trusted, and we hold that unique trust to be inviolable."

"Eloquent speech," said Gurney.

"One I've made before," admitted Ashton, "and will probably make again."

"So even if a list of students Jillian knew or staff members in whom she may have confided could help us find her killer, that would make no difference to you?"

"If you wish to put it that way."

"Suppose giving us those lists could save your own life. Would that make a difference?"

"None."

"Doesn't the teacup incident bother you?"

"Not nearly so much as dealing a fatal blow to Mapleshade. If that covers all your questions . . . ?"

"How about enemies outside the school?"

"For Jillian, I imagine there might be quite a few, but I have no names."

"And for you?"

"Academic competitors, professional enviers, ego-bruised patients, fools not gladly suffered—perhaps a few score souls in all."

"Any names you'd be willing to share?"

"Afraid not. Now I must move on to my next meeting."

"You have a lot of meetings."

"Good-bye, Detective."

Gurney's phone didn't ring again until he was passing through Dillweed, pulling over in front of Abelard's, thinking he might get a decent cup of coffee to wash the taste of the awful one out of his mouth.

The name of the caller made him smile.

"Detective Gurney, this is Agatha Smart, Dr. Perry's assistant. You're requesting an appointment, as well as information about Dr. Perry's hunting rifle. Is that correct?"

"Yes. I was wondering how soon I could——"

She interrupted. "You may submit your questions in writing. The doctor will decide if an appointment is warranted."

"I'm not sure if I made this clear in the message I left, but this is part of the inquiry into the murder of his stepdaughter."

"We realize that, Detective. As I said, you may submit your questions in writing. Would you like the address?"

"That won't be necessary," said Gurney, struggling to suppress his irritation. "It all comes down to one very simple question. Can he say for sure where his rifle was on the afternoon of May seventeenth?"

"As I said before, Detective——"

"Just pass the question along, Ms. Smart. Thank you."

Chapter 28

A different perspective

He almost missed seeing her.

As he approached the point where the narrow dirt-and-gravel road reached his property and faded into the grassy farm track that rose through the pasture to the house, a red-tailed hawk took wing from the top of a tall hemlock on his left and flew over the road and over the pond. As he watched the rising bird disappear above the far treetops, he glimpsed Madeleine sitting on a weathered bench at the pond's edge, half hidden by a clump of cattails. He stopped the car by the old red barn, got out, and waved.

She responded with what seemed to be a small smile. He couldn't be sure at that distance. He wanted to talk to her, felt he needed to talk to her. As he followed the curving path around the grassy margin of the pond to the bench, he began to feel the stillness of the place. "Okay if I sit with you for a bit?"

She nodded gently, as if a larger response would disturb the peace.

He sat and gazed out over the quiet surface of the pond, seeing in it the upside-down reflection of the sugar maples on the opposite side, some of their leaves turning toward muted versions of their autumn colors. He looked at her and was overcome by the strange notion that the tranquillity in her at that moment was not the product of her surroundings but that, in some fantastical reversal, her surroundings were absorbing that very quality from a reservoir within her. He'd had that idea about her before, but that part of his mind that scorned the sentimental had always brushed it aside.

"I need your help," he heard himself saying, "to sort out some things." When she didn't answer, he went on, "I've had a confusing day. More than confusing."

She gave him one of those looks of hers that either communicated a great deal—in this instance that a confusing day would be a predictable result of getting involved in the Perry case—or that simply presented him with a blank slate on which his uneasy mind might write that message.

In any event he kept talking. "I don't think I've ever felt so overloaded. You found the note I left for you this morning?"

"About meeting your friend from Ithaca?"

"She's not what I would call a friend."

"Your 'adviser'?"

He resisted an urge to debate the terminology, to defend his innocence. "The Reynolds Gallery has been approached by a wealthy art collector who's interested in the mug-shot art portraits I was doing last year."

Madeleine raised a mocking eyebrow at his substituting the name of the business for the name of the person.

He went on, dropping his bombshell calmly. "He'll give me a hundred thousand dollars each for unique one-off prints."

"That's ridiculous."

"Sonya insists the guy is serious."

"What mental hospital did he escape from?"

There was a loud splash on the far side of the cattail clump. She smiled. "Big one."

"You're talking about a frog?"

"Sorry."

Gurney closed his eyes, more annoyed than he'd be willing to admit at Madeleine's apparent disinterest in his windfall. "From what I know of the art world, it's pretty much one giant mental hospital, but some of the patients have an awful lot of money. Apparently this guy is one of them."

"What is it he wants for his hundred thousand dollars?"

"A print that only he would own. I'd have to take the prints I did last year, enhance them somehow, introduce a variation into each one that would make it different from anything the gallery sold to anyone else."

"He's for real?"

"So I'm told. I'm also told he may want more than one. Sonya's imagining the possibility of a seven-figure sale." He turned to see Madeleine's reaction.

"Seven-figure sale? You mean some amount over a million dollars?"

"Yup."

"Oh, my, that's . . . certainly something."

He stared at her. "Are you purposely trying to show as little reaction to this as possible?"

"What reaction should I have?"

"More curiosity? Happiness? Some thoughts about what we could do with a chunk of money that size?"

She frowned thoughtfully, then grinned. "We could spend a month in Tuscany."

"That's what you'd do with a million dollars?"

"What million dollars?"

"Seven figures, remember?"

"I heard that part. What I'm missing is the part where it becomes real."

"According to Sonya, it's real right now. I have a dinner meeting Saturday in the city with the collector, Jay Jykynstyl."

"In the *city*?"

"You make it sound like I'm meeting him in a sewer."

"What does he 'collect'?"

"No idea. Apparently stuff he pays a lot for."

"You find it credible that he wants to pay you hundreds of thousands of dollars for fancied-up mug shots of low-life scum? Do you even know who he is?"

"I'll find out Saturday."

"Are you listening to yourself?"

To the extent that he was capable of perceiving his own emotional tone and rhythm, he wasn't entirely comfortable with it, but he wasn't ready to admit it. "What's your point?"

"You're good at poking holes in things. Nobody better at it than you."

"I don't get it."

"Don't you? You can rip anything to shreds—'an eye for discrepancy,' you once called it. Well, if anything ever cried out for a little poking and ripping, this sounds like it. How come you're not doing it?"

"Maybe I'm waiting to find out more, find out how real it is, get a sense of who this Jykynstyl character is."

"Sounds reasonable." She said this in such a reasonable way that he knew she meant the opposite. "By the way, what kind of name is that?"

"Jykynstyl? Sounds Dutch to me."

She smiled. "Sounds to me like a monster in a fairy tale."

Chapter 29

Among the missing

While Madeleine was creating a shrimp-and-pasta combination for dinner, Gurney was in the basement going through old copies of the Sunday *Times* that were being saved for a gardening project. (One of Madeleine's friends had gotten her interested in a type of garden bed in which newspapers were used to create layers of mulch.) He was searching the magazine sections of the paper for the advertising spread he remembered seeing that featured the provocative photograph of Jillian. What he was ultimately looking for was the company name and photo credit. He was about to give up and call Ashton for the information when he found the most recent insertion of the ad—which he noted had appeared, by macabre coincidence, on the day of the murder.

Instead of just making a note of the credit line, "Karnala Fashion, Photo by Alessandro," he decided to bring the magazine section upstairs. He laid it open on the table where Madeleine was setting their dinner plates. Apart from the credit line, there was only one sentence on the page, in very small, fashionably understated type: "Custom-designed wardrobes, starting at $100,000."

She scowled at it. "What's that?"

"An ad for expensive clothes. Insanely expensive. It's also a picture of the victim."

"The vic— You don't mean . . . ?"

"Jillian Perry."

"The bride?"

"The bride."

Madeleine looked closely at the ad.

"The two images in the photo are both of her," Gurney explained.

Madeleine nodded quickly, meaning that this had already occurred to her. "That's what she did for a living?"

"I don't know yet whether it was a job or an occasional thing. When I first saw the photo hanging in Scott Ashton's house, I was too amazed to ask."

"He has *that* hanging in his home? He's a widower, and that's the picture he . . ." She shook her head, her voice fading.

"He talks about her the same way her mother talks about her—like she was some kind of uniquely brilliant, sick, seductive maniac. The thing of it is, the whole damn case is like that. Everyone connected with it is either a genius or a lunatic or . . . a pathological liar or . . . I don't know what. Christ, Ashton's next-door neighbor, whose wife presumably ran off with the murderer, is playing with a Lionel train set under a Christmas tree in his basement. I don't think I've ever felt so goddamn adrift. It's like the trail—the scent trail the K-9 team was able to follow that led to the murder weapon in the woods, but it didn't go any farther, which suggests that the killer went back to the cottage and hid there—except there's no place in the cottage to hide. One minute I think I know what's going on, the next minute I realize I have no evidence at all for what I think. We have lots of interesting scenarios, but when you look under them, there's nothing there."

"What does that mean?"

"It means that we need to come up with hard data, firsthand observations by credible witnesses. So far none of the narratives has any verifiable facts to support it. It's too damn easy to get carried away by a good story. You can get so emotionally invested in a certain view of the case that you don't notice it's all wishful thinking. Let's eat. Maybe food will help my brain."

Madeleine put a large bowl of shrimp and pappardelle with a tomato-and-garlic sauce in the middle of the table, along with small bowls of shredded asiago and chopped basil, and they began eating.

After a few mouthfuls, Madeleine started toying with a shrimp. "The little apple didn't fall far from the tree."

"Hmm?"

"Mother and daughter have a lot in common."

"Both a bit erratic, you mean?"

"That's a way of putting it."

There was another silence as Madeleine lightly tapped her shrimp with the tines of her fork. "You're sure there was no place to hide?"

"Hide?"

"In the cottage."

"Why do you ask?"

"There was a terrifying movie I saw a long time ago—about a landlord who had secret spaces between the walls of the apartments, and he'd watch his tenants through tiny pinholes."

Their landline phone rang. "The cottage is pretty small, only three rooms," he said as he stood to go and answer it.

She shrugged. "Just a thought. It still gives me the shivers."

The phone was on his desk in the den. He got to it on the fourth ring. "Gurney here."

"Detective Gurney?" The female voice was young, tentative.

"That's right. Who am I speaking to?" He could hear the caller breathing, apparently in some distress. "You still there?"

"Yes, I . . . I shouldn't be calling, but . . . I wanted to talk to you."

"Who is this?"

The caller answered after another hesitation. "Savannah Liston."

"What can I do for you?"

"Do you know who I am?"

"Should I?"

"I thought he might have mentioned my name."

"Who might have mentioned it?"

"Dr. Ashton. I'm one of his assistants."

"I see."

"That's why I'm calling. I mean, maybe that's why I shouldn't be calling, but . . . Is it true you're a private detective?"

"Savannah, you need to tell me why you're calling me."

"I know. But you won't tell anyone, will you? I'd lose my job."

"Unless you're planning to hurt someone, I can't think of any legal reason I'd have to divulge anything." That answer, which he'd used a few hundred times in his career, was about as meaningless as it could be, but it seemed to satisfy her.

"Okay. I should just tell you. I overheard Dr. Ashton on the phone with you earlier today. It sounded like you wanted the names of girls in Jillian's class that she hung out with, but he couldn't give them to you?"

"Something like that."

"Why do you want them?"

"I'm sorry, Savannah, but I'm not allowed to discuss that. But I would like to know more about the reason you're calling me."

"I could give you two names."

"Of girls Jillian hung out with?"

"Yes. I know them because when I was a student here, once in a while we hung out together, which is kind of why I'm calling you. There's this weird thing going on." Her voice was getting shaky, like she was about to cry.

"What weird thing, Savannah?"

"The two girls Jillian hung out with—they've both disappeared since they graduated."

"How do you mean, 'disappeared'?"

"They both left home during the summer, their families haven't seen them, nobody knows where they are. And there's another horrible thing about it." Her breathing now was so uneven it was more like quiet sobbing.

"What's the horrible thing, Savannah?"

"They both talked about wanting to hook up with Hector Flores."

Chapter 30

Alessandro's models

By the time he got off the phone with Savannah Liston, he'd asked her a dozen questions and ended up with half a dozen useful answers, the names of the two girls, and one anxious request: that he not tell Dr. Ashton about the call.

Did she have some reason to be afraid of the doctor? No, of course not, Dr. Ashton was a saint, but it made her feel bad to be going behind his back, and she wouldn't want him to think that she didn't trust his judgment completely.

And did she trust his judgment completely? Of course she did—except maybe she was worried that he *wasn't* worried about the missing girls.

So she'd told Ashton about the "disappearances"? Yes, of course she had, but he'd explained that Mapleshade graduates often made clean breaks for good reasons, and it wouldn't be unusual for a family not to have contact with an adult daughter who wanted some breathing room.

How did the missing girls happen to know Hector? Because Dr. Ashton had brought him to Mapleshade sometimes to work on the flower beds. Hector was really hot, and some of the girls got very interested in him.

When Jillian was a student, was there anyone in particular on staff in whom she might have confided? There was a Dr. Kale who was in charge of a lot of things—Dr. Simon Kale—but he'd retired to Cooperstown. She'd found Gurney's home phone number through the Internet, and he could probably find Kale's number the same way. Kale was a cranky old man. But he might know stuff about Jillian.

Why was she telling Gurney all this? Because he was a detective, and sometimes she lay awake at night and scared herself with questions about the missing girls. In the daylight she could see that Dr. Ashton was probably right, that a lot of the students had come from sick families—like her own—and it would make sense to get away from them. Get away and not leave any forwarding address. Maybe even change your name. But in the dark . . . other possibilities came to her mind. Possibilities that made it hard to sleep.

And oh, by the way, the missing girls had another thing in common besides both of them having shown a major interest in Hector with his shirt off working on the flower beds.

What was that?

After they'd graduated from Mapleshade, they'd both been hired to pose, just like Jillian, "for those really hot fashion ads."

When Gurney returned to the kitchen, to the table where they'd been eating when the phone rang, Madeleine was standing there with the *Times Magazine* open on the table. As he joined her, staring down at that unsettling depiction of rapacity and self-absorption, he could feel the hairs rising on the back of his neck.

She glanced at him curiously, which he interpreted as her way of asking if he wanted to tell her about the phone call.

Grateful for her interest, he recounted it in detail.

Her curiosity sharpened into concern. "Someone needs to find out why those girls are unreachable."

"I agree."

"Shouldn't their local police departments be notified?"

"It's not that simple. The girls Savannah is talking about were in Jillian's class, presumably her age, so they'd be at least nineteen by now—all legal adults. If their relatives or other people who saw them regularly haven't officially reported them as missing, there's not much the police can do. However . . ." He pulled his cell phone out of his pocket and entered Scott Ashton's number.

It rang four times and was switching to voice mail when Ashton picked up and responded, apparently, to the caller-ID display. "Good evening, Detective Gurney."

"Dr. Ashton, sorry to bother you, but something's come up."

"Progress?"

"I don't know what to call it, but it's important. I understand Mapleshade's privacy policy, as you've explained, but we've got a situation that requires an exception—access to past enrollment records."

"I thought I'd been clear about that. A policy to which exceptions are made is no policy at all. At Mapleshade privacy is *everything*. There are no exceptions. None."

Gurney felt his adrenaline rising. "Do you have any interest in knowing what the problem is?"

"Tell me."

"Suppose we had reason to believe that Jillian wasn't the only victim."

"What are you talking about?"

"Suppose we had reason to believe that Jillian was one of a number of Mapleshade graduates targeted by Hector Flores."

"I fail to see . . ."

"There's anecdotal evidence suggesting that some Mapleshade graduates who were friendly with Hector Flores are not locatable. Under the circumstances we should find out how many of Jillian's classmates can be accounted for at this time and how many can't."

"God, do you realize what you're saying? Where is this so-called anecdotal evidence coming from?"

"The source is not the issue."

"Of course it's an issue. It's a matter of credibility."

"It may also be a matter of saving lives. Think about it."

"I'll do that."

"I'd suggest you think about it right now."

"I don't care for your tone, Detective."

"You think my *tone* is the problem? Think about this instead: Think about the possibility that some of your graduates might die because of your precious privacy policy. Think about explaining that to the police. And to the media. And to the parents. After you've thought about it, get back to me. I have other calls to make." He broke the connection and took a deep breath.

Madeleine studied his face, smiled crookedly, and said, "Well, that's one approach."

"You have others?"

"Actually, I kind of liked yours. Shall I reheat the dinner?"

"Sure." He took another deep breath, as though adrenaline could be exhaled away. "Savannah gave me the names and phone numbers of the families of the girls—the women, I should say— who she claims are missing. You think I should call them now?"

"Is that your job?" She picked up their pasta plates and carried them over to the microwave.

"Good point," he conceded, sitting at the table. Something in Ashton's attitude had gotten to him, was pushing him to respond impulsively. But how to pursue the issue of the "missing" Maple-shade graduates, as he forced himself to think about it calmly, was a question for the police. There were procedural requirements for the "missing person" designation and for the subsequent entry of the descriptive and last-sighting information into state and national databases. More important, it was a manpower issue. If, in fact, it turned out that the case involved multiple mis-pers with a suspicion of felony abduction or worse, a lone investigator was not the answer. The following day's meeting with the district attorney and the promised BCI representative would provide an ideal forum for discussing Savannah's call and for passing the matter on.

In the meantime, however, it might be interesting to speak to Alessandro.

Gurney got his laptop from the den and set it up where his plate had been.

A search of the Internet white pages for New York City turned up twelve individuals with that surname. Of course, "Alessandro" was far more likely to be a first name, or a professional name in-vented to convey a certain image. However, there were no business listings involving the name Alessandro in any of the categories that might relate to the *Times* ad: photography, advertising, marketing, graphics, design, fashion.

It seemed odd that a commercial photographer would be so elusive—unless he were so successful that the people who mattered knew already how to contact him and his invisibility to the masses was part of his appeal, like an "in" nightclub with no signage.

It occurred to Gurney that if Ashton had acquired his photo of Jillian directly from Alessandro, he'd have the man's phone number, but this was not the best moment to ask for it. Conceivably, Val Perry would know something about it, might even know Alessandro's full name. Either way the following day would be the appropriate time to pursue it. And, very important, he needed to keep an open mind. The fact that two former Mapleshade students whom Ashton's assistant was having trouble contacting had posed for the same fashion photographer as Jillian might be a meaningless coincidence, even if they did have an eye for Hector. Gurney closed his laptop and laid it on the floor beside his chair.

Madeleine returned to the table with their plates, the shrimp and pasta steaming again, and sat across from him.

He picked up his fork, then put it down. He turned to look out through the French doors, but the dusk had deepened and the glass panes, instead of providing a view of the patio and garden, offered only a reflection of the two of them at the table. His eye was drawn to the stern lines on his face, the serious set of his mouth, a reminder of his father.

It set him off on a tangent of loosely linked bits of memories—images from long ago.

Madeleine was watching him. "What are you thinking?"

"Nothing. I don't know. About my father, I guess."

"What about him?"

He blinked, looked at her. "Did I ever tell you the rabbit story?"

"I don't think so."

He cleared his throat. "When I was a little kid—five, six, seven years old—I'd ask my father to tell me stories about the things he did when he was a little kid. I knew he grew up in Ireland, and I had an idea of what Ireland looked like from a calendar we got from a neighbor who went there on vacation—all very green, rocky, kind of wild. To me it was a strange, wonderful place—wonderful, I guess, because it was nothing like where we lived in the Bronx."

Gurney's distaste for his childhood neighborhood, or maybe for his childhood itself, showed in his face. "My father didn't talk much, at least not to me or my mother, and getting him to tell me anything about how he grew up was almost impossible. Then finally, one day, maybe to stop me from pestering him, he told me this story. He said there was a field behind his father's house—that's what he called it, his *father's* house, an odd way to put it, since he lived there, too—a big grassy field with a low stone wall separating it from an even bigger field with a stream running through it, and a distant hillside beyond that. The house was a beige cottage with a dark thatched roof. There were white ducks and daffodils. I'd lie in bed every night picturing it—the ducks, the daffodils, the field, the hill—wishing I were there, determined that someday I *would* be there." His expression was a mixture of sourness and wistfulness.

"What was the story?"

"Hmm?"

"You said he told you a story."

"He said that he and his friend Liam used to go hunting for rabbits. They had slingshots, and they'd go off into the fields behind his father's house at dawn while the grass was still covered with dew, and they'd hunt for rabbits. The rabbits had narrow pathways through the tall grass, and he and Liam would follow the pathways. Sometimes the pathways ended in bramble patches, and sometimes they went under the stone wall. He described the size of the openings of the burrows the rabbits dug and how he and Liam would set snares for the rabbits along their pathways, or at their burrows, or at the holes they dug under the stone wall."

"Did he tell you if they ever caught any?"

"He said if they did, they'd let them go."

"And the slingshots?"

"A lot of near misses, he said." Gurney fell silent.

"That's the story?"

"Yes. The thing is, the images it painted in my mind became so real, and I thought so much about them, spent so much time imagining myself there, following those little narrow pathways in the grass, that those images became in some peculiar way the most vivid memories of my childhood."

Madeleine frowned a little. "We all do that, don't we? I have vivid memories of things I never actually saw—memories of scenes someone else described. I remember what I've pictured."

He nodded. "There's a piece of this I haven't told you yet. Years later, decades later, when I was in my thirties and my father was sixty-something, I happened to bring it up on the phone with him. I said, 'Remember the story you told me about you and Liam going out in the field at dawn with your slingshots?' He didn't seem to know what I was talking about. So I added all the other details: the wall, the brambles, the stream, the hillside, the rabbit paths. 'Oh, that,' he said. 'That was all bullshit. None of that ever happened.' And he said it in that tone of his that seemed to imply I was a fool to ever have believed it." There was a rare, barely perceptible tremor in Gurney's voice. He coughed loudly as if trying to clear whatever obstruction had caused it.

"He made it all up?"

"He made it all up. Every speck of it. And the damnable part of it is, it's the only thing he ever told me about his childhood."

Chapter 31

Scottie dogs

Gurney was leaning back in his chair, studying his hands. They were more creased and worn than he would have pictured them had he not been looking at them. His father's hands.

As Madeleine cleared the table, she appeared deep in thought. When the dishes and pans were all in the sink and she'd covered them with hot, soapy water, she turned off the tap and spoke in a very matter-of-fact way. "So I guess he had a pretty awful childhood."

Gurney looked up at her. "I would imagine so."

"Do you realize that during the twelve years of our marriage that he was alive, I only saw him three times?"

"That's the way we are."

"You mean you and your father?"

He nodded vaguely, focusing on a memory. "The apartment where I grew up in the Bronx had four rooms—a small eat-in kitchen, a small living room, and two small bedrooms. There were four people—mother, father, grandmother, myself. And you know what? There was almost always just one person in each room, except for the times when my mother and grandmother would watch television together in the living room. Even then my father would stay in the kitchen and I'd be in one of the bedrooms." He laughed, then stopped with an empty feeling, having heard in that sardonic sound an echo of his father.

"You remember those little toy magnets in the shape of Scottie dogs? If you aligned them one way, they attracted each other; the other way, they repelled each other. That's what our family was like, four little Scottie dogs aligned so we repelled one another into the four corners of our apartment. As far from one another as possible."

Madeleine said nothing, just turned the water back on and busied herself washing the dinner things, rinsing them, stacking them in the drying rack next to the sink. When she was finished, she turned off the hanging light over the sink island and went to the opposite end of the long room. She sat in an armchair by the fireplace, switched on the lamp next to it, and withdrew her current knitting project, a woolly red hat, from a tote bag on the floor. She glanced every so often in Gurney's direction but remained silent.

Two hours later she went to bed.

Gurney, in the meantime, had gotten the Perry case folders from the den, where they'd been piled since they were cleared from the main table when the Meekers came to dinner. He'd been reading the summaries of the interviews conducted in the field, as well as verbatims of those that had been conducted and recorded at BCI headquarters. It struck him as a lot of material that failed to paint a coherent picture.

Some of it made virtually no sense at all. There was, for example, the Naked in the Pavilion incident recounted by five Tambury residents. They said that Flores had been seen one month prior to the murder standing on one foot, eyes closed, hands clasped prayerfully in front of him in what was taken to be some sort of yoga pose, stark naked in the center of Ashton's lawn pavilion. In each interview summary, the interviewing officer had noted that the individual describing the incident had not actually witnessed it but was presenting it as "common knowledge." Each one reported hearing about it from other people. Some could remember who mentioned it to them, some couldn't. None could remember when. Another widely reported incident concerned an argument between Ashton and Flores one summer afternoon on the main street of the village, but again none of the individuals reporting it, including two who described it in detail, had been present at the event.

Anecdotes were abundant, eyewitnesses in short supply.

Almost everyone interviewed saw the murder itself through the lens of one of a handful of paradigms: the Frankenstein Monster, the Revenge of a Jilted Lover, Inherent Mexican Criminality,

Homosexual Instability, the Poisoning of America by Media Violence.

No one had suggested a connection to Mapleshade's sexual-
abuser clientele or the possibility of a revenge motive arising out of
Jillian's past behavior—areas where Gurney believed that the key
to the killing would eventually be found.

Mapleshade and Jillian's past: two general headings under which
he had many more question marks than facts. Maybe that retired
therapist whom Savannah had mentioned could help with both.
Simon Kale, easy name to remember. Simon Legree. Simon Says.
Simon Kale of Cooperstown. Went to jail and wore a gown. Christ! He
was slipping fast into the giddiness of total exhaustion.

He went to the sink and splashed cold water on his face. Coffee
seemed like a good idea, then a bad idea. He went back to the table,
set up his laptop again, and found Kale's phone number and address
in less than a minute through an Internet directory. Problem was,
he'd been absorbed by the interview reports longer than he'd realized, and it was now 11:02 P.M. To call or not to call? Now or in the
morning? He was itchy to talk to the man, to follow a concrete lead,
a route to some piece of the truth. If Kale was already in bed, the
call would not be a welcome event. On the other hand, its very lateness and inconvenience could serve to emphasize the urgency of the
issue. He made the call.

After three or four rings, an androgynous voice answered. "Yes?"

"Simon Kale, please."

"Who is this?" The voice, still of uncertain gender though tend-
ing toward male, sounded anxious and irritated.

"David Gurney."

"May I tell Dr. Kale the reason for your call?"

"Who am I speaking to?"

"You're speaking to the person who answered the phone. And
it is rather late. Now, would you please tell me why—" There was
another voice in the background, a pause, the sound of the phone
being handed over.

A prissy, authoritative voice announced, "This is Dr. Kale. Who
is this?"

"David Gurney, Dr. Kale. Sorry to bother you so late in the

evening, but there's some urgency involved. I'm working as a consultant on the Jillian Perry murder case, and I'm trying to get some perspective on Mapleshade. You were suggested to me as a person who could be helpful." There was no response. "Dr. Kale?"

"*Consultant?* What does that mean?"

"I've been retained by the Perry family to provide them with an independent view of the investigation."

"Is that so?"

"I was hoping you might be able to enlighten me regarding Mapleshade's clientele and general philosophy."

"I would have thought Scott Ashton would be the perfect source for that sort of enlightenment." There was acid in this comment, which he softened by adding in a more casual tone, "I'm no longer part of the Mapleshade staff."

Gurney tried for a foothold in what sounded like a rift between the two men. "I thought your position might give you more objectivity than someone still involved with the school."

"That's not a subject I'd care to discuss on the phone."

"I can understand that. The fact is, I live over in Walnut Crossing, and I'd be happy to come to Cooperstown, if you could spare me even half an hour."

"I see. Unfortunately, I'll be away on a one-month vacation starting the day after tomorrow." The way he said it made it sound more like a legitimate impediment than a brush-off. Gurney got the feeling that Kale was not only intrigued but might have something interesting to say.

"It would be enormously helpful, Doctor, if I could see you before then. It just so happens that I have a meeting with the district attorney tomorrow afternoon. If I could spend some time with you, perhaps I could make a detour on my way?"

"You have a meeting with Sheridan Kline?"

"Yes, and it would be really helpful to get your input prior to that."

"Well . . . I suppose . . . Still, I would need to know more about you before . . . before it would be appropriate to discuss anything. Your credentials and so forth."

Gurney responded with his résumé highlights and the name of

a deputy commissioner Kale could talk to at the NYPD. He even
mentioned, half apologetically, the existence of the five-year-old
New York magazine article that glorified his contributions to the solution of two infamous serial-murder cases. The article had made
him sound like a cross between Sherlock Holmes and Dirty Harry,
which he found embarrassing. But it had its uses.

Kale agreed to meet with him at 12:45 P.M. the next day, Friday.

When Gurney tried to organize his thoughts for that meeting,
to make a mental list of the topics he wanted to cover, he
discovered for the hundredth time that excitement and weariness
formed a lousy foundation on which to organize anything. He concluded that sleep would be the most efficient use of his time. But
no sooner had he taken off his clothes and slipped into bed next to
Madeleine than the ring of his cell phone summoned him back to
the kitchen counter where he'd absentmindedly left it.

The voice on the other end was born and bred in a Connecticut
country club. "This is Dr. Withrow Perry. You called. I can give you
precisely three minutes."

It took Gurney a moment to focus. "Thank you for calling back.
I'm investigating the murder of—"

Perry cut in sharply. "I know what you're doing. I know who you
are. What do you want?"

"I have some questions that might help me to—"

"Go ahead, ask them."

Gurney suppressed an impulse to comment on the man's attitude.
"Do you have any idea why Hector Flores killed your daughter?"

"No, I don't. And for the record, Jillian was my wife's daughter,
not mine."

"Do you know of anyone besides Flores who might have had a
grudge against her—a reason to hurt or kill her?"

"No."

"No one at all?"

"No one and, I suppose, everyone."

"Meaning?"

Perry laughed—a harsh, unpleasant sound. "Jillian was a lying, manipulative bitch. I doubt I'm the first to tell you that."

"What's the worst thing she ever did to you?"

"That's not a subject I'm willing to discuss."

"Why do you think Dr. Ashton wanted to marry her?"

"Ask him."

"I'm asking you."

"Next question."

"Did she ever talk about Flores?"

"Not to me, certainly. We had no relationship at all. Let me be clear, Detective. I'm speaking to you solely because my wife has decided to pursue this unofficial inquiry and asked that I return your call. I really don't have anything to contribute, and to be honest with you, I personally consider her endeavor a waste of time and money."

"How do you feel about Dr. Ashton?"

"Feel? What do you mean?"

"Do you like him? Admire him? Pity him? Despise him?"

"None of the above."

"What then?"

There was a pause, a sigh. "I have no interest in him. I consider his life none of my business."

"But there's something about him that . . . what?"

"Just the obvious question. The question you already asked, in a way."

"Which one?"

"Why would such a competent professional marry a train wreck like Jillian?"

"Did you hate her that much?"

"I didn't hate her, Mr. Gurney, no more than I would hate a cobra."

"Would you kill a cobra?"

"That's a childish question."

"Humor me."

"I'd kill a cobra that threatened my life, just as you would."

"Did you ever want to kill Jillian?"

He laughed humorlessly. "Is this some sort of sophomoric game?"

"Just a question."

"You're wasting my time."

"Do you still own a Weatherby .257 rifle?"

"What the hell does that have to do with anything?"

"Are you aware that someone with a rifle like that took a shot at Scott Ashton a week after Jillian's murder?"

"With a .257 Weatherby? For Godsake, you're not suggesting . . . you're not daring to suggest that somehow . . . What the hell *are* you suggesting?"

"I'm just asking you a question."

"A question with offensive implications."

"Shall I assume you still have the rifle in your possession?"

"Assume whatever you like. Next question."

"Can you say for sure where that rifle was on May seventeenth?"

"Next question."

"Did Jillian ever bring friends home?"

"No—thank God for small favors. I'm afraid your time is up, Mr. Gurney."

"Final question. Do you happen to know the name or address of Jillian's biological father?"

For the first time in the conversation, Perry hesitated. "Some Spanish-sounding name." There was a kind of revulsion in his voice. "My wife mentioned it once. I told her I never wanted to hear it again. Cruz, perhaps? Angel Cruz? I don't know his address. He may not have one. Considering the life expectancy of the average methamphetamine addict, he's probably been dead for quite a few years."

He broke the connection without another word.

Getting to sleep proved difficult. If Gurney's mind was engaged after midnight, turning it off wasn't easy. It could take hours to loosen its obsessive grip on the problems of the day.

He'd been in bed, he guessed, for at least forty-five minutes without any respite from the kaleidoscope of images and questions embedded in the Perry case when he noted that the rhythm of Madeleine's breathing had changed. He was convinced she'd been asleep when he came to bed, but now he had the distinct feeling that she was awake.

He wanted to talk to her. Well, actually, he wasn't sure about that. And he wasn't sure, if he did talk to her, what it was that he wanted to talk to her about. Then he realized that he wanted her advice, wanted her guidance out of the swamp in which he was getting mired—a swamp composed of too many shaky stories. He wanted her advice, but he wasn't sure how to ask for it.

She cleared her throat softly. "So what are you going to do with all your money?" she asked matter-of-factly, as though they'd been discussing some related matter for the past hour. This was not an unusual way for her to bring something up.

"The hundred thousand dollars, you mean?"

She didn't reply, which meant she considered the question unnecessary.

"It's not *my* money," he said. "It's *our* money. Even if it's still theoretical."

"No, it's definitely *your* money."

He turned his head toward her on the pillow, but it was a moonless night, too dark to make out her expression. "Why do you say that?"

"Because it's true. It's your hobby, now your very lucrative hobby. And it's your gallery contact, or your representative, or agent, or whatever she is. And now you're going to meet your new fan, the art collector, whoever he is. So it's your money."

"I don't understand why you're saying this."

"I'm saying it because it's true."

"No it's not. Whatever *I* own, *we* own."

She uttered a rueful little laugh. "You don't see it, do you?"

"See what?"

She yawned, suddenly sounded very tired. "The art project is yours. All I ever did was complain about how much time you spent on it, how many beautiful days you spent cooped up in your den staring at your screen, staring at the faces of serial killers."

"That's got nothing to do with how we think about the money."

"It's got everything to do with it. You earned it. It's yours." She yawned again. "I'm going back to sleep."

Chapter 32

An intractable madness

Gurney left at 11:30 A.M. the next day for his meeting with Simon Kale, allowing himself a little over an hour for the drive to Cooperstown. Along the way he drank a sixteen-ounce container of Abelard's house blend, and by the time Lake Otsego was in sight, he was feeling awake enough to take note of the classic September weather, the blue sky, the hint of chill in the air.

His GPS brought him along the hemlock-shaded west shore of the lake to a small white Colonial on its own half-acre peninsula. The open garage doors revealed a shiny green Miata roadster and a black Volvo. Parked at the edge of the driveway, away from the garage, was a red Volkswagen Beetle. Gurney parked behind the Beetle and was getting out of his car just as an elegant gray-haired man emerged from the garage with a pair of canvas tote bags.

"Detective Gurney, I presume?"

"Dr. Kale?"

"Correct." He smiled perfunctorily and led the way along a flag-stone path from the garage to the side door of the house. The door was open. Inside, the place looked very old but meticulously cared for, with the heat-conserving low ceilings and hand-hewn beams typical of the eighteenth century. They were standing in the middle of a kitchen that featured an enormous open hearth as well as a chrome-and-enamel gas stove from the 1930s. From another room came the unmistakable strains of "Amazing Grace" being played on a flute.

Kale laid his tote bags on the table. They were imprinted with the logo of the Adirondack Symphony Orchestra. Leafy vegetables and loaves of French bread were visible in one, bottles of wine in the other. "The elements of dinner. I was sent out to hunt and gather," he said rather archly. "I do not myself cook. My partner, Adrian, is both chef and flautist."

"Is that . . . ?" Gurney began, tilting his head in the direction of the faint melody.

"No, no, Adrian is far better than *that*. That would be his twelve-o'clock student, the Beetle person."

"The . . . ?"

"The car outside, the one in front of yours, the cutesy red thing."

"Ah," said Gurney. "Of course. Which would leave the Volvo for you and the Miata for your partner?"

"You're sure it's not the other way around?"

"I wouldn't think so."

"Interesting. What exactly is it about me that screams Volvo to you?"

"When you came out of the garage, you came out of the Volvo side of it."

Kale emitted a sharp cackle. "You're not clairvoyant, then?"

"I doubt it."

"Would you care for tea? No? Then come, follow me to the parlor."

The parlor turned out to be a tiny room next to the kitchen. Two floral-printed armchairs, two tufted fussy-floral hassocks, a tea table, a bookcase, and a small red-enameled woodstove just about filled the space. Kale gestured to one of the chairs for Gurney, and he sat in the other.

"Now, Detective, the purpose of your visit?"

Gurney noticed for the first time that Simon Kale's eyes, in contrast with his giddy manner, were sober and assessing. This man would not be easily fooled or flattered—although his dislike of Ashton, revealed on the phone, might be helpful if handled carefully.

"I'm not a hundred percent sure what the purpose is." Gurney shrugged. "Maybe I'm just on a fishing expedition."

Kale studied him. "Don't overdo the humility."

Gurney was surprised by the jab but responded blandly. "Frankly, it's more ignorance than humility. There's so damn much about this case that I don't know—that no one knows."

"Except for the bad guy?" Kale looked at his watch. "You do have questions you want to ask me?"

"I'd like to know whatever you're willing to tell me about Mapleshade—who goes there, who works there, what it's all about, what you did there, why you left."

"Mapleshade before or Mapleshade after the arrival of Scott Ashton?"

"Both, but mainly the period when Jillian Perry was a student."

Kale licked his lips thoughtfully, seemed to be savoring the question. "I'd sum it up this way: For eighteen of the twenty years I taught at Mapleshade, it was an effective therapeutic environment for the amelioration of a wide range of mild to moderate emotional and behavioral problems. Scott Ashton arrived on the scene five years ago with great fanfare, a celebrity psychiatrist, a cutting-edge theoretician, just the thing to nudge the school into the premier position in the field. Once he had a foothold, however, he began shifting the focus of Mapleshade to sicker and sicker adolescents—violent sexual predators, manipulative abusers of other children, highly sexualized young women with long histories of incest as both victims and perpetrators. Scott Ashton turned our school, with its broad history of success with troubled kids, into a disheartening repository for sex addicts and sociopaths."

Gurney thought it had the ring of a carefully constructed speech polished by repetition, yet the emotion in it seemed real enough. Kale's arch tone and mannerisms had been replaced, at least temporarily, by a stiff and righteous anger.

Then, into the open silence that followed the diatribe, from the flute in the other room flowed the haunting melody of "Danny Boy."

It assaulted Gurney slowly, debilitatingly, like the opening of a grave. He thought he would have to excuse himself, find a pretext for abandoning the interview, flee the premises. Fifteen years, and still the song was unbearable. But then the flute stopped. He sat, hardly breathing, like a shell-shocked soldier awaiting the resumption of distant artillery.

"Is something wrong?" Kale was eyeing him curiously.

Gurney's first impulse was to lie, hide the wound. But then he thought, why? The truth was the truth. It was what it was. He said, "I had a son by that name."

Kale looked baffled. "What name?"

"Danny."

"I don't understand."

"The flute . . . It . . . it doesn't matter. An old memory. Sorry for the interruption. You were describing the . . . the transition from one type of clientele to another."

Kale frowned. *"Transition*—such a benign term for so massive a dislocation."

"But the school continues to be successful?"

Kale's smile sparkled like glare ice. "There's money to be made in housing the demented offspring of guilty parents. The more terrifying they are, the more their parents will pay to get rid of them."

"Regardless of whether they get any better?"

Kale's laugh was as cold as his smile. "Let me be perfectly clear about this, Detective, so that I leave no doubt in your mind what we're talking about. If you were to discover that your twelve-year-old has been raping five-year-olds, you might be willing to pay anything for that lunatic child of yours to disappear for a few years."

"That's who's sent to Mapleshade?"

"Precisely."

"Like Jillian Perry?"

Kale's expression moved through a small series of tics and frowns. "Mentioning individual student names in a context like this puts us on the edge of a legal minefield. I don't feel that I can give you a specific answer."

"I already have reliable descriptions of Jillian's behavior. I only mention her because the timing raises a question. Wasn't she sent to Mapleshade before Dr. Ashton altered the school's focus?"

"That's true. However, without saying anything one way or the other about the Perry girl, I can tell you that Mapleshade traditionally accepted students with a wide range of problems, and there were always a few who were far sicker than the others. What Ashton did was focus Mapleshade's enrollment policy entirely on the sickest. Give any one of them a gram of coke and they'd seduce a horse. Does that answer your question?"

Gurney's gaze rested thoughtfully on the little red woodstove. "I understand your reluctance to violate confidentiality commitments. However, Jillian Perry can no longer be harmed, and finding her murderer may depend on finding out more about her own past contacts. If Jillian ever confided anything to you about—"

"Stop right there. Whatever was confided to me remains confidential."

"There's a great deal at stake, Doctor."

"Yes, there is. Integrity is at stake. I will not reveal anything that was told to me with the understanding that I would not reveal it. Is that clear?"

"Unfortunately, yes."

"If you want to know about Mapleshade and its transmogrification from a school to a zoo, we can discuss that in general terms. But the details of individual lives will not be discussed. It's a slippery world we live in, Detective, in case you hadn't noticed. We have no secure footing beyond our principles."

"What principle dictated your departure from Mapleshade?"

"Mapleshade became a home for female sexual psychopaths. Most of them don't need therapists, they need exorcists."

"When you left, did Dr. Ashton hire someone to replace you?"

"He hired someone for the same position." There was acid in the neat distinction and something like real hatred in Kale's eyes.

"What sort of person?"

"His name is Lazarus. That says it all."

"How so?"

"Dr. Lazarus has all the warmth and animation of a cadaver." There was a bitter finality in Kale's voice that told Gurney the interview was over.

As if on cue, the flute began again, and the plaintive strains of "Danny Boy" propelled him from the house.

Chapter 33

A simple reversal

The living fable, the pivotal dream, the vision that had changed everything, was as vivid to him now as when it first came to him.

It was like watching a movie and being in the movie at the same time, then forgetting that it was a movie, and living it, feeling it— an experience more real than so-called real life had ever been.

It was always the same.

John the Baptist was barefoot and naked except for a homespun brown loincloth that barely covered his genitals. It was secured by a rough leather belt from which hung a primitive hunting knife. He stood beside a rumpled bed in a space that seemed to be both a bedroom and a dungeon cell. There were no visible restraints upon him, yet he could move neither his arms nor his legs. The feeling was claustrophobic, and he feared that if he lost his balance and fell onto the bed, he would suffocate.

Into the dungeon, descending on dark stone steps, came Salome. She came toward him in a swirling air of perfume and translucent silk, stood before him, swaying, dancing. Moving more like a snake than a human being. The silk slipped away, dissolving, revealing creamy skin, breasts surprisingly ample for the lithe body, full round buttocks, breathtakingly perfect, breathtakingly deadly. The body writhing in the anticipation of pleasure.

The archetype of degradation.

Eve the succubus.

Avatar of the serpent.

Essence of evil.

Incarnation of lust.

Writhing, dancing like a snake.

Dancing around him, against him. Slime of sweat forming on her swaying breasts, pinpricks of sweat around her mouth. Electric shock of her legs brushing against his legs, her legs parting, the rasp of pubic hair against his thigh, a scream of horror building in his chest, horror racing through his blood. The scream in his heart struggling to burst out. At first a tiny constricted whine, building, straining through his clenched teeth. Her eyes burning, her groin pressed against his, burning, his scream rising, bursting out, a roar now, a torrent of sound, the roar of a cyclone leveling the world, freeing his arms and legs of their paralysis, his hunting knife transformed now into a sword, a blessed scimitar. With all the strength of heaven and earth, he swings the great scimitar—swings it in a sweet, perfect arc—hardly feeling it pass through her sweating neck, the head falling, falling free. As it falls, disappearing through the stone floor, the damp body dries into gray dust and is gone, blown away by a wind that warms his soul, filling him with light and peace, filling him with the knowledge of his true identity, filling him with his Mission and Method.

They say that God comes to some men slowly and to others in a flash of light that illuminates everything. And so it was with him.

The power and clarity of it had stunned him the first time, as it did each time he recalled it, each time he reexperienced the Great Truth that had been revealed to him in the "dream."

Like all great ideas, it was astonishingly simple: Salome cannot have John the Baptist beheaded by Herod if John the Baptist strikes first. John the Baptist, alive in him. John the Baptist, destroyer of the evil Eve. John the Baptist, vessel of the baptism of blood. John the Baptist, scourge of the slimy snakes of the earth. Severer of the head of Salome the serpent.

It was a wonderful insight. A source of purpose, serenity, and solace. He felt uniquely blessed. So many people in the modern world had no idea who they really were.

He knew who he was. And what he had to do.

Chapter 34

Ashton uneasy

As Gurney was pulling in to the parking lot of the county building that housed the office of the district attorney, his phone rang. He was surprised to hear the voice of Scott Ashton, and more surprised at its new insecurity and informality.

"David, after your call last evening ... your comments about people who couldn't be found ... I know what I said about the privacy issue, but ... I thought perhaps I could make a few discreet phone calls myself. That way there wouldn't be any question of my having given out names or phone numbers to a third party."

"Yes?"

"Well, I made some calls, and ... the fact is ... I don't want to jump to any conclusions, but ... it's possible that something strange is going on."

Gurney pulled in to the first parking space he could find. "Strange in what way?"

"I made a total of fourteen phone calls. I had the number for the former student herself in four cases, in the other ten the number of a parent or a guardian. One of the students I was able to reach and speak to. For one other I was able to leave a voice-mail message. Phone service to the other two had been discontinued. Of the ten calls I made to the families, I got through to two and left messages for the other eight, two of whom called me back. So I ended up having four conversations with family members."

Gurney wondered where all this arithmetic was going.

"In one case there was no problem. However, in the other three—"

"Sorry to cut you off, but what do you mean by 'no problem'?"

"I mean they were aware of their daughter's location, said she was away at college, said they had spoken to her that very day. The problem is with the other three. The parents have no idea where they are—which in itself has no great significance. In fact, I strongly recommend to some of our graduates that they separate themselves from their parents when those relationships have a toxic history. Reintegration with one's family of origin is sometimes not advisable. I'm sure you can understand why."

Gurney almost slipped and said that Savannah had told him as much, but he caught himself. Ashton went on. "The problem is what the parents told me had happened, how the girls actually left home."

"How?"

"The first parent I spoke to said her daughter was unusually calm, had behaved well for about four weeks after coming home from Mapleshade. Then, one evening at the dinner table, she demanded money to buy a new car, specifically a twenty-seven-thousand-dollar Miata convertible. The parents of course refused. She then accused them of not caring about her, aggressively resurrected all the traumas of her early childhood, and gave them the absurd ultimatum that they must give her the money for the car or she would never speak to them again. When they refused, she literally packed her bags, called a car service, and left. After that, she called once to say that she was sharing an apartment with a friend, that she needed time to sort out her 'issues,' and that any effort they made to find her or communicate with her would be an intolerable assault on her privacy. And that was the last word they ever heard from her."

"You obviously know more about your ex-students than I do, but on the surface of it that story doesn't sound that incredible to me. It sounds like something an emotionally unstable spoiled brat might do." When the words were out, Gurney wondered if Ashton might object to that characterization of Mapleshade's alumnae.

"It sounds exactly that way," he replied instead. "A 'spoiled brat' stamping her feet, storming out, punishing her parents by rejecting them. Not particularly shocking, not even unusual."

"Then I don't get the point of the story. Why are you disturbed by it?"

"Because it's the same story told by all three families."

"The same?"

"The same story, except for the brand and price of the car. Instead of a twenty-seven-thousand-dollar Miata, the second girl demanded a thirty-nine-thousand-dollar BMW, and the third wanted a seventy-thousand-dollar Corvette."

"Jesus."

"So you see why I'm concerned?"

"What I see is a mystery about the nature of the connection. Did your conversations with the parents give you any ideas about that?"

"Well, it can't be a coincidence. Which makes it a conspiracy of some kind."

Gurney could see two broad possibilities. "Either the girls devised this among themselves as a way of leaving home—although why they would need to do it that way is unclear—or each of them was following the directions of an outside party without necessarily being aware that other girls were following the same directions. But, again, *why* is the real question."

"You don't think it was just a crazy scheme to see if they could force their parents to buy them their dream cars?"

"I doubt it."

"If it was a story they devised among themselves, or under the direction of some mysterious third party—for reasons yet unknown—why would each girl come up with a different brand of car?"

A possible answer occurred to Gurney, but he wanted more time to think about it. "How did you pick the names of the girls you tried to reach?"

"Nothing systematic. They were just girls from Jillian's graduating class."

"So they were all approximately the same age? All around nineteen or twenty?"

"I believe so."

"You do realize now that you'll have to turn over Mapleshade's enrollment records to the police?"

"I'm afraid I don't quite see it that way—at least not yet. All I know at the moment is that three girls, legally adults, left their homes after having similar arguments with their parents. I'll grant you there's something about it that seems peculiar—which is why I'm telling you about it—but so far there's no evidence of criminality, no evidence of any wrongdoing at all."

"There are more than three."

"How do you know that?"

"As I explained before, I was told—"

Ashton cut in. "Yes, yes, I know, some unnamed person told you that they couldn't reach some of our former students, also unnamed. That in itself means nothing. Let's not mix apples and oranges, leap to some awful conclusion, and use it as a pretext for destroying the school's guarantees of privacy."

"Doctor, you just called me. You sounded concerned. Now you're telling me there's nothing to be concerned about. You're not making a lot of sense."

He could hear Ashton breathing a bit shakily. After a long five seconds, the man spoke in a more subdued voice.

"I just don't want to pull the whole structure of the school down on our heads. Look, here's what I propose: I'll continue making calls. I'll try to call every contact number I have for recent graduates. That way we can find out if there's a serious pattern here before we cause irreversible damage to Mapleshade. Believe me, I'm not trying to be pointlessly obstructive. If we discover any additional examples . . ."

"All right, Doctor, make the calls. But be aware that I intend to pass along what I already know to BCI."

"Do what you have to do. But please remember how little you actually *know*. Don't destroy a legacy of trust on the basis of a guess."

"I get your point. Eloquently expressed." Ashton's easy eloquence was, in fact, starting to get on Gurney's nerves. "But speaking of the institution's legacy, or mission, or reputation, or whatever you want to call it, I understand you made some dramatic changes in that area yourself a few years ago—some might say risky changes."

Ashton answered simply, "Yes, I did. Tell me how the changes were described to you, and I'll tell you the reason for them."

"I'll paraphrase: 'Scott Ashton upended the institution's mission, turned it from a facility that treated the treatable into a holding pen for incurable monsters.' I think that captures the gist of it."

Ashton uttered a small sigh. "I suppose that's the way *someone* might see it, especially if his career didn't benefit from the change."

Gurney ignored the apparent swipe at Simon Kale. "How do *you* see it?"

"This country has an overabundance of therapeutic boarding schools for neurotics. What it lacks are residential environments where the problems of sexual abuse and destructive sexual obsessions can be addressed creatively and effectively. I'm trying to correct that imbalance."

"And you're happy with the way it's working?"

There was the sound of a longer sigh. "The treatment of certain mental disorders is medieval. With the bar set so low, making improvements is not as difficult as you might think. When you have a free hour or two, we can go into it in more detail. Right now I'd rather proceed with those phone calls."

Gurney checked the time on his car dashboard. "And I have a meeting I'm already five minutes late for. Please let me know what you can, as soon as you can. Oh—one last thing, Doctor. I assume you have phone numbers and addresses for Alessandro and for Karnala Fashion?"

"I beg your pardon?"

Gurney said nothing.

"You're talking about the ad? Why would I have their numbers?"

"I assumed you'd gotten that photo on your wall from either the photographer or the company that commissioned it."

"No. As a matter of fact, Jillian was the one who got it. She gave it to me as a wedding present. She gave it to me that morning. The morning of the wedding."

Chapter 35

A hell of a lot more

The County Office Building had an unusual history. Prior to 1935 it was known as the Bumblebee Lunatic Asylum— named after the eccentric British transplant Sir George Bumblebee, who endowed it with his entire estate in 1899 and who, his disinherited relatives argued, was as insane as any prospective resident. It was a history that provided endless fodder for local wags commenting on the workings of the government agencies that had been located there ever since the county took the place over during the Great Depression.

The dark brick edifice sat like an oppressive paperweight holding down the north side of the town square. The much-needed sandblasting to remove a century of grime was put off each year to the following year, the victim of a perennial budget crisis. In the mid-sixties, the inside had been gutted and redone. Fluorescent lights and plasterboard were installed in place of cracked globes and warped wainscoting. The elaborate lobby security apparatus that Gurney remembered from his visits to the building during the Mellery case was still in place and still frustratingly slow. Once one was past that barrier, however, the rectangular layout of the building was simple, and a minute later he was opening a frosted-glass door on which DISTRICT ATTORNEY appeared in elegant black letters.

He recognized the woman in the cashmere sweater behind the reception desk: Ellen Rackoff, the DA's intensely sexy, though far from young, personal assistant. The look in her eyes was arrestingly cool and experienced.

"You're late," she said in her cashmere voice. The fact that she didn't ask his name was the only acknowledgment that she remembered him from the Mellery case. "Come with me." She led him back out through the glass door and down a corridor to a door with a black plastic sign on it that read CONFERENCE ROOM.

"Good luck."

He opened the door and thought for a moment he'd been brought to the wrong meeting. There were several people in the room, but the one person he'd expected to be there, Sheridan Kline, wasn't among them. He realized he was probably in the right place after all when he saw Captain Rodriguez of the state police glowering at him from the opposite side of the big round table that filled half the windowless room.

Rodriguez was a short, fleshy man with a closed face and a carefully coiffed mass of thick black hair, obviously dyed. His blue suit was immaculate, his shirt whiter than white, his tie bloodred. Glasses with thin steel frames emphasized dark, resentful eyes. Sitting on his left was Arlo Blatt, who was looking at Gurney with small, unfriendly eyes. The colorless man on Rodriguez's right showed no emotion beyond a faintly depressed quality that Gurney guessed was more constitutional than situational. He gave Gurney the appraising once-over that cops automatically give strangers, looked at his watch, and yawned. Across from this trio, his chair pushed back a good three feet from the table, Jack Hardwick sat with his eyes closed and his arms folded on his chest, as if being in the same room with these people had put him to sleep.

"Hello, Dave." The voice was strong, clear, female, and familiar. The source was a tall, auburn-haired woman standing by a separate table in the far corner of the room—a woman with a striking resemblance to the young Sigourney Weaver.

"Rebecca! I didn't know that . . . that you . . ."

"Neither did I. Sheridan called this morning, asked if I could find the time. It worked out, so here I am. Like some coffee?"

"Thank you."

"Black?"

"Sure." He preferred it with milk and sugar but for some reason didn't want to tell her she'd guessed wrong.

Rebecca Holdenfield was a well-known profiler Gurney had met and come to respect, despite his doubts about profilers in general, when they were both working on the Mellery case. He wondered what her presence might signify about the DA's view of the case.

Just then the door opened, and the DA himself strode into the room. Sheridan Kline was, as usual, radiating a sparky sort of energy. His rapidly moving gaze, like a burglar's flashlight, took in the room in a couple of seconds. "Becca! Thank you! Appreciate your making the time to be here. Dave! Detective Dave, the man who's been stirring the pot! Reason we're all here. And Rod!" He grinned brightly at Rodriguez's sour face. "Good of you to make it on such short notice. Glad you were able to bring your people along." He glanced without interest at the bodies flanking the captain, his gladness a transparent lie. Kline liked an audience, Gurney reflected, but he liked it to be composed of people who mattered.

Holdenfield came to the table with two black coffees, gave Gurney one of them, and sat down next to him.

"Senior Investigator Hardwick here is not currently assigned to the case," Kline went on to no one in particular, "but he was involved at the beginning, and I thought it would be helpful to have all our relevant resources in the room at the same time."

Another transparent lie, Gurney thought. What Kline found "helpful" was to throw cats and dogs in together and watch what happened. He was a rabid fan of the adversarial process for getting at the truth and motivating people—the angrier the adversaries, the better. The vibe in the room was hostile, which Gurney figured accounted for the energy level in Kline, which was now approaching the hum of a high-voltage transformer.

"Rod, while I get some coffee here, why don't you summarize BCI's approach to the case so far. We're here to listen and learn."

Gurney thought he heard Hardwick, slouching in his chair on the far side of Rebecca Holdenfield, groan.

"I'll keep this brief," said the captain. "In the matter of the Jillian Perry murder, we know what was done, when it was done, and how it was done. We know who did it, and our efforts have been concentrated on finding that individual and taking him into custody. In pursuit of this objective, we've mobilized one of the largest manhunts in the history of the bureau. It is massive, painstaking, and ongoing."

Another muted sound emanated from Hardwick's direction.

The captain's elbows were planted on the table, his left fist buried in his right hand. He shot Hardwick a warning glance. "So far we've conducted over three hundred interviews, and we're continuing to expand the radius of our inquiries. Bill—Lieutenant Anderson—and Arlo here are responsible for guiding and monitoring the day-to-day progress."

Kline came to the table with his coffee but remained standing. "Maybe Bill could give us a feeling for the current status. What do we know today that we didn't know, say, a week after the beheading?"

Lieutenant Anderson blinked and cleared his throat. "What we didn't know . . . ? Well, I'd say we've eliminated a lot of possibilities." When it became apparent from the stares fixed on him that this was not an adequate response, he cleared his throat again. "There were a lot of things that might have happened that we know now didn't happen. We've eliminated a lot of possibilities, and we've developed a sharper picture of the suspect. A real nutcase."

"What possibilities have you eliminated?" asked Kline.

"Well, we know that no one observed Flores leaving the Tambury area. There's no record of his calling any cab company, no car-rental record, and none of the bus drivers who make local pick-ups recall anyone like him. In fact, we couldn't find anyone who saw him at any time after the murder."

Kline blinked in confusion. "Okay, but I don't quite understand . . ."

Anderson continued blandly. "Sometimes what we don't find is as important as what we do. Lab analyses showed that Flores had scoured the cottage to the point where there was zero trace evidence of himself or anyone other than the victim. He took incredible care in erasing everything that might carry analyzable DNA. Even the traps under the bathroom and kitchen sinks had been scrubbed. We've also interviewed every available Latino laborer within a fifty-mile radius of Tambury, and not a single one was able or willing to tell us anything about Flores. Without prints or DNA or a date of entry into the country, Immigration can't help us. Ditto the authorities in Mexico. The identikit composite is too generic to be of much use. Everyone we interviewed thought it looked like somebody they knew, but no two people identified the same person. As for Kiki Muller, the next-door neighbor who disappeared with Flores, no one has seen her since the murder."

Kline look exasperated. "Sounds like you're telling me the investigation has gotten nowhere."

Anderson glanced at Rodriguez. Rodriguez studied his fist.

Blatt made his first comment of the meeting. "It's a matter of time."

Everyone looked at him.

"We have people in that community keeping their eyes and ears open. Eventually Flores will surface, shoot his mouth off to the wrong person. Then we scoop him up."

Hardwick was peering at his fingernails as though they were suspicious growths. "What 'community' would that be, Arlo?"

"Illegal aliens, who else?"

"Suppose he's not Mexican."

"So he's Guatemalan, Nicaraguan, whatever. We've got people poking around in all those communities. Eventually..." He shrugged.

Kline's antenna tuned in to the conflict. "What are you getting at, Jack?"

Rodriguez stepped in stiffly. "Hardwick has been out of the loop for some time. Bill and Arlo are your best sources for current information."

Kline acted like he didn't hear him. "Jack?"

Hardwick smiled. "Tell you what. Why don't you listen to what Ace Detective Gurney here has uncovered in less than four days, which is a shitload more than we've come up with in four months."

Kline's voltage was rising. "Dave? What have you got?"

"What I've uncovered," began Gurney slowly, "are mostly questions—questions that suggest new directions for the investigation." He placed his forearms on the table and leaned forward. "One key element that deserves more attention is the victim's background. Jillian was sexually abused as a child and became an abuser of other children. She was aggressive, manipulative, and reportedly had sociopathic traits. The possibility of a revenge motive arising out of that kind of behavior is significant."

Blatt's expression was screwed up in a knot. "You're trying to tell us that Jillian Perry sexually abused Hector Flores when he was a little kid and that's why he killed her? That sounds nuts."

"I agree. Especially since Flores was probably at least ten years older than Jillian. But suppose he was taking revenge for something done to someone else. Or suppose he himself had been so severely abused, so traumatically, that it affected the balance of his mind, and he decided to take out his rage on all abusers. Suppose Flores found out about Mapleshade, about the nature of its clientele, about Dr. Ashton's work. Is it possible that he might show up at Ashton's house, try to get odd jobs, ingratiate himself, wait for an opportunity to make a dramatic gesture?"

Kline spoke up excitedly. "What do you think, Becca? Is that possible?"

Her eyes widened. "It's possible, yes. Jillian could have been chosen as a specific revenge target based on her actions against some individual Flores knew, or as a proxy target representing abusers in general. Do you have any evidence pointing in one direction or the other?"

Kline looked to Gurney.

"The dramatic details of the murder—the beheading, the placement of the head, the choice of the wedding day—have a ritual feeling. That would be consistent with a revenge motive. But we sure as hell don't know enough yet to say whether she was an individual target or a proxy target."

Kline finished his coffee and headed for a refill, speaking to the room in general as he went. "If we take this revenge angle seriously, what investigatory actions would that require? Dave?"

What Gurney believed it would require—to start with—was a much more detailed disclosure of Jillian's past problems and childhood contacts than her mother or Simon Kale had so far been willing to provide, and he needed to figure out how to make that happen. "I can give you a written recommendation on that within the next couple of days."

Kline seemed satisfied with that and moved on. "So what else? Senior Investigator Hardwick gave you credit for what he called a 'shitload' of discoveries."

"We may be a couple short of a shitload, but there's one thing I'd put at the top of the list. A number of girls from Mapleshade seem to be missing."

The three BCI detectives came to attention, more or less in unison, like men awakened by a loud noise.

Gurney continued. "Both Scott Ashton and another person connected with the school have tried to contact certain recent graduates and haven't been able to."

"That doesn't necessarily mean—" began Lieutenant Anderson.

But Gurney cut him off. "By itself it wouldn't mean much, but there's an odd similarity among the individual instances. All the girls in question started the same argument with their parents— demanding an expensive new car, then using their parents' refusal as a pretext for leaving home."

"How many girls are we talking about?" asked Blatt.

"A former student who was trying to reach some of her fellow graduates told me about two instances in which the parents had no idea where their daughter was. Then Scott Ashton told me about three more girls he was trying to reach, who he discovered had left home after an argument with their parents—the same kind of car argument in all three instances."

Kline shook his head. "I don't get it. What's it all about? And what's it got to do with finding Jillian Perry's killer?"

"The missing girls had at least one thing in common, besides the argument they started with their parents. They all knew Flores."

Anderson was looking more dyspeptic by the minute. "How?"

"Flores volunteered to do some work for Ashton at Mapleshade. Good-looking man, apparently. Attracted the attention of some Mapleshade girls. Turns out that the ones who showed interest, the ones who were seen speaking to him, are the ones who've gone missing."

"Have they been put on the NCIC missing-persons list?" asked Anderson, in the hopeful tone of a man trying to shift a problem onto another lap.

"None of them," said Gurney. "Problem is, they're all over

eighteen, free to come and go as they wish. Each one announced her plan to leave home, her intention to keep her whereabouts a secret, her desire to be left alone. All of which is contrary to the entry criteria for mis-pers databases."

Kline was pacing back and forth. "This gives the case a new slant. What do you think, Rod?"

The captain looked grim. "I'd like to know what the hell Gurney is really telling us."

Kline answered. "I think he's telling us that there might be more to the Jillian Perry case than Jillian Perry."

"And that Hector Flores might be more than a Mexican gardener," added Hardwick, staring pointedly at Rodriguez. "A possibility I recall mentioning some time ago."

This had the effect of raising Kline's eyebrows. "When?"

"When I was still assigned to the case. The original Flores narrative felt wrong to me."

If Rodriguez's jaws were clenched any tighter, Gurney mused, his teeth would start disintegrating.

"Wrong how?" asked Kline.

"Wrong in the sense that it was all too fucking right."

Gurney knew that Rodriguez would be feeling Hardwick's delight like an ice pick in the ribs—never mind the touchy issue of airing an internal disagreement in front of the district attorney.

"Meaning?" asked Kline.

"I mean too fucking smooth. The illiterate laborer, too rapidly educated by the arrogant doctor, too much advancement too soon, affair with the rich neighbor's wife, maybe an affair with Jillian Perry, feelings he couldn't handle, cracking under the strain. It plays like a soap opera, like complete fucking bullshit." He delivered this judgment with such a steady focus on Rodriguez that there could be no doubt about the source of the scenario he was attacking.

From what Gurney knew of Kline from the Mellery case, he was sure the man was loving the confrontation while he was hiding the feeling under a thoughtful frown.

"What was your own theory of the Flores business?" prompted Kline.

Hardwick settled back in his chair like a wind dying down. "It's easier to say what isn't logical here than what is. When you combine all the known facts, it's hard to make any sense at all out of Flores's behavior."

Kline turned to Gurney. "That the way you see it, too?"

Gurney took a deep breath. "Some facts seem contradictory. But facts don't contradict each other—which means there's a big piece of the puzzle missing, the piece that'll eventually make the others make sense. I don't expect it to be a simple narrative. As Jack once said, there are definitely hidden layers in this case." He was concerned for a moment that this comment might reveal Hardwick's role in Val's decision to hire him, but no one seemed to pick it up. Blatt looked like a rat trying to identify something by sniffing it, but Blatt always looked like that.

Kline sipped his coffee thoughtfully. "Which facts are bothering you, Dave?"

"To start with, the rapid Flores transition from leaf raker to household manager."

"You think Ashton is lying about that?"

"Lying to himself, maybe. He explains it as a kind of wishful thinking, something that supported the concept of a book he was writing."

"Becca, that make sense to you?"

She smiled noncommittally, more of a facial shrug than a real smile. "Never underestimate the power of self-deception, especially in a man trying to prove a point."

Kline nodded sagely, turned back to Gurney. "So your basic idea is that Flores was working a con?"

"That he was playing a role for some reason, yes."

"What else bothers you?"

"Motivation. If Flores came to Tambury for the purpose of killing Jillian, why did he wait so long to do it? But if he came for another purpose, what was it?"

"Interesting questions. Keep going."

"The beheading itself seems to have been methodical and well planned, but also spontaneous and opportunistic."

"I don't follow that."

"The arrangement—of the body—was precise. The cottage had very recently, perhaps that same morning, been scoured to eliminate any traces of the man who'd lived there. The escape route had been planned, and some way had been devised to create the scent-trail problem for the K-9 team. However it was that Flores managed to disappear, it had been carefully thought through. It has the feeling of a *Mission: Impossible* scheme that relies on split-second timing. But the actual circumstances would appear to defy any attempt at planning at all, much less perfect timing."

Kline cocked his head curiously. "How so?"

"The video indicates that Jillian made her visit to the cottage on a kind of whim. A little bit before the scheduled wedding toast, she told Ashton she wanted to persuade Hector to join them. As I recall, Ashton told the Luntz couple—the police chief and his wife—about Jillian's intentions. No one else seemed to be crazy about the idea, but I got the impression that Jillian pretty much did whatever she felt like doing. So on the one hand we have a meticulously premeditated murder that depended on perfect timing, and on the other hand, we have a set of circumstances completely beyond the murderer's control. There's something wrong with that picture."

"Not necessarily," said Blatt, his rat nose twitching. "Flores could have set up everything ahead of time, had everything ready, then waited for his opportunity like a snake in a hole. Waited for the victim to come by, and . . . bam!"

Gurney looked doubtful. "Problem is, Arlo, that would require Flores to get the cottage perfectly clean, almost sterile, prepare himself and his escape route, wear the clothes he intended to wear, have whatever he was taking with him at hand, have Kiki Muller equally prepared, and then . . . and then what? Sit in the cottage with a machete in his hand hoping that Jillian would pop in to invite him to the reception?"

"You're making it sound stupid, like it couldn't happen," said Blatt with hatred in his eyes. "But I think that's exactly what happened."

Anderson pursed his lips. Rodriguez narrowed his eyes. Neither seemed willing to endorse their colleague's view.

Kline broke the awkward silence. "Anything else?"

"Well," said Gurney, "there's the matter of the new elephant in the room—the missing graduates."

"Which," said Blatt, "may not even be true. Maybe they just don't want to be found. These girls are not what you'd call stable. And even if they're, like, really *missing,* there's no proof of any connection to the Perry case."

There was another silence, this time broken by Hardwick. "Arlo might be right. But if they *are* missing and there *is* a connection, there's a good chance they're all dead by now."

No one said anything. It was well known that, when young females went missing under suspicious circumstances with no further contact, the odds of their safe return were not high. And the fact that the girls in question had all started the same peculiar argument before disappearing definitely qualified as suspicious.

Rodriguez looked pained and angry, looked like he was about to offer an objection, but before any words came out, Gurney's cell phone rang. Gurney glanced at the ID on the screen and decided to answer it.

It was Scott Ashton. "Since we last spoke, I made six more calls and got through to two more families. I'm continuing the calls, but . . . I wanted to let you know that both girls in the families I got through to left home after the same outrageous argument. One demanded a twenty-thousand-dollar Suzuki, the other a thirty-five-thousand-dollar Mustang. The parents said no. Both girls refused to say where they were going and insisted that nobody should try to contact them. I have no idea what it means, but obviously something strange is going on. And another distressing coincidence: They'd both posed for those Karnala Fashion ads."

"How long have they been missing?"

"One for six months, one for nine months."

"Tell me something, Doctor. Are you ready to provide us with names, or do we get an immediate court order for your records?"

All eyes in the room were on Gurney. Kline's coffee was inches from his lips, but he seemed to have forgotten he was holding it.

"What names do you want?" said Ashton in a beaten voice.

"Let's start with the names of the missing girls, plus the names of all the girls who were in the same classes."

"Fine."

"One other question: How did Jillian get her modeling job?"

"I don't know."

"She never told you? Even though she gave you the photograph as a wedding present?"

"She never told me."

"You didn't ask?"

"I did, but . . . Jillian wasn't fond of questions."

Gurney felt an urge to shout, *WHAT THE HELL IS GOING ON? IS EVERYONE CONNECTED WITH THIS CASE OUT OF HIS GODDAMN MIND?*

Instead he said simply, "Thank you, Doctor. That's it for now. You'll be contacted by BCI for the relevant names and addresses."

As Gurney slipped the phone back into his pocket, Kline barked, "What on earth was that?"

"Two more girls are missing. After having the same argument: One girl demanded that her parents buy her a Suzuki, the other a Mustang." He turned toward Anderson. "Ashton is ready to provide BCI with the names of the missing girls, plus the names of their classmates. Just let him know what format you want the list in and how to send it to you."

"Fine, but we're ignoring the point that nobody is *legally missing,* which means we can't devote police resources to finding them. These are eighteen-year-old women, adults, who made apparently free decisions to leave home. The fact that they haven't told their families how to reach them does not give us a legal basis for tracking them down."

Gurney got the impression that Lieutenant Anderson was coasting toward a Florida retirement and had a coaster's fondness for inaction. It was a state of mind for which Gurney, a driven man in his police career, had little patience. "Then find a basis. Declare them all material witnesses to the Perry murder. Invent a basis. Do what you have to do. That's the least of your problems."

Anderson looked riled enough to escalate the argument into

something unpleasant. But before he could launch his reply, Kline interrupted. "This may seem a small point, Dave, but if you're implying that these girls were following the directions of some third party—presumably Flores—who rehearsed them in the argument they were supposed to start with their parents, why is the make of car different from case to case?"

"The simplest answer is that different cars might be necessary in order to achieve the same effect on families in different economic circumstances. Assuming that the purpose of the argument was to provide a credible excuse for the girl to storm out—to disappear without the disappearance becoming a police matter—the car demand would need to have two results. One, it would have to involve enough money to guarantee that it would be refused. Two, the parents would have to believe that their daughter was serious. The different makes may not have any significance per se; the key point may be the difference in the prices. Different prices would be necessary in order to achieve the same impact in families of different financial means. In other words, a demand for a twenty-thousand-dollar car in one family might have the same impact as a demand for a forty-thousand-dollar car in another family."

"Clever," said Kline, smiling appreciatively. "If you're right, Flores is a thinker. A maniac, maybe, but definitely a thinker."

"But he's also done things that make no sense." Gurney stood to get himself some more coffee. "That damn bullet in the teacup—what the hell was the point of that? He stole Ashton's hunting rifle so he could shatter his teacup? Why take a risk like that? By the way," said Gurney in an aside to Blatt, "were you aware that Withrow Perry had a gun of the same caliber?"

"The hell are you talking about?"

"The bullet that was fired at the teacup came from a .257 Weatherby. Ashton owns one, which he reported stolen, but Perry also owns one. You might want to look into that."

There was an uncomfortable silence as Rodriguez and Blatt both made hurried notes.

Kline looked accusingly at both of them, then turned his attention to Gurney. "Okay, what else do you know that we don't?"

"Hard to say," said Gurney. "How much do you know about Crazy Carl?"

"Who?"

"Husband of Kiki Muller."

"What's he got to do with it?"

"Maybe nothing, except for having a credible motive for killing Flores."

"Flores wasn't killed."

"How do we know? He disappeared without a trace. He could be buried in somebody's backyard."

"Whoa, whoa, what's all this?" Anderson was appalled, Gurney guessed, at the prospect of more work. Digging up backyards. "What are we doing here, inventing imaginary murders?"

Kline looked confused. "Where are you going with this?"

"The assumption seems to be that Flores fled the area in the company of Kiki Muller, maybe even hid out at the Muller house for a few days before leaving the area. Suppose Flores was still around when Carl came home from his stint on that ship he worked on? I assume the interview team noticed that Carl is bonkers?"

Kline took a step backward from the table, as if the panorama of the case were too broad to see from where he'd been standing. "Wait a second. If Flores is dead, he can't be connected to the disappearances of these other girls. Or the gunshot on Ashton's patio. Or the text message Ashton received from Flores's cell phone."

Gurney shrugged.

Kline shook his head in frustration. "It sounds to me like you just took everything that was starting to fit together and kicked it off the table."

"I'm not kicking anything off the table. Personally, I don't believe Carl is involved. I'm not even sure his wife was involved. I'm just trying to loosen things up a bit. We don't have as many solid facts as you might think. My point is, we need to keep our minds open." He weighed the risk of ill will inherent in what he was about to add and decided to add it, anyway. "Getting committed to the wrong hypothesis early on may be the reason the investigation hasn't gotten anywhere."

Kline looked at Rodriguez, who was staring at the table surface as if it were a painting of hell. "What do you think, Rod? You think we need to take a new look at it? You think maybe we've been trying to solve the puzzle ass backwards?"

Rodriguez just shook his head slowly. "No, that's not what I think," he said, his voice hoarse, tense with suppressed emotion.

Judging from the expressions around the table, Gurney wasn't the only one taken aback when the captain, a man obsessed with projecting an aura of control, rose awkwardly from his chair and left the room as though he couldn't bear to be in it for another minute.

Chapter 36

Into the heart
of darkness

After the captain left, the meeting lost focus. Not that it had much focus to begin with, but the strangeness of his departure seemed to underline the incoherence of the investigation, and the discussion disintegrated. Star profiler Rebecca Holdenfield, expressing confusion about her role there, was the next to flee. Anderson and Blatt were restless, caught between the gravitational fields of their boss who was gone and the DA who was still present.

Gurney asked if any progress had been made identifying the significance of the Edward Vallory name, but none had. Anderson looked blank at the question, and Blatt dismissed it with a wave of his hand that conveyed what a useless avenue of inquiry he considered it to be.

The DA mouthed a few meaningless sentences about how profitable the meeting had been in getting everyone on the same page. Gurney didn't think it had done that. But at least it might have gotten everyone wondering what kind of story they were reading. And it got the question of the disappearing graduates on the table.

Gurney's final contribution to the meeting was a strong suggestion that BCI dig up some background and contact information on Alessandro and Karnala Fashion, since they constituted a common factor in the lives of the missing girls and a link between them and Jillian. Just as Kline was endorsing this pursuit, Ellen Rackoff came to the door and pointed at her watch. He checked his, looked startled, and announced with stern self-importance that he was late for a conference call with the governor. As he departed, he expressed his confidence that they all could find their own way out. Anderson and Blatt left together, followed by Gurney and Hardwick.

Hardwick had one of the NYSP's ubiquitous black Ford sedans. In the parking lot, he leaned against the trunk, lit a cigarette, and, without being asked, offered Gurney his take on the captain. "Little fucker is coming apart. You know what they say about control freaks—that they have to control everything outside them because everything inside's a fucking mess. That's Captain Rod, except the little fucker can't keep the craziness hidden anymore." He took a long drag on his cigarette, grimaced as he blew the smoke out. "His daughter's a fucking cokehead. You knew that, right?"

Gurney nodded. "You told me that during the Mellery case."

"I told you she was in Greystone? The nuthouse down in Jersey?"

"Right." Gurney remembered a damp, bitter day the previous November when Hardwick had told him about the Rodriguez girl's addiction problem and how it skewed her father's judgment in cases where drugs might be involved.

"Well, she got booted out of Greystone for smuggling in roxies and for fucking her fellow patients. Latest news is that she was arrested for dealing crack at an NA meeting."

Gurney wondered where this was going. It didn't have the tone of a compassionate explanation of the captain's behavior.

Hardwick took the kind of drag he'd take if he were trying to set a new record for how much smoke he could get into his lungs in three seconds. "I see you looking at me like, so what, what does this have to do with anything? Am I right?"

"The question crossed my mind."

"The answer is, nothing. It doesn't have a fucking thing to do with anything. Except that Rodriguez's decisions aren't worth shit these days. He's a liability to the case." He flung the half-finished cigarette down, put his foot on it, ground it into the asphalt.

Gurney took a shot at changing the subject. "Do me a favor. Follow up on Alessandro and Karnala. I don't get the impression anyone else in there is particularly interested."

Hardwick didn't respond. He stood there for another minute,

staring down at the crushed butt next to his foot. "Time to go," he finally said. He opened his car door and wrinkled his face as though assailed by a sour smell.

"Just watch out, Davey boy. The little fucker's a time bomb, and he's gonna go off. They always do."

Chapter 37

The deer

The drive home was miserable in a way Gurney couldn't at first identify. He was both distracted and seeking distraction, seeking distraction and unable to find it. Every radio station was more intolerable than the one before it. Music that failed to reflect his mood struck him as idiotic, while music that did only made him feel worse. Every human voice carried within it an irritant, a revelation of stupidity or cupidity or both. Every commercial made him want to scream, *Lying bastards!*

Turning off the radio refocused him on the road—refocused him on the shabby villages, the dead and dying farms, and the poisonous economic carrots being dangled in front of poor upstate towns by the gas-drilling industry.

Jesus, he was in a hell of a mood.

Why?

He let his mind drift back over the meeting, see what it would fasten on.

Ellen Rackoff, of course, in cashmere. Zero pretense of innocence. Warm and cozy as a snake. The danger itself a perverse part of the attraction.

The original evidence team's report on the crime scene, reprised by Lieutenant Anderson, that made the murder sound like a professional assassination: *Even the traps under the bathroom and kitchen sinks had been scrubbed.*

The facts uniting the missing graduates: their common arguments with their parents, their extravagant demands that were sure to be refused, their prior contacts with Hector and Karnala Fashion and the elusive photographer, Alessandro.

Jack Hardwick's cold prognosis: *There's a good a chance they're all dead by now.*

Rodriguez's personal agony, as the father of a troubled daughter, echoed and magnified by the potential horrors of the case in front of him.

Gurney could hear the hoarseness in the man's voice as clearly as if he were sitting next to him in the car. It was the sound of a man being stretched out of shape, stretched like a rubber band too small to encompass everything it was given to hold—a man whose constitution lacks the flexibility to absorb the accidental elements of his own life.

Which set Gurney to wondering: Are there really any *accidental* elements? Don't we, in some undeniable way, place ourselves in the positions in which we find ourselves? Don't our choices, our priorities, make all the difference? He felt sick to his stomach, and suddenly he knew the reason. He was identifying with Rodriguez: the career-obsessed cop, the father without a clue.

And then—as though the turmoil of this realization were not enough, as though some malignant god were seeking to contrive the perfect external disaster to match the collision of emotions within him—he hit the deer.

He had just passed the sign that read ENTERING BROWNVILLE. There was no village, just the overgrown remnants of a long-abandoned river-valley farm on the left and a forested upslope on the right. A medium-size doe had emerged from the woods, hesitated, then dashed across the road far enough ahead of him that there was hardly any need to brake. But then her fawn followed her, it was too late to brake, and although he swerved as far to the left as he could, he heard and felt the terrible thump.

He pulled over onto the shoulder and stopped. He looked into his rearview mirror, hoping to see nothing, hoping that it was one of those fortunate collisions from which the remarkably resilient deer ran off into the woods with only superficial damage. But that was not the case. A hundred feet behind him, a small brown body lay sprawled at the edge of the roadside drainage ditch.

He got out of the car and walked back along the shoulder, holding on to a faint hope that the fawn was only stunned and would at any moment stagger to its feet. As he got closer, the twisted position of the head and the empty stare of the open eyes took that hope away. He stopped and looked around helplessly. He saw the doe standing in the ruined farm field, watching, waiting, motionless.

There was nothing he could do.

He was sitting in his car with no recollection of having walked back to it, his breathing interrupted by small sobs. He was halfway to Walnut Crossing before he thought of checking the damage to the front end, but even then he continued on, pierced by regret, wanting only to get home.

Chapter 38

The eyes of
Peter Piggert

The house had that peculiarly empty feeling it had when Madeleine was out. On Fridays she had dinner with three of her friends, to talk about knitting and sewing, things they were making and things they were doing, and everyone's health, and the books they were reading.

He had the idea, formed at the emotional nadir of the drive from Brownville to Walnut Crossing, that he would follow Madeleine's prodding and call Kyle—have an actual conversation with his son instead of another exchange of those carefully drafted, antiseptic e-mails that provided them both with the illusion of communication. Reading the edited descriptions of life's events on the screen of a laptop bore little resemblance to hearing them related in a living voice without the smoothing process of rewrites and deletions.

He went into the den with good intentions but decided to check his voice mail and e-mail before making the call. There was one message in each format. They were both from Peggy Meeker, social-worker wife of the spider man.

On voice mail she sounded excited, almost bouncy. *"Dave, Peggy Meeker. After you mentioned Edward Vallory the other night, the name kept gnawing at me. I knew that I knew it from somewhere. Well, I found it! I remembered it from a college English course. Elizabethan drama. Vallory was a dramatist, but none of his dramas survive, which is why almost no one has ever heard of him. All that exists is the prologue to one play. But get this—his stuff was all supposedly misogynistic. He absolutely hated women! In fact, the play that this prologue was part of was reputedly about a man who killed his own* mother! I e-mailed you the existing prologue. Does this have something to do with the Perry case? I was wondering, because you were talking about that earlier in the evening. I thought about that when I read Vallory's prologue, and it gave me the chills. Look at the e-mail. Let me know if it helps. And let me know if there's anything more I can do for you. This is soooo exciting. Talk to you soon. Bye. Oh, and hello to Madeleine."

Gurney opened her e-mail and scanned down quickly to get to the Vallory quote:

> There is on earth no woman chaste. There is
> no purity in her. Her aspect, speech,
> and heart sing never three as one. She seems
> but this, and seems but that, and seeming's all.
> With slipp'ry oils and powders bright
> she colours o'er her dark designs, and paints
> upon herself a portrait we might love.
> But where's the honest heart that with
> a single note doth ring its true content?
> Fie! Ask her not for pure, direct,
> and honest music. Purity's no part of her.
> She drew from Eden's serpent all its wiles
> into her serpent heart that she might spew
> o'er every man a slime of lies and trickery.

Gurney read it several times, trying to absorb the intended meaning and purpose of it.

It was the prologue to a play about a man who killed his own mother. A prologue written centuries ago by a playwright famous for his hatred of women. The playwright whose name was appended to the text message sent from Hector's cell phone to Jillian's the morning she was killed—and sent again, just two days ago, to Ashton. A text message that read simply, FOR ALL THE REASONS I HAVE WRITTEN.

And the reasons given in his only extant writing seemed to add up to this: Women are impure, seductive, deceptive, satanic creatures—spewing, like monsters, a *slime* of lies and trickery. The more closely he read Vallory's words, the more he sensed in them a twisted sexual nightmare.

Gurney prided himself on his caution, his balance, but it was difficult not to conclude that the quotation constituted a demented justification for Jillian Perry's murder. And possibly for other murders as well.

Of course there was nothing certain about it. No way of proving that Edward Vallory, the purported seventeenth-century women hater, was the Edward Vallory whose name was appropriated for the text messages. No proof that Edward Vallory was a pseudonym for Hector Flores—although the fact that the messages came from Flores's cell phone made it a fair assumption.

It did all seem to fit together, did seem to make a kind of awful sense. The Vallory prologue offered the first motive hypothesis that wasn't based entirely on speculation. For Gurney it was a motive that held the additional attraction of being compatible with his own growing sense that Jillian's murder was driven by revenge for past sexual offenses—either hers or those of Mapleshade students in general. Moreover, the receipt of the Vallory message by Scott Ashton supported a view of the murder as part of a complex enterprise— an enterprise that seemed to be ongoing.

Maybe Gurney was reading too much into it, but it suddenly occurred to him that the fact that the surviving snippet of Vallory's play was its *prologue* might have more than accidental significance. Might it, in addition to being the prologue to a lost drama, also be intended as a prologue to future events—a hint of murders yet to come? Exactly how much was Hector Flores telling them?

He clicked "reply" on Peggy Meeker's e-mail and asked, "What else is known about the play? Plot line? Characters? Any surviving comments from Vallory's contemporaries?"

For the first time in the case, Gurney felt an undeniable excitement—and an irresistible urge to call Sheridan Kline, hoping he'd still be in the office.

He placed the call.

"He's in conference." Ellen Rackoff spoke with the confidence of a powerful gatekeeper.

"There's been a development in the Perry matter he'd want to know about."

"Be more specific."

"It may be turning into a serial-murder case."

Thirty seconds later Kline was on the phone—edgy, pressured, and intrigued. "Serial murder? What the hell are you talking about?"

Gurney described the Vallory discovery, pointing out the sexual anger in the words of the prologue, explaining how it might relate not only to Jillian but to the missing girls.

"Isn't all that pretty iffy? I don't get how anything has really changed. I mean, this afternoon you were saying that Hector Flores might be at the center of everything, or then again he might not be, we didn't really have any solid facts, we needed to keep an open mind. So what happened to the open mind? How did this suddenly turn into serial murder? And by the way, why are you calling me with this, not the police?"

"Maybe it's just that the focus got clearer once I read that Vallory thing and felt the hatred in it. Or maybe it's just that word: *prologue.* A promise of something to come. The fact that Flores sent that text message to Jillian before she was killed and sent it again to Ashton this week. It makes the murder four months ago look like part of something bigger."

"You honestly think that Flores was persuading girls to leave home under the smoke screen of an argument so he could kill them without anyone bothering to look for them?" Kline's voice conveyed a mixture of worry and incredulity.

"Until we find them alive, I think it's a possibility we have to take seriously."

The defensive reflex in Kline spit back, "I wouldn't take it any other way." Then he added earnestly, as though he were being taped for broadcast, "I can't think of anything more serious than the possibility of a kidnapping-and-murder conspiracy—if, God forbid, that's what we're dealing with here." He paused, his tone turning suspicious. "Returning to the protocol issue, how come I'm getting this call instead of BCI?"

"Because you're the only decision maker who's making any sense to me."

"Why do you say that?" Kline's fondness for flattery was obvious in his voice.

"The emotional undercurrent in that conference room today was nuts. I know that Rodriguez and Hardwick never cared much for each other, which was obvious on the Mellery case, but whatever the hell's going on now, it's becoming dysfunctional. There's zero objectivity. It's like a war, and I have the impression that every new development is going to be evaluated by those guys on the basis of which side it helps. You don't seem to be entangled in that mess, so I'd rather talk to you."

Kline paused. "You don't know what happened with your buddy?"

"Buddy?"

"Rodriguez nailed him for an over-the-limit BAC on duty."

"What!?"

"Suspended him for drinking on the job, hung a possible DWI over his head, threatened his pension, forced him to go to rehab as a condition for ending the suspension. I'm surprised you don't know about this."

"When did it happen?"

"Month and a half ago? Twenty-eight-day rehab. Jack's back on the job maybe ten days."

"Jesus." Gurney had figured that part of Hardwick's reason for setting him up with Val Perry was the hope that some new discovery would put Rodriguez in a bad light, but this news went a long way toward explaining the negative energy bouncing around that conference room.

"I'm surprised you didn't know about it," Kline repeated, enough disbelief in his tone to make it an accusation.

"If I'd known, I'd never have gotten involved," said Gurney. "But it's all the more reason to keep my exposure limited to my client and to you—assuming that a direct line of contact with me isn't going to poison your relationship with BCI."

Kline took so long to mull this over that Gurney imagined the man's risk-reward calculator starting to smolder from an overload of permutations.

"Okay—with one major caution. It has to be perfectly clear

that you're working for the Perry family, independently of this office. Which means that under no circumstances can you imply that you're covered by our investigatory authority or by any form of immunity. You proceed as Dave Gurney, private citizen, period. With that understanding, I'd be happy to listen to whatever you have to say. Believe me, I have nothing but respect for you. Based on your NYPD homicide record and your role in solving the Mellery case, how could I not? We just need to be clear about your *unofficial* position. Any questions?"

Gurney smiled at Kline's predictability. The man never strayed from the one guiding principle of his life: *Get everything you possibly can from other people, while covering your own ass absolutely.*

"One question, Sheridan: How do I get in touch with Rebecca Holdenfield?"

Kline's voice tightened with an attorney's skepticism. "What do you want from her?"

"I'm starting to get a sense of our killer. Very hypothetical, nothing that firm yet, but it might help me to have someone with her background as a sounding board."

"There some reason you don't want to call the killer by his name?"

"Hector Flores?"

"You have a problem with that?"

"Couple of problems. Number one, we don't know that he was alone in the cottage when Jillian went in, so we don't know that he's the killer. Come right down to it, we don't know that he was in the cottage at all. Suppose someone else was in there instead, waiting for her? I realize it's unlikely—all I'm saying is, we don't *know.* It's all circumstantial, assumptions, probabilities. Second problem is the name itself. If the Cinderella gardener is really a cool, think-ahead murderer, then 'Hector Flores' is almost certainly an alias."

"Why am I getting the feeling I'm on a merry-go-round— that every damn thing I think is settled comes flying around at me again?"

"Merry-go-round doesn't sound so bad. To me it feels more like being sucked down a drain."

"And you want to suck Becca down with you?"

Gurney chose not to react to whatever nasty suggestion Kline was making. "I want her to help me stay realistic—provide boundaries for the image I'm forming of the man I'm after."

Perhaps jarred by the commitment in those last four words, perhaps reminded of Gurney's unparalleled record of homicide arrests, Kline's tone changed.

"I'll have her call you."

An hour later Gurney was sitting in front of his computer screen at the desk in his den, staring into the emotionless black eyes of Peter Piggert—a man who might have something in common with the murderer of Jillian Perry and quite a lot in common with the villain in Edward Vallory's lost play. Gurney wasn't sure whether he'd been drawn back to the computer-art portrait he'd done of the man a year earlier because of its possible relevance to the psychology of his current quarry or because of its new financial potential.

A hundred thousand dollars? For this? The moneyed art world must be a strange place indeed. A hundred thousand dollars for Peter Piggert's picture. The price was as absurd as the alliteration. He needed to talk to Sonya. He'd get in touch with her first thing in the morning. Right now he wanted to concentrate not so much on the portrait's possible value but on the man it depicted.

Piggert at the age of fifteen had murdered his father in order to pursue without obstruction a profoundly sick relationship with his mother. He got her pregnant twice and had two daughters with her. Fifteen years later, at the age of thirty, he murdered his mother in order to pursue without obstruction an equally sick relationship with their daughters, then thirteen and fourteen.

To the average observer, Piggert appeared to be the most ordinary of men. But to Gurney there had seemed from the beginning to be something not quite right about the eyes. Their dark placidity seemed eerily bottomless. Peter Piggert seemed to view the world in a way that justified and encouraged any action that might please him, regardless of its effect on anyone else. Gurney wondered if it was a man like Piggert whom Scott Ashton had in mind when he floated his provocative theory that a sociopath is a creature with "perfect boundaries."

As he stared into the disconcerting stillness of those eyes, Gurney was more certain than ever that the man's principal drive was an overwhelming need to control his environment. His vision of the proper order of things was inviolable, his whims absolute. That was what Gurney had endeavored to highlight in his manipulation of the original mug-shot photo. The rigid tyrant behind the bland features. Satan in the skin of Everyman.

Was that what Jay Jykynstyl was fascinated by? The veiled evil? Was that what he prized, what he was offering to pay a small fortune for?

Of course, there was a crucial difference between the reality of the killer and the portrait of the killer. The object on the screen derived its appeal in part from its evocation of the monster and in part, ironically, from its own essential harmlessness. The serpent defanged. The devil paralyzed and laminated.

Gurney leaned back from his desk, away from the computer screen, folded his arms across his chest, and gazed out the west window. His focus initially was inward. When he began to notice the crimson sunset, it seemed at first a smear of blood across the aqua sky. Then he realized he was remembering a bedroom wall in the South Bronx, a turquoise wall against which a shooting victim had leaned, sliding slowly to the floor. Twenty-four years ago, his first murder case.

Flies. It was August, and the body had been there for a week.

Chapter 39

Real, unreal, crazy, not crazy

For twenty-four years he'd been up to his armpits in murder and mayhem. Half his life. Even now, in retirement . . . What was it Madeleine had said to him during the Mellery carnage? That death seemed to call to him more strongly than life?

He'd denied it. And argued the point semantically: It wasn't *death* that drew his attention and energy; it was the challenge of unraveling the mystery of murder. It was about justice.

And of course she had given him her wry look. Madeleine was unimpressed by principled motives, or at least by the invocation of principles to win arguments.

Once he had disengaged from the debate, the truth would sneak up on him. The truth was that he was *drawn*, almost physically, to criminal mysteries and the process of exposing the people behind them. It was a far more primal and powerful force than whatever it was that pushed him toward weeding the asparagus patch. Murder investigations captured the fullness of his attention as nothing else in his life ever had.

That was the good news. It was also the bad news. Good because it was real, and some men went through life with nothing to excite them but their fantasies. Bad because it was a tidal force that drew him away from everything else in his life that mattered, including Madeleine.

He tried to remember where she was at that very moment and found that it had slipped his mind—displaced by God-knows-what. By Jay Jykynstyl and his hundred-thousand-dollar carrot? By the toxic rancor at BCI and its warping effect on the investigation? By

the teasing significance of Edward Vallory's lost play? By the eagerness of Peggy, the spider man's wife, to join the hunt? By the echo of
Savannah Liston's fearful voice, reporting the disappearance of her
former classmates? The truth is, any of a score of items could easily
have edged Madeleine's whereabouts off his radar screen.

Then he heard a car driving up the pasture lane, and it came
back to him: her Friday-evening meeting with her knitting friends.
But if that was her car, she was coming home a lot earlier than usual.
As he headed for the kitchen window to check, the phone rang on
the den desk behind him, and he went back to answer it.

"Dave, so glad I caught you live on the phone, not your machine. I've got a couple of curveballs for you, but not to worry!" It
was Sonya Reynolds, a dash of anxiety coloring her characteristic
excitement.

"I was going to call you——" Gurney began. He'd planned to ask
more questions in order to get a more grounded feeling about the
following evening's dinner with Jykynstyl.

Sonya cut him off. "Dinner is now lunch. Jay has to catch a plane
for Rome. Hope that's not a problem for you. If it is, you'll have to
make it not be. And curveball number two is that I won't be there."
That was the part that obviously bothered her. "Did you hear what
I said?" she asked after Gurney failed to react.

"Lunch is not a problem for me. You can't be there?"

"I certainly *could* be there, would certainly *like* to be there,
but . . . well, instead of trying to explain, why don't I just tell you
what he said. Let me preface this by reminding you how incredibly impressed he is with your work. He referred to it as potentially
seminal. He's very excited. But here's what he said: 'I want to see for
myself who this David Gurney is, this incredible artist who happens
to be a detective. I want to understand who I'm investing in. I want
to be exposed to the mind and imagination of this man without the
obstruction of a third party.' I told him that was the first time in
my life I'd ever been referred to as an obstruction. I told him I don't
think I like that very much, being told not to come. But for him I
make an exception. I stay home. You're very quiet, David. What are
you thinking?"

"I'm wondering if this man is a lunatic."

"This man is Jay Jykynstyl. *Lunatic* is not the word I would use. I would say that he is quite unusual."

Gurney heard the side door opening and shutting, followed by sounds from the mudroom off the kitchen.

"David—why so quiet? More thinking?"

"No, I just . . . I don't know, what does he mean by 'investing' in me?"

"Ah, that's the really good news. That's the biggest part of the reason I would have wanted to be there at dinner, or lunch, or whatever. Listen to this. This is life-changing information. He wants to own all of your work. Not one or two things. All of it. And he expects it to increase in value."

"Why would it?"

"Everything Jykynstyl buys increases in value."

Gurney caught a movement out of the corner of his eye, turned, and saw Madeleine at the den door. She was frowning at him—a worried frown.

"You still there, David?" Sonya's voice was both bubbly and incredulous. "Are you always so quiet when someone offers you a million dollars to start with and sky's the limit after that?"

"I find it bizarre."

A little twist of annoyance was added to Madeleine's worried frown, and she went back out to the kitchen.

"Of course it's bizarre!" cried Sonya. "Success in the art world is always bizarre. Bizarre is normal. You know what Mark Rothko's colored squares sell for? Why should bizarre be a problem?"

"Let me absorb this, okay? Can I call you later?"

"You *better* call me later, David, my million-dollar baby. Tomorrow's a big day. I need to get you ready for it. I can feel that you are thinking again. My God, David, what are you thinking now?"

"I'm just having a hard time believing that any of this is real."

"David, David, David, you know what they tell you when you're learning to swim? Stop fighting the water. Relax and float. Relax and breathe and let the water hold you up. Same thing here. Stop struggling with real, unreal, crazy, not crazy—all these words. Accept the magic. The magic Mr. Jykynstyl. And his magic millions. Ciao!"

Magic? There was no concept on earth quite so alien to Gurney as magic. No concept quite so meaningless, so aggravatingly empty-headed.

He stood by his desk gazing out through the west window. The sky above the ridge, so recently a bloody red, had faded to a murky pall of mauve and granite, and the grass of the high field behind the house had only the memory of green in it.

There was a crash and a clatter in the kitchen, the sound of pot covers sliding from the overloaded dish drainer into the sink, then the sound of Madeleine restacking them.

Gurney emerged from the darkened den into the lighted kitchen. Madeleine was wiping her hands on one of the dish towels.

"What happened to the car?" she asked.

"What? Oh. A deer collision." The recollection was clear, sickening.

She looked at him with alarm, pain.

He went on. "Ran out of the woods. Right in front of me. No way to . . . to get out of the way."

She was wide-eyed, uttered a small gasp. "What happened to the deer?"

"Dead. Instantly. I checked. No sign of life at all."

"What did you do?"

"Do? What could I . . . ?" His mind was suddenly swamped by the image of the fawn on the shoulder of the road, head twisted, unseeing eyes open—an image infused with emotions from long ago, from another accident, emotions that seized his heart with such frozen fingers it almost stopped.

Madeleine watched him, seemed to know what he was thinking, reached out and touched his hand lightly. As he slowly recovered himself, he looked into her eyes and saw a sadness that was simply part of all the things she felt, even of joy. He knew that she had dealt long ago with the death of their son in a way he had not, in a way that he'd never been willing or able to. He knew that one day he would have to. But not yet, not now.

Perhaps that was part of what stood between him and Kyle, his grown son from his first marriage. But theories like that had the feel of therapist-think, and for that he had no use at all.

He turned to the French doors and stared out at the dusky evening, dark enough now that even the red barn was drained of its color.

Madeleine turned to the sink and began drying the stacked pots. When she finally spoke, her question came from an unexpected direction. "So you plan to have it all wrapped up in another week— bad guy safely delivered to the good guys in a box with a bow?" He could hear it in her voice before he looked at her and saw it: the querying, humorless smile.

"If that's what I said, then that's the plan."

She nodded, her skepticism unconcealed.

There was a long silence as she continued to wipe the pots with more than her usual attention, moving the dried items to the pine sideboard, lining them up with a neatness that began to get on his nerves.

"By the way," he said, the question popping back into his mind, coming out more aggressively than he intended, "why are you home?"

"I beg your pardon?"

"Isn't this knitting night?"

She nodded. "We decided to end a bit early."

He thought he heard something odd in her voice.

"How come?"

"There was a little problem."

"Oh?"

"Well . . . actually . . . Marjorie Ann puked."

Gurney blinked. "What?"

"She puked."

"Marjorie Ann Highsmith?"

"That's right."

He blinked again. "What do you mean, puked?"

"What the hell do you think I mean?"

"I mean, where? Right there at the table?"

"No, not at the *table*. She got up from the table and ran for the bathroom and . . ."

"And?"

"And she didn't quite make it."

Gurney noted that a certain almost imperceptible light had come back into Madeleine's eyes, a flicker of the subtle humor with which she viewed almost everything, a humor that balanced her sadness—a light that had lately been missing. He wanted so much, right then, at that moment, to fan the flame of that light but knew that if he tried too hard, he'd only succeed in blowing it out.

"I guess there was a bit of a mess?"

"Oh, yes. A bit of a mess. And it . . . uh . . . it didn't stay in one place."

"Didn't . . . what?"

"Well, she didn't just throw up on the floor. Actually, she threw up on the cats."

"Cats?"

"We met tonight at Bonnie's house. You remember Bonnie has two cats?"

"Yes, sort of."

"The cats were lying down together in a cat bed that Bonnie keeps in the hall outside the bathroom."

Gurney started to laugh—a sudden giddiness taking hold of him.

"Yes, well, Marjorie Ann made it as far as the cats."

"Oh, Jesus . . ." He was doubled over now.

"And she threw up quite a bit. I mean, it was . . . substantial. Well, the cats sort of exploded out of the cat bed and came flying out into the living room."

"Covered . . ."

"Oh, yes, covered with it. Racing around the room, over couches, chairs. It was . . . really something."

"Good God . . ." Gurney couldn't remember the last time he'd laughed so hard.

"And of course," Madeleine concluded, "after that no one could eat. And we couldn't stay in the living room. Naturally, we wanted to help Bonnie clean up, but she wouldn't let us."

After a short silence he asked, "Would you like to eat something now?"

"No!" She shuddered. "Don't mention food."

The image of the cats got him laughing again.

His food suggestion, however, had seemed to trigger in Madeleine's mind a delayed association that extinguished the sparkle in her eyes.

When his laughter finally subsided, she asked, "So is it just you, Sonya, and the mad collector at dinner tomorrow night?"

"No," he said, glad for the first time that Sonya wasn't going to be present. "Just the mad collector and me."

Madeleine raised a quizzical eyebrow. "I would've thought she'd kill to be at that dinner."

"Actually, dinner's been switched to lunch."

"*Lunch?* Are you being downgraded already?"

Gurney showed no reaction, but, absurdly, the comment stung.

Chapter 40

A faint yipping

Once Madeleine had finished with the pots and pans and dishes, she made herself a cup of herbal tea and settled with her knitting bag into one of the overstuffed armchairs at the far end of the room. Gurney, with one of the Perry case folders in hand, soon followed to the armchair's twin on the opposite side of the fireplace. They sat in companionable isolation, each in a separate pool of lamplight.

He opened the folder and extracted the ViCAP crime report. Curious thing about that acronym. At the FBI it stood for the Violent Criminal Apprehension Program. At New York's Bureau of Criminal Investigation, it stood for the Violent Crime Analysis Program. But it was the same form, processed by the same computers and distributed to the same recipients. Gurney liked New York's version better. It said what it was, made no promises.

The thirty-six-page form itself was comprehensive, to say the least, but useful only to the extent that the officer filling it out had been accurate and thorough. One of its purposes was to uncover MO similarities to other crimes on file, but in this case there was no notation of any subsequent hits by the comparative-analysis program. Gurney was poring over the thirty-six pages to make sure he hadn't overlooked anything significant the first time around.

He was having a hard time focusing, kept thinking he should call Kyle, kept looking for excuses to put it off. The time difference between New York and Seattle had provided a convenient obstruction for the past three years, but now Kyle was back in Manhattan, enrolled at Columbia Law School, and Gurney's procrastination had lost its enabler. Which is not to say that the procrastination had ceased, or even that its true causes had become transparent to him.

Sometimes he dismissed it as the natural product of his cold Celtic genes. That was the most comfortable way of looking at it. Hardly any personal responsibility at all. Other times he was convinced it was related to one of his downward spirals of guilt: the guilt that was created by not calling, creating in turn an increasing resistance to calling, and more guilt. For as long as he could remember, he'd had an abundance of that gnawing rat of an emotion—an only child's feeling of responsibility for his parents' strained and staggering marriage. At still other times, he suspected that the problem was that he saw too much of his first wife in Kyle—too many reminders of too many ugly disagreements.

And then there was the disappointment factor. In the midst of the stock-market meltdown, when Kyle announced he was leaving investment banking for law school, Gurney had entertained for a delusional moment the belief that the young man might have an interest in following him into law enforcement. But it soon became clear that Kyle was simply taking a new route to the old goal of material success.

"Why don't you just call him?" Madeleine was watching him, her knitting needles resting in her lap atop a half-finished orange scarf.

He stared at her, a little startled but not so utterly amazed as he once would have been at this uncanny sensitivity.

"It's a certain look you get when you're thinking about him," she said, as if explaining something obvious. "Not a happy look."

"I will. I'll call."

He began scanning the ViCAP form with a fresh urgency, like a man in a locked room searching for a hidden exit. Nothing emerged that seemed new or different from what he'd remembered. He shuffled through the other reports in the folder.

One of several analyses of the wedding-reception DVD material concluded with this summary: *"Locations of all persons present on the Ashton property during the time frame of the homicide have been verified through time-coded video imagery."* Gurney had a pretty good idea what this meant, recalling what Hardwick had told him the evening they watched the video, but given its critical significance, he wanted to be sure.

He got his cell phone from the sideboard and called Hardwick's number. He was shunted immediately into voice mail: *"Hardwick. Leave a message."*

"It's Gurney. I have a question about the video."

Less than a minute after he left the message, his phone rang. He didn't bother to check the caller ID. "Jack?"

"Dave?" It was a woman's voice—familiar, but he couldn't immediately place it.

"Sorry, I was expecting someone else. This is Dave."

"It's Peggy Meeker. I got your e-mail, and I just e-mailed you back. Then I thought I should call you in case you might need to know this right away." Her voice was racing with excitement.

"What is it?"

"You wanted to know about Edward Vallory's play, plot, characters, whether anything was known about it. Well, you're not going to believe this, but I called the English department at Wesleyan, and guess who's still there—Professor Barkless, who taught the course."

"The course?"

"The English course I took. The Elizabethan-drama course. I left a message, and he got back to me. Isn't that amazing?"

"What did he tell you?"

"Well, that's the really, really amazing part. Are you ready for this?"

There was a call-waiting beep on Gurney's phone, which he ignored. "Go ahead."

"Well, to begin with, the name of the play was *The Spanish Gardener.*" She paused for a reaction.

"Go on."

"The name of the central character was Hector Flores."

"You're serious?"

"There's more. It gets better and better. The plot, which was partially described by a contemporary critic, is one of those complicated things where people wear disguises and people in their own families don't recognize them and all that kind of nonsense, but the basic story line"—there was another call-waiting beep—"which is pretty wild, is that Hector Flores was sent away from home by his mother, who killed his father and seduced his brother. Years later Hector returns, disguised as a gardener, and to make a long story short, he tricks his brother—through more disguises and mistaken identities—into cutting off his mother's head. It was all pretty much over the top, which is maybe why all the copies of the play were destroyed after the first performance. It's not clear if the plot was based on some ancient variant of the Oedipus myth or if it was just a piece of grotesquerie cooked up by Vallory. Or maybe it was somehow influenced by Thomas Kyd's *Spanish Tragedy,* which is kind of emotionally over the top, too, so who knows? But those are the basic facts—straight from Professor Barkless."

Gurney's brain was racing faster than Peggy Meeker's breathless voice.

After a moment she asked, "You want me to go through that again?"

Another beep.

"You said it was all in an e-mail you sent me?"

"Yes, all spelled out. And I put in my professor's phone number, in case you want to call him directly. It's so exciting, isn't it? Does it give you, like, a whole new perspective on the case?"

"Maybe more like a reinforcement of one of the existing perspectives. We'll see how it plays out."

"Right. Okay. Let me know."

Beep.

"Peggy, I seem to have a persistent caller here. Let me say good-bye for now. And thank you. This could be very helpful."

"Sure, glad to do it. Great. Let me know what else I can do."

"I will. Thank you again."

He switched to the other call.

"Took you long enough to answer. Question mustn't be too fucking urgent."

"Ah, yes. Jack. Thanks for getting back."

"And the question is . . . ?"

Gurney smiled. Hardwick made a fetish of brusqueness, when

he wasn't too busy making a fetish of vulgarity. "How sure are you about the location of every individual at the reception during the time Jillian was in the cottage?"

"Sure enough."

"How do you know?"

"The way the cameras were set up, there were no blind spots. Guests, catering staff, musicians—they were all on tape, all the time."

"Except for Hector."

"Except for Hector, who was in the cottage."

"Who you *think* was in the cottage."

"What's your point?"

"Just trying to sort out what we know from what we think we know."

"Who the fuck else would be in there?"

"I don't know, Jack. And neither do you. By the way, thanks for the heads-up on that rehab jam-up."

There was a long silence. "Fuck told you about that?"

"You sure as hell didn't."

"Fuck's that got to do with anything?"

"I'm a big fan of full disclosure, Jack."

"Full disclosure? I'll give you full fucking disclosure. Dickbrain Rodriguez took me off the Perry case because I told him that chasing down every fucking Mexican illegal in upstate New York was the biggest fucking waste of time I'd ever been assigned to. First of all, no one was going to admit working there illegally, evading taxes. And they sure as hell weren't going to admit having any contact with someone wanted for murder. Two months later, on my day off, I get called into an emergency manhunt situation for a couple of idiots who shot a gas-station attendant on the thruway, and somebody at the scene tells Captain Marvel that I smelled of alcohol, so I get jammed up. The little fuck had been dreaming of ways to get me on the wrong foot. Now he's got his opportunity. So what does he do? Little fuck sticks me in a fucking dump rehab full of crackhead scumbags. Twenty-eight miserable fucking days. With scumbags, Davey! Fucking nightmare! Scumbags! All I could think about for twenty-eight days was killing little Dickbrain Captain Fuckface, tearing his fucking head off! That enough full disclosure for you?"

"Plenty, Jack. Problem is, the investigation went off the rails, and it needs to start over from scratch. And it needs to have people assigned to it who are more interested in solving it than they are in messing each other up."

"Is that a fucking fact? Well, good fucking luck, Mr. Voice of Fucking Reason."

The connection was broken.

Gurney put the phone down on top of the case folder. He became aware of the clicking of Madeleine's knitting needles and looked over at her.

She smiled without looking up. "Problems?"

He laughed humorlessly. "Only that the investigation needs to be completely reorganized and redirected, and I have no power to make that happen."

"Think about it. You'll find a way."

He thought about it. "You mean through Kline?"

She shrugged. "You told me during the Mellery case that he had big ambitions."

"I wouldn't be surprised if he imagined himself president one day. Or at least governor."

"Well, there you go."

"There I go where?"

She concentrated for a minute on an alteration in her stitching technique. Then she looked up, seemingly bemused by his failure to grasp the obvious. "Help him see how this connects to his big ambitions."

The more he pondered it, the more perceptive her comment seemed. As a political animal, Kline was super-sensitive to the media dimension of any investigation. It was the surest route to the center of his being.

Gurney picked up his phone and called the DA's number. The recorded message offered three options: call again between 8:00 A.M. and 6:00 P.M. Monday through Friday, or leave a name and phone number to receive a return call during business hours, or call the

emergency twenty-four-hour number for matters requiring immediate assistance.

Gurney entered the emergency number in his phone list, but
before making the call he decided to devote a little more time to
structuring what he was going to say—first to the screener, then
to Kline if the call was passed through—because he realized it was
crucial to lob exactly the right grenade over the wall.

The needles stopped clicking.

"Do you hear that?" Madeleine leaned her head slightly in the
direction of the nearest window.

"What?"

"Listen."

"What am I listening for?"

"Shhh . . ."

Just as he was about to insist that he could hear nothing, he heard
it: the faint yipping of distant coyotes. Then, again, nothing. Only
the lingering image in his mind of animals like small, lean wolves,
running in a loosely spaced pack, running wild and heartless as the
wind through a moonlit field beyond the north ridge.

The phone, still in his hand, rang. He checked the ID: REYNOLDS
GALLERY. He glanced at Madeleine. Nothing in her expression suggested a clairvoyant insight into the identity of the caller.

"This is Dave."

"I want to go to bed. Let's talk."

After an awkward silence, Gurney replied, "You first."

She uttered a soft, intimate laugh—really more purring than
laughing. "I mean I want to go to bed early, go to sleep, and in case
you were going to call later to talk about tomorrow, it would be better to talk now."

"Good idea."

Again the velvety laugh. "So what I'm thinking is very simple.
I can't tell you what to say to Jykynstyl, because I don't know what
he'll ask you. So you must be yourself. The wise homicide detective.
The quiet man who has seen everything. The man on the side of the
angels who wrestles with the devil and always wins."

"Not always."

"Well, you're human, right? Being human is important. This

makes you real, not some fake hero, you see? So all you need to do is be yourself. You are a more impressive man than you think, David Gurney."

He hesitated. "Is that it?"

This time the laugh was more musical, more amused. "That's it for you. Now for me. Did you ever read our contract, the one you signed for the show last year?"

"I suppose I did at the time. Not recently."

"It says that the Reynolds Gallery is entitled to a forty percent commission on displayed works, thirty percent on cataloged works, and twenty percent on all future works created for customers introduced to the artist through the gallery. Does this sound familiar?"

"Vaguely."

"Vaguely. Okay. But is it all right, or do you have any problem with it now, going forward?"

"It's fine."

"Good. Because we'll have a very good time working together. I can feel it, can't you?"

Madeleine, inscrutable, seemed fixated on the ornamental border of her slowly growing scarf. Stitch after stitch after stitch. Click. Click. Click.

Chapter 41

The big day

It was a glorious morning, a calendar picture of autumn. The sky was a thrilling blue without a hint of a cloud. Madeleine was already out on one of her bike rides through the winding river valley that extended for nearly twenty miles to both the east and west sides of Walnut Crossing.

"A perfect day," she'd said before she left, managing to suggest by her tone that his decision to spend a day like this in the city talking about big money for ugly art made him as crazy as Jykynstyl. Or maybe he'd reached that conclusion himself and was blaming it on her.

He was sitting at the breakfast table by the French doors, gazing out over the pasture at the barn, a startling crimson in the limpid morning light. He took the first energizing sip of his coffee, then picked up his phone and called Sheridan Kline's twenty-four-hour number.

It was answered by a dour, colorless voice—which brought to Gurney's mind a vivid recollection of the man who owned it.

"Stimmel. District Attorney's Office."

"This is Dave Gurney." He paused, knowing that Stimmel would remember him from the Mellery case and being not at all surprised when the man didn't acknowledge it. Stimmel had the warmth and loquacity, as well as the thick physiognomy, of a frog.

"Yes?"

"I need to talk to Kline ASAP."

"That so?"

"Matter of life or death."

"Whose?"

"His."

The dour tone hardened. "What does that mean?"

"You're familiar with the Perry case?" Gurney took the ensuing silence for a yes. "It's about to explode into a media circus, maybe the biggest mass-murder case in the history of the state. Thought Sheridan might want a heads-up."

"What are you talking about?"

"You asked me that already, and I told you."

"Give me the facts, wiseass, and I'll pass them along."

"No time to go through it all twice. I need to talk to him *right now*, even if you have to drag his ass off the can. Tell him this one's going to make the Mellery murder look like a misdemeanor."

"This better not be bullshit."

Gurney figured that was Stimmel's way of saying, *Good-bye, we'll get back to you.* He laid down his phone, picked up his coffee, and took another sip. Still nice and warm. He looked out at the asparagus ferns leaning away from a gentle westerly breeze. The fertilizer questions—if, when, how much—that had filled his mind less than a week ago now seemed infinitely postponable. He hoped he hadn't overstated the situation to Stimmel.

Two minutes later Kline was on the phone, excited as a fly on fresh manure. "What is this? What media explosion?"

"Long story. You have time to talk?"

"How about you give me the one-sentence summary?"

"Imagine a news story that starts like this: 'Police and DA clueless as serial murderer abducts Mapleshade girls.' "

"Didn't we go through this yesterday?"

"New information."

"Where are you right now?"

"Home, but I'm heading into the city in an hour."

"This is real? Not some wild-ass theorizing?"

"Real enough."

There was a pause. "How secure is your phone?"

"I have no idea."

"You can take the thruway to the city, right?"

"I guess so."

"So you could stop at my office en route?"

"I could."

"Can you leave now?"

"Maybe in ten minutes."

"Meet me at my office at nine-thirty. Gurney?"

"Yes?"

"This goddamn better be real."

"Sheridan?"

"What?"

"If I were you, I'd pray for it not to be."

Ten minutes later Gurney was on the road, heading east into the sun. His first stop was Abelard's for a container of coffee to substitute for the nearly full cup he'd left on the kitchen table in his rush to get out.

He sat for a while in the gravelly little patch in front that passed for a parking area, reclined his seat about a third of the way, and tried to relax his mind by concentrating on nothing but the flavor of the coffee. It wasn't a technique that worked particularly well for him, and he wondered why he kept trying it. It did have the effect of changing what was on his mind, but not necessarily to anything less worrisome. In this case it moved his focus from the dysfunctional mess of the investigation to the dysfunctional mess of his relationship with Kyle—and the growing pressure he felt to call him.

It was ludicrous, really. All he had to do was stop procrastinating and make the call. He knew very well that procrastination was nothing but a short-term escape that creates a long-term problem—that it just occupies more and more storage space in the brain, creating more and more discomfort. Intellectually, there was no argument. Intellectually, he knew that most of the misery in his life arose from the avoidance of discomfort.

He had Kyle's new number on his speed dial. *Christ! Just do it!*

He took out his phone, called the number, got voice mail: *"Hi, this is Kyle. I can't pick up right now. Please leave a message."*

"Hi, Kyle, it's Dad. Thought I'd call, get your impressions of

Columbia. The apartment share working out okay?" He hesitated, almost asked about Kate, Kyle's ex-wife, thought better of it. "Nothing urgent, just wondering how you're doing. Give me a call whenever you can. Talk to you soon." He pushed the "end call" button.

A curious experience. A bit tangled, like the rest of Gurney's emotional life. He was relieved that he'd finally called. He was also relieved, to be honest about it, that he'd gotten his son's voice mail instead of his son. But maybe now he could stop thinking about it, at least for a while. He took a couple more swallows of his coffee, checked the time—8:52 A.M.—and got back on the county road.

Except for a gleaming black Audi and a handful of not-so-gleaming Fords and Chevys with official plates, the parking lot of the County Office Building was empty, as it usually was on a Saturday morning. The looming dirty-brick edifice looked cold and deserted, every bit the wretched institution it had once been.

Kline emerged from the Audi as Gurney pulled in to a nearby space. Another car, a Crown Victoria, entered the lot and parked on the far side of the Audi. Rodriguez got out from behind the wheel.

Gurney and Rodriguez approached Kline from opposite directions. They exchanged nods with the DA, but not with each other. Kline led the way in through a side door to which he had his own key, then up a flight of stairs. Not a word was spoken until they were seated in the leather chairs around the coffee table in his inner office. Rodriguez folded his arms tightly across his chest. His dark eyes were uncommunicative behind his steel-rimmed glasses.

"Okay," said Kline, leaning forward. "Time to cut to the chase." He was giving Gurney the kind of piercing look he might give a hostile witness on the stand. "We're here because of your promised bombshell, my friend. Let's have it."

Gurney nodded. "Right. The bombshell. You may want to take notes." A twitch under one of the captain's eyes told Gurney he heard the suggestion as an insult.

"Just get to the point," said Kline.

"The bombshell comes in parts. I'll toss them on the table. You fit them together. First of all, it turns out that Hector Flores is the name of a character in an Elizabethan play—a character who pretends to be a Spanish gardener. Interesting coincidence, no?"

Kline gave Gurney a questioning frown. "What kind of play?"

"That's where it gets interesting. The plot involves the violation of a major sexual taboo, incest—which happens to be a common element in the childhood formation of sex offenders."

Kline's frown deepened. "So you're saying . . . what?"

"I'm saying that the man who was living in Ashton's cottage almost certainly took the name Hector Flores from that play."

The captain let out a little snort of disbelief.

"I think we need a bit more detail here," said Kline.

"This play is about incest. The Hector Flores character in the play shows up disguised as a gardener. And . . ." Gurney couldn't resist the dramatic pause. "It just so happens that he kills the guilty female character in the play by cutting off her head."

Kline's eyes widened. "What?"

Rodriguez gave Gurney a disbelieving stare. "Where the hell is this play?"

Rather than get bogged down in the argument sure to ensue if he revealed that the full text of the play no longer existed, Gurney gave the captain the name and affiliation of Peggy Meeker's old college professor. "I'm sure he'd be happy to discuss it with you. And by the way, there's no doubt at all that the play relates to Jillian Perry's murder. The playwright's name was Edward Vallory."

It took a couple of seconds for this to register with Kline. "The text-message signature?"

"Right. So now we know for sure that the 'Mexican laborer' identity was a con from day one, a con that everyone fell for."

The captain looked furious enough to burst into flames.

Gurney went on. "This guy came to Tambury with a long-term plan and a lot of patience. The obscurity of the literary reference means we're dealing with a pretty sophisticated individual. And the content of the Vallory play makes it clear that Jillian Perry's sexual history was almost certainly the motive for her murder."

Kline looked like he was trying not to look stunned. "Okay, so we've got . . . we've got a new slant here."

"Unfortunately, it's just the tip of the iceberg."

Kline's eyes widened. "What iceberg?"

"The missing graduates."

The captain shook his head. "It's been said before, and I'll say it again: There's no proof that anyone's *missing.*"

"Sorry," said Gurney. "Didn't mean to misuse a legal term. You're right—nobody's name has been entered yet in an official mis-pers database. So let's call them . . . what? 'Mapleshade graduates of currently unverifiable location'? That work better for you?"

Rodriguez came forward in his seat, his voice rasping. "I don't have to take this wiseass crap from you!"

Kline raised his hand like a traffic cop. "Rod, Rod, take it easy. We're all a little . . . you know . . . Just take it easy." He waited until the man began to settle back in his chair before turning his attention to Gurney. "Let's say, just for the sake of argument, that one or more of these girls is actually missing, or unlocatable, or whatever the proper term would be. If that were the case, your conclusion is what?"

"If they've been abducted by the man calling himself Hector Flores, my conclusion is that either they're dead or soon will be."

Rodriguez lurched forward again in his chair. "There's no evidence! *If, if, if, if.* It's just one assumption on top of another."

Kline took a slow breath. "That does seem like a hell of an end point to jump to, Dave. You want to give us a little help with the logic?"

"The content of the play, plus the Vallory text messages, suggest that Jillian Perry's murder was an act of revenge for sexual abuse. A history of perpetrating sexual abuse happens to be a common factor among Mapleshade students, making them all potential targets. It would make Mapleshade the perfect place for a killer motivated by that issue to find his victims."

" 'Potential targets'—did you hear that? 'Potential,' he just said. That's my point." Rodriguez shook his head. "All of this is—"

"Hold it, Rod, please," Kline broke in. "I get your point. Believe me, I'm on your side. I'm a proof-oriented guy just like you are. But let's hear him out. You know, no stone unturned. Let's just hear him out. Okay?"

Rodriguez stopped talking, but he kept shaking his head like he hardly knew he was doing it. Kline gave Gurney a small nod to proceed.

"Regarding the missing girls, the similarity in the arguments leading to their departures is prima facie proof of a conspiracy. It's inconceivable they would all have come up with the expensive-car demand by pure coincidence. A reasonable explanation is that it was a conspiracy created to facilitate their abductions."

Kline looked like he had a case of Tabasco reflux. "Do you have any other facts that support the abduction hypothesis?"

"Hector Flores had asked Ashton for opportunities to work at Mapleshade, and the currently unlocatable girls were seen in conversations with him there."

Rodriguez was still shaking his head. "That's a pretty thin connection."

"You're right, Captain," said Gurney wearily. "In fact, most of what we know is pretty thin. All the missing or abducted girls had previously appeared in sexually oriented ads for Karnala Fashion, as did Jillian Perry, but we know nothing about that company. How those modeling assignments were set up has not been determined, or even investigated. As of today the total number of girls who may be missing is still unknown. Whether the girls we can't get in touch with are alive or dead is unknown. Whether abductions are occurring as we sit here is unknown. All I'm doing is telling you what I think. What I fear. Maybe I'm completely nuts, Captain. I hope to God I am, because the alternative is horrendous."

Kline swallowed drily. "So you admit there's a fair amount of supposition built into your . . . your view of this."

"I'm a homicide cop, Sheridan. Without a few suppositions . . ." Gurney shrugged, his voice trailing off.

There was a long silence.

Rodriguez seemed deflated, smaller, as though half his anger were gone but hadn't been replaced by anything else.

"Let's assume, just for the sake of argument," said Kline, "that you're a hundred percent right." He extended both hands, palms up, as though conveying open-mindedness to even the most outlandish theory. "What would you do?"

"The crucial task is to get up to speed on who's missing. Get ahold of those Mapleshade class lists with the family contact information. Get them from Ashton this morning if possible. Interview every family, every graduate you can reach in Jillian's class, then everyone from the year before and the year after. In any family where the daughter's location is not verifiable, get all the descriptive and circumstantial detail you can to enter in the ViCAP, NamUs, NCIC databases—especially if the family's last contact included the argument we've heard about."

Kline glanced at Rodriguez. "Sounds like something we could be doing regardless."

The captain nodded.

"Okay, go on."

"In any case where the daughter can't be reached, collect a DNA sample from a first-degree biological relative—mother, father, brother, sister. As soon as the BCI lab does the profile, run it against the profile of every unidentified female decedent of the right age within the time frame of the disappearance."

"Geography?"

"National."

"God! You realize what you're asking? That stuff is all state by state, sometimes county by county. Some jurisdictions don't save it. Some don't even collect it."

"You're right—big pain in the ass. Costs money, takes time, coverage is incomplete. But it'll be a bigger pain in the ass down the road if you have to explain why it wasn't done."

"Fine." The word came out of Kline like an exclamation of disgust. "Next?"

"Next, track down Alessandro and Karnala Fashion. They both seem way too elusive for normal commercial enterprises. Next, interview all current Mapleshade students regarding anything they might know about Hector, Alessandro, Karnala, or any of the missing girls. Next, interview every current and recent Mapleshade employee."

"You have any idea what kind of man-hours you're talking about?"

"Sheridan, this is what I do for a living." He paused at the significance of the slip. "I mean, *did* for a living. BCI needs to throw a dozen investigators against this ASAP, more if they can. Once this hits the media, you'll be eaten alive for doing anything less."

Kline's eyes narrowed. "Way you're talking about it, we'll be eaten alive no matter what."

"The media will take whatever route attracts the biggest audience," said Gurney. "So-called news reporting is a cartoon business. Give them a big, hot, cartoony story line and they'll run with it. Guaranteed."

Kline regarded him warily. "Like what?"

"The story here needs to be that you've pulled out all the stops. Totally proactive. The instant you and the BCI team discovered the difficulty some of the parents were having getting in touch with their daughters, you and Rod launched the biggest five-alarm, all-hands-on-deck, all-vacations-canceled serial-murder investigation in history."

Kline's mental hard drive seemed to be racing through the possible outcomes. "Suppose they pounce on the cost?"

"Easy. 'In a situation like this, being proactive costs money. Inaction costs lives.' It's a cartoon answer that's hard to argue with. Give them the 'Giant Mobilization' story and maybe they'll stay away from the 'Screwed-Up Investigation' story."

Kline was opening and closing his fists, flexing his fingers, the uncertainty in his eyes shifting in the direction of excitement.

"Okay," he said. "We better start thinking about the press conference."

"First," said Gurney, "you need to get the actual ball rolling. If the press discovers it's all bullshit, the narrative instantly changes from you guys being the heroes of the hour to the jerks of the year. As of this moment, you need to treat this like the potentially huge case it probably is—or kiss your careers good-bye."

Maybe something in the set of Gurney's jaw got through to Kline, or maybe a jagged sliver of the potential horror of the case finally pierced his self-absorption. For whatever reason, he blinked, rubbed his eyes, sat back in his chair, and gave Gurney a long, bleak look. "You really think we've got a major psycho on our hands, don't you?"

"Yes, I do."

Rodriguez roused himself from whatever dark preoccupation he was mired in. "What makes you so sure? Some sick play written four hundred years ago?"

What makes me so sure? Gurney thought about it. A gut feeling? Although it was one of the oldest clichés in the business, there was truth in it. But there was something else, too.

"The head."

Rodriguez stared at him.

Gurney took a steadying breath. "Something . . . about the head. Arranged on the table the way it was, facing the body."

Kline's mouth opened as if he were about to speak, but he didn't. Rodriguez just stared.

Gurney went on. "I believe that whoever did that, in that particular way, was announcing that he's on a mission."

Kline frowned. "Meaning that he intends to do it again?"

"Or already has done it again. I believe he has an appetite for it."

Chapter 42

The magic Mr. Jykynstyl

The weather remained perfect for Gurney's late-morning drive from the Catskills to New York City. As he sped down the thruway, the crisp air and clear sky energized his thoughts, made him optimistic about the impact he'd had on Kline and, to a lesser extent, on Rodriguez.

He wanted to follow up with Kline, find a way to ensure that he'd be kept in the loop. And he wanted to call Val, bring her up to date. But he also needed, right then and there, to give some thought to the meeting he was heading for. The meeting with the man from "the art world." A man who wanted to give him a hundred thousand dollars for a graphically enhanced portrait of a lunatic. A man who might very well be a lunatic himself.

The address Sonya had given him turned out to be a brownstone residence in the middle of a hushed, tree-shaded block in Manhattan's East Sixties. The neighborhood exuded the aroma of money, a genteel miasma that insulated the place from the bustle of the avenues around it.

He parked in a no-parking zone directly in front of the building—as she had instructed him, passing along Jykynstyl's assurance that there would be no problem, that the car would be taken care of.

An oversize black-enameled front door led into an ornately tiled and mirrored vestibule, which led to a second door. Gurney was about to press the bell on the wall next to it when it was opened by a striking young woman. At second glance he realized that she was a rather ordinary-looking young woman whose overall appearance was elevated, or at least dominated, by extraordinary eyes—eyes that were now assessing him as one might assess the cut of a sport jacket or the freshness of a pie on a bakery shelf.

"Are you the artist?" He caught something volatile in her tone, something he couldn't quite identify.

"I'm Dave Gurney."

"Follow me."

They entered a large foyer. There was a coatrack, an umbrella stand, several closed doors, and a broad mahogany staircase rising to the next floor. The dark luster of her hair matched the dark wood. She led him past the staircase to a door, which she opened to reveal a small elevator with its own separate sliding door.

"Come," she said with a slight smile that he found oddly disconcerting.

They got in, the door slid shut without a sound, and the elevator rose with hardly any sensation of motion.

Gurney broke the silence. "Who are you?"

She turned toward him, her remarkable eyes amused by some private joke. "I'm his daughter." The elevator had stopped so smoothly that Gurney hadn't felt it. The door slid open. She stepped out. "Come."

The room was furnished in the style of an opulent Victorian parlor. Large-leafed tropical plants stood in floor pots at each side of a large fireplace. Several others stood next to armchairs. Beyond a wide arch at one end was a formal dining room, with table, chairs, sideboard, and carved woodwork, all of deeply polished mahogany. Dark green damask curtains covered the tall windows in both rooms, obscuring the time of day, the time of year—creating the illusion of an elegant, unanchored world where cocktails were always about to be served.

"Welcome, David Gurney. So good of you to come so far so quickly."

Gurney followed the oddly accented voice to its source: a colorless little man dwarfed by the enormous leather club chair in which he was seated next to a towering rain-forest plant. He held in his small hand a diminutive cordial glass filled with a pale green liqueur.

"Forgive me if I don't rise to greet you. I have difficulty with my back. Perversely, it is worst in the best weather. A troublesome mystery, no? Please seat yourself." He gestured toward a matching chair facing his across a small Oriental rug. He wore faded jeans and a burgundy sweatshirt. His hair was short, thin, gray, perfunctorily combed. His hooded eyes created a superficial impression of sleepy detachment.

"You would like a drink. One of the girls will bring you something." His indefinite accent seemed to have multiple European origins. "Myself, I have made again the mistake of choosing absinthe." He raised his greenish liqueur and regarded it as one might a disloyal friend. "I do not recommend it. Since it has become legal and perfectly safe, it has, in my opinion, lost its soul." He put the glass to his lips and drained off about half the contents. "Why do I keep going back to it? An interesting question. Perhaps I am a sentimentalist. But you, obviously, are no such thing. You are a great detective, a man of clarity, unencumbered by foolish attachments. So no absinthe for you. But something else. Whatever you would like."

"A small glass of water?"

"*L'acqua minerale? Ein Mineralwasser? L'eau gazéifiée?*"

"Tap water."

"Of course." His sudden grin was as bright as bleached bones. "I should have known." He raised his voice only slightly, in the way of someone accustomed to having servants in his vicinity. "A glass of cold tap water for our guest." The strangely smiling girl who called herself his daughter left the room.

Gurney sat calmly in the chair to which the little man had directed him. "Why should you have known that I'd want tap water?"

"Because of what Ms. Reynolds told me of your character. You frown at that. That also I should have predicted. You look at me with your detective eyes. You ask yourself, 'How much does this Jykynstyl know about me? How much has the Reynolds woman told him?' Am I right?"

"You're way ahead of me. I was just wondering about the connection between tap water and my character."

"She told me that you are so complicated inside that you like to keep things simple on the outside. You agree with this?"

"Sure. Why not?"

"That's very good," he said, like an expert savoring an interesting wine. "She also warned me that you are always thinking and you always know more than you say."

Gurney shrugged. "Is that a problem?"

Music began playing in the background, so softly that its low notes were hardly audible. It was a sad, slow, pastoral melody on a cello. Its whispered presence in the room reminded Gurney of the English garden scents that subtly penetrated the interior of Scott Ashton's house.

The wispy-haired little man smiled and sipped his absinthe. A young woman with a dramatic figure on display in low-cut jeans and an even lower-cut T-shirt entered the room through the arch at the far end and approached Gurney with a crystal glass of water on a silver tray. She had the eyes and mouth of a cynic twice her age. As Gurney took the glass, Jykynstyl was answering his question.

"It's certainly not a problem for me. I love a man of substance, a man whose mind is larger than his mouth. This is the kind of man you are, no?" When Gurney didn't answer, Jykynstyl laughed. It was a dry, humorless sound. "I see that you are also a man who likes to get to the point. You want to know exactly why we are here. Very well, David Gurney. Here is the point: I am perhaps your greatest fan. Why am I? For two reasons. First, I believe that you are a great portrait artist. Second, I intend to make a lot of money on your work. Please notice which of these reasons I put first. I can tell from the work you've done already that you have a rare talent for bringing the mind of a man into the lines of his face, for letting the soul show through the eyes. This is a talent that thrives on purity. It is not the talent of a man who is mad for money or attention, a man who strives to be agreeable, a man who talks too much. It is the talent of a man who values the truth in all his affairs—business, professional, artistic. I suspected you were such a man, but I wanted to be sure." He held Gurney's steady gaze for what seemed like a very long time before going on. "What would you like for lunch? There is cold sea bass rémoulade, a lime seviche of shellfish, quenelles de veau, a lovely Kobe steak tartare—whichever you prefer, or perhaps a bit of each?"

As he spoke, he began slowly extricating himself from his chair. He paused, searching for a place to deposit his little glass, shrugged, and placed it delicately into the overgrown plant pot next to him. Then, grasping the arms of his chair with both hands, he pushed himself with considerable effort to his feet and led the way through the arched doorway to the dining room.

The most arresting feature of the space was a life-size portrait in a gilded frame hanging in the center of the long wall facing the arch. Gurney's limited knowledge of art history placed its source somewhere in the Dutch Renaissance.

"It is remarkable, no?" said Jykynstyl.

Gurney agreed.

"I'm glad you like it. I will tell you about it as we eat."

Two places were set across from each other at the table. The entrées that Jykynstyl had named were arrayed between them on four china platters, along with bottles of Puligny-Montrachet and Château Latour, wines that even a non-oenophile like Gurney recognized as wildly expensive.

Gurney opted for the Montrachet and the bass, Jykynstyl for the Latour and the tartare.

"Are both of the girls your daughters?"

"That is correct, yes."

"And you live here together?"

"From time to time. We are not a family of a fixed location. I come and go. It is the nature of my life. My daughters live here when they are not living with someone else." He spoke of these arrangements in a tone that seemed to Gurney as deceptively casual as his sleepy gaze.

"Where do you spend most of your time?"

Jykynstyl laid his fork down on the edge of his plate as though ridding himself of an obstruction to clear expression. "I don't think in that way, of being *here* for a length of time or *there* for another length of time. I am . . . *in motion.* Do you understand?"

"Your answer is more philosophical than my question. I'll ask it another way. Do you have homes like this anywhere else?"

"Family members in other countries sometimes *put me up,* or they *put up with me.* In English you have these two phrases—close but not the same, correct? But maybe in my case they are both true." He displayed his cold ivory smile. "So I am a homeless man with many homes." The mongrelized accent, from nowhere and everywhere, seemed to grow stronger to reinforce his nomadic claim. "Like the wonderful Mr. Wordsworth, I wander lonely as a cloud. In search of golden daffodils. I have a good eye for these daffodils. But having a good eye is not enough. One must also *look*. This is my double secret, David Gurney: *a good eye and I am always looking*. This to me is far more important than living in a particular place. I do not live *here* or live *there*. I live in the activity, in the movement. I am not a resident. I am a searcher. This is maybe a little like your own life, your own profession. Am I right?"

"I can see your point."

"You can see my point, but you don't really agree with it." He seemed more amused than offended. "And like all policemen, when it comes to questions you would rather ask them than answer them. A characteristic of your profession, is it not?"

"Yes, it is."

He made a sound that might have been a laugh or a cough. His eyes supplied no clue as to which. "Then let me give you answers rather than questions. I am thinking you want to know why this crazy little man with the funny name wants to pay you so much money for these portraits that you do maybe pretty quickly and easily."

Gurney felt a spark of annoyance. "Not that quickly, not that easily." And then a spark of chagrin at voicing the objection.

Jykynstyl blinked. "No, of course not. Forgive my English. I think I speak it better than I do, but I am inadequate at the nuance. Shall I try again, or do you understand what I am trying to say?"

"I think I do."

"So then, the basic question: Why do I offer so much money for this art of yours?" He paused, flashed the chilly grin. "Because it is worth it. And because I want it, exclusively, without competition. So I make you what I believe is a preemptive offer, an offer you can accept without question, without quibble, without negotiation. You understand?"

"I think I do."

"Good. You noticed, I think, the painting on the wall behind me. The Holbein."

"That's an actual Hans Holbein?"

"Actual? Yes, of course. I do not own reproductions. What do you think of it?"

"I don't have the right words."

"Say the first words that come to mind."

"Startling. Astonishing. Alive. Unnerving."

Jykynstyl studied him for a long minute before speaking again. "Let me tell you two things. First, these words that you claim are not the right words come closer to the truth than the bullshit of the professional art critics. Second, these are the same words that came to my mind when I saw your portrait of Piggert, the murderer. The very same words. I looked into the eyes of your Peter Piggert and I could feel him in the room with me. Startling. Astonishing. Alive. Unnerving. All these things that you say about the Holbein portrait. For the Holbein I paid a little over eight million dollars. The amount is a secret, but I tell you, anyway. Eight million, one hundred fifty thousand dollars—for one golden daffodil. One day, perhaps, I will sell it for three times that much. So now I pay one hundred thousand each for a few David Gurney daffodils, and one day, perhaps, I will sell them for ten times that. Who can say? You will toast this future with me, please? A toast—that we may both get from the transaction the satisfaction that we wish?"

Jykynstyl seemed to sense Gurney's skepticism. "It only seems like a lot of money because you aren't yet accustomed to it. It's not because your work isn't worth it. Remember that. You are being rewarded for your extraordinary insight and your ability to convey that insight—not unlike Hans Holbein. You are a detective not only of the criminal mind but of human nature. Why should you not be paid appropriately?"

Jykynstyl raised his glass of Latour. Gurney followed the gesture uncertainly with his Montrachet.

"To your insight and your work, to our business arrangement, and to you yourself, Detective David Gurney."

"And to you, Mr. Jykynstyl."

They drank. The experience surprised Gurney pleasantly. Although he was far from being a connoisseur, he thought the Montrachet was the best wine he'd ever tasted—and one of the few in his memory that ignited an instant desire for a second glass. As he finished the first, the young woman who had brought him up in the elevator appeared at his side with an odd glimmer in her eyes to provide the desired refill.

For the next few minutes, the two men ate in silence. The cold bass was wonderful, and the Montrachet only seemed to make it more so. When Sonya had broached the subject of Jykynstyl's interest two days earlier, Gurney's mind had wandered briefly into fantasies of what the money could buy, geographical fantasies that carried him to the northwest coast—to Seattle and Puget Sound and the San Juan Islands in the summer sun, blue sky and blue water, the Olympic Mountains on the horizon. Now that image returned, seemingly fueled by the firming up of the financial promise of the Mug Shot Art project—fueled also by the second, even more delightful, glass of Montrachet.

Jykynstyl was speaking again, lauding Gurney's perception, his psychological subtlety, his eye for detail. But it was the rhythm of the words that captivated Gurney's attention now, more than their meaning, the rhythm lifting him, rocking him gently. Now the young women were smiling serenely and clearing the table, and Jykynstyl was describing exotic desserts. Something creamy with rosemary and cardamom. Something silky with saffron, thyme, and cinnamon. It made Gurney smile to imagine the man's strangely complex accent as though it were itself a dish made with seasonings not normally combined.

He felt a thrilling, and wholly uncharacteristic, rush of freedom, optimism, and pride in his accomplishments. It was the way he had always wanted to feel—full of clarity and strength. The feeling blended into the glorious blues of water and sky, a boat racing forward in full white sail on the wings of a breeze that would never die.

And then he felt nothing at all.

Part Three

Fatal
Oversight

Chapter 43

Waking up

No bone shatters as painfully as the illusion of invulnerability. Gurney had no idea how long he'd been sitting in his car, nor how it had gotten to where it was parked, nor what time it was. What he knew was that it was late enough to be dark, that he had a dizzying headache along with feelings of anxiety and nausea, and no memory of anything that had occurred after his second glass of wine at lunch. He checked his watch. It told him it was 8:45 P.M. He'd never had so devastating a reaction to any amount of alcohol, much less two glasses of white wine.

The first explanation that came to mind was that he'd been drugged.

But why?

Staring blankly at that question intensified his anxiety. Staring helplessly into the empty space that should have been filled with recollections of the afternoon made it worse. Then he realized with a slap-in-the-face kind of surprise that he was sitting not behind the steering wheel of his car but in the passenger seat. The fact that it had taken a full minute of consciousness for him to become aware of this ratcheted his anxiety in the direction of panic.

He looked out the windows, front and back, and discovered that he was in the middle of a long block—probably a crosstown block somewhere in Manhattan—too far from either corner for him to read the street signs. The street was busy enough with normal traffic, mostly cabs tailgating other cabs, but no nearby pedestrians. He opened the door and got out cautiously, stiffly, achingly. He felt like he'd been sitting for a long time in an awkward position. He looked up and down both sides of the street for some identifiable structure.

The unlighted building directly across the street from his car was some sort of institutional building, perhaps a school, with broad stone steps and massive doors at least ten feet high. The classical façade was colonnaded.

Then he saw it.

Above the high Greek columns, in the center of a kind of frieze extending the length of the four-story building, just below the heavily shadowed roofline, an engraved motto was barely visible: AD STUDIUM VERITATIS.

Ad Studium Veritatis? Genesius Prep? His own high school? What the hell . . . ?

He stared, blinking, at the dark stone edifice, trying to make sense of the situation. He'd been in the passenger seat of his own car, so someone else must have driven him here. Who? He had no idea, no memory of driving or being driven.

Why here?

Surely it wasn't a coincidence that he'd been driven to this particular spot on this particular block out of a thousand blocks in Manhattan, directly across the street from the front door of the high school from which he'd graduated thirty years earlier—the academically revered institution to which he'd been awarded a scholarship, commuted to from his parents' apartment in the Bronx, hated, and hadn't visited since. A school he never spoke of. A school very few people knew he'd attended.

What in the name of God was going on?

Again he looked up and down the street, as if someone familiar might appear out of the darkness with a simple explanation. No one appeared. He got back into his car, this time into the driver's seat. Finding his key in the ignition was a momentary relief, certainly better than not finding it, but did little to calm his jumping thoughts.

Sonya. Sonya might know something. She might have been in touch with Jykynstyl. But if Jykynstyl was responsible, if Jykynstyl had drugged him . . .

Was it possible that Sonya was part of it all? Had she set him up?

Set him up for what? And why? What sense did any of it make? And why bring him here? Why go to the trouble? How would Jykynstyl know what high school he'd gone to? And what would the point be? To prove that the details of his personal life were accessible? To focus him on the past? To remind him of something specific from his teenage years, some person or event from those wretched years at St. Genesius? Give him a panic attack? But why on earth would the world-renowned Jay Jykynstyl want to do any of that?

It was ridiculous.

On the other hand, to pile conundrum on conundrum, was there any proof that the man he'd met in the brownstone was in fact Jay Jykynstyl? But if he wasn't—if the man was an impostor—what could be the point of so elaborate a deception?

And if in fact he'd been drugged, what was the nature of the drug? Had it knocked him out in the manner of a powerful sedative or anesthetic, or was it something like Rohypnol—a disinhibiting amnesiac—a more problematic possibility?

Or was there something organically wrong with him? Severe dehydration could produce disorientation, even some memory confusion.

But not like this. Not a total eight-hour memory blackout.

A brain tumor? Embolism? Stroke?

Was it conceivable that he had left Jykynstyl's brownstone, gotten into his car, decided on some nostalgic whim to take a look at his old school, gotten out of his car, maybe even gone inside, and then . . . ?

And then what? Come back out, maybe gotten into the passenger seat to put something into the glove box or take something out of it, and then had some sort of seizure? Passed out? A certain type of seizure could produce retroactive amnesia, blocking recall of the period preceding as well as following it. Was that it—some acute brain pathology?

Questions and more questions. And no answers. There was a tightness in the pit of his stomach like a fistful of gravel.

He looked in the glove box but found nothing unusual. The car manual, a few old service receipts, a small flashlight, the plastic cap from a water bottle.

He patted his jacket pockets and found his cell phone. There were seven voice-mail messages and one text message waiting for him. Apparently he'd been in demand during the missing hours. Maybe among the messages would be the explanation he was looking for.

The first voice mail, received at 3:44 P.M., was from Sonya. *"David? You still at lunch? I guess that's a good sign. I want to know everything. Call me the minute you can. Kiss, kiss."*

Voice mail number two, at 4:01, was from the DA. *"David, Sheridan Kline here. Wanted to fill you in as a matter of courtesy. A question you had raised regarding the Karnala Fashion angle—you might want to know that that's been checked out, and there's some interesting information on that. You know anything about the Skard family? S-K-A-R-D. Give me a call ASAP."*

Skard? A peculiar name, and there was something familiar about it, a feeling that he had come upon it before, perhaps seen it in print somewhere, not all that long ago.

Number three, at 4:32, was from Kyle. *"Hi, Dad. What's up? So far Columbia's great, I think. I mean, it's read, read, read, lecture, lecture, lecture, read, read, read. But it's going to be worth it. Really worth it. You have any idea what a good class-action trial attorney can make? Monster bucks! Got to run. Late for another class. Keep forgetting what time it is. Call you later."*

Number four, at 5:05, was Sonya again. *"David? What's happening? Is this the world's longest lunch or what? Call me. Call me!"*

Number five, the shortest, at 5:07, was from Hardwick. *"Hey, ace, I'm back on the case!"* He sounded nasty, triumphant, and drunk.

Number six, at 5:50, was from Kline's favorite forensic psychologist. *"Hi, David, this is Rebecca Holdenfield. Sheridan said you were getting some ideas about the machete murderer that you wanted to discuss. I'm pretty busy, but for this I can find time. Mornings are terrible, later in the day is better. Call me with some days and hours that work for you, and we'll figure something out. From what little I know so far, I'd say you're chasing a very sick man."* The animation bubbling beneath her professional tone made it clear that she liked nothing better than chasing a very sick man. She concluded by leaving a number with an Albany area code.

The seventh and final voice mail, received at 8:35, was from Sonya. *"Shit, David, are you alive?"*

He checked his watch again: 8:58 P.M.

He listened again to the last message, and then again, searching for a serious meaning in Sonya's question. There didn't seem to be any, beyond the exasperation of someone whose calls weren't being returned. He started to call her back, then remembered he also had a text message and decided to check that first.

It was short, anonymous, ambiguous: SUCH PASSIONS! SUCH SE-CRETS! SUCH WONDERFUL PHOTOGRAPHS!

He sat and stared at it. On second thought, although it left much to the imagination, it wasn't ambiguous at all. In fact, what it left to the imagination was far too clear.

He could feel the imagined contents of those photos exploding in his life like a roadside bomb.

Chapter 44

Déjà vu

Keeping his balance, staying focused, and subjecting the facts to a dispassionate analysis had been the pillars of Gurney's success as a homicide cop.

At the moment he was having a hell of a time doing any of those things. His mind was churning with unknowns, with terrible possibilities.

Who the hell was this Jykynstyl character? Or was the proper question, who the hell was this character posing as Jykynstyl? What was the nature of the threat, the purpose of the threat? It was fairly certain that the scenario, whatever it was, was criminal. The hope that he'd gotten harmlessly drunk or that the text message had a harmless meaning seemed delusional. He needed to face the fact that he'd been drugged and that the worst-case scenario—involving a massive dose of Rohypnol in that first glass of white wine—was the most likely scenario.

Rohypnol plus alcohol. The disinhibiting amnesiac cocktail. The date-rape cocktail that dissolves clear judgment, fears, and second thoughts. That strips the mind of moral and practical inhibitions, that blocks the intervention of reason and conscience, that has the power to reduce you to the sum of your primal appetites. The drug combo with the potential to convert one's impulses, however foolish, into actions, however damaging. The nasty elixir that prioritizes the wants of the primitive lizard brain, regardless of the expense to the whole person, then cloaks the experience—which might last anywhere from six to twelve hours—in an impenetrable amnesia. It was as though it had been invented to facilitate disasters. The kinds of disasters Gurney was imagining as he sat in his car, helpless and scattered, trying to get his head around facts that refused to cohere.

Madeleine had made him a believer in small, simple actions, in putting one foot in front of the other, but when nothing made sense and every direction held a shadowy threat, it wasn't easy to decide where to put that first foot.

However, it did occur to him that remaining parked on that dark block was accomplishing nothing. If he drove away, even if he hadn't decided where he was going, he might at least be able to tell if he was being watched or followed. Before he could get tangled up in reasons not to, he started the car, waited for the light at the end of the street to turn green, waited for three taxis in a row to race by, switched on his headlights, pulled out quickly, and made it through the Madison Avenue intersection just before the light turned red behind him. He drove on, turning randomly at a series of intersections until he was positive no one was tailing him, working his way down the east side of Manhattan from the Eighties to the Sixties.

Without having made a conscious decision to do so, Gurney arrived at the block where Jykynstyl's residence was located. He drove through the block once, came around, and entered it again. There were no lights showing in the windows of the big brownstone. He parked in the same illegal space he'd occupied nine hours earlier.

He was jittery and unsure what he was going to do next, but taking even the action he had so far was calming him. He remembered he had a phone number for Jykynstyl in his wallet—a number Sonya had given him in case he got delayed in traffic. He called the number now without bothering to plan what he'd say. Maybe something like, *Hell of a party, Jay! Got photos?* Or something a little more Hardwick-like: *Hey, fuckface, fuck with me, you get a bullet between your fucking eyes.* He ended up not saying any of those things, because when he called the number Sonya gave him, a recorded voice announced that it was out of service.

He had an urge to bang on the door until someone answered it. Then he remembered something Jykynstyl had said about always being in motion, never staying anywhere very long, and he was suddenly convinced that the brownstone was empty, the man was gone, and banging on the door would be utterly pointless.

He should call Madeleine, let her know how late he'd be. But how late was that going to be? Should he tell her about the amnesia? Waking up across the street from St. Genesius? The photo threat? Or would all that just worry her sick for no reason?

Maybe he should call Sonya first, see if she could throw any light on what was going on. How much did she really know about Jay Jykynstyl? Was there any reality at all to the hundred-thousand-dollar offer? Was all that just a ruse to get him to come to the city for a private lunch? So he could be drugged and . . . and what?

Maybe he ought to get to an ER and have them run a tox screen—find out before they were metabolized away exactly what chemicals he'd ingested, replace his suspicions with evidence. On the other hand, the record of a tox screen could create questions and complications. He found himself in the catch-22 of wanting to find out what had happened before taking any official steps to find out what had happened.

As he felt himself slipping into a pit of indecision, a large white van came to a stop less than thirty feet away, directly in front of the brownstone. The wash of headlights from a passing car made the green lettering on the side of the van legible: WHITE STAR COMMER-CIAL CLEANING.

Gurney heard a sliding door open on the far side of the van, followed by a few comments in Spanish, then the door sliding shut. The van pulled away, leaving a drably uniformed man and woman in the semidarkness at the door of the brownstone. The man opened it with a key affixed to a ring at his belt. They entered the building, and moments later a light came on in the foyer. Shortly after that a light came on in another ground-floor window. That was followed at approximately two-minute intervals by the appearance of lights in windows on each of the building's four stories.

Gurney decided to bluff his way in. He looked like a cop, sounded like a cop, and his membership card in an association of retired de-tectives could be mistaken for active credentials.

When he came to the front door, he found it still open. He walked into the vestibule and listened. There were no footsteps, no voices. He tried the door that led from the vestibule into the rest of the house. It, too, was unlocked. He opened it and listened again. He heard nothing except the muted whine of a vacuum from one of the upper floors. He stepped inside and closed the door gently behind him.

The cleaning people had turned on all the lights, giving the large, foyerlike room a colder, barer look than he remembered. The brightness had diminished the richness of the mahogany staircase that was the room's main feature. The wood-paneled walls had been cheapened as well, as though the unflattering light had stripped off their antique patina.

In the far wall, there were two doors. One of them, he recalled, was the door to the little elevator into which he'd been escorted by Jykynstyl's daughter—if in fact that's who she was, which he now doubted. The door next to it was ajar, and the room beyond it was as brightly illuminated as the large foyer in which he stood.

It appeared to be what real-estate ads refer to as a "media" room. It was visually dominated by a flat-panel video screen with half a dozen armchairs arranged at various angles to it. There was a wet bar in the rear corner, and against an adjoining wall there was a sideboard with an array of wine and cocktail glasses and a stack of glass plates appropriate for elegant desserts or lines of coke. He checked the drawers of the sideboard and found them empty. The wet bar's cabinets and small refrigerator were locked. He left the room as quietly as he'd entered it and headed for the staircase.

The Persian runner cushioned his rapid steps as he climbed the risers two at a time to the second floor, then to the third. The vacuum sound was louder here, and he imagined that at any moment the cleaning team might descend from the floor above, so reconnaissance time was limited. An archway led into a corridor with five doors. He assumed that the one at the far end would be for the elevator and the other four would open into bedrooms. He went to the nearest door and turned the knob as soundlessly as he could. As he did so, he heard the muffled thump of the elevator stopping farther down the hall, followed by the smooth whoosh of its sliding door.

He stepped quickly into an unlit room he assumed was a bedroom and eased the door shut behind him, hoping that whoever had emerged from the elevator, presumably one of the cleaning people, had been looking in another direction.

It dawned on him that he was in a bit of a situation: unable to conceal himself because the room was too dark for him to locate an appropriate spot and unable to turn on a light for fear it would give him away. And if he were caught hiding pathetically behind a bedroom door, he could hardly bluff his way out at that point by flashing a set of retired-detective credentials. What the hell was he doing there, anyway? What was it he hoped to discover? Jykynstyl's wallet with a clue to another identity? Conspiratorial e-mail? The photographs referred to in the text message? Something incriminating enough to Jykynstyl to neutralize any threat? Those possibilities were the stuff of implausible caper movies. So why had he put himself in this ridiculous position, lurking in the dark like an idiot burglar?

The vacuum roared to life in the hall outside the door, its shadow passing back and forth across the half inch of light that intruded between the door bottom and the carpet pile. He stepped back gingerly against the wall, feeling his way. He heard a door opening directly across the hall. A few seconds later, the roar of the vacuum diminished, suggesting that it and its operator had entered the opposite room.

Gurney's eyes were beginning to adjust to the darkness, which the crack of light shining under the door was diluting just enough for him to make out a few large shapes: the footboard of a king-size bed, the curving wings of a Queen Anne chair, a dark armoire against a lighter wall.

He decided to take a chance. He felt along the wall behind him for the light switch and found a dimmer knob. He turned it until it was approximately in the middle of its range, then depressed it to its "on" position and immediately back to its "off" position. He was betting that the cleaners were sufficiently busy that the resulting half-second flash of muted light beneath the door would go unnoticed.

What he saw in the brief moment of illumination was a spacious bedroom with the furnishings whose outlines he'd discerned in the semidarkness, plus two smaller chairs, a low chest of drawers with an elaborate mirror above it, and a pair of nightstands with ornate lamps. There was nothing unexpected or strange—except for his reaction. In the instant it was visible, the scene ignited in him the experience of déjà vu. He was sure he had seen before everything exactly as it appeared in that flash of light.

The visceral sense of familiarity was followed a few seconds later by a chilling question: Had he been in this bedroom earlier that day? The chill grew into a kind of nausea. *He must have been here, in this room.* Why else would he have such an intense feeling about it, about the bed, the position of the chairs, the scalloped crest of the armoire?

More important, how far might the disinhibiting power of alcohol and Rohypnol take one? How much of what one believed, how much of one's true value system, how much of what was precious to one—how much of all that could be swept away by that chemical mixture? Never in his whole life had he felt so vulnerable, such a stranger to himself—so unsure of who he was or of what he might be capable of doing—as he did at that moment.

Then, gradually, the vertiginous feeling of helplessness and incomprehension was replaced by alternating currents of fear and rage. Uncharacteristically, he embraced the rage. The steel of the rage. The strength and willfulness of the rage.

He opened the door and stepped out into the light.

The drone of the vacuum was coming from a room farther down the corridor. Gurney walked rapidly the other way, back to the big staircase. His recollection of the brevity of his noontime elevator ride told him that the sitting room and dining room were almost certainly on the second floor. Hoping that something in those rooms might provide a thread of memory he could follow, he descended the stairs.

An archway led from the landing to the rest of the second floor. Passing through it, Gurney found himself in the Victorian parlor where he'd met Jykynstyl. As elsewhere in the house, all the lights had been turned on by the cleaners, with a similarly bleak effect. Even the giant potted plants had lost their luxuriance. He walked through the sitting area into the dining room. Dishes, glasses, silverware had all been removed. So had the Holbein portrait. Or Holbein fake.

Gurney realized he knew nothing for certain about his lunch

visit that day. The safest assumption would be that every element of it was phony. Especially the extravagant purchase offer for his mug-shot portraits. The idea that all of that was bogus, that there never was any money on the table, never any admiration for his insights or talents, brought with it a surprising shock to his ego—followed by chagrin at how much the offer and the accompanying flattery had meant to him.

He recalled a therapist once telling him that the only way one can judge the strength of one's attachment to something is by the level of pain caused by its removal. It seemed clear now that the potential rewards of the Jykynstyl fantasy had been as important to him as . . . as believing that they weren't important at all. Which made him feel like an idiot doubled.

He looked around the dining room. His ecstatic vision of a sailboat on Puget Sound returned with the sourness of regurgitated wine. He studied the freshly polished surface of the table. Not a hint of a smudge or fingerprint anywhere. He went back into the sitting room. There was a faint, complex smell in the air of which he'd been dimly aware as he'd passed through the room minutes before. Now he tried to isolate its elements. Alcohol, stale smoke, ashes in the fireplace, leather, moist plant soil, furniture polish, old wood. Nothing surprising. Nothing out of place.

He sighed with a sense of frustration and failure, the pointless risk of having entered the house. The place radiated a hostile emptiness—no feeling that anyone actually lived there. Jykynstyl had admitted as much with his vague description of a traveling lifestyle, and God only knew where the "daughters" spent their time.

The vacuum sound on the floor above grew louder. Gurney took a last look around the room, then headed for the staircase. He was halfway down to the first floor when a vivid recollection brought him to a full stop.

The smell of alcohol.

The little glass.

Christ!

He strode back up the stairs, two at time, back into the sitting room, over to the cavernous leather armchair from which Jykynstyl had greeted him upon his arrival, the chair from which the apparently infirm man had had such difficulty rising that he needed two free hands on the arms to support himself. And having no convenient table on which to lay his little glass of absinthe . . .

Gurney reached into the base of the thick tropical plant. And there it was—shielded from casual sight by the high rim of the pot and the dark, drooping leaves. He carefully wrapped it in his handkerchief and slipped it into his jacket pocket.

The question facing him, back in his car a minute later, was what to do with it.

Chapter 45

A curious dog

The fact that the Nineteenth Precinct station house was just a few blocks away on East Sixty-seventh Street focused Gurney on a mental list of the contacts he had there. He knew at least half a dozen detectives in the Nineteenth, maybe two of them well enough to approach for an awkward favor. And getting a set of prints lifted from the pilfered cordial glass and run against the FBI database—a process that would demand some wiggling around the need for a case number—was definitely awkward. He wasn't about to explain his interest in knowing more about his luncheon host, but he wasn't about to invent a lie that could later blow up in his face.

He decided he'd have to find another way to go about it. He placed the little glass carefully in the console compartment, put his cell phone on the seat beside him, started the car, and headed for the George Washington Bridge.

The first call he made along the way was to Sonya Reynolds.

"Where the hell have you been? What the hell have you been doing all afternoon?" She sounded angry, anxious, and completely ignorant of the day's events, which he found reassuring.

"Great questions. I don't know the answer to either one."

"What happened? What are you talking about?"

"How much do you know about Jay Jykynstyl?"

"What's this about? What the hell happened?"

"I'm not sure. Nothing good."

"I don't understand."

"How much do you know about Jykynstyl?"

"I know what's reported in the art media. Big buyer, very

selective. Huge financial influence on the market. Likes to be anonymous. Doesn't allow his photograph to be taken. Likes there to be a lot of confusion about his personal life, even where he lives. Even whether he's straight or gay. The more confusion, the more he likes it. Kind of obsessed with his privacy."

"So you'd never met him, never even seen a photo of him, before he dropped into your gallery one day and said he wanted to buy my stuff?"

"What are you getting at?"

"How do you know that the man you spoke to is Jay Jykynstyl? Because he said so?"

"No. Exactly the opposite."

"He said he *wasn't* Jay Jykynstyl?"

"He said his name was Jay. Just Jay."

"So how . . . ?"

"I kept asking him, told him it would be very difficult to do business with him without knowing his full name, that it was ridiculous for me not to know who I was dealing with when so much money would be involved."

"And he said . . . what?"

"He said Javits. His name was Jay Javits."

"Like Jacob Javits? The guy who used to be a senator?"

"Right, but he said it sort of odd like, like the name just occurred to him and he felt he had to say something because I was making a big issue out of it. Dave, tell me why the fuck we're talking about this. I want to know right now what happened today."

"What happened is . . . it became plain that this whole deal is bullshit. I believe I was drugged and that lunch was some kind of setup that had nothing to do with my artwork."

"That's insane."

"Getting back to the man's identity—he told you his name was Jay Javits and you concluded from that that his name was Jay Jykynstyl?"

"Not like that, no. Don't be silly. During the course of our conversation, we were talking about how pretty the lake was, and he mentioned he could see it from his room, so I asked him where he was staying, and he told me at a very beautiful inn, like he didn't want me to know the name. So later I called the Huntington, the most exclusive inn on the lake, and I asked if they had a Jay Javits registered there. At first the guy sounded confused, and then he asked me if maybe I had the name wrong. And I said sure, I'm getting older and my hearing is bad and sometimes I get names wrong. I tried to sound pathetic."

"And you think you succeeded?"

"I must have. He said, 'Could the person you want be named Jykynstyl?' "

"I asked him to spell the name, and he did, and I thought to myself, *'Holy fucking Christ, is it really possible?'* So I asked him to describe this Jykynstyl guest, and he did, and it was obviously the same guy who had come to the gallery. So, you see, he didn't want me to know who he was, but I found out."

Gurney was silent. He thought a far more likely possibility was that Sonya had been smoothly manipulated into believing that the man was Jykynstyl—in a way that would leave her with no doubts about her conclusion. The subtlety and expertise of the con job was almost more disturbing than the con itself.

"You still there, David?"

"I need to make some more calls, and then I'll get back to you."

"You still haven't told me what happened."

"I have no idea what happened—other than the fact that I was lied to, drugged, driven around the city in a blackout, and threatened. Why and by whom I have no idea. I'm doing my best to find out. And I will find out." The optimism in those last five words bore little relationship to the anger, fear, and confusion he felt. He promised again to get back to her.

His next call was to Madeleine. He made it without thinking about what he was going to say or checking the time. It wasn't until she picked up with a sleepy sound in her voice that he glanced at the dashboard clock and saw that it was 10:04 P.M.

"I was wondering when you'd finally call," she said. "Are you all right?"

"Pretty much. Sorry I didn't call sooner. Things were a little nuts this afternoon."

"What do you mean, 'pretty much'?"

"Huh? Oh, I mean I'm okay, just in the middle of a little mystery."

"How little?"

"Hard to say. But it seems that the Jykynstyl thing is some kind of con. I've been sort of running around tonight trying to get a handle on it."

"What happened?" She was totally alert now, speaking in the perfectly calm voice that both masked and exposed her concern.

He was aware that he had a choice. He could relate everything he knew and feared, regardless of the effect on her. Or he could present a less complete, less disturbing version. In what he would later see as a self-deluding bit of fancy dancing, he chose the latter *as a first step* and told himself he would present the whole story as soon as he understood it better himself.

"I started feeling funny at lunch, and later, in the car, I was having trouble remembering the conversation we'd had." He told himself that this was true, albeit somewhat minimized.

"Sounds like you were drunk." Her voice was more questioning than assertive.

"Maybe. But . . . I'm not sure."

"You think you were drugged?"

"It's one of the possibilities I've been considering. Even though it doesn't make any sense. Anyway, I've been checking the place out, and all I know for sure is that there's something wrong about the whole situation—and the hundred-thousand-dollar offer is almost certainly baloney. But what I actually called to say is that I'm just leaving Manhattan and I should be home in about two and a half hours. I'm really sorry I didn't call earlier."

"Don't race."

"See you soon. Love you."

He nearly missed the last exit from the Harlem River Drive to the GW Bridge. With a quick glance to his right, he swerved into the exit lane and onto the ramp, triggering the blare of an indignant car horn.

It was too late to call Kline. But if Hardwick was indeed back on the case, he might know something about the Karnala inquiry and Kline's phone-message reference to the Skard family. With a little luck, Hardwick would be awake, would answer the phone, and be willing to talk.

All three turned out to be true.

"What's up, Sherlock? You couldn't wait till morning to congratulate me on my reinstatement?"

"Congratulations."

"Apparently you got everybody believing that Mapleshade grads are dropping like flies and everybody in the world has to be interviewed—which has created this huge manpower crunch that forced Rodriguez to bring me back into it. Almost made his head explode."

"I'm glad you're back. I have a couple of questions."

"About the pooch?"

"Pooch?"

"The one that dug up Kiki."

"The hell are you talking about, Jack?"

"Marian Eliot's curious Airedale. You haven't heard?"

"Tell me."

"She was out working in her rose garden with Melpomene tied to a tree."

"Who?"

"The Airedale's name is Melpomene. Very sophisticated bitch. Somehow Melpomene manages to untie her rope. She wanders over behind the Muller house, starts rooting around in back of the woodshed. By the time Old Lady Eliot gets over there to retrieve her, Melpomene's got a pretty good hole going. Something catches Old Lady Eliot's eye. Guess what?"

"Jack, for Christ's sake, just tell me."

"She thought it was one of her gardening gloves."

"For Christ's sake, Jack . . ."

"Think about it. What might look like a glove?"

"Jack . . ."

"It was a decomposed hand."

"And this hand was attached to Kiki Muller, the woman who supposedly ran off with Hector Flores?"

"The very same."

Gurney was silent for a good five seconds.

"You got the wheels turning, Sherlock? Deducing, inducing, whatever the hell you do?"

"How did Kiki's husband react to this?"

"Crazy Carl? Trainman under the tree? No reaction at all. I think his shrink has him so zapped on Xanax he's beyond reaction. Fucking zombie. Or he's putting on a hell of an act."

"Is there any cause or approximate date of death?"

"She only got dug up this morning. But she'd definitely been in the ground awhile. Maybe a few months, which would put it back to the time of Hector's disappearance."

"What about the cause?"

"The ME hasn't put it in writing yet, but based on my observation of the body I'd be willing to take a guess."

Hardwick paused. Gurney clenched his teeth. He knew what was coming.

"I'd say her death might be related to the fact that her head was chopped off."

Chapter 46

Nothing on paper

Arriving home well after midnight, Gurney got so little sleep that night that it hardly felt like sleep at all.

The next morning over coffee with Madeleine, he attributed his restlessness to his suspicions regarding "Jykynstyl" and to the growing intensity of the Perry case. Without saying so, he also attributed it to the metabolites of whatever chemical he'd been dosed with.

"You should have gone to the hospital."

"I'll be okay."

"Maybe you should go back to bed."

"Too much going on. Besides, I'm too wound up to sleep."

"What are you going to do?"

"Work."

"You know it's Sunday, right?"

"Right." But he'd forgotten that it was. His confusion was scaring him. He had to do something to focus his mind on something concrete, a path to clarity, one foot after another.

"Maybe you should call Dichter's office, ask if he can fit you in today."

He shook his head. Dichter was their family doctor. Dr. Dichter. The silliness of it almost always made him smile, but not today.

"You said you might have been drugged. Are you taking that seriously enough? What kind of drug are you talking about?"

He wasn't going to raise the specter of Rohypnol. Its sexual associations would trigger an explosion of questions and concerns he didn't feel capable of discussing. "I'm not sure. I'm guessing it was something with blackout effects similar to alcohol."

She gave him that assessing look of hers that made him feel naked.

"Whatever it was," he said, "it's wearing off." He knew he was sounding too casual, or at least too eager to move to another subject.

"Maybe there's something you should be taking to counteract it."

He shook his head. "I'm sure my body's natural detoxing process will take care of it. What I need in the meantime is something to focus on." That thought led him directly back to the Perry case, which led him to the call he'd made to Hardwick the previous evening, which led him to the sudden realization that their discussion of Melpomene and Kiki Muller's decomposing hand had caused him to forget why he'd called Hardwick in the first place.

A moment later he was back on the phone to him.

"Skard?" rasped Hardwick unhappily. "Yeah, that name came up in connection with Karnala Fashion. By the way, it's Sunday fucking morning. How urgent is this?"

Nothing with Hardwick was easy. But if you played the game, you could make it less difficult. One way to play was to escalate the vulgarity.

"How about a shotgun-to-your-balls level of urgency?"

For a couple of seconds, Hardwick was quiet, as if considering the number of points to award for artfulness of expression. "Karnala Fashion turns out to be a complicated outfit, hard to pin down. It's owned by another corporation, which is owned by another corporation, which is owned by another corporation in the Cayman Islands. Very hard to say what business they're actually in. But there seems to be a Sardinian connection, and the Sardinian connection seems to be connected to the Skard family. The Skards are reputed to be very bad people."

"*Reputed* to be?"

"I don't mean to suggest there's any doubt about it. There's just no legal proof of it. According to our friends at Interpol, no member of the Skard family has ever been convicted of anything. Potential witnesses always change their minds. Or they disappear."

"The Skards own Karnala Fashion?"

"Probably. Everything about them is *probably* this, *probably* that. They don't put much on paper."

"So what the hell is Karnala Fashion all about?"

"Nobody knows. We can't find a single fabric supplier or clothing retailer who's ever done business with them. They run ads for incredibly expensive women's clothes, but we can't find evidence that they actually sell them."

"What do their representatives say about that?"

"We can't find any representatives."

"Jesus, Jack, who places the ads? Who pays for them?"

"It's all done by e-mail."

"E-mail from where?"

"Sometimes from the Cayman Islands. Sometimes from Sardinia."

"But . . ."

"I know. It doesn't make sense. It's being pursued. We're waiting for more stuff from Interpol. Also from the Italian police. Also from the Cayman Islands. It's tricky, since nobody's been convicted of anything and the missing girls aren't officially missing. Even if they were, their connection to Karnala wouldn't prove anything, and there's nothing on paper connecting Karnala to the Skards. *Reputed* is as good as it gets. Legally, we're in a minefield in a fog. Plus, thanks to the observations you shared with the DA, the whole case is now being run like a cover-your-ass panic attack."

"Meaning?"

"Meaning that instead of a couple of guys in that minefield, we've got a dozen tripping over one another."

"Admit it, Jack, you love it."

"Fuck you."

"Right. So I guess this wouldn't be a good time to ask you for a favor."

"Like what?" He was suddenly placid. Hardwick was strange that way. His reactions were backward, like a hyperactive kid being calmed by an upper. The best time to ask him for a favor was the exact time you'd think would be the worst, and vice versa. The same upside-down principle governed his response to risk. He tended to view it as a positive factor in any equation. Unlike most cops, who tend by nature to be hierarchical and conservative, Hardwick had the true maverick gene. He was lucky to be alive.

"It's a rule breaker," said Gurney, feeling for the first time in nearly twenty-four hours that he was on solid ground. Why hadn't he thought of Hardwick sooner? "It might involve a little deviousness."

"What is it?" The man sounded like he'd just been offered a surprise dessert.

"I need to get some prints lifted off a small glass and run against the FBI database."

"Let me guess—you don't want anyone to know why, you don't want a case file opened, and you don't want the inquiry to be traced back to you."

"Something like that."

"Where and when do I get this glass?"

"How about at Abelard's in ten minutes?"

"Gurney, you're a presumptuous dick."

Chapter 47

An impossible situation

After entrusting the glass to Hardwick in the tiny parking area in front of Abelard's, Gurney was struck by the idea of continuing on to Tambury. Abelard's, after all, was nearly halfway there, and the scene of the crime might have more to reveal to him. He also wanted to keep moving, keep the anxiety of the Jykynstyl business from enveloping him.

He thought about those outdoorsy aristocrats Marian Eliot and Melpomene, Melpomene rooting up the dirt behind the Muller shed, Kiki's hand sticking out of the ground like a grungy garden glove. And Carl. Christmas Carl. Carl who might very well end up in the frame for his wife's murder. Of course, the fact that her head was cut off would point the finger at Hector. But if Carl were clever . . .

Had he discovered her affair with Hector? And decided to kill her the way Hector had killed Jillian Perry? Conceivable but un-likely. If Carl were guilty, that would make Kiki's murder a tangent off the main course of the Mapleshade business. It would also mean that Carl had been furious enough to kill his wife, rational enough to mimic Hector's MO, and foolish enough to bury her in a shallow grave in his own backyard. Gurney had seen stranger sequences of events, but that didn't make this scenario feel any more credible.

He suspected there was a better explanation for Kiki Muller's murder than the rage of a jealous husband, something that would attach it more directly to the larger mystery at Mapleshade. As he turned into Badger Lane from Higgles Road, he was starting to feel like himself again. He was far from whistling a happy tune, but at least he felt like a detective. And he didn't feel like throwing up.

Two tattooed clones of Calvin Harlen were standing with the man himself next to the manure pile that separated the wreck of a house from the wreck of a barn. Their dull eyes followed Gurney's car into the lane with a lazy malevolence.

Driving up toward Ashton's house, he half expected to see Marian Eliot and Melpomene, exposer of buried sins, striking a dour pose on their front porch, but there was no sign of either. Nor was there any sign of life at the Muller house.

When he got out of his car in Ashton's brick-paved driveway, he was struck again by the English ambience of the place—its subtle communication of wealth and quiet exclusivity. Rather than proceeding straight to the front door, he walked over to the arched trellis that served as an entryway to the broad lawn extending far behind the house. Although the surrounding shrubs were still primarily green, scattered tinges of yellow and red were beginning to appear in the trees.

"Detective Gurney?"

He turned toward the house. Scott Ashton was standing at the open side door.

Gurney smiled. "Sorry to bother you on a Sunday morning."

Ashton mirrored his smile. "I wouldn't expect any distinction between weekday and weekend in a murder investigation. Is there anything specific . . . ?"

"Actually, I was wondering if I could take a closer look at the area around the cottage."

"A closer look?"

"That's right. If you don't mind?"

"Anything in particular you're interested in?"

"I'm hoping I'll know it when I see it."

Ashton's even smile was as measured as his voice. "Let me know if you need any help. I'll be with my father in the library."

Some people have "dens," thought Gurney, and some people have "libraries." Who said America was a classless society? Certainly no one whose home was built of Cotswold stone and whose father was named Hobart Ashton.

He walked from the driveway across the side lawn through the trellis to the main area of the rear lawn. He'd been so preoccupied

that he hadn't noticed until that very moment what a strangely perfect day it was, one of those autumn days when the altered angle of
the sun, the altered color of the leaves, and an absolute stillness in
the air conspired to create a world of timeless peace, a world that
required nothing of him, a world whose peace took his breath away.

Like all the moments of serenity in Gurney's life, this one was
short-lived. He had come here to focus on a murder, to absorb more
fully the nitty-gritty reality of the place in which it happened, the
locale in which the murderer went about his business.

He continued around the back of the house to the broad stone
patio, to the small round table—the table where four months earlier
a bullet from a .257 Weatherby rifle had shattered Ashton's teacup.
He wondered where Hector Flores was at that very moment. He
might be anywhere. He might be in the woods watching the house,
keeping an eye on Ashton and his father, keeping an eye on Gurney.

Gurney's attention moved to the cottage, to what had happened
the day of the murder, the day of the wedding. From where he was
standing, he could see the front and one side, as well as the part of
the woods that Flores would have had to pass through in order to deposit the machete where it was found. In May the leaves would have
been coming out, as now they were thinning, making the visibility
conditions in the thicket roughly the same.

As he'd done many times during the past week, Gurney envi-
sioned an athletic Latino male climbing out the back window of the
cottage, running with the evasive steps of a soccer player through
the trees and thornbushes to a point approximately 150 yards away,
and half concealing the bloodied machete under some leaves. And
then . . . then what? Slipping some sort of plastic bags over his feet?
Or spraying them with some chemical to destroy the continuity of
the scent trail? So he could proceed tracelessly to some other des-
tination in the copse or on the road beyond it? So he could meet
up with Kiki Muller, waiting in her car to drive him safely out of
the area before the police arrived? Or take him to her own house?
To her own house where he then killed and buried her? But why?
What sense did any of that make? Or was that the wrong question,
assuming as it did that the scenario had to make practical sense?
Suppose a large part of it had been driven by pure pathology, by

some warped fantasy? But that was not a useful avenue to explore. Because if nothing made sense, there was no way to make sense of it. And he had the feeling that, under the cloak of fury and lunacy, it all somehow *did* make sense.

So why was the machete only partially concealed? It seemed senseless to go to the trouble of covering the blade while leaving the handle in plain sight. For some reason that small discrepancy was the one that bothered him the most. Perhaps *bothered* was the wrong word. He was actually quite fond of discrepancies, because his experience told him that they eventually provided a window into the truth.

He sat down at the table and gazed into the woods, imagining as best he could the path of the running man. The view of those 150 yards from cottage to machete site was almost entirely obscured, not only by the foliage of the copse itself but by the rhododendron border that separated the wild area from the lawn and the flower beds. Gurney tried to estimate how deeply into the woods someone could see, and he concluded that it was not very deeply at all—making it easy for a man to pass where Flores had evidently passed without anyone on the lawn noticing him. In fact, by far the most distant object in the woods Gurney could see through the foliage from where he was sitting was the black trunk of a cherry tree. And he could see only a narrow slice of it through a gap in the bushes no more than a few inches wide.

True, that visible bit of tree trunk was on the far side of the route Flores would have to have taken, and theoretically, if someone had been staring into the woods, focused on that spot at the right moment, he or she might have caught a split-second glimpse of a person passing it. But it would have meant nothing at the time. And the chance of someone's attention being focused on that precise spot at that time was about as likely as . . .

Jesus Christ!

Gurney's eyes widened at the obvious thing he'd almost missed.

He stared through the foliage at the black, scaly bark of the cherry tree. Then, keeping it in sight, he walked toward it—straight across the patio, through the flower bed where Ashton had collapsed, through the rhododendron border of the lawn, and into the copse.

His direction was approximately perpendicular to the route he as-sumed Flores would have traveled from the cottage to the machete site. He wanted to be sure there was no way the man could have avoided passing in front of the cherry tree.

When Gurney reached the edge of the ravine that he remem-bered from his first examination of the copse a couple of days ear-lier, his assumption was confirmed. The tree was on the far side of the ravine, which was long and deep with precipitous sides. Any route from the cottage that would pass *behind* the tree would in-volve crossing that ravine at least twice—a time-consuming task that would have been impossible to accomplish before the area was swarming with people after the discovery of the body—not to men-tion the fact that the scent trail ran along the near side of the ravine, not the far side. Which meant that anyone going from the cottage to the machete site had to pass *in front of* the tree. There was simply no way not to.

Gurney made the trip home from Tambury to Walnut Crossing in fifty-five minutes instead of the normal hour and a quarter. He was in a hurry to take a closer look at the video material from the wedding reception. He also realized that his rush might be arising from a need to stay as involved as possible in the Perry murder—a murder that, however horrendous, caused him far less anxiety than did the Jykynstyl situation.

Madeleine's car was parked next to the house, and her bicycle was leaning against the garden shed. He guessed she'd be in the kitchen, but when he went in through the side door and called out, "I'm home," there was no answer.

He went straight to the long table that separated the big kitchen from the sitting area—the table where his copies of the case mate-rials were laid out, much to Madeleine's annoyance. Amid the fold-ers was a set of DVDs.

The one on top, the one he sat through with Hardwick, bore a label that said "Perry-Ashton Reception, Comprehensive BCI Edit." But it was another DVD, one of the unedited originals, that Gurney was looking for. There were five to choose from. The first was labeled "Helicopter, General Aerial Views and Descent." The other four, each containing the video captured by one of the stationary ground cameras at the reception, were labeled according to the compass orientation of each camera's field of view.

He took the four DVDs into the den, opened his laptop, went to Google Earth, and typed in, *"Badger Lane, Tambury, NY."* Thirty seconds later he was looking at a satellite photo of Ashton's property, complete with altitude and compass points. Even the tea table on the patio was identifiable.

He chose the approximate point in the woods where he figured the visible tree trunk would be. Using the Google compass points, he calculated the heading from the table to the tree. The heading was eighty-five degrees—close to due east.

He shuffled through the DVDs. The last one was labeled "East by Northeast." He popped it into the player across from the couch, located the point at which Jillian Perry had entered the cottage, and settled down to give the next fourteen minutes of the video his total attention.

He watched it once, twice, with increasing bafflement. Then he watched it again, this third time letting it run to the point when Luntz, the local police chief, had secured the scene and the state cops were arriving.

Something was wrong. More than wrong. Impossible.

He called Hardwick, who, in no hurry, answered on the seventh ring.

"What can I do for you, ace?"

"How sure are you that the input tapes of the wedding reception are complete?"

"What do you mean, 'complete'?"

"One of the four fixed cameras was set up so that its field of view covered the cottage and a broad stretch of woods to the left of the cottage. That stretch of woods includes all the space that Flores had to pass through in order to ditch the murder weapon where he did."

"So?"

"So there's a tree trunk in back of that area that's visible through gaps in the foliage from the angle of the patio, which was also the angle of one of the cameras."

"And?"

"That tree trunk, I repeat, is *in back of* the route Flores would have to have taken to place the machete where it was found. That tree trunk is clearly and continually visible on the high-def video recorded by that camera."

"Your point being what?"

"I watched the video three times to be absolutely sure. Jack, no one passed in front of that tree."

Hardwick sounded subdued. "I don't get it."

"Neither do I. Is there any possibility that the machete in the woods wasn't the murder weapon?"

"We have a perfect DNA match. The fresh blood on the machete was Jillian Perry's. Potential error factor is less than one in a million. Not to mention the fact that the ME report refers to a powerful blow from a heavy, sharp blade. And what's the alternative, anyway? That Flores secretly disposed of a second bloody machete, the real murder weapon, after wiping some of the blood from it onto the first one? But he'd still have to get it to where we found it. I mean, what the hell are we talking about? How could it not be the murder weapon?"

Gurney sighed. "So what we have, basically, is an impossible situation."

Chapter 48

Perfect memories

If the facts contradict each other, it means that some of them aren't facts.

One of his instructors at the NYPD academy had made that observation in class one day. Gurney never forgot it.

If he was going to base any conclusions on the content of the video, he needed to test its factualness a little further. On the DVD case, there was a phone number for the company, Perfect Memories, that had handled the videography.

He called the number, left a message mentioning the names Ashton and Perry, and had barely concluded when his phone rang and Perfect Memories appeared as the caller ID.

A professionally pleasant and alert female voice asked, "How can I help you?"

Gurney explained who he was and how he was trying to assist Val Perry, mother of the late bride, and how important he believed the video material produced by Perfect Memories would be in capturing the madman who'd killed Jillian and providing closure for her family. All he needed was an absolutely certain answer to one question, but he needed to hear it from the person who'd supervised the project.

"That would be me."

"And you are . . . ?"

"Jennifer Stillman. I'm the managing director here."

Managing director. British-sounding title. Nice touch for the upscale market. "What I need to know, Jennifer, is whether there were any time breaks in any of the original recordings."

"Absolutely not." Her response was crisp and immediate.

"Not even for a fraction of a second?"

"Absolutely not."

"You seem remarkably sure. Has the question come up before?"

"Not the question, but that specific requirement."

"Requirement?"

"It was actually written into the production contract that the video had to cover the entire venue during the entire reception, start to finish, with absolutely nothing left out. Apparently the bride wanted literally *all* of it recorded—every inch of that reception, for every second it lasted."

Jennifer Stillman's tone told Gurney this was not exactly a standard request, or at least the client's emphasis on it was not standard. He asked about it, just to be sure.

"Well . . ." She hesitated. "I'd say that it was unusually important to them. Or at least to her. When Dr. Ashton passed along the request to us, he seemed a little . . ." Again she hesitated. "I shouldn't be saying any of this. I'm not a mind reader."

"Jennifer, this is important. As you know, it's a murder case. My main concern is that I can be confident that the DVDs contain an uninterrupted video record—nothing missing, no dropped frames."

"There were certainly no dropped frames. Holes would create glitches in the time code, and the computer would flag that."

"Okay. Good to know. Thank you. Just one more thing—you were starting to say something about Dr. Ashton?"

"Not really. Just . . . it was just that he seemed a little embarrassed talking about his fiancée's obsession with every instant of the reception being recorded. Like maybe he was embarrassed by the romantic sentimentality of it, or maybe he thought it sounded childish, I really don't know. It's not my place to judge why people want what they want. The customer is always right, right?"

"Thank you, Jennifer. You've been extremely helpful."

It might not be Jennifer Stillman's job to judge why people wanted what they wanted, but it was a big part of Gurney's job. Understanding motivations could make all the difference, and in this instance a weird one came to mind: One reason a person might want total video coverage of an event was security. Either because they believed that the deterrent effect of multiple cameras in continuous recording mode would keep some feared event from occurring or because they wanted to have an indisputable record of anything that did occur.

And then there was the question of who it was that wanted all those cameras running. It hadn't escaped Gurney's notice that the request had been positioned to Ms. Stillman as coming from Jillian, but that Jillian herself hadn't been present, and the request had been "passed along" by Ashton. So it might have been his idea and he had chosen to present it as hers. But why would he do that? What difference did it make whose idea it was?

The possibility that he or she had been motivated by the security aspect of the cameras—the possibility that at least one of them, maybe both, had reason to be apprehensive about what might happen that day—was intriguing.

Their most likely focus of concern would have been Flores, who reportedly had been acting strangely. Maybe the camera emphasis had come from Jillian, just as Ashton had said. Maybe she had reasons to fear Flores. After all, her cell records for the weeks preceding the murder indicated numerous text messages from Flores's phone—including the final one, the only one that hadn't been deleted: FOR ALL THE REASONS I HAVE WRITTEN. EDWARD VALLORY. In light of the prologue to Vallory's play, that message could certainly be interpreted as a threat. So maybe she went to see him in the cottage to discuss something a lot less pleasant than a wedding toast.

When Gurney was engaged in stitching together the pieces of evidence, interpretation, hearsay, and logical leaps that constituted his understanding of a crime, the process filled his mind completely, obliterating his sense of time and place. Thus, when he looked at the clock on the den bookcase and saw that it was 5:05 P.M., it both surprised him and didn't surprise him—like the stiffness in his legs when he stood up.

Madeleine was still out. Perhaps he should get something started for dinner, or at least check to see if she'd left anything on the countertop that needed to go into the oven. He was heading in that direction when the phone on his desk rang and brought him back. The caller ID said Jack Hardwick.

"Golly, Supercop, you've got one hell of a creepy friend!"

"Meaning?"

"Hope you weren't near a school yard with this guy."

Gurney had a sinking feeling about where this was heading. "The hell are you talking about, Jack?"

"Touchy, touchy. This sweetheart a close buddy of yours?"

"Enough bullshit. What's this about?"

"The gentleman you were drinking with? Whose glass you walked off with? Whose prints you asked me to run? Sound familiar, Sherlock?"

"What did you find out?"

"Quite a bit."

"Jack . . ."

"I found out that his name is Saul Steck. Professional name Paul Starbuck."

"His profession being . . . ?"

"Nothing currently. At least nothing on record. Until fifteen years ago he was a Hollywood actor on the come. TV commercials, couple of movies." Hardwick was in arch storyteller mode, with a dramatic pause after each sentence. "Then he had a little problem."

"Jack, can we move this along? What little problem?"

"Accused of raping an underage girl. Once that hit the media, other victims started coming out of the woodwork. Saul-Paul was indicted on a bunch of rape and molestation charges. Fond of drugging fourteen-year-old girls. Took a lot of very explicit pictures. Ended his acting career. Could have gone to prison for the rest of his life. Too bad he didn't. Best place for the little scumbag. However, family money bought enough expert medical testimony to get him committed to a psych hospital, from which he was quietly released five years ago. Dropped off the radar screen. Current address unknown. Except maybe by you? I mean, you got that cute little glass somewhere, right?"

Chapter 49

Little boys

Gurney stood at the French doors facing the lavender remnants of a spectacular sunset that he hadn't really noticed, trying to assimilate the latest aftershock of the Jykynstyl earthquake.

Information. He needed information. What did he need to find out first? He should grab a pad and start listing the questions, prioritizing. An obvious one came immediately to mind: Who owned the brownstone?

How to pursue the question was not so obvious.

The old catch-22 again. To disentangle himself from the snare, he needed to know whose snare it was. But pursuing that question naïvely, without any idea what the answer might be, could get him more deeply entangled. Unanswered questions were threatening to make other questions unanswerable.

"Hello!"

It was Madeleine's voice. Like a voice that awakens you in the morning, jarring you into the room, into the specific day of the week.

He turned toward the little hall that led from the kitchen to the mudroom. "Is that you?" he asked. Of course it was. An inane question. When she didn't answer, he asked it again, louder.

She responded by appearing in the kitchen doorway, frowning at him.

"Did you just come in?" he asked.

"No, I've been standing in the mudroom all afternoon. What kind of question is that?"

"I didn't hear you come in."

"And yet," she said cheerily, "here I am."

"Yes," he said. "Here you are."

"Are you all right?"

"Fine."

She raised an eyebrow.

"I'm fine. Maybe a little hungry."

She glanced at a bowl on the sideboard. "The scallops should be defrosted by now. Do you want to sauté them while I get the water on for the rice?"

"Sure." He was hoping that the simple task might provide at least a partial escape from the Saul-Paul whirlpool that was engulfing his mind.

He sautéed the scallops in olive oil, garlic, lemon juice, and capers. Madeleine boiled some basmati rice and made a salad of oranges, avocados, and diced red onions. He was having a hell of a time staying focused, staying in the room, staying in the present. *Fond of drugging fourteen-year-old girls. Took a lot of very explicit pictures.*

Halfway through dinner he realized that Madeleine had been describing a hike she'd taken that afternoon through the meandering trails that linked their 50 acres with their neighbor's 350. Hardly a word had registered with him. He smiled gamely and made a belated effort to listen.

". . . amazingly intense green, even in the shade. And underneath the blanket of ferns there were the smallest purple flowers you can imagine." As she spoke, there was a light in her eyes brighter than any light in the room. "Almost microscopic. Like the teeniest blue-and-purple snowflakes."

Blue-and-purple snowflakes? Mother of God! The tension, the incongruity, the gap he felt between her elation and his anxiety brought him close to groaning aloud. Her field of perfect emerald ferns and his own nightmare of poisonous thorns. Her lively honesty and his . . . his what?

His encounter with the devil?

Get a grip, Gurney. Get a grip. What the hell are you so afraid of?

The answer only darkened the pit and greased the walls.

You're afraid of yourself. Afraid of what you might have done.

He sat in a kind of emotional paralysis through the rest of dinner, trying to eat enough to conceal the fact that he wasn't really eating, pretending to appreciate Madeleine's descriptions of her outing. But the more she enthused over the beauty of the black-eyed Susans, the perfume in the air, the azure of the wild asters, the more isolated, dislocated, and crazy he felt. He became aware that Madeleine had stopped talking. She was watching him with concern. He wondered if she'd asked him something and was waiting for an answer. He didn't want to admit how distracted he was, or why.

"Have you spoken to Kyle?" Her question seemed to arise out of nothing. Or had she already asked it? Or segued to it while he was immersed in himself?

"Kyle?"

"Your son."

He hadn't actually been asking a question, just repeating the word, the name, as a way of stepping ashore, of being present. Too tangled a thing to explain. "I've tried. We've traded calls, left messages. A few times."

"You should try harder. Keep at it until you get him."

He nodded, didn't want to argue, didn't know what to say.

She smiled. "It would be good for him. Good for both of you."

He nodded again.

"You're his father."

"I know."

"Well, then." It was a conclusive statement. She began to clear the dishes.

He watched her make two trips to the sink. When she came back with a damp sponge and paper towel to wipe the table, he said, "He's very focused on money."

She lifted the tray that held the napkins so she could wipe under it. "So what?"

"He wants to be a trial lawyer."

"Not necessarily a bad thing."

"It seems to be all about the big money, big house, big car."

"Maybe he wants to be noticed."

"Noticed?"

"Little boys like to be noticed by their fathers," she said.

"Kyle is hardly a little boy."

"But that's exactly what he is," she insisted. "And if you refuse to notice him, then he'll have to settle for impressing the rest of the world."

"I'm not *refusing* to do anything. That's psychobabble bullshit."

"Maybe you're right. Who knows?" Madeleine had perfected the art of sidestepping an attack, of remaining untouched. It left him lurching into empty space.

He continued to sit at the table as she washed the dishes. His eyes began to close. As he'd discovered many times before, the by-product of intense anxiety is exhaustion. He drifted into a kind of half sleep.

Chapter 50

Loose cannon

"You should come to bed." It was Madeleine's voice.

He opened his eyes. She'd turned off all but one light and was on her way out of the kitchen with a book under her arm. The drooping position of his head on his chest had produced a sharp pain in his collarbone. As he straightened himself, he discovered a matching pain in the back of his neck. Instead of refreshing him, his doze at the table had reconstituted his worries.

His level of agitation would make real sleep impossible. But he had to do something to avoid bouncing from one Saul Steck horror scenario to another.

He could return Sheridan Kline's phone call. The man had left that vague message for him about the Skard family. He'd already followed up on it with Hardwick, but maybe the DA knew more than Hardwick. Of course, the DA's office would be closed. It was Sunday night.

He did have Kline's personal cell number. Because he had it from the days of the Mellery case, it hadn't seemed appropriate to use it, uninvited, in connection with the current matter. But right now protocol seemed less important than maintaining his sanity.

He went into the den, got the number, and made the call. He was prepared to leave a message and get a return call later, figuring that the odds were in favor of a control freak like Kline wanting phone conversations to occur on his own schedule. So he was surprised when the man answered.

"Gurney?"

"I apologize for calling so late."

"I thought you'd call me back this afternoon at the office. Chasing down that Karnala thing was your idea."

"Sorry, I got a little tangled up. In your phone message, you asked if I'd heard of the Skard family."

"That's where the Karnala thread led us. Familiar name to you?"

"Yes and no."

"That's not an answer."

"What I meant, Sheridan, is that it struck me as familiar, but I don't know why. Jack Hardwick filled me in on the fact that the Skards are bad guys with Sardinian roots. But I still can't place where I know the name from. I do know that I came upon it very recently."

"That's all Hardwick told you?"

"He told me that no Skard has ever been convicted of anything. And that whatever business Karnala Fashion may be in, it's not the fashion business."

"So you know as much I know. What else did you call me for?"

"I'd like to be involved on a more official basis."

"Meaning what?"

"Updates, invitations to meetings."

"Why?"

"I've gotten kind of attached to the case. And so far my instincts about it have been pretty good."

"That's an open question."

"Look, Sheridan, all I'm saying is, we can help each other. The more I know and the quicker I know it, the more help I can be."

There was a long silence. Gurney's intuition told him it was more technique than indecision on Kline's part. He waited.

Kline emitted a humorless laugh. Gurney kept waiting.

"You know Rodriguez can't stand you, right?"

"Sure."

"And you know Blatt can't stand you, right?"

"Absolutely."

"And that even Bill Anderson isn't very fond of you?"

"Right."

"So you'll be about as welcome at BCI as a fart in an elevator. You realize that?"

"I wouldn't doubt it for a minute."

There was another silence, followed by another chilly Kline chuckle.

"Here's what I'll do: I'm going to tell everyone we have a Gurney problem. Gurney is a loose cannon. And the best way to control a loose cannon is to keep an eye on it, keep it on a short leash, keep it in the corral. And the way I plan to keep an eye on you is to have you over here a lot, sharing your loose-cannon thoughts with us. How does that sound to you?"

Keeping a loose cannon on a short leash in a corral sounded to Gurney like a symptom of mental disintegration. "Sounds workable, sir."

"Good. There's a meeting at BCI tomorrow morning at ten. Be there." Kline hung up without saying good-bye.

Chapter 51

Total confusion

For the rest of the evening, Gurney felt both energized and calmed by the conversation and its promise of ongoing involvement.

He was pleased and rather surprised to still feel the same way when he awoke at sunrise the following day. In an effort to feed that feeling, to stay within the comparatively safe and solid confines of a world in which he was the hunter and not the quarry, he reviewed the Perry file for the tenth time while he had his morning coffee. Then he called Rebecca Holdenfield's number and left a message asking if he could drop by her Albany office that afternoon following his meeting at BCI.

Making calls, returning calls, making appointments—the activity created a sense of momentum. He called Val Perry's number and was shunted into her voice mail. He'd barely said, "This is Dave Gurney," when she picked up, surprising him. He hadn't figured her for an early riser.

"What's happening?" she asked.

Unprepared for an actual conversation, he replied, "Just wanted to touch base."

"Oh? And . . . ?" She sounded edgy, but maybe no edgier than usual.

"Does the name Skard mean anything to you?"

"No. Should it?"

"I was just wondering if Jillian had ever mentioned it."

"Jillian never mentioned anything. It wasn't like she *shared* things with me. I thought I'd made that clear."

"Perfectly clear, several times. But some questions have to be asked, even if I'm ninety-nine percent sure what the answer's going to be."

"Okay. Anything else?"

"Did Jillian ever ask you or your husband to buy her an expensive car?"

"There was hardly anything Jillian didn't demand at some point, so I suppose she must have. On the other hand, she made it clear from the time she was twelve that Withrow and I were irrelevant to her happiness, that she could always find a rich man to give her whatever she wanted, so as far as she was concerned, we could go fuck ourselves." She paused, perhaps savoring the shock value of her observations. "I'm on my way out. Any more questions?"

"That's it for now, Mrs. Perry. Thank you for your time."

Like Sheridan Kline the night before, Val Perry hung up without bothering to say good-bye. Whatever it was that Gurney was contributing to the investigation of her daughter's murder, it clearly wasn't what she'd been hoping for.

At 9:50 A.M. he pulled in to the parking lot of the fortresslike state police facility where his 10:00 A.M. meeting was to take place. During the minute or so that he was searching for a space, his phone rang twice. The first was a voice call, the second a text message. He was looking forward to at least one of them being from Rebecca Holdenfield.

As soon as he'd parked, he took out his phone and checked the text message first. The source was a cell number with a Manhattan area code.

As he read the message, a flood of fear rose from his gut into his chest.

ARE YOU THINKING ABOUT MY GIRLS? THEY'RE THINKING ABOUT YOU.

He reread it, then reread it again. He looked at the originating number. The fact that the sender hadn't bothered to block it surely meant it was assigned to an untraceable prepaid phone. But it also meant he could send a reply message.

After dismissing the expressions of fury and bravado that came

to mind, he decided on three unemotional little words: TELL ME
MORE.

As he pressed "send," he noted that the time was 9:59. He hurried into the building.

When he arrived in the bleak institutional conference room, the
six chairs at the oblong table were already taken. The closest thing
to a greeting he received was Hardwick pointing at a handful of
folding chairs leaning against the wall by the coffee urn. Rodriguez,
Anderson, and Blatt ignored him. Gurney could imagine their un-
enthusiastic reactions to the DA's artful nonsense about controlling
the loose cannon by inviting him to their meetings.

Sergeant Wigg, a wiry redhead familiar to Gurney as the efficient evidence-team coordinator from the Mellery affair, was sitting
at the far end of the table studying the screen of her laptop—
exactly the way he'd remembered her. Her main agenda would
be the pursuit of factual certainty and logical coherence. Gurney
opened his folding chair and placed it at the end of the table facing
her. It was 10:05 on the wall clock.

Sheridan Kline frowned at his watch. "Okay, people. We're running a little late. I've got a tight schedule today. Maybe we could
start with anything new, significant progress, promising directions?"

Rodriguez cleared his throat.

"Dave's got some news," interjected Hardwick, "a peculiar thing
at the crime scene. Might make a good way to kick off the meeting."

Kline's eyes widened. "What now?"

Gurney had intended to wait until later in the meeting to bring
up the problem, in the hope that some piece of information along
the way might cast light on it. But now that Hardwick was forcing
the issue, it would be awkward to delay it.

"We're imagining that after killing Jillian, Flores went out
through the woods to the spot where we found the machete, is that
right?" said Gurney.

Rodriguez adjusted his steel-rimmed glasses. *"Imagining?* I'd
say we have conclusive evidence to that effect."

Gurney sighed. "Problem is, we have some video data that
doesn't support that hypothesis."

Kline went into rapid-blinking mode. "Video data?"

Gurney painstakingly explained how the continuous visibility of the tree trunk in the reception video proved that Flores could not have taken the necessary route through the woods, since anyone taking such a route would have to pass between the camera in that corner of the property and the tree, and he would have to appear, albeit fleetingly, in the picture.

Rodriguez was frowning like a man who suspected he was being tricked but didn't know how. Anderson was frowning like a man trying to stay awake. Wigg looked up from her laptop screen, which Gurney interpreted as a sign of high interest.

"So he went around the long way, in back of the tree," said Blatt. "I don't see the problem."

"The problem, Arlo, is the terrain. I'm sure you've checked it out?"

"What terrain problem are you talking about?"

"The ravine. In order to get from the cottage to the place the machete was found without walking in front of that tree would require someone to go straight back from the cottage, then slide down a long, steep slope with a lot of loose stones, then travel another five hundred feet on the rocky, uneven bottom of the ravine to get to the first place where there's any possibility of climbing back out. And even there the loose stones and dirt make it no easy thing. Not to mention that the point at which you get back on level ground is nowhere near the place where the machete was found."

Blatt sighed as though he were already aware of all this and it made no difference. "Just because it wasn't easy doesn't mean he didn't do it."

"Another problem is the time it would take."

"Meaning?" asked Kline.

"I checked out that area pretty carefully. Going via the ravine route to the machete site would just take too damn long. I don't think he'd want to be scrambling around back there when the body was discovered and people started swarming all over the place. Plus, there are two bigger problems. One: Why make it so god-awfully difficult, when he could have ditched the machete anywhere? Two—and this is pretty much the clincher: The scent trail follows the route in front of the tree, not behind it."

"Wait a second," said Rodriguez. "Aren't you contradicting yourself? You're saying that all those factors prove that Flores took the route in front of the tree, but the video proves he didn't. What on earth does that add up to?"

"An equation with a serious flaw," said Gurney, "but I'll be damned if I can see what it is."

For the next hour and a half, the group questioned him about the reliability of the video's time code, the potential for dropped frames, the position of the cherry tree in relation to the cottage and the machete and the ravine. They retrieved the crime-scene sketches from the master case file, passed them around the room, studied them. They went off on brief tangents about the fabled talents and accomplishments of K-9 teams. They debated the alternative scenarios for Flores's disappearance after depositing the murder weapon, for Kiki Muller's possible involvement as an accessory after the fact, and when and why she'd been killed. They pursued a few speculative notions concerning the psychopathology of cutting off a victim's head. At the end of it all, however, the basic puzzle seemed no closer to solution.

"So," said Rodriguez, summing up the central conundrum as simply as anyone could, "according to Dave Gurney, we can be absolutely certain of two things. First, Hector Flores had to pass in front of the cherry tree. Second, he couldn't have."

"A very interesting situation," said Gurney, feeling the electricity in the contradiction.

"This might be a good time to take a short lunch break," said the captain, who seemed to be feeling more frustration than electricity.

Chapter 52

The Flores factor

L unch was not a social occasion, which was fine with Gurney, who was about as far from being a social animal as a man could be and still be married. Instead of gravitating to the cafeteria, everyone scattered for the allotted half hour to commune with BlackBerrys and laptops.

He might have been happier, however, with thirty minutes of macho camaraderie than he was sitting alone on a chilly bench outside the state police fortress, absorbing the latest text message he found on his phone—evidently a response to his "Tell me more" request.

It said, YOU'RE SUCH AN INTERESTING MAN, I SHOULD HAVE KNOWN MY DAUGHTERS WOULD ADORE YOU. IT WAS SO GOOD OF YOU TO COME TO THE CITY. NEXT TIME THEY WILL COME TO YOU. WHEN? WHO CAN SAY? THEY WANT IT TO BE A SURPRISE.

Gurney stared at the words, even as they slammed his mind back to the unsettling smiles of those young women, back to the pale Montrachet lifted in a toast, back to the looming black wall of his amnesia.

He toyed with the idea of sending a message that began, "Dear Saul . . ." But he decided to keep his knowledge of the identity of Jykynstyl's impersonator to himself, at least for now. He didn't know how much that card might be worth, and he didn't want to play it before he understood the game. Besides, holding on to it gave him, in a minuscule way, a feeling of power. Like carrying a penknife in a bad neighborhood.

. . .

By the time he reentered the conference room, he was desperate to get his mind back on the Perry case. Kline, Rodriguez, and Wigg were already seated. Anderson was approaching the table, focused fiercely on a coffee cup so full that it made walking a challenge. Blatt was at the urn, tilting it forward to extract a final black trickle. Hardwick was missing.

Rodriguez looked at his watch. "It's time, people. Some of us are here, some of us aren't, but that's their problem. Time for a status report on the family interviews. Bill, you're up."

Anderson set his coffee on the table with the concentration of a man defusing a bomb. "Okay," he said. He sat, opened a file folder, and began examining and rearranging its contents. "Okay. Here's where we are. We started with a master list of all graduates for all twenty years Mapleshade has been in operation, and then we narrowed that to a list of graduates from the past five years. Five years ago is when the focus of the place changed from a general adolescent population with behavioral problems to female adolescent sex abusers."

"Convicted offenders?" asked Kline.

"No. All private interventions through family members, therapists, doctors. Mapleshade's population is basically warped sicko kids whose families are trying to keep them out of the juvie court system or just get them the hell out of town, out of the house, before they get caught doing what they're doing. The parents send them to Mapleshade, pay the tuition, and hope that Ashton solves the problem."

"And does he?"

"Hard to say. The families won't talk about it, so all we have to go by is a cross-check of graduate names against the national sex-offender database to see if any of them got tangled up with the legal system as adults since leaving Mapleshade. So far that isn't turning up much. A couple from the graduating classes of four and five years ago, none from the past three years. Hard to say what that means."

Kline shrugged. "Could mean that Ashton knows what he's doing. Or it could just reflect the fact that abuse perpetrated by females is grossly underreported to the police and tends not to be prosecuted."

"How grossly?" asked Blatt.

"Excuse me?"

"How grossly underreported and underprosecuted do you think it is?"

Kline leaned back in his chair, looking annoyed at what he obviously considered a distraction. His tone was stiff, academic, impatient. "Some data suggests that approximately twenty percent of all women and ten percent of all men were sexually abused as children, and that the perpetrator was female in about ten percent of the total cases. Bottom line, we're talking about millions of instances of sexual abuse and hundreds of thousands of instances in which the perp was female. But you know as well as I do, there's always been a double standard—a reluctance by families to report mothers, sisters, and baby-sitters to the police, a reluctance by law enforcement to take abuse accusations against young women seriously, a reluctance by courts to convict them. Society can't quite seem to accept the reality of female sexual predators like we accept the reality of male predators. But some studies suggest that a lot of men convicted of rape were sexually abused by females when they were children." Kline shook his head, hesitated. "Jesus, I could tell you stories from right here in this county—cases that come into family court through social services. You know about this stuff—mothers pimping out their own kids, selling porno videos of them having sex with each other. Jesus. And what finally works its way into the legal system is just a fraction of what's going on. But you get my point. Enough said, okay? We should get back to the agenda."

Blatt shrugged.

Rodriguez nodded in agreement. "Okay, Bill, let's move on with the phone-call report."

Anderson shuffled once more through his papers, which were spreading out over a larger area of the table. "The addresses, phone numbers, and other contact information we used were the most recent on file. The number of graduates within the five-year target period is a hundred and fifty-two. Average is about thirty per year. Of the hundred and fifty-two, we think we have currently valid contact information for a hundred and twenty-six. Initial calls have been placed to all hundred and twenty-six. Of those calls, forty resulted in immediate contact, with either the graduate herself or a family member. Of the remaining eighty-six for whom we left messages, twelve had gotten back to us as of nine forty-five this morning."

"That makes fifty-two live contacts," said Kline quickly. "What's the bottom line?"

"Hard to say." Anderson sounded like everything in his life was hard.

"Jesus, Lieutenant . . ."

"What I mean is, the results are mixed." He fished another sheet of paper out of his pile. "Out of the fifty-two, we spoke directly to the graduate herself in eleven instances. No problem there, right? I mean, if we spoke to them, they're not missing."

"How about the other forty-one?"

"In twenty-nine instances, the individual we spoke to—parent, spouse, sibling, roommate, significant other—claimed to know the location of the graduate and to be in contact with her."

Kline was keeping a running tally on a pad. "And the other twelve?"

"One told us her daughter had died in an automobile accident. One was extremely vague, probably high on something, didn't seem to know much of anything. One other claimed to know the exact whereabouts of the subject but refused to provide any further information."

Kline scribbled something on his pad. "And the other nine?"

"The other nine—all parents or stepparents—said they had no idea where their daughter was."

There was a speculative silence in the room, broken by Gurney. "How many of those disappearances began with an argument about a car?"

Anderson consulted his notes, frowning at them as though they were the cause of his weariness. "Six."

"Wow," said Kline with a soft little whistle. "And that's in addition to the ones Ashton and the Liston girl already told Gurney about?"

"Right."

"Jesus. So the total is close to a dozen. And there are still a hell of a lot of families we haven't spoken to yet. Wow. Anyone want to comment on this?"

"I think we owe a thank-you to Dave Gurney!" said Hardwick, who had slipped into the room unnoticed. He glanced at Rodriguez. "If he hadn't nudged us in this direction . . ."

"Nice you could find time to join us," said the captain.

"Let's not get carried away with crazy theories," said Anderson glumly. "There's still no evidence of abduction and no evidence of any other related crime. We could be overreacting. All this might be nothing more than a few rebellious kids cooking up a little scheme together."

"Dave?" said Kline, ignoring Anderson. "You want to say anything at this juncture?"

"One question for Bill. What's the pattern of distribution of the missing girls over the five graduating classes you looked at?"

Anderson gave his head a little shake as if he hadn't heard right. "Excuse me?"

"The girls who disappeared—which graduating classes were they in?"

Anderson sighed, went back to flipping through his pile of papers. "Whatever you need," he muttered, generalizing to no one in particular, "it's always on the bottom." He poked through at least a dozen pieces of paper before he fastened on one of them. "Okay . . . looks like . . . 2009 . . . 2008 . . . 2007 . . . 2006. And that's it. None from 2005. Earliest disappearances, if you want to call them that, were from the May 2006 graduating class."

"So, all within the past four years," concluded Kline. "Or, actually, the past three and a half years."

"So what?" said Blatt, shrugging. "What's that supposed to mean?"

"For one thing," suggested Gurney, "it means that the disappearances began occurring shortly after Hector Flores arrived on the scene."

Chapter 53

Game changer

Kline turned toward Gurney. "That ties in with what Ashton's assistant told you. Didn't she say that the two graduates she couldn't get in touch with had gotten interested in Flores when he was working on the grounds at Mapleshade?"

"Yes."

"This is the damnedest thing," Kline went on excitedly. "Let's assume for a minute that Flores is the key to everything—that once we figure out what brought him here, we'll understand everything else. We'll understand Jillian Perry's murder, Kiki Muller's murder, how and why he hid the machete where he did, why the camera didn't pick him up, the disappearance of God only knows how many Mapleshade graduates . . ."

"That last thing could be a harem thing," said Blatt.

"A what?" said Kline.

"Like Charlie Manson."

"You're saying he might have been looking for followers? For impressionable young women?"

"For female sex maniacs. That's what Mapleshade's all about, right?"

Gurney looked at Rodriguez to see how he might react to Blatt's comment in light of the situation with his daughter, but if he felt anything, he was hiding it under a thoughtful scowl.

Kline's mental computer seemed to be back in high gear, as he presumably weighed the media benefits of trying and convicting his very own Manson. He tried to build on Blatt's idea. "So you're

imagining that Flores had a little commune tucked away somewhere, and he talked these women into leaving home, covering
their tracks, and going there?"

He turned to the captain, seemed deterred by the scowl, and addressed Hardwick instead. "You have any thoughts on that?"

Hardwick responded with the ironic leer. "I was thinking Jim
Jones myself. Charismatic leader with a congregation of nubile
acolytes."

"The hell is Jim Jones?" asked Blatt.

Kline answered. "Jonestown. The massacre-suicide thing. Cya-
nide in the Kool-Aid. Wiped out nine hundred people."

"Oh, yeah, the Kool-Aid." Blatt grinned. "Right, Jonestown. Totally fucked up."

Hardwick raised a cautionary finger. "Beware of men who invite you to places in the jungle they've named after themselves."

The captain's scowl was reaching thunderstorm intensity.

"Dave?" said Kline. "You have any ideas about Flores's grand
plan?"

"The problem with the commune thing is that Flores lived on
Ashton's property. If he was gathering these women and stashing
them somewhere, it would have to be nearby. I don't think that's
what it was about."

"What, then?"

"I think it's about what he told us it's about. 'For all the reasons
I have written.' "

"And those reasons add up to what?"

"Revenge."

"For?"

"If we take the Edward Vallory prologue seriously, for some
major sexual offense."

It was clear that Kline loved conflict. So it didn't surprise Gurney that the next opinion he solicited was from Anderson.

"Bill?"

The man shook his head. "Revenge usually takes the form of
a physical attack, broken bones, murder. In all these so-called disappearances there isn't even a hint of that." He leaned back in

his chair. "Not a single *hint* of it. I think we need to take a more evidence-based approach." He smiled, seemingly pleased with this neat summation.

Kline's gaze settled on Sergeant Wigg, whose own gaze was, as always, on her computer screen. "Robin, anything you want to add?"

She answered immediately, without looking up. "Too many things don't make sense. There's bad data somewhere in the equation."

"What kind of bad data?"

Before she could respond, the conference room's door opened and a lean woman who could have inspired a Grant Wood painting stepped into the room. Her gray eyes settled on the captain.

"Sorry to interrupt, sir." Her voice sounded like it was sharpened by the same cold winds as her face. "There's been a significant development."

"Come in," commanded Rodriguez. "And close the door."

She closed it, then stood as rigidly as an army private awaiting permission to speak.

Rodriguez seemed pleased by her formality. "All right, Gerson, what is it?"

"We've been informed that one of the young women on our call-and-locate list was the victim of a homicide three months ago."

"*Three months ago?*"

"Yes, sir."

"You have the specifics?"

"Yes, sir."

"Go ahead."

Her expression was as stiff as the starched collar of her shirt. "Name, Melanie Strum. Age eighteen. Graduated May first of this year from Mapleshade Academy. Last seen by her mother and stepfather in Scarsdale, New York, on May sixth. Her body was recovered from the basement of a mansion in Palm Beach, Florida, on June twelfth."

Rodriguez grimaced. "Cause of death?"

Gerson's lips tightened.

"Cause of death?" he repeated.

"Her head was cut off. Sir."

Rodriguez stared at Gerson. "How did this information come to us?"

"Through our outgoing calling process. Melanie Strum's name was on the list subset assigned to me. I made the call."

"Who did you speak to?"

She hesitated. "May I get my notes, sir?"

"Quickly, if you don't mind."

During the minute she was gone, the only person who spoke was Kline. "This could be it," he said with an excited smile. "This could be the breakthrough."

Anderson made a face like a man with a sore on the inside of his lip. Hardwick looked intensely interested. Wigg was inscrutable. Gurney was less disturbed than he would have been comfortable admitting. He told himself that his lack of shock or sadness was due to the fact that he had from the beginning assumed that the missing girls were dead. (On occasion, when he was alone and exhausted, some inner defense system would be breached and he would see himself as a man so emotionally disconnected from the lives of others, so lopsidedly devoted to his puzzle-solving agenda, that he hardly qualified as a member of the human family at all. However, that troubling vision would pass with a good night's sleep, after which he would rationalize his lack of feeling as the normal by-product of a law-enforcement career.)

Gerson stepped back into the room, carrying a flip-top notepad. Her brown hair was pulled back severely into a tight ponytail, giving her features a skull-like immobility.

"Captain, I have the information on the Strum call."

"Go ahead."

She consulted her pad. "The phone was answered by Roger Strum, Melanie's stepfather. When I explained the purpose of the call, he expressed confusion, then anger at the fact that we didn't already know that Melanie was dead. His wife, Dana Strum, joined the conversation on the extension. They were upset. They provided the following facts: Acting on a tip, the Palm Beach police had entered the home of Jordan Ballston and discovered Melanie's body in a basement freezer. The police——"

Kline interrupted. "Jordan Ballston, the hedge-fund guy?"

"There was no specific mention of a hedge fund, but in my follow-up call to the Palm Beach PD, they did say Ballston lived in a multi-million-dollar mansion."

"The fucking freezer?" muttered Blatt, as though food-contamination concerns were making him queasy.

"Okay," said Rodriguez, "keep going."

"Mr. and Mrs. Strum mostly went on about how outraged they were that Ballston was out on bail. Who was he paying off? Did he have the judge in his pocket? Remarks like that. Mr. Strum indicated that if Ballston managed to buy himself out of this, he would per-sonally 'put a bullet in the bastard's head.' He repeated that several times. I was able to ascertain that they did have an argument with Melanie on May sixth, the day she left home, about a car she wanted them to buy for her—a Porsche Boxster that costs forty-seven thou-sand dollars. They say that she flew into a rage when they refused, said she hated them, didn't want to live with them anymore, didn't want to speak to them anymore. She said she was going to live with a friend. The following morning she was gone. The next time they saw her was when they ID'd the body in the Palm Beach morgue."

"You said the local cops were acting on a tip when they found the body," said Gurney. "Do we know anything more about that?"

She glanced at Rodriguez, apparently to confirm Gurney's right to ask questions.

"Go ahead," said the captain, with obvious mixed feelings.

She hesitated. "I told the chief investigating officer in Palm Beach that we had an interest in the case and we'd like as much in-formation as possible. He said he'd be willing to talk to the person in charge of whatever investigation we had going on up here. He said he'd be available for the next half hour."

After a few minutes of waffling on the pros and cons, the DA and the captain agreed that the call, with whatever information ex-change would occur, would be a net plus all around. The conference room's landline phone was moved to the center of the table around which they were all seated. Gerson dialed the direct number she'd been given by the detective in Palm Beach. She explained to him briefly who was in the room, then pushed the speakerphone button.

Rodriguez deferred to Kline, who provided the names and

titles of the people at the table and described the case as a possible missing-persons investigation in its earliest stages.

The faint southern accent of the man on the other end made him sound like he might be a native Floridian, a rare breed in that state and almost unheard-of in Palm Beach. "Being alone in my office here, I feel kind of outnumbered. I'm Detective Lieutenant Darryl Becker. I understand from the officer I spoke to earlier that you folks would like to know more about the Strum murder."

"We sure would appreciate knowing as much as you can tell us, Darryl," said Kline, who seemed to be absorbing and reflecting Becker's drawl. "One question we have right off the bat here—what kind of tip was it that led you fellas to the body?"

"Not a particularly voluntary one."

"How so?"

"The gentleman who offered the information was not what you'd call a public-spirited citizen helping out the forces of good. He acquired his information in a somewhat compromising manner."

"The hell's he talking about?" murmured Blatt, not quite under his breath.

"How so?" repeated Kline.

"Man's a burglar. A professional burglar. That's what he does for a living."

"He was caught in Ballston's house?"

"No, sir, he wasn't. He was apprehended emerging from another house a week after breaking into the Ballston place. Burglar's name happens to be Edgar Rodriguez—no relative of your captain there, I'm sure."

A snorting one-syllable laugh burst out of Blatt.

The captain's jaw muscles bulged. The remark seemed to anger him far out of proportion to its mindlessness.

"Let me guess," said Kline. "Edgar was looking at serious prison time, and he offered to trade some information about Ballston's basement, something he'd seen there, for a more lenient approach to his situation?"

"That would be it in a nutshell, Mr. Kline. By the way, how do you spell that?"

"Excuse me?"

"Your name. How do you spell your name?"

"K-L-I-N-E."

"Ah, with a *K.*" Becker sounded disappointed. "Thought it might be like Patsy."

"Excuse me?"

"Patsy Cline. Not important. Sorry for the diversion. Go ahead with your questions."

It took Kline a moment to get back on track. "So . . . what he told you was sufficient for a warrant?"

"It was indeed."

"And when you exercised that warrant, you found what?"

"Melanie Strum. In two pieces. Wrapped in aluminum foil. In the bottom of a freezer chest. Underneath a hundred pounds of chicken breasts. And a fair amount of frozen broccoli."

Hardwick produced a snorting laugh of his own, louder than Blatt's.

Kline looked baffled. "Why was your burglar unwrapping aluminum foil packages at the bottom of a freezer?"

"He said it's the first place he always looks. He said people think it's the *last* place a burglar would look, so that's where they put their valuable stuff. He said you want to find the diamonds, look in the freezer. He thought it was pretty funny, all those people thinking they had a bright idea, thinking they were going to fool him, thinking they were smarter than he was. Had a good laugh about it."

"So he went to the freezer and started unwrapping the body, and—"

"Actually," Becker interrupted, "he started unwrapping the head."

Various guttural exclamations of disgust around the room were followed by a silence.

"You gentlemen still there?" There was a touch of amusement in Becker's voice.

"We're here," said Rodriguez coldly. There was another silence.

"You gentlemen have any more questions, or does that pretty much wrap up your missing-person case?"

"I have a question," said Gurney. "How'd you make the positive ID?"

"We got a DNA near hit on the sex-offender segment of the NCIC database."

"Meaning a close family member?"

"Yep. Turned out to be Melanie's biological heroin-addict father, Damian Clark, who'd been convicted of rape, aggravated sexual assault, sexual abuse of a minor, and several other unpleasant offenses about ten years ago. We tracked down the mother, who had divorced her rapist husband and remarried a man by the name of Roger Strum. She came down and ID'd the body. We also took a DNA sample from her and got a first-degree family confirmation like we did with the biological father. So there's no doubt about the identity of the murdered girl. Any other questions?"

"You have any doubt about the identity of the murderer?" asked Gurney.

"Not a lot. There's just something about Mr. Ballston."

"The Strums seem pretty upset that he's out on bail."

"Not as upset as I am."

"He managed to convince the judge he's not a flight risk?"

"What he managed to do was post a ten-million-dollar bail bond and agree to what amounts to house arrest. He has to remain within the confines of his estate here in Palm Beach."

"You don't sound happy with that."

"Happy? Did I mention that the ME concluded that before she was decapitated, Melanie Strum had been forcibly raped maybe a dozen times and that virtually every inch of her body had been lacerated with a razor blade? Am I happy that the man who did that is sitting next to his million-dollar swimming pool in his five-hundred-dollar designer sunglasses while the most expensive law firm in the state of Florida and the fanciest public-relations outfit in New York City are doing everything possible to position him as the innocent victim of an incompetent and corrupt police department? Are you asking me if I'm happy about that?"

"So it would be an understatement to say he's not cooperating with the investigation?"

"Yes, sir. Yes indeed. That would be an understatement. Mr. Ballston's attorneys have made it clear that their client will not say one word to anyone in law enforcement about the bogus case fabricated against him."

"Before he decided to say nothing, did he offer any explanation for the presence of a murdered woman in his freezer?"

"Only that he has had frequent work done on his home, has had many household employees, and Lord only knows how many people might have had access to his basement—not to mention the burglar himself."

Kline looked around the room, his hands palms up in a questioning gesture, but no one had anything to add. "Okay," he said. "Detective Becker, I want to thank you for your help. And for your candor. And good luck with your case."

There was a pause. Then the soft drawl. "Just wondering . . . if you gentlemen might know anything about this case up there on your end that could be useful to us down here?"

Kline and Rodriguez looked at each other. Gurney could see the wheels turning as they weighed the potential risks and rewards of openness. The captain finally offered a glum little shrug, deferring the decision to the DA.

"Well," said Kline, making it all sound iffier than it really was, "we think it's possible we may be looking for more than one mis-per."

"Oh?" There was a silence, suggesting that Becker was either taking time to absorb this or wondering why it hadn't been mentioned sooner. When he spoke again, his voice had lost its softness. "Exactly how many are we talking about?"

Chapter 54

Unpleasant stories

On the long drive home, Gurney was obsessed by the situation in Palm Beach, by the image of Jordan Ballston beside his pool, by the desire to get to the man and get to the bottom of this bizarre case. But getting to the man would not be easy. Having insulated himself behind a wall of legal and PR spokespeople, Ballston sure as hell was not about to sit down for a friendly chat about the body in his basement.

Just outside the little village of Musgrave, Gurney pulled in to a Stewart's convenience store for coffee. It was close to 3:00 P.M., and he was on the verge of caffeine withdrawal.

As he was getting back into his car with a steaming sixteen-ounce container, his phone was ringing.

It was Hardwick. "So what do you think, Davey? Whole new ball game?"

"Same game. New camera angle."

"You see something you didn't see before?"

"An opportunity. Just not sure how to get at it."

"Ballston? You think he's going to tell you anything? Good luck!"

"Only key we've got, Jack. Got to find a way to turn it."

"You think he's somehow behind this whole thing?"

"I don't know enough yet to think anything. I can't imagine any way he could have killed Jillian Perry. But I'll say it again—he's the only key we've got. He's got a real name, a real business and personal background, and his ass is planted at a real address. Compared to him, Hector Flores is a ghost."

"Okay, ace, you let us know when that genius brain of yours

figures out how to turn the key. But that's not why I called. Some more stuff on Karnala and its owners just drifted in."

"Kline told me you discovered it wasn't really a clothing company?"

Hardwick cleared his throat. "Tip of the proverbial iceberg. Or more like the tip of an insane asylum. We still don't know for sure what business Karnala is in, but I got some data on the Skards. Definitely not people you want to fuck with."

"Hold on a second, Jack." Gurney opened his coffee container and took a long swallow. "Okay, talk to me."

"We're getting this in bits and pieces. Before they came to the U.S. and went international, the Skards originally operated out of Sardinia, which is part of Italy. Italy's got three separate law-enforcement agencies, each with its own records, plus local stuff, and then there's Interpol, which has access to some of it but not all of it. Plus, I'm getting snatches of stuff that's not in any file—old rumors, hearsay, whatever—from a guy at Interpol I've done some favors for. So what I have is disconnected chunks, some of it unique, some of it repetitive, some of it contradictory. Some reliable, some not, but no way of knowing which is which."

Gurney waited. It never helped to tell Hardwick to skip the preamble.

"At the visible level, the Skards are high-end international investors. Resorts, casinos, thousand-dollar-a-night hotels, companies that build million-dollar yachts, shit like that. But the betting is that the money they use to acquire those legal assets comes from somewhere else."

"From a nastier enterprise they're concealing?"

"Right, and the Skards are very effective concealers. In the whole bloody history of the family, there has been only one arrest—for an atrocious assault ten years ago—and not a single conviction. So there are no real criminal files, almost nothing on paper. Rumors keep surfacing that they're into very-high-end prostitution, sex slavery, extreme S&M pornography, extortion. But none of that can be verified. They also have very aggressive legal representation that pounces with an instant libel suit when anything remotely critical appears in the press. There aren't even any photographs of them."

"What happened to the mug shot from the assault arrest?"

"Mysteriously disappeared."

"Nobody has ever testified against these guys?"

"People who might know something, people who might be persuaded to say something, even just people who happen to be in the general vicinity of the Skards in times of stress, have a hell of a time staying alive. The few people who cooperated with media stories about the Skards, even anonymously, disappeared within days. The Skards have only one response to trouble—they erase it, totally, without compunction, and without a hint of concern for collateral damage. Perfect example: According to my Interpol contact, about ten years ago Giotto Skard, presumed head of the family, had a business disagreement with an Israeli real-estate developer. After a meeting in a small Tel Aviv nightclub during which Giotto appeared to agree to the Israeli's terms, he said good-night, stepped outside, barred the exits, and burned the place down. He managed to kill the real-estate developer, along with fifty-two other people who just happened to be in there."

"Their organization has never been penetrated?"

"Never."

"Why not?"

"They have no organization in the usual sense."

"What do you mean?"

"The Skards are the Skards. A biological family. The only way in is by birth or marriage—and right off the bat I can't think of any female undercovers devoted enough to the job to marry into a pack of mass murderers."

"Big family?"

Hardwick cleared his throat again. "Surprisingly small. Of the oldest generation, only one of three brothers is believed to still be alive. Giotto Skard. He may have killed the other two. But no one will say that. Not even whisper it. Not even as a joke. Giotto has—or maybe had—three sons. No one knows how many of them are still alive, or exactly how old they are, or where they might be. As I said, small as they are in numbers, the Skards operate internationally, so it's presumed that the sons are in various places around the world where Skard interests need to be looked after."

"Wait a second. If only family members are involved, what do they do for muscle?"

"The word is, they take care of problems themselves. The word is, they're very prompt and very efficient. The word is, the Skards over the years have personally eliminated at least two hundred human obstacles to the family's business objectives, not counting the nightclub massacre."

"Nice people. With three sons, presumably Giotto had a wife?"

"Oh, indeed he did. Tirana Magdalena—the only member of the whole rotten Skard menagerie about which anything is actually known. And maybe the only person on earth who ever seriously inconvenienced Giotto and lived to tell it."

"How'd she manage that?"

"She was the daughter of the head of an Albanian mafia family. I should say she *is* his daughter—she's still alive, somewhere in her mid-sixties, in an institution for the criminally insane. The Albanian don is about ninety. Not that Giotto would be afraid of a mafia don. The word is, it was purely a business decision on Giotto's part to let his wife live. He didn't want to have to waste time and money killing the angry Albanians who would try to avenge her death."

"How the hell do you know all this?"

"I don't, really. Like I said, it's mostly rumors from the guy at Interpol. Maybe mostly bullshit. But it sounds good to me."

"Hold on. A second ago you said she was the only member of the Skard family about which anything is actually known. *Known,* you said."

"Ah. But I haven't gotten yet to the part that's *known.* I was saving that till the end."

Chapter 55

Tirana Magdalena Skard

“Tirana Magdalena was Adnan Zog's only daughter.”

“Zog being the don?”

“Zog being the don, or whatever they call that exalted position in Albania. Anyway, his daughter was drop-dead gorgeous.”

“How do you know that?”

“Her beauty was the stuff of legend. At least in the seedy underbelly of Eastern Europe. At least according to my Deep Throat contact at Interpol. Also, there are photographs. Many photographs. Unlike the Skards, the Zogs, particularly Tirana Magdalena, had no problem with fame. In addition to being gorgeous, she was also high-strung, weird, artsy, and obsessed with wanting to be a dancer. Papa Zog didn't give a shit about what she wanted. He just saw her as something of potential value. So when the ambitious young Giotto Skard took an interest in the sixteen-year-old Tirana at the same time as he was negotiating a business alliance with Zog, Zog tossed her in as part of the deal. Probably saw it as a win-win. Zog gives Skard something Skard values that costs Zog nothing, plus he gets rid of his nutty, pain-in-the-ass daughter. This makes him and Giotto like blood brothers without even having to prick their thumbs.”

“Very efficient,” said Gurney.

“Very efficient. So now this wacky sixteen-year-old who has been raised by a lunatic Albanian murderer is married to a lunatic Sardinian murderer. And all she wants to do is dance. But all Giotto wants is sons—a lot of sons. Good for the business. So she starts having Giotto's babies, which turn out to be all sons, just like he wants.

Tiziano, Raffaello, Leonardo. Which makes him pretty happy. But all Tirana wants to do is dance. And each kid is making her a little crazier. By the time she has number three, she's ready for the loony bin. Then she makes her big discovery. Coke! She discovers that snorting coke is almost as good as dancing. She snorts a lot of coke. When she can't steal any more money from Giotto—a very dangerous activity, by the way—she starts fucking the local coke dealer. When Giotto finds out, he chops him up."

"Chops him up?"

"Yeah. Literally. Into little pieces. To make a statement."

"Impressive."

"Right. So then Giotto decides to move the family to America. Better for everyone, he says. What he really means is, better for business. Business is all Giotto cares about. Once they're over here, Tirana starts fucking American coke dealers. Giotto chops them up. Everyone she fucks gets chopped up. She's fucking so many guys he can hardly keep up with it. Finally he kicks her out, along with son number three, Leonardo, who is now about ten years old and either gay or schizo or just too fucking oddball for Giotto to deal with. She takes the money Giotto gives her as a good-bye-and-get-lost present, and she opens a modeling agency for kids whose parents would love to get them into commercials, TV, whatever—offers acting and dancing classes to enhance their budding careers. Giotto meanwhile settles down with his two older sons to focus on their sex-and-extortion empire. Sounds like a happy ending for all concerned. But there was a flaw in the ointment."

"Fly."

"What?"

"A *fly* in the ointment, not a flaw."

"Fly, flaw, whatever. The problem with cokehead Tirana's modeling agency is that she's molesting the kids. Not only is she still fucking coke dealers, now she's fucking every ten-, eleven-, twelve-year-old boy she can get her hands on."

"Jesus. How did it end?"

"It ended with her being arrested and charged with about two dozen counts of sexual abuse, assault, sodomy, rape, you name it.

She ended up being committed to a state mental hospital, where she remains to this day."

"And her son?"

"By the time she was arrested, he was gone."

"Gone?"

"Either ran away or was taken back by his father or was spirited off through some kind of private adoption. Or, knowing the Skards, he could very well be dead. Giotto would never let sentimentality keep him from tying up a loose end."

Chapter 56

A matter of control

Halfway between his Stewart's stop and Walnut Crossing, Gurney's phone rang again. Rebecca Holdenfield's voice was smart, edgy—as reminiscent of the young Sigourney Weaver as were her face and hair. "So I guess you're not coming?"

"Beg pardon?"

"Don't you check your messages?"

He remembered. That morning there had been one text and one voice mail. He'd checked the text first—the message that had spun him off into a world of speculation about his brownstone blackout. He'd never checked the voice mail.

"Christ, I'm sorry, Rebecca. I'm running too damn fast. You expected me this afternoon?"

"It was your request in your voice mail to me. So I said fine, come."

"Any chance we could do it tomorrow? What's tomorrow, anyway?"

"Tuesday. And I'm jammed all day. How about Thursday? That's my next free time."

"Too far away. Can we talk now?"

"I'm free till five. Which means we have about ten minutes. What's the topic?"

"I've got a few: the effects of being raised by a promiscuous mother, the mind-set of women who sexually abuse children, the psychological weaknesses of male sex murderers ... and the behavior range of adult males under the influence of a Rohypnol cocktail."

After a two-second silence, she burst into laughter. "Sure. And in the time we have left after that, we can discuss the causes of divorce, ways to eliminate war, and—"

"Okay, okay, I get it. Pick the topic you think we have enough time to talk about."

"You planning on spiking your next martini with Rohypnol?"

"Hardly."

"Just an academic question, then?"

"Sort of."

"Hmm. Well, there's no standard range of behavior for intoxication in general. Different chemicals skew behavior in different directions. Cocaine, for example, tends to produce a heightened sexual drive. But if what you're asking is, are there limits to the behavior that a nonhallucinogenic disinhibitor will allow, the answer is yes and no. There's no specific limit that applies to everyone, but there are individual limits."

"Like what?"

"There's no way of knowing. The limitations on our behavior depend on the accuracy of our perceptions, the strength of our instinctive desires, and the strength of our fears. If the drug is a disinhibitor that removes our fear of consequences, then our behavior will reflect our desires and be limited mainly by pain, satisfaction, or exhaustion. We'll do whatever we would do in a world with no consequences, but not things we have no desire to do. Disinhibitors give free rein to one's existing impulses, but they don't manufacture impulses that are inconsistent with the underlying psychic structure of the individual. Am I answering your question?"

"Bottom line, give people a drug like that and they might act out their fantasies?"

"They might even do things they'd been afraid to fantasize about."

"I see," he said, feeling sick to his stomach. "Let me change the subject to something completely different. A recent Mapleshade graduate has turned up dead—a sex murder in Florida. Rape, torture, decapitation, body in the suspect's freezer."

"How long?" As usual, Holdenfield was unfazed by gory details—or adept at making it seem that way.

"What do you mean?"

"How long was the body in the freezer?"

"ME thought a couple of days, maybe. Why do you ask?"

"Just wondering what he was saving it for. It was a *he,* right?"

"Jordan Ballston, hotshot in the financial-derivatives business."

"Ballston, the super-rich guy? I remember reading about that. First-degree murder charge. But that was months ago."

"Right, but the identity of the victim was originally withheld from the media, and the connection to the other disappearances at Mapleshade was just discovered."

"You're sure there *is* a connection?"

"Hell of a coincidence if there isn't one."

"Do you guys get to interview Ballston?"

"Apparently not. He's hunkering down behind a thorny hedge of attorneys."

"Then what can I do for you?"

"Suppose I manage to get to him."

"How?"

"I don't know yet. Just suppose I do."

"Okay. I'm supposing. Now what?"

"What would he be most afraid of?"

"Surrounded by his thorny attorneys?" She clucked her tongue repeatedly, rapidly, making it sound like a finger-tapping accompaniment to fast thinking. "Not much . . . unless . . ."

"What?"

"Unless he thinks someone else knows what he's done, someone who might have an agenda in conflict with his own. That kind of situation would leave a gap in his span of control. Sadistic sex murderers are control freaks to the max, and the one thing that will blow a control freak's circuits is being at the mercy of someone else." She paused for a moment. "Do you have a way of contacting Ballston?"

"Not yet."

"Why do I have the feeling that you're about to come up with one?"

"I appreciate your confidence."

"I need to hang up now. Sorry I don't have more time. Just re-member, Dave, the more power he believes you have over him, the more likely he is to come apart."

"Thanks, Becca. I appreciate your help."

"I hope I didn't make it sound like it's going to be easy."

"Don't worry. 'Easy' is not what I'm imagining."

"Good. Keep me up to date, okay? And good luck!"

The same mental-overload factor that caused him to neglect that morning's phone message from Holdenfield kept him, for the rest of his trip home, oblivious to another spectacular mountain sunset. By the time he had turned off the county highway and driven up the winding road to his property, all that was left of it was a subdued wash of faded rose in the western sky, and even that he barely noticed.

At the transition area in front of his barn, where the town's dirt road faded into his narrower and grassier driveway, he pulled over to his mailbox, which was cantilevered out from a fence post. As he was about to open it, a little patch of yellow on the hillside ahead caught his eye. The patch of yellow was moving slowly along the arc of the path over the high pasture. He recognized it as Madeleine's light Windbreaker.

Because of the intervening ryegrass and milkweed, she was visible only from the waist up, but he imagined he could perceive the gentle rhythm of her steps. He sat and watched her until the trajectory of the path and the rolling contour of the field took her gradually out of sight, a solitary figure moving calmly into an obscuring ocean of tall grass.

He remained there awhile longer, gazing up at the deserted hillside, until all the color in the sky was gone, replaced by a gray as monotone as the note that registers the absence of a heartbeat. He blinked, found some dampness in his eyes, swiped at it with his knuckles, and drove the rest of the way up to the house.

He decided to take a shower in the hope that it might restore in him some sense of normalcy. As he stood in the heavy spray of hot water, its tingly massage relaxing his neck and shoulders, he let his mind drift into the sound: the soft roar of a summer downpour. For a strange second or two, his brain was filled with the pure and peaceful scent of rain. He scrubbed himself with soap and a rough sponge, rinsed, got out, and toweled himself dry.

Too drowsy now to dress, still warm from the shower, he pulled back the quilted cover on their bed and lay down on the cool sheet. For a wonderful minute, the whole world consisted of that cool sheet, grass-scented air wafting over him from an open window, imagined sunlight sparkling through the leaves of giant trees ... as he descended the free-associating staircase of dreams into a deep sleep.

He awoke in the dark with no sense of the time. A pillow had been placed under his head, and the quilt had been drawn up to his chin. He got up, turned on the bedside lamp, and checked the clock. It was 7:49 P.M. He put on the clothes he'd had on before his shower and went out to the kitchen. Something baroque was faintly audible on the stereo. Madeleine was sitting at the smaller of the room's two tables with a bowl of orange-colored soup and half a baguette, reading a book. She looked up as he entered the room.

She said, "I thought maybe you'd gone to bed for the night."

"Apparently not," he muttered. Finding his voice hoarse, he coughed to clear it.

Her eyes returned to her book. "If you feel like eating, there's carrot soup in the pot and a stir-fried chicken thing in the wok."

He yawned. "What are you reading?"

"The Natural History of Moths."

"History of what?"

She articulated the word as one might to a lip-reader. "Moths." She turned the page. "Was there any mail?"

"Mail? I ... I don't know. I think ... Oh, right, I was about to get it, and then I saw you up on the hill and got distracted."

"You've been distracted for a while."

"Is that a fact?" He immediately regretted his defensive tone, but not enough to admit it.

"You don't think so?"

He sighed nervously. "I suppose." He went to the pot on the stove and ladled out a bowl of soup.

"Is there anything you want to talk about?"

He delayed answering until he was seated across from her with his soup and the other half of the baguette. "There's a major development in the case. A former Mapleshade girl has turned up dead in Florida. Victim of a sex murderer."

Madeleine closed her book, stared at him. "So you're thinking . . . what?"

"It's possible that the other girls who've disappeared have ended up the same way."

"Murdered by the same person?"

"It's possible."

Madeleine studied his face as if unspoken information were written on it.

"What?" he asked.

"Is that what's on your mind?"

A rush of unease passed through his stomach. "That's part of it. Another part is that the police haven't been able to get a single word out of the man they've charged with the murder—nothing beyond a categorical denial. Meanwhile his law firm and PR firm are creating alternative scenarios to feed to the media—lots of innocent reasons that a woman's raped, tortured, and beheaded body might have been in his freezer."

"And you're thinking, if only you could sit down and talk to this monster . . ."

"I'm not saying that I'd get a confession, but . . ."

"But you'd do a better job than the locals?"

"That wouldn't be so difficult." He winced inwardly at his own arrogance.

Madeleine frowned. "It wouldn't be the first time the star detective rose to the challenge and deciphered the mystery."

He stared at her uncomfortably.

Again she seemed to be examining the message encoded in his expression.

"What?" he asked.

"I didn't say anything."

"But you're thinking something. What is it? Tell me."

She hesitated. "I thought you liked puzzles."

"I admit that I do. So what?"

"So why do you look so miserable?"

The question jarred him. "Maybe I'm just exhausted. I don't know." But he did know. The reason he felt as bad as he did was that he couldn't bring himself to tell her why he felt bad to begin with. His reluctance to reveal the full chagrin of being duped and the intensity of his worry over what may have happened during his period of amnesia had isolated him in a terrible way.

He shook his head, as if refusing the pleas of his better self, the small voice within that was begging him to lay the facts of the matter before this woman who loved him. His fear was so great that it blocked the very action that would have removed it.

Chapter 57

The plan

As strained as it often was, Gurney's relationship with Madeleine had always been the chief pillar of his stability. But that relationship depended on a degree of openness he felt incapable of at the moment.

With the desperation of a drowning man, he embraced his only other pillar, his detective identity, and attempted to channel all his energies into Solving the Crime.

The most productive next step in that process, he was convinced, would be a conversation with Jordan Ballston. He needed to devise a way to bring that about. Rebecca had insisted that fear would be the key to cracking the shell of the rich psycho, and Gurney had no reason to disagree. Nor did he have any reason to disagree with her warning that it wouldn't be easy.

Fear.

It was a subject with which Gurney had a raw, current, intimate familiarity. Perhaps that experience could be of some use. What exactly was it that frightened him so much? He retrieved the three alarming text messages and reread them carefully.

SUCH PASSIONS! SUCH SECRETS! SUCH WONDERFUL PHOTOGRAPHS!

ARE YOU THINKING ABOUT MY GIRLS? THEY'RE THINKING ABOUT YOU.

YOU'RE SUCH AN INTERESTING MAN, I SHOULD HAVE KNOWN MY DAUGHTERS WOULD ADORE YOU. IT WAS SO GOOD OF YOU TO COME TO THE CITY. NEXT TIME THEY WILL COME TO YOU. WHEN? WHO CAN SAY? THEY WANT IT TO BE A SURPRISE.

The words generated a sick, hollow feeling in his chest.

Such virulent threats wrapped in such airy banalities.

So nonspecific, yet so malignant.

So nonspecific. Yes, that was it. It brought to mind his favorite English professor's explanation of the emotional power of Harold Pinter: *The perils that strike the greatest terror in us are not those which have been spelled out but those that our imaginations conjure. We are chilled to the bone not by the lengthy rants of an angry man but by the menace in a placid voice.*

He remembered it because the truth of it had struck him immediately, and experience had reinforced it over the years. What we're able to imagine is always worse than what reality places before us. The greatest fear by far is the fear of what we imagine is lurking in the dark.

So perhaps the best way to panic Ballston would be to give him an opportunity to panic himself. A frontal attack would be rebuffed by his legal army. Gurney needed a back door through the fortifications.

Ballston's current defense strategy was a categorical denial of any knowledge of Melanie Strum dead or alive, plus the creation of an alternative hypothesis, involving the access other individuals had to his home, to explain the presence of her body. Such a strategy would collapse, disastrously for Ballston, if a prior link could be established between him and the girl. In the best possible outcome, the nature of that link would also explain how the murders of Melanie Strum, Jillian Perry, and Kiki Muller, as well as the disappearances of the other Mapleshade graduates, were connected. But whether it did or not, Gurney was sure that discovering Melanie's route to Ballston's basement freezer would be a giant step toward the final solution. And the possible exposure of that link would be Ballston's greatest fear.

The question was how to trigger that fear—how to use it as an entry point into Ballston's psyche, a way around the battlements manned by his lawyers. Was there a person, place, or thing the mention of which would open the door? Mapleshade? Jillian Perry? Kiki Muller? Hector Flores? Edward Vallory? Alessandro? Karnala Fashion? Giotto Skard?

And as hard as it would be to pick the magic name, the harder part would lie in managing whatever dialogue ensued—the Pinter-

esque art of implying without specifying, unnerving without providing details. The challenge would be to provide the dark space in
which Ballston could imagine the worst, the platform on which he
might hang himself.

Madeleine had gone in to bed. Gurney, however, was wide awake,
pacing the length of the big kitchen, on fire with possibilities, risk
evaluations, logistics. He narrowed the names of his potential door
openers to the three he thought most promising: Mapleshade,
Flores, Karnala.

Of those he finally put Karnala, by a millimeter, at the top of
the list. Because all the Mapleshade girls known to be missing had
appeared in near-pornographic Karnala Fashion ads, because Karnala did not seem to be in the business it pretended to be in, because Karnala was connected to the Skards, and the Skards were
rumored to be involved in a criminal sex enterprise, and Melanie
Strum's murder was a sex crime. In fact, the Edward Vallory dimension and Mapleshade's admissions policy suggested that everything
connected with the case so far was in some way a sex crime or the
result of a sex crime.

Gurney was aware that the logical chain back to Karnala was
less than perfect, but demanding perfect logic (much as the concept
appealed to him) did not lead to solutions, it led to paralysis. He'd
learned that the key question in police work, as in life, was not "Am
I *absolutely sure* of what I believe?" The question that mattered was
"Am I *sure enough to act* on that belief?"

In this case Gurney's answer was yes. He was willing to bet that
there was something about Karnala that would unnerve Jordan
Ballston. According to the old clock over the sideboard, it was just
after ten when he placed a call to the Palm Beach Police Department to get Ballston's unlisted number.

No one assigned to the Strum case was on duty that night, but
the desk sergeant was able to give him Darryl Becker's cell number.

Surprisingly, Becker picked up on the first ring.

Gurney explained what he wanted.

"Ballston's not talking to anybody," said Becker testily. "Communications go in and out through Markham, Mull & Sternberg, his
main law firm. Thought I'd made that clear."

"I may have a way of getting through to him."

"How?"

"I'm going to toss a bomb through his window."

"What kind of bomb?"

"The kind he'll want to talk to me about."

"This some kind of game, Gurney? I had a long day. I'd like some facts."

"You sure about that?"

Becker was silent.

"Look, if I can knock this scumbag off balance, that's a plus for everyone. Worst case, we're maybe back where we started. All you're giving me is a phone number, no official authorization to do anything, so if there's any fallout at all, which I don't think there will be, it doesn't land on you. In fact, I've already forgotten in advance where I got the number from."

There was another short silence, followed by a few clicks on a keypad, followed by Becker's voice reading off a number that began with a Palm Beach area code. Then the connection was broken.

Gurney spent the next several minutes picturing and then immersing himself in a simple version of the kind of layered undercover persona he advocated in his academy lectures—in this case a reptilian ice man, lurking under a thin veneer of civilized manners.

Once he was satisfied with his sense of the attitude and tone, he activated the ID blocker on his phone and made the call to the Palm Beach number. It went straight into voice mail.

A spoiled, imperious voice announced, *"This is Jordan. If you wish to receive a response, please leave a substantive message regarding the subject of your call."* He managed to imbue the *please* with a grating condescension that reversed its normal meaning.

Gurney spoke deliberately and a little awkwardly, as though he found the intricacies of polite speech a strange and difficult dance. He also added the subtlest hint of a Southern European accent. "The subject of my call is your relationship with Karnala Fashion, which I need to discuss with you as soon as possible. I'll call you back in approximately thirty minutes. Please be available to answer the phone, and I'll be more... *substantive*... at that time."

Gurney was making some major assumptions: that Ballston was

at home, as the stipulations of his bail arrangement required, that a man in his perilous position would be screening his calls and checking his messages obsessively, and that how he chose to handle the promised call thirty minutes later would reveal the nature of his involvement with Karnala.

Making one assumption was risky. Making three was crazy.

Chapter 58

Into action

At 10:58 P.M., Gurney made his second call. It was picked up after the third ring.

"This is Jordan." The live voice sounded stiffer, older than the one on the recorded greeting.

Gurney grinned. It appeared that *Karnala* was indeed the magic word. Having hit it on the first shot gave him a burst of adrenaline. He felt like he'd gained entry to a high-stakes tournament in which the challenge was to deduce the rules of the game from the behavior of your opponent. He closed his eyes and stepped into his snake-pretending-to-be-harmless persona.

"Hello, Jordan. How are you this evening?"

"Fine."

Gurney said nothing.

"What . . . what's this about?"

"What do you think?"

"What? Who am I speaking to?"

"I'm a police officer, Jordan."

"I have nothing to say to the police. That's been made clear by—"

Gurney broke in. "Not even about Karnala?"

There was a pause. "I don't know what you're talking about."

Gurney sighed, made a bored little sucking noise with his teeth.

"I have no idea what you're talking about," Ballston reiterated.

If he really didn't, thought Gurney, he'd have hung up by now. Or he never would have taken the call. "Well, Jordan, the thing is, if you had any information you were willing to share, perhaps something could be worked out to your advantage."

Ballston hesitated. "Look . . . uh, why don't you give me your name, Officer?"

"That's not a good idea."

"Sorry? I don't . . ."

"See, Jordan, this is a preliminary exploration here. You understand what I'm saying?"

"I'm not sure I do."

Gurney sighed again, as though speech itself were a burden. "No formal offer can be made without some indication that it would be seriously considered. A willingness to provide useful information about Karnala Fashion could result in a very different prosecutorial attitude toward your case, but we would need to feel a sense of cooperation from you before we discuss the possibilities. I'm sure you understand."

"No, I really don't." Ballston's voice was brittle.

"*No?*"

"I don't know what you're talking about. I never heard of Caramel Fashion, or whatever the name of it is. So it's impossible to tell you anything about it."

Gurney laughed softly. "Very good, Jordan. That's very good."

"I'm serious. I know nothing about that company, that name, whatever it is."

"That's good to know." Gurney let a glimpse of the reptile creep into his voice. "That's good for you. Good for everybody."

The glimpse seemed to have a stunning effect. Ballston was absolutely quiet.

"You still with us, Jordan?"

"Yes."

"So we got that piece of it out of the way, right?"

"Piece of it?"

"That piece of the situation. But we got more to talk about."

There was a pause. "You're not really a cop, are you?"

"Of course I'm a cop. Why would I say I was a cop if I wasn't a cop?"

"Who are you really, and what do you want?"

"I want to come see you."

"See me?"

"I don't like the phone so much."

"I don't understand what you want."

"Just a little talk."

"About what?"

"Enough bullshit. You're a smart guy. Don't talk like I'm stupid."

Again Ballston seemed stunned into silence. Gurney thought he could hear a tremor in the man's breathing. When Ballston spoke again, his voice had dropped to a frightened whisper.

"Look, I'm not sure who you are, but . . . everything is under control."

"Good. Everyone will be glad to hear that."

"Really. I mean it. *Everything . . . is . . . under . . . control.*"

"Good."

"Then, what more . . ."

"A little talk. Face-to-face. We just want to be sure."

"*Sure?* But why? I mean . . ."

"Like I said, Jordan . . . *I don't like the fucking phone!*"

Another silence. This time Ballston hardly seemed to be breathing at all.

Gurney brought his tone back down to a velvety calm. "Okay, nothing to worry about. So here's what we do. I come up to your place. We talk a little bit. That's all. See? No problem. Easy."

"When do you want to do this?"

"How about half an hour from now?"

"Tonight?" Ballston's voice was close to breaking.

"Yeah, Jordan, tonight. When the fuck else would half an hour from now be?"

In Ballston's silence, Gurney imagined he could sense pure fear. The ideal moment to end the call. He broke the connection and laid the phone down on the end of the dinner table.

In the dim light beyond the far end of the table, Madeleine was standing in the kitchen doorway in her pajamas. The top didn't match the bottom. "What's going on?" she asked, blinking sleepily.

"I think we have a fish on the line."

"We?"

With a twinge of annoyance, he rephrased his comment. "The fish in Palm Beach seems to be hooked, at least for the moment."

She nodded thoughtfully. "Now what?"

"Reel him in. What else?"

"So who are you meeting with?"

"Meeting with?"

"In half an hour."

"You heard me say that? Actually, I'm not meeting with anyone in half an hour. I wanted to give Mr. Ballston the idea that I was in the neighborhood. Ratchet up the uneasiness. I also said that I'd come *up* to his place, create the impression that I might be driving up from Lake Worth or South Palm."

"What happens when you don't show up?"

"He worries. Has some trouble sleeping."

Madeleine looked skeptical. "Then what?"

"I haven't worked that out yet."

Despite the fact that this was partly true, Madeleine's antenna seemed to detect the dishonesty in it. "So do you have a plan or don't you?"

"I have sort of a plan."

She waited, staring at him expectantly.

He couldn't picture any way out of the spot he was in other than straight ahead. "I need to get in closer to him. It's obvious he has some connection with Karnala Fashion, that the connection is dangerous, and that it frightens him. But I need to find out a lot more about it—exactly what the connection is, what Karnala is all about, how Karnala and Jordan Ballston are connected to the other pieces of the case. There's no way I can do all that over the phone. I need to see his eyes, read his expressions, watch his body language. I also need to take advantage of the moment, while the son of a bitch is wriggling on the hook. Right now I have his fear working for me. But that won't last."

"So you're on your way to Florida?"

"Not tonight. Maybe tomorrow."

"*Maybe* tomorrow?"

"Most likely tomorrow."

"Tuesday."

"Right." He wondered if he'd forgotten something. "Do we have some other commitment?"

"What difference would it make?"

"Well, do we?"

"As I said, what difference would it make?"

Such a simple question, yet how strangely difficult to answer. Perhaps because Gurney heard it as a proxy for the larger questions that these days never seemed far from Madeleine's mind: *Will anything we plan to do together ever make a difference? Will any piece of our life together ever be more important than the next step in some investigation? Will our being together ever outweigh your being a detective? Or will chasing whatever you're chasing always be at the heart of your life?*

Then again, maybe he was reading too damn much into a cranky comment, a passing mood in the middle of the night. "Look, tell me if I'm supposed to be doing something tomorrow that I somehow forgot about," he said earnestly, "and I'll tell you if it makes a difference."

"You're such an accommodating man," she said, mocking his earnestness. "I'm going back to bed."

For some time after she left, his priorities were jumbled. He went to the unlit end of the room, the sitting area between the fieldstone fireplace and the iron woodstove. The air smelled cold and ashy. He sank into his dark leather armchair. He felt uneasy, unmoored. A man without a harbor.

He fell asleep.

He awoke at 2:00 A.M. He pushed himself up out of the chair, stretching his arms and back to work out the kinks.

The customary currents of his mind had reasserted themselves and seemingly resolved whatever doubts he might have had about his plans for the coming day. He got his credit card out of his wallet, went to the computer in the den, and typed on the search line, *"Flights from Albany NY to Palm Beach FL."*

As his round-trip electronic tickets were printing out, along with a Palm Beach Tourist Guide, he was heading into the shower. And forty-five minutes later, having scribbled a note to Madeleine promising he'd be home that evening around seven, he was on his way to the airport, carrying nothing but his wallet, cell phone, and printouts.

During the sixty-mile drive east on I-88, he made four phone calls. The first was to a high-end limousine service, open twenty-four hours a day, to arrange for the right kind of car to meet him in Palm Beach. The next was to Val Perry, because he was going to be spending her money on some expensive but necessary purchases, and he wanted it on the record, if only by voice mail in the wee hours of the morning.

His third call, at 4:20 A.M., was to Darryl Becker. Amazingly, Becker not only picked up but sounded wide awake—or as wide awake as a man with a drawl could sound to northern ears.

"I'm just on my way out to the gym," Becker said. "What's up?"

"I have some good news, and I need a big favor."

"How good and how big?"

"I took a wild swing at Ballston on the phone, and I hit a soft spot. I'm on my way to see him, to see what happens if I keep punching."

"He doesn't talk to cops. What the hell did you say to get through to him?"

"Long story, but the son of a bitch is going down." Gurney was sounding a lot more confident than he really was.

"I'm impressed. So what's the favor?"

"I need a couple of big guys, nastiest-looking big guys you know, to stand next to my car while I'm in Ballston's house."

Becker sounded incredulous. "You afraid someone's going to steal it?"

"I need to create a certain impression."

"When does this impression need to get created?"

"Around noontime today. By the way, the pay is pretty good. They get five hundred bucks apiece for an hour's work."

"For standing next to your car?"

"For standing next to my car and looking like mob muscle."

"For five hundred an hour, that can be arranged. You can pick them up at my gym in West Palm. I'll give you the address."

Chapter 59

Undercover

Gurney's plane departed from Albany on schedule at 5:05 A.M. He switched planes in D.C., barely making a tight connection, and arrived in Palm Beach International Airport at 9:55 A.M.

In the designated limo-pickup area, among the dozen or so uniformed drivers awaiting incoming passengers, there was one driver with a sign bearing Gurney's name.

He was a young Latino with high Indian cheekbones, hair as black as squid ink, and a diamond stud in one ear. He seemed at first a bit thrown off, even annoyed, by the absence of luggage—until Gurney handed him the address of their first stop: the Giacomo Emporium on Worth Avenue. Then he brightened, perhaps reasoning that a man who traveled light for convenience, later picking up what he needed at Giacomo, might be a lavish tipper.

"Car is right outside, sir," he said, with an accent Gurney guessed to be Central American. "Very nice one."

A power-assisted revolving door propelled them from the controlled, seasonless, indoor climate common to airports everywhere into a tropical steam bath—reminding Gurney there is nothing autumnal about southern Florida in September.

"Right over there, sir," said the driver, his smile revealing surprisingly bad teeth for a young man. "First one."

The car, as Gurney had specified in his predawn call, was a Mercedes S600 sedan, the sort of six-figure vehicle you might see once a year in Walnut Crossing. In Palm Beach it was as common as five-hundred-dollar sunglasses. Gurney slipped into the backseat—a quiet, dehumidified cocoon of soft leather, soft carpet, and softly tinted windows.

The driver closed the door for him, got in the front seat, and they glided soundlessly into the stream of taxis and shuttle buses.

"Temperature okay?"

"It's fine."

"You want music?"

"No, thank you."

The driver sniffed, coughed, slowed to a crawl as the car passed through a pond-size puddle. "Been raining like a bitch."

Gurney did not answer. He'd never been prone to conversing simply for the sake for conversing, and in the company of strangers he was more comfortable with silence. Not another word was spoken until the car came to a stop at the entrance to the very posh little shopping plaza where the Giacomo Emporium was located.

The driver looked at him through the rearview mirror. "You know how long you want to be here?"

"Not long," said Gurney. "Fifteen minutes, max."

"Then I stay here. Cops tell me no, then I circle." He made an orbital gesture with his forefinger to illustrate the intended process. "I circle, keep coming around, passing this spot, until you're here. Okay?"

"Okay."

The shock of stepping back out into the hot, humid atmosphere was intensified by the visual impact of moving from the car's tinted light into the full glare of the midmorning Florida sun. The plaza was landscaped with planting beds of palms and ferns and potted Asiatic lilies. The air smelled like boiled flowers.

Gurney hurried into the store, where the air smelled more like money than flowers. Customers, blond women from thirty to sixty, drifted through the meticulously crafted displays of clothes and accessories. Salespeople, anorexic boys and girls in their twenties, looked like they were trying to look like the anorexic boys and girls in Giacomo ads.

Gurney's eagerness to flee this chic environment had him back on the street in ten minutes. Never had he spent so much on so little: an amazing $1,879.42 for one pair of jeans, one pair of moccasins,

one polo shirt, and one pair of sunglasses—selected with the assistance of a willowy male exhibiting the fashionable ennui of a
recent vampire victim.

In a changing room, Gurney had removed his battered jeans,
T-shirt, sneakers, and socks and put on his pricey new apparel. He
removed the tags and gave them to the salesperson along with his
old clothes, which he asked to be wrapped in a Giacomo box.

It was then that the salesperson offered the first small smile Gurney had seen since entering the shop. "You're like a Transformer,"
he said, presumably referring to the popular toy that is instantly
convertible from one thing into another.

The Mercedes was waiting. Gurney got in, checked his printed-
out tourist guide, and gave the driver the next address, less than a
mile away.

Nails Delicato was a tiny place, staffed by four dramatically
coiffed manicurists who appeared to be teetering on the shaky fence
that separated high-fashion models from high-priced hookers. No
one seemed to notice or care that Gurney was the only male customer. The manicurist to whom he was assigned looked sleepy. Apart
from apologizing several times for yawning while she was working
on his nails, she said nothing until she was almost at the end of the
process, applying a transparent polish.

"You have nice hands," she observed. "You should take better
care of them." Her voice was both young and weary, and it seemed
to resonate with the matter-of-fact sadness in her eyes.

As he was paying on the way out, he bought a small tube of hair
gel from the display of creams and cosmetics on the counter. He
opened the tube, spread a bit of the gel on his palms, and rubbed
it into his hair, aiming for the disarranged look so popular at the
moment.

"What do you think?" he asked the blankly beautiful young
woman in charge of collecting the money. The question engaged
her to a degree that surprised him. She blinked several times as if
being summoned from a dream, came around to the front of the
counter, and studied his head from various angles.

"Can I . . . ?" she asked.

"Absolutely."

She ran her fingers through his hair in rapid zigzags, flicking it this way and that and pulling up on bits of it to make it spikier. After a minute or two, she stepped back, her eyes lighting up with pleasure.

"That's it!" she declared. "That's the real you!"

He burst out laughing, which seemed to confuse her. Still laughing, he took her hand and, on an impulse, kissed it for no sensible reason he could think of—which also seemed to confuse her, but more pleasantly. Then he stepped out into the Florida steam bath and back into the Mercedes and gave the driver the address of Darryl Becker's gym.

"We need to pick up a couple of guys in West Palm," he explained. "Then we're going to visit a man on South Ocean Boulevard."

Chapter 60

Dancing with the devil

As anyone who'd attended one of his academy lectures quickly realized, Gurney's approach to undercover work was more complex than the average detective's. It wasn't just a matter of wrapping yourself in the manners, attitudes, and backstory of an assumed identity. It was more devious than that, and proportionally more difficult to manage. His "layered" approach involved creating a complex persona for the target to penetrate, a code for the target to break, a path the target could follow to arrive at the beliefs Gurney wanted him to embrace.

The current situation, however, added another dimension of difficulty. He had in past instances always known precisely what end-point belief about his identity he wanted his target to arrive at. But this time he didn't. Because the appropriate identity would depend on the exact nature of the Karnala operation and Ballston's connection to it—both still unknowns in the equation. It left Gurney in the position of having to feel his way forward, knowing that a misstep could be fatal.

As the car turned onto South Ocean Boulevard a couple of miles from Ballston's address, the absurd difficulty of what Gurney was attempting began to sink in. He was walking into the home of a psychopathic sex murderer, unarmed. His only defense and only chance of success lay in the creation of a persona he would have to make up as he went along, following the currents of Ballston's reactions as best he could, moment by moment. It was a challenge out of *Alice in Wonderland*. A sane man would probably turn back. A sane man with a wife and a son would certainly turn back.

He realized he was running too fast, that adrenaline was driving his decisions. It was a mistake that could easily lead to more mistakes. Worse, it deprived him of his main strength. It was in his analytic ability that he excelled, not in the quality of his adrenaline. He needed to *think*. He asked himself what he knew for sure, whether he had anything resembling a firm starting point for his conversation with Ballston.

He knew that the man was afraid and that his fear was related to Karnala Fashion. He knew that Karnala was reputedly controlled by the Skard family—who were, among other ugly things, high-end procurers. It also appeared that Melanie Strum had been sent to Ballston to satisfy his sexual needs. It was not too great a leap to imagine Karnala involved in that process. If evidence could be uncovered linking Karnala to both Ballston and Strum, then Ballston's conviction would be assured. That could explain his fear. Except . . . Gurney had gotten the impression that the man had been frightened not only by his mention of Karnala, and therefore by Gurney's knowledge of some link, but by Karnala itself.

And what was the significance of Ballston's odd insistence on the phone that everything was "under control"? That wouldn't make sense if Ballston believed that Gurney was any sort of legitimate detective. But it might make sense if he thought Gurney was a representative of Karnala or of some other dangerous organization with whom he was doing business.

This was the logic that led to the presence in the car of the two hulking, granite-faced men he'd just picked up in front of Darryl Becker's gym. Apart from minimally identifying themselves as Dan and Frank and informing Gurney that Becker had filled them in and they "knew the routine," they hadn't said another word. They looked like linebackers on a prison football team, whose idea of communication was to smash into something at full speed, preferably another person.

As the car glided to a stop at the Ballston address, Gurney realized with a sinking feeling that his assumptions were, in reality, too iffy to support the course of action he was taking. Yet it was all he had. And he had to do something.

At his request, the two big men got out, and one of them opened his door. Gurney checked his watch. It was eleven forty-five. He put on his five-hundred-dollar Giacomo sunglasses and stepped out of the car in front of an ornate iron gate at the end of a yellow-pebbled driveway. The gate was the only break in the high stone wall that enclosed the oceanfront estate on its three land-facing sides. Like its neighbors on that stretch of luxury coastline, the property had been converted from a barrier sandbar of coarse grasses, sea oats, and saw palmettos into a lushly loamed and mulched botanical garden of frangipani, hibiscus, oleander, magnolia, and gardenia blossoms.

It smelled to Gurney like a gangster's wake.

With his two hired companions standing by the car, radiating a barely suppressed violence, he approached the intercom on the stone pillar beside the gate. In addition to the camera built into the intercom, two separate security cameras were mounted on poles on either side of the driveway—at intersecting angles, which covered the approach to the gate as well as a wide segment of the adjacent boulevard. The gate was also directly observable from at least one second-floor window of the Spanish-style mansion at the end of the yellow driveway. In such a leafy, flowery environment, it said something about the owner's obsessiveness that not a single fallen leaf or petal had been allowed to remain on the ground.

When Gurney pressed the intercom button, the response was immediate, the tone mechanically polite. *"Good morning. Please identify yourself and the nature of your business."*

"Tell Jordan I'm here."

There was a brief pause. *"Please identify yourself and the nature of your business."*

Gurney smiled, then let the smile fade to zero. "Just tell him."

Another pause. *"I need to give Mr. Ballston a name."*

"Of course," said Gurney, smiling again.

He recognized that he was at a fork in the road. He ran through the options and chose the one that offered the greatest reward, at the greatest risk.

He let the smile fade. "My name is Fuck You."

Nothing happened for several seconds. Then there was a muted metallic click, and without another sound the gate swung slowly open.

One thing Gurney had forgotten to do in the rush to do everything else was to check the Internet for photos of Ballston. However, when the mansion door opened as he approached it, he had no doubt at all about the identity of the man standing there.

His appearance fulfilled the expectations one might have of a criminally decadent billionaire. There was a pampered look about his hair and skin and clothes; a disdainful set to his mouth, as though the world in general fell far below his standards; a self-indulgent cruelty in his eyes. There also seemed to be a sniffly twitch in his nose, suggestive of a coke addiction. It was abundantly apparent that Jordan Ballston was a man to whom nothing on earth was remotely as important as getting his own way, and getting it quickly, at whatever cost to others the process might entail.

He regarded Gurney with ill-concealed anxiety. His nose twitched. "I don't understand what this is all about." He looked past Gurney down the driveway at the well-guarded Mercedes, his eyes widening just a fraction.

Gurney shrugged, smiled like he was unsheathing a knife. "You want to talk outside?"

Ballston apparently heard this as a threat. He blinked, shook his head nervously. "Come in."

"Nice pebbles," said Gurney, ambling past Ballston into the house.

"What?"

"The yellow pebbles. In your driveway. Nice."

"Oh." Ballston nodded, looked confused.

Gurney stood in the middle of the grand foyer, affecting the gimlet eye of an assessor at a foreclosure. On the main wall facing him, between the curving arms of a double staircase, was a huge painting of a lawn chair—which he recognized from the art-appreciation course he'd attended with Madeleine a year and a half earlier, the course taught by Sonya Reynolds, the course that had launched him on his fateful mug-shot art "hobby."

"I like that," announced Gurney, pointing at it as though his benediction were a form of triage that saved it from the trash bin.

Ballston seemed vaguely relieved by the approval but no less confused.

"Guy's a fucking faggot," Gurney explained, "but his shit is worth a lot."

Ballston made a hideous attempt at a grin. He cleared his throat but couldn't seem to think of anything to say.

Gurney turned toward him, adjusting his sunglasses. "So, Jordan, you collect a lot of fag art?"

Ballston swallowed, sniffled, twitched. "Not really."

"Not really? That's very interesting. So where can we sit down and have a little talk?" From the trial-and-error experience of countless interrogations, Gurney had come to appreciate the unsettling effect of casual non sequiturs.

"Uh . . ." Ballston looked around him as though he were in someone else's house. "In there?" He extended his arm cautiously toward a broad archway that led to an elegant, antique-furnished living room. "We could sit in there."

"Wherever you're comfortable, Jordan. We'll sit down. Relax. Have a conversation."

Ballston led the way stiffly to a pair of white-brocaded armchairs on opposite sides of a baroque card table. "Here?"

"Sure," said Gurney. "Very nice table." His expression contradicted the compliment. He sat down and watched Ballston do the same.

The man crossed his legs awkwardly, hesitated, uncrossed them, sniffled.

Gurney smiled. "Coke got you by the balls, huh?"

"Excuse me?"

"Not my concern."

A long silence passed between them.

Ballston cleared his throat. It sounded dry. "So you . . . you said on the phone you're a cop?"

"Right. I did say that. You got a good memory. Very important, a good memory."

"That doesn't look like a cop's car out there."

"Course not. I'm undercover, you know? Actually, I'm retired."

"You always ride with bodyguards?"

"Bodyguards? What bodyguards? Why would I need bodyguards? Some friends gave me a ride, that's all."

"Friends?"

"Yeah. Friends." Gurney sat back, stretching his neck from side to side, letting his gaze drift around the room. It was a room that could be on the cover of *Architectural Digest.* He waited for Ballston to speak.

Finally the man asked in a low voice, "Is there a particular problem?"

"You tell me."

"Something must have brought you here . . . a specific concern."

"You're under a lot of pressure. Stress, you know?"

Ballston's face tightened. "It's nothing I can't handle."

Gurney shrugged. "Stress is a terrible thing. It makes people . . . unpredictable."

The tightness in Ballston's face spread through his body. "I assure you the situation here will be resolved."

"There's a lot of different ways things get resolved."

"I assure you that the situation will be resolved in a favorable way."

"Favorable to who?"

"To . . . everyone concerned."

"Suppose everyone's interests don't line up the same way."

"I assure you that won't be a problem."

"I'm glad to hear you say that." Gurney gazed lazily at the big pampered pig of a man across from him, allowing just enough of his disgust to seep through. "You see, Jordan, I'm a problem solver. But I got enough of them on my plate. I don't want to be distracted by a new one. I'm sure you can appreciate that."

Ballston's voice was breaking. "There . . . won't . . . be . . . any . . . new . . . problems."

"How can you be so sure?"

"The problem this time was a freak one-in-a-million accident!"

"This time"? Mother of God, this is it! I've got the bastard! But for Christ's sake, Gurney, don't let it show. Relax. Take it easy. Relax.

Gurney shrugged. "That's the way you see it, huh?"

"A fucking burglar, for shit sake! A fucking burglar who just happened to break in on exactly the wrong fucking night, the one fucking night that fucking cunt was in the fucking freezer!"

"So it was, like, a coincidence?"

"Of course it was a fucking coincidence! What else could it be?"

"I don't know, Jordan. Only time anything ever went wrong, huh? Only time? You sure about that?"

"Absolutely!"

Gurney went back to stretching his neck slowly from side to side. "Too much fucking tension in this business. You ever try that yoga shit?"

"What?"

"You remember the Maharishi? What a fuckin' hand job."

"Who?"

"Before your time. I forget what a young man you are. So tell me, Jordan. How do we know nothing's going to pop up and surprise us?"

Ballston blinked, sniffled, started to smile with jerky little movements of his lips.

"Did I ask a funny question?"

Ballston's breathing became as jerky as his facial tics. Then his whole torso began to shake, and a series of sharp staccato sounds burst from his throat.

He was laughing. Horribly.

Gurney waited for the bizarre fit to subside. "You want to let me in on the joke?"

"Pop up," said Ballston, the phrase triggering a renewed display of crazy machine-gun giggling.

Gurney waited, didn't know what else to say or do. He remembered the wisdom an undercover partner had once shared with him: *When in doubt, shut up.*

"Sorry," said Ballston. "No offense. But it's such a funny image. Popping up! Two headless bodies, popping up out of the fucking ocean halfway to the fucking Bahamas! Shit, that is a picture!"

Mission accomplished! Probably. Maybe. Maintain credibility. Stay in character. Patience. See where it goes.

Gurney studied the fingernails on his right hand, then buffed their glossy surface on his jeans.

Ballston's exhilaration faded.

"So you're telling me everything's under control?" asked Gurney, still buffing.

"Completely."

Gurney nodded slowly. "So why am I still concerned?" When Ballston just stared at him, he continued. "Couple of things. Small questions. I'm sure you got good answers. First, suppose I was really a cop, or working for the cops. How the fuck do you know I'm not wired?"

Ballston smiled, looked relieved. "You see that thing on the credenza that looks like a DVD player? See the little green light? That would be a red light if there was any kind of recording or transmitting equipment operating anywhere in this room. It's very reliable."

"Good. I like reliable things. Reliable people."

"Are you suggesting I'm not reliable?"

"How the fuck do you know I'm not a cop? How the fuck do you know that I'm not a cop who came here to find out exactly what you just told me with all that giggly crap, you fucking moron?"

Ballston looked like a rotten little boy who'd been slapped in the face. The ugly shock was replaced by an uglier grin. "Despite your opinion of me, I am an excellent judge of character. You don't get as rich as I am by misreading people. So let me tell you something. The odds of you being a cop are about the same as the odds of the cops ever finding those headless cunts. I'm not going to lose sleep over either possibility."

Gurney mirrored Ballston's grin. "Confidence. Good. Very good. I like confidence." Gurney stood suddenly. Ballston flinched. "Good luck, Mr. Ballston. We'll be in touch if there are any unforeseen developments."

As Gurney was passing through the front door, Ballston added a little twist. "You know, if I did think you were a cop, everything I told you would have been bullshit."

Chapter 61

Homeward bound

"Maybe that's exactly what it was," drawled Becker.

As Gurney emerged from the cool indulgence of the chauffeured Mercedes onto the broiling pavement in front of the airport terminal, he was on the phone to Darryl Becker, giving him as detailed a verbatim report as he could on his meeting with Jordan Ballston.

"I don't think it was bullshit," said Gurney. "I've had some experience with decompensating psychos. And I'd be willing to bet that some real energy was starting to come loose in that loony laugh and the image of decapitated women that went with it. But the bottom line is, we don't have time to debate it. I strongly recommend you take what he said at face value and take immediate appropriate action."

"I assume you're not suggesting we search the Atlantic Ocean, so what are you suggesting?"

"The son of a bitch has a boat, right? He has to have a boat. Find the goddamn boat, put every tech you've got on it. Assume that he transported at least two bodies on that boat. Assume there's still trace evidence somewhere on that boat—in some crack, crevice, corner—and don't stop looking till you find it."

"I hear what you're saying. However, just to introduce a tiny speck of rational perspective here, let me point out that we don't even know for a fact that Ballston has a boat. We don't—"

Gurney broke in, "I'm telling you he has a boat. If anyone in this whole goddamn state owns a boat, he does."

"As I was saying," Becker drawled, "we have no evidence that he owns a boat, much less what kind of boat it might be, or where it might be, or when these alleged transportations of bodies took place, or whose bodies they were, or even if there were any bodies to begin with. You see my point?"

"Darryl, I have other calls to make. I'll say this one last time. He has a boat. He's had the bodies of at least two victims on it. Find the boat. Find the evidence. Do it now. We have to make this creep talk. We have to find out what the hell is going on. This thing is a lot bigger than Ballston, and I have a very bad feeling about it. A very urgent very bad feeling." There was a silence too long for Gurney's comfort. "You there, Darryl?"

"I promise nothing. We'll do what we can do."

As he made his way down an endless concourse to his flight gate, he placed a call to Sheridan Kline. He got Ellen Rackoff.

"He's in court all afternoon," she said. "Absolutely not interruptible."

"How about Stimmel?"

"I think he's in his office. You'd rather talk to him than to me?"

"It's a practical need, not a personal preference." Gurney couldn't imagine *wanting* to talk to Kline's relentlessly dour deputy. "There's some super-urgent stuff he's going to have to handle if Sheridan's tied up."

"Okay, just call this number again. If I don't pick up, it'll bounce over to him."

He did what she said, and thirty seconds later Stimmel was on the line, his voice radiating all the charm of a swamp.

Gurney related enough of the story to convey his current view of the case: that it was potentially huge, that it combined elements of ruthless efficiency with sexual insanity, that Hector Flores and Jordan Ballston and the known deaths so far were just the visible pieces of an underground monster—and that if it turned out that as many as fifteen or twenty Mapleshade graduates were missing, then it was likely that all fifteen or twenty were going to end up raped, tortured, and decapitated.

He concluded, "Either you or Kline needs to get on the phone with the Palm Beach County district attorney within the next hour to accomplish two things. Number one, make sure that the PBPD is allocating sufficient resources to find Ballston's boat and put it under a microscope ASAP. Number two, you guys need to convince the Palm Beach DA that full cooperation is the way to go here. You need to be very persuasive on the point that New York is holding the bigger end of the stick on this one—and that some kind of deal may have to be worked out with Ballston in order for us to get to Karnala Fashion, or whatever organization is at the root of whatever the hell is going on."

"You think the DA in Florida is going to give Ballston a pass to make Sheridan's life easier?" His tone made it plain he considered this idea absurd.

"I'm not talking about a pass. I'm talking about Ballston being made to understand that lethal injection is an absolute certainty for him unless he cooperates fully. And immediately."

"And if he cooperates?"

"If he does—fully, truthfully, with no reservations—then maybe other outcomes could be considered."

"That's a tough sell." Stimmel sounded like if he were the Florida DA, it would be an impossible sell.

"The fact is," said Gurney, "getting Ballston to talk may be our only shot."

"Our only shot at what?"

"A bunch of girls are missing. Unless we crack Ballston, I doubt we'll ever find a single one of them alive."

The rapid-fire pressures of the day caught up with Gurney on the second leg of the flight home, and his brain began shutting down. With the jet engines droning in his ears like a formless white noise, loosening his grip on the present, he drifted through unpleasant scenes and disjointed moments that hadn't come to mind in over a decade: the visits he made to Florida after his parents moved from the Bronx to a rented bungalow in Magnolia, a little town that seemed to be the mother lode of bleakness and decay; a brown palmetto bug the size of a mouse, scuttling under the leafy detritus on the bungalow porch; tap water that tasted like recycled sewage but that his parents insisted had no taste at all; the times when his mother drew him aside to complain with tearful bitterness about her marriage, about his father, about his father's selfishness, about her migraines, about her lack of sexual satisfaction.

Disturbing dreams, dark memories, and increasing dehydration through the remainder of the flight put Gurney in a state of anxious depression. As soon as he got off the plane in Albany, he bought a liter bottle of water at the inflated airport price and drank half of it on the way to the bathroom. In the relatively roomy wheelchair-accessible stall, he removed his chic jeans, polo shirt, and moccasins. He opened the Giacomo Emporium box he'd been carrying that contained his own original clothes and put them on. Then he put the new clothes into the box, and when he left the stall, he tossed the box into the garbage bin. He went to the basin and rinsed the gel out of his hair. He dried it roughly with a paper towel and looked at himself in the mirror, reassuring himself that he was again himself.

It was exactly 6:00 P.M., according to the parking booth's clock, as he paid the twelve-dollar fee and the striped yellow barrier arm rose to let him pass. He headed for I-88 West with the late sun glaring through his windshield.

By the time he got to the exit for the county route that led from the interstate down through the northern Catskills to Walnut Crossing, an hour had passed; he'd finished his liter of water and was feeling better. It always surprised him that such a simple thing—you couldn't get much simpler than water—could have such power to calm his thoughts. His emotional restoration gradually continued, and by the time he reached the little road that meandered up through the hills to his farmhouse, he was feeling close to normal.

He walked into the kitchen just as Madeleine was removing a roasting pan from the oven. She laid it on top of the stove, glanced at him with raised eyebrows, and said with a bit more sarcasm than surprise, "This is a shock."

"Nice to see you, too."

"Are you interested in having dinner?"

"I told you in the note I left for you this morning that I'd be home for dinner, and here I am."

"Congratulations," she said, getting a second dinner plate out of an overhead cabinet and laying it next to the one already on the countertop.

He gave her a narrow-eyed look. "Maybe we ought to try this again? Should I go out and come back in?"

She returned an extended parody of his look, then softened. "No. You're right. You're here. Get out another knife and fork, and let's eat. I'm hungry."

They filled their plates from the pan of roasted vegetables and chicken thighs and carried them to the round table by the French doors.

"I think it's warm enough to open them," she said—which he did.

As they sat down, a bath of sweetly fragrant air washed over them. Madeleine closed her eyes, a slow-motion smile wrinkling her cheeks. In the stillness Gurney thought he could hear the faint, soft cooing of mourning doves from the trees beyond the pasture.

"Lovely, lovely, lovely," Madeleine half whispered. Then she sighed happily, opened her eyes, and began to eat.

At least a minute passed before she spoke again. "So tell me about your day," she said, eyeing a parsnip on the tip of her fork.

He thought about it, frowning.

She waited, watching him.

He placed his elbows on the table, interlocking his fingers in front of his chin. "My day. Well. The highlight was the point at which the psychopath dissolved into giggles. A funny image occurred to him. An image involving two women he had raped, tortured, and decapitated."

She studied his face, her lips tightening.

After a while he added, "So that's the kind of day it was."

"Did you accomplish what you set out to accomplish?"

He rubbed the knuckle of his forefinger slowly across his lips. "I think so."

"Does that mean you've solved the Perry case?"

"I think I have part of the solution."

"Good for you."

A long silence passed between them.

Madeleine stood, picked up their plates, then the knives and forks. "She called today."

"Who?"

"Your client."

"Val Perry? You spoke to her?"

"She said that she was returning your call, that she had your home phone number with her but not your cell number."

"And?"

"And she wanted you to know that three thousand dollars is not an amount of money you need to bother her about. 'He should spend whatever the hell he needs to spend to find Hector Flores.' That's a quote. Sounds like an ideal client." She let the dishes clatter into the sink. "What more could you ask for? Oh, by the way, speaking of decapitation . . ."

"Speaking of what?"

"The man in Florida you mentioned who decapitates people—it just reminded me to ask you about that doll."

"Doll?"

"The one upstairs."

"Upstairs?"

"What is this, the echo game?"

"I don't know what you're talking about."

"I'm asking you about the doll on the bed in my sewing room."

He shook his head, turned up his palms in bafflement.

There was a flicker of concern in her eyes. "The doll. The broken doll. On the bed. You don't know anything about it?"

"You mean like a little girl's doll?"

Her voice rose in alarm. "Yes, David! A little girl's doll!"

He stood and walked quickly to the hall stairs, took two at a time, and in a matter of seconds was standing in the doorway of the spare bedroom Madeleine used for her needlework. The dying dusk threw only a dim gray light across the double bed. He flipped the wall switch, and a bright bedside lamp provided all the illumination he needed.

Propped against one of the pillows was an ordinary doll in a sitting position, unclothed—ordinary except for the fact that the head had been removed and was placed on the bedspread a few feet from the body, facing it.

Chapter 62

Tremors

The dream was coming apart, cracking like the compartments of a brittle carton, no longer able to keep its unruly contents firmly in place.

Each night his scimitar victory over Salome was less clear, less certain. It was like an old-time television transmission being interrupted by a program on an adjoining frequency. Competing voices broke back and forth across each other. Images of Salome dancing were replaced in vivid flashes by those of another dancer.

In place of the strong and reassuring Vision of His Mission and His Method—the courage and conviction of John the Baptist—there were shards of memories, sudden sharp pieces he recoiled from, moments overwhelmingly familiar, nauseatingly familiar.

A woman dancing, her silky dress rising, showing her long legs, showing the little girls how to dance like Salome, how to dance in front of the little boys.

Salome doing the samba on a peach rug amid tropical plants, huge moist leaves, dripping. Showing the boys how to do the samba. How to hold her.

The peach rug and tropical plants were in her bedroom. She was showing him and his best friend from school how to do the samba. How to hold her.

The serpent moving from her mouth into his, searching, slithering.

Later he threw up, and she laughed. Threw up on the peach rug under the giant tropical plants, sweating, gasping. The world spinning, his stomach heaving.

She took him into the shower, her legs pressing against him.

She was crawling on the peach rug toward a boy and a girl, exhausted and inexhaustible. "Wait in the hall, darling." Gasping. "I'll be with you in a minute." Her face gleaming with sweat, flushed. Biting her lip. Wild eyes.

Chapter 63

Just like Ashton's cottage

The BCI investigation team arrived in two installments—Jack Hardwick at midnight and the evidence team an hour later.

The techs in their white anticontamination suits were initially skeptical of a crime scene in which the only "crime" was the unexplained presence of a broken doll. They were accustomed to carnage, to the bloody remnants of mayhem and murder. So perhaps it was understandable that their first reactions were raised eyebrows and sideways glances.

Their initial suggestions—that the doll might have been put there by a visiting child or that it might be a practical joke—were perhaps understandable as well, but that did not make them tolerable to Madeleine, whose blunt question to Hardwick they probably overheard, judging by the expressions on their faces: "Are they drunk or just stupid?"

However, once Hardwick took them aside and explained the uncanny resemblance of the doll's position to that of Jillian Perry's body, they did as thorough and professional a job of processing the scene as if it had been riddled with bullets.

The results, unfortunately, didn't amount to anything. All their fine-combing, print-lifting, and fiber- and soil-vacuuming efforts produced nothing of interest. The room contained the prints of one person, no doubt Madeleine's. Ditto the few hairs found on the back of the chair by the window where Madeleine worked on her knitting. The inside of the frame of the adjoining window, the one Gurney was called upon to open when it got stuck, bore a second set, no doubt his. There were no prints on the body or head of the doll. The brand of doll was a popular one, sold at every Walmart in America. The downstairs entry doors had multiple prints identical to the prints found in the bedroom. No door or window in the house showed any sign of being forced. There were no prints on the outside of the windows. Luma-Lite examination of the floors showed no clear footprints that didn't match either Dave's or Madeleine's shoe size. Examination of all the doors, banisters, countertops, faucets, and toilet handles for fingerprints produced the same results.

When the techs finally packed up their equipment and departed at around 4:00 A.M. in their van, they took with them the doll, the bedspread, and the throw rugs they had removed from the floor on either side of the bed.

"We'll run the standard tests," Gurney overheard them telling Hardwick on their way out, "but ten to one everything's clean." They sounded tired and frustrated.

When Hardwick came back into the kitchen and sat at the table across from him and Madeleine, Gurney commented, "Just like the scene in Ashton's cottage."

"Yeah," said Hardwick with a bone-tired disconnectedness.

"What do you mean?" asked Madeleine, sounding antagonistic.

"The antiseptic quality of it all," said Gurney. "No prints, no nothing."

She made an almost agonized little sound in her throat. She took several deep breaths. "So . . . what . . . what are we supposed to do now? I mean, we can't just . . ."

"There'll be a cruiser here before I leave," said Hardwick. "You'll have protection for at least forty-eight hours, no problem."

"No problem?" Madeleine stared at him, uncomprehending. "How can you . . . ?" She didn't finish the sentence, just shook her head, stood up, and left the room.

Gurney watched her go, at a loss for any comforting thing to say, as jarred by her emotion as he was by the event that had caused it.

Hardwick's notebook was on the table in front of him. He opened it, found the page he wanted, and took a pen out of his shirt pocket. He didn't write anything, just tapped idly with it on the open page. He looked exhausted and vaguely troubled.

"So . . ." he began. He cleared his throat. He spoke as if he were pushing the words uphill. "According to what I wrote down earlier . . . you were away all day."

"Right. In Florida. Extracting a near confession from Jordan Ballston. Which I hope is being followed up as we speak."

Hardwick laid down his pen, closed his eyes, and massaged them with his thumb and forefinger. When he opened them again, he looked back at his notebook. "And your wife told me she was out of the house all afternoon—from sometime around one till sometime around five-thirty—bike riding, then hiking through the woods. She does that a lot?"

"She does that a lot."

"It's a reasonable assumption, then, that the doll was . . . installed, shall we say, during that time window."

"I'd say so," said Gurney, becoming irritated at the reiteration of the obvious.

"Okay, so as soon as the morning shift comes on, I'll send someone over to talk to your neighbors down the road. A passing car must be a big event up here."

"Having live neighbors is a big event. There are only six houses on the road, and four of them belong to city people, only here on weekends."

"Still, you never know. I'll send someone over."

"Fine."

"You don't sound optimistic."

"Why the hell should I be optimistic?"

"Good point." He picked up his pen and started tapping again on his notebook. "She says she's sure she locked the doors when she went out. That sound right to you?"

"What do you mean, does it *sound right*?"

"I mean, is that something she normally does, lock the doors?"

"What she normally does is tell the truth. If she says she locked the doors, she locked the doors."

Hardwick stared at him, seemed as if he were about to respond, and then changed his mind. More tapping. "So . . . if they were locked and there's no sign of forced entry, that means someone came in with a key. You give keys to anyone?"

"No."

"Any instances you can think of when your keys were out of your possession long enough for someone to make dupes?"

"No."

"Really? Only takes twenty seconds to make a key."

"I know how long it takes to make a key."

Hardwick nodded, as though this were actual information. "Well, chances are, somebody got one somehow. You might want to change your locks."

"Jack, who the hell do you think you're talking to? This isn't Home Safety Night at the PTA."

Hardwick smiled, leaned back in his chair. "Right. I'm talking to Sherlock fucking Gurney. So tell me, Mr. Brilliant Fucking Detective, you have any bright ideas about this?"

"About the doll?"

"Yeah. About the doll."

"Nothing that wouldn't already be obvious to you."

"That somebody's trying to scare you off the case?"

"You have a better idea?"

Hardwick shrugged. He stopped tapping and began studying his pen as though it were a complex piece of evidence. "Anything else odd been happening?"

"Like what?"

"Like . . . odd. Have there been any other little . . . oddities in your life?"

Gurney uttered a short, humorless laugh. "Apart from every single aspect of this miserably odd case and all the miserably odd people involved in it, everything's perfectly normal." It wasn't really an answer, and he suspected that Hardwick knew it wasn't. For all the man's bluster and vulgarity, he had one of the sharpest minds Gurney had encountered in all his years in law enforcement. He could easily have been a captain at thirty-five if he gave a damn about any of the things that captains need to give a damn about.

Hardwick looked up at the ceiling, his eyes following the crown molding as though it were the subject of what he was saying. "Remember the guy whose fingerprints were on that little cordial glass?"

A bad feeling seized Gurney's stomach. "Saul Steck, aka Paul Starbuck?"

"Right. You remember what I told you?"

"You told me he was a successful character actor with a nasty interest in young girls. Got a psych commitment, eventually got out. What about him?"

"The guy who helped me lift the prints and run them through the system called me back last night with an interesting little addendum."

"Yeah?"

Hardwick was squinting across the room at the farthest corner of the molding. "Seems that back before he was arrested, Steck used to have a porno website, and Starbuck wasn't his only alias. His website, which featured underage girls, was called Sandy's Den."

Gurney waited for Hardwick's gaze to return to him before replying. "You're struck by the possibility that the name Sandy could be a nickname for Alessandro?"

Hardwick smiled. "Something like that."

"World is full of meaningless coincidences, Jack."

Hardwick nodded. He stood up from the table and looked out the window. "Cruiser's here. Like I said, full coverage for two twenty-fours, minimum. After that, we'll see. You okay?"

"Yeah."

"She going to be okay?"

"Yeah."

"I got to get home and get some sleep. I'll call you later."

"Yeah. Thanks, Jack."

Hardwick hesitated. "You still have your weapon from the job?"

"No. Never liked carrying it. Didn't even like having it around."

"Well . . . considering the situation . . . you might want to pick up a shotgun."

For a long while after Hardwick's taillights receded down the pasture lane, Gurney sat alone at the table—absorbing the shock of the doll, contemplating the shifting landscape of the case.

It was conceivable, of course, that the names Sandy and Alessandro had each popped up with coincidental insignificance, but that was the definition of wishful thinking. A realistic man would have to accept that Sandy, the former photographer of the pornographic website, might very well be Alessandro, the current photographer of the near-pornographic Karnala ads—and that both names were aliases of the sex criminal Saul Steck.

But who was Hector Flores?

And why was Jillian Perry beheaded?

And Kiki Muller?

Had the women discovered something about Karnala? About Steck? About Flores himself?

And why had Steck drugged him? In order to photograph him with his "daughters"? To threaten him with public embarrassment, or worse? To have the leverage to control his input into the investigation? To blackmail him into providing inside information into its progress?

Or was the purpose of the drugging, like that of the decapitated doll, to demonstrate Gurney's accessibility and vulnerability? To frighten him into backing away?

Or were both events prompted by something even sicker? Were they both part of a control freak's game, an exciting way of demonstrating power and dominance? Something he did to prove he could do it? Something he did for a thrill?

Gurney's hands were cold. He rubbed them hard against his thighs in an effort to warm them. It didn't seem to be working very well. He started to shiver. He stood, tried rubbing his hands on his chest and upper arms, tried walking back and forth. He walked to the far end of the room, where sometimes the iron woodstove held some residual warmth from an earlier fire. But the dusty black metal was colder than his hand, and touching it made him shiver again.

He heard the click of the lamp switch in the bedroom, followed shortly by the squeak of the bathroom door. He'd talk to Madeleine, calm her nerves—after he managed to calm himself. He looked out the window, was reassured by the sight of the police cruiser by the side door.

He took the deepest breath he could, exhaled slowly. Slow, controlled breathing. Deliberation, determination. Positive thoughts. Thoughts of achievement and competence.

He reminded himself that the fingerprint trail that led to Steck existed because of his personal initiative in retrieving the glass under difficult circumstances.

That discovery had also connected the "Jykynstyl" drugging mystery with the Mapleshade murder-and-disappearance mysteries. And since he had a foot planted in each area, he was in a unique position to use one situation to illuminate the other.

His original insights and prodding had pulled the investigation out of the ditch it had been mired in—the search for an insane Mexican laborer—and put it on a new path.

His urging that all former Mapleshade graduates be contacted led not only to the discovery that the whereabouts of an extraordinary number of them were unknown but also to knowledge of the fate of Melanie Strum.

His judgment regarding the likely significance of Karnala had shaken loose a crazed revelation from Jordan Ballston that could well lead to a final solution.

Even the killer's devotion of time, energy, and resources to the apparent goal of halting his efforts proved that he was on the right track.

He heard the bathroom door hinge squeak again and twenty seconds later the click of the lamp being switched off. Perhaps now that he had his feet on the ground, now that the chill was leaving his fingers, he could talk to Madeleine. But first he took the precaution of locking the side door not only with the knob lock but also with the dead bolt they never used. Then he latched all the ground-floor windows.

He went into the bedroom in what he considered to be a good frame of mind. He approached the bed in the dark. "Maddie?"

"You bastard!"

He'd expected her to be in bed, in front of him, but her voice, shocking in its anger, came from the far corner of the room.

"What?"

"What have you done?" Her voice, hardly above a whisper, was furious.

"Done? What . . . ?"

"This is my home. This is my sanctuary."

"Yes?"

"*Yes? Yes?* How could you? How could you bring this horror into my home?"

Gurney was rendered speechless by the question and by its intensity. He felt his way along the edge of the bed and turned on the lamp.

The antique rocker that was usually near the foot of the bed had been pushed into the corner farthest from the windows. Madeleine was sitting in it, still fully dressed, her knees pulled up in front of her body. Gurney was startled first by the raw emotion in her eyes, then by the sharp pair of scissors in each of her clenched fists.

He'd had much training and practice in the technique of talking an overwrought person down into a calmer state of mind, but none of it seemed appropriate at that moment. He sat on the corner of the bed closest to her.

"Someone invaded my home. Why, David? Why did they do that?"

"I don't know."

"Of course you do! You know exactly what's happening."

He watched her, watched the scissors. Her knuckles were white.

"You're supposed to protect us," she went on in a trembling whisper. "Protect our home, make it safe. But you've done the opposite. The opposite. You've let horrible people come into our lives, come into our home. MY HOME!" she shouted at him, her voice breaking. "YOU LET MONSTERS INTO MY HOME!"

Gurney had never seen this kind of rage in her before. He said nothing. He had no words in his mind, not even thoughts. He hardly moved, hardly took a breath. The emotional explosion seemed to clear the room, the world, of all other realities. He waited. No other option occurred to him.

After a while, he wasn't sure how long, she said, "I can't believe what you've done."

"This wasn't my intention." His voice sounded strange to him. Small.

She made a sound that might have been mistaken for laughter but sounded to him more like a brief convulsion in her lungs. "That horrible mug-shot art—that was the beginning. Pictures of the most disgusting monsters on earth. But that wasn't enough. It wasn't enough having them in our computer, having them on the screen staring at us."

"Maddie, I promise you—whoever got into our house, I'll find them. I'll put an end to them. This will never happen again."

She shook her head. "It's too late. Don't you see what you've done?"

"I see that war has been declared. We've been attacked."

"No! *You*—don't you see what *you've* done?"

"What I did is kick a rattlesnake out from under a rock."

"You brought this into our lives."

He said nothing, just bowed his head.

"We moved to the country. To a beautiful place. Lilacs and apple blossoms. A pond."

"Maddie, I promise you, I'll kill the snake."

She seemed not to be listening. "Don't you see what you've done?" She gestured slowly with one of her scissors to the dark window beside him. "Those woods, the woods where I take my walks, he was hiding in those woods, watching me."

"What makes you think you were being watched?"

"God, it's obvious! He put that hideous thing in the room I work in, the room I read in, the room with my favorite window, the window I sit next to with my knitting. The room overlooking the woods. He knew it was a room I used. If he'd put that thing in the spare bedroom across the hall, I might not have found it for a month. So he *knew*. He saw me in the window. And the only way he could see me in the window was from the woods." She paused, stared at him accusingly. "You see what I mean, David? You've destroyed my woods. How can I ever walk out there again?"

"I'll kill the snake. It'll be all right."

"Until you kick the next one out from under its rock." She shook her head and sighed. "I can't believe what you've done to the most beautiful place in the world."

It seemed to Gurney that once in a while, unpredictably, the elements of an otherwise indifferent universe conspired to produce in him an eerie frisson, and so it was that at that very moment behind the farmhouse, beyond the high pasture, out on the northern ridge, the coyotes began to howl.

Madeleine closed her eyes and lowered her knees. She rested her fists on her lap and loosened her grip on the two scissors enough for the blood to flow back into her knuckles. She tilted her head back against the headrest of the chair. Her mouth relaxed. It was as though the howling of the coyotes, weird and unsettling to her at other times, touched her that night in an entirely different way.

As the first gray swath of dawn appeared in the bedroom's east-facing window, she fell asleep. After a while Gurney took the scissors from her hands and switched off the light.

Chapter 64

A very strange day

As the yellow rays of the rising sun slanted across the pasture, Gurney sat at the breakfast table drinking a second cup of coffee. A few minutes earlier, he'd watched the changing of the guard as the day-shift trooper cruiser arrived to replace the one summoned by Hardwick. He'd gone out to offer the new trooper breakfast, but the young man had declined with crisp, military politeness. "Thank you, sir, but I've already had breakfast, sir."

A dull sciatic ache had settled in Gurney's left leg, as he grappled with questions whose resolutions were eluding his grasp like slippery fish.

Should he ask Hardwick to get him a copy of the mug shot that must have been taken at the time of Saul Steck's arrest—so he could be sure there was no mistake about the fingerprints—or might the paper trail generated between BCI and the original prosecuting jurisdiction raise too many questions?

Should he ask Hardwick, or maybe one of his old partners at the NYPD, to check the city tax rolls for ownership information on the brownstone, or might even that simple exercise raise a chain of sticky questions?

Was there any reason to doubt Sonya's claim to have been as thoroughly duped by the "Jykynstyl" story as he was—apart from the fact that she struck Gurney as the sort of woman not likely to be duped by anyone?

Should he get a shotgun for the house, or would Madeleine be more upset than reassured by its presence?

Should they move out, live in a hotel until the case was resolved? But suppose it wasn't resolved for weeks, or months, or ever?

Should he follow up with Darryl Becker on the status of the search for Ballston's boat?

Should he follow up with BCI on the progress of the calls being made to the Mapleshade graduates and their families?

Was everything that had happened—from the arrival of Hector Flores in Tambury through the murders of Jillian and Kiki and the disappearances of all those girls, right up to the complex brownstone deception, the Ballston sex murders, and the beheaded doll—was all that the product of a single mind? And if so, was the driving force of that mind a practical criminal enterprise or a psychotic mania?

Most disturbingly to Gurney, why was he finding these knots so difficult to untangle?

Even the simplest of questions—should he continue weighing alternatives, or return to bed and try to empty his mind, or busy himself physically—had become ensnared in a mental process that conjured an objection to every conclusion. Even the idea of taking a few ibuprofens for his aching sciatic nerve met with an unwillingness to go into the bedroom to get the bottle.

He stared out at the asparagus ferns, motionless in the dead morning calm. He felt disconnected, as though his customary attachments to the world had been broken. It was the same unmoored sense he'd had when his first wife announced her intention to divorce him, and years later when little Danny was killed, and again when his own father died. And now . . .

And now that Madeleine . . .

His eyes filled with tears. And as his sight grew blurry, he had the first perfectly clear thought he'd had in a long time. It was so simple. He would quit the case.

The purity and rightness of the decision was reflected in an immediate feeling of freedom, an immediate impulse to action.

He went into the den and called Val Perry.

He got her voice mail, was tempted to leave his resignation message, but felt that doing it that way was too impersonal, too avoidant. So he left a message saying only that he needed to speak to her as soon as possible. Then he got a glass of water, went into the bed-room, and took three ibuprofens.

Madeleine had moved from the rocking chair to the bed. She was still dressed, lying on top of the spread rather than under it, but she was sleeping peacefully. He lay down next to her.

When he awoke at noon, she was no longer there. He felt a small stab of fear, relieved a moment later by the sound of the kitchen sink running. He went to the bathroom, splashed water on his face, brushed his teeth, changed his clothes—did the things that would make it feel as much as possible like a new day.

When he went out to the kitchen, Madeleine was transferring some soup from a large pot to a plastic storage container. She put the container in the refrigerator and the pot in the sink and dried her hands on a dish towel. Her expression told him nothing.

"I've made a decision," he said.

She gave him a look that told him she knew what he was about to say.

"I'm backing out of the case."

She folded the towel and hung it over the edge of the dish drainer. "Why?"

"Because of everything that's happened."

She studied him for a few seconds, turned, and looked thought-fully out the window nearest the sink.

"I left a message for Val Perry," he said.

She turned back toward him. Her Mona Lisa smile came and went like a flicker of light. "It's a beautiful day," she said. "Do you want to come for a little walk?"

"Sure." Normally he would have resisted the suggestion or, at best, accompanied her reluctantly, but at that moment he had no resistance in him.

It had turned into one of those soft September days when the temperature outside was the same as inside, and the only difference he sensed as they stepped out onto the little side porch was the leafy smell of the autumn air. The trooper sitting in his cruiser by the asparagus patch lowered his window and looked questioningly at them.

"Just stretching our legs," said Gurney. "We'll stay in sight."

The young man nodded.

They followed the swath they kept mowed along the edge of the woods to prevent saplings from encroaching on the field. They circled slowly down to the bench by the pond, where they sat in silence.

It was quiet around the pond in September—unlike May and June, when the croaking frogs and screeching blackbirds maintained a constant territorial ruckus.

Madeleine took his hand in hers.

He lost track of time, a casualty of emotion.

At some point Madeleine said softly, "I'm sorry."

"For what?"

"My expectation . . . that everything should always be exactly the way I want it."

"Maybe that's the way everything should be. Maybe the way you want things is right."

"I'd like to think so. But . . . I doubt that it's true. And I don't think you should give up the job you agreed to do."

"I've already made up my mind."

"Then you should change your mind."

"Why?"

"Because you're a detective, and I have no right to demand that you should magically turn into something else."

"I don't know much about magic, but you have every right in the world to ask me to see things another way. And God knows I have no right at all to put anything ahead of your safety and happiness. Sometimes . . . I look at things I've done . . . situations I've created . . . dangers I didn't pay enough attention to—and I think I must be insane."

"Maybe sometimes," she said. "Maybe just a little." She looked out over the pond with a sad smile and squeezed his hand. The air was perfectly still. Even the tops of the tall cattail rushes were as motionless as a photograph. She closed her eyes, but the expression on her face grew more poignant. "I shouldn't have attacked you the way I did, shouldn't have said what I did, shouldn't have called you a bastard. That's the last thing on earth anyone should ever call you." She opened her eyes and looked directly at him. "You're a good man, David Gurney. An honest man. A brilliant man. An amazingly talented man. Maybe the best detective in the whole world."

A nervous laugh burst from his throat. "God save us all!"

"I'm serious. Maybe the best detective in the whole world. So how can I tell you to stop being that, to be something else? It's not fair. It's not right."

He looked out over the glassy pond at the upside-down reflections of the maples that grew on the far side. "I don't see it in those terms."

She ignored his response. "So here's what you should do. You agreed to take on the Perry case for two weeks. Today is Wednesday. Your two weeks will be up this Saturday. Just three more days. Finish the job."

"There's no need for me to do that."

"I know. I know you're willing to give it up. Which is exactly what makes it all right not to."

"Say that again?"

She laughed, ignoring his question. "Where would they be without you?"

He shook his head. "I hope you're joking."

"Why?"

"The last thing on earth I need is for my arrogance to be reinforced."

"The last thing on earth you need is a wife who thinks you should be someone else."

After a while they ambled, hand in hand, back up through the pasture, nodded pleasantly to their bodyguard, and went into the house.

Madeleine made a small cherrywood fire in the big fieldstone fireplace, opening the window next to it to keep the room from getting too warm.

For the rest of the afternoon, they did something they rarely did: nothing at all. They lounged on the couch, letting themselves be lazily hypnotized by the fire. Later Madeleine thought out loud about possible planting changes in the garden for the following spring. Still later, perhaps to keep a flood of worries at bay, she read a chapter of *Moby-Dick* aloud to him—both pleased and perplexed by what she continued to refer to as "the most peculiar book I've ever read."

She tended the fire. He showed her pictures of garden pavilions and screened gazebos in a book he'd picked up months earlier at Home Depot, and they talked about building one next summer, maybe by the pond. They dozed on and off, and the afternoon passed. They had an early supper of soup and salad while the sunset was still bright in the sky, illuminating the maples on the opposite hillside. They went to bed at dusk, made love with a kind of tenderness that grew quickly into a desperate urgency, slept for over ten hours, and awoke simultaneously at the first gray light of dawn.

Chapter 65

Message from the monster

Gurney had finished his scrambled eggs and toast and was about to take his plate to the sink. Madeleine looked up at him from her bowl of oatmeal and raisins and said, "I assume you've forgotten already where I'm going today."

Over supper the night before, he'd persuaded her with some difficulty to spend the next couple of days with her sister in New Jersey—a prudent precaution, under the circumstances—while he wrapped up his commitment to the case. But now he wrinkled his face in concentration, making a show of bafflement. She laughed at his exaggerated expression. "Your undercover acting technique must have been a lot more persuasive than that. Or you were dealing with idiots."

After she finished her oatmeal and had a second cup of coffee, she took a shower and got dressed. At eight-thirty she gave him a tight hug and a kiss, a worried look, then another kiss, and left for her sister's suburban palace in Ridgewood.

When her car was well down the road, he got into his own car and followed her. Knowing the route she would take, he was able to stay far behind her, keeping her only occasionally in sight. His goal was not to follow her but to make sure no one else was following her.

After a few deserted miles, he was sure enough, and he returned home.

As he parked by the trooper's car, they exchanged small, friendly salutes.

Before going into the house, he stood by the side door and looked around. He had for a moment a timeless feeling, the feeling of standing in a painting. As he entered the house, the feeling of peace was disturbed by his cell phone with the short ring that signaled the arrival of a text message—and utterly shattered by the message itself:

SORRY I MISSED YOU THE OTHER DAY. I'LL TRY AGAIN. HOPE YOU ENJOY THE DOLL.

Gurney felt an irrational impulse to charge into the woods, as though the message had been sent by someone who was at that moment lurking behind a tree trunk watching him—to shout obscenities at his invisible foe. Instead he read the message again. It included the originating number, unblocked, just like the previous messages, making it a virtual certainty that the cell phone was the untraceable prepaid variety.

It might be helpful to know the originating cell tower location, but that was a process with some sticky strings attached.

Since the intrusion of the doll into the house had been reported, it had the status of an open investigation. In that context an anonymous text message referring to the doll was a form of evidence that should be reported. However, a cell-records warrant with its ensuing data search would reveal that previous text messages had been sent to Gurney's number from the same phone, and that he had replied to them. He felt trapped in a box of his own making, a box in which every solution would create a bigger problem.

He cursed himself for his ego-driven agreement to take on one more murder case no one else could solve; for his ego-driven willingness to let Sonya Reynolds back into his life; for his ego-driven blindness to the Jykynstyl deception; for his ego-driven desire to keep the consequences, and possible photographs, from Madeleine; for the absurd and dangerous bind in which he now found himself.

But cursing himself for his failings was getting him nowhere. He had to *do* something. But what?

The phone ringing on the kitchen sideboard answered the question for him.

It was Sheridan Kline, exuding his oiliest enthusiasm. "Dave! Glad you picked up. Get on your horse, my friend. We need you here pronto."

"What's happening?"

"What's happening is that Darryl Becker of Palm Beach's Finest found Ballston's boat, just like you said he would. Guess what else he found."

"I'm not a guesser."

"Hah! Fact is, you made a damn good guess about that boat—and the possibility that the Palm Beach techs would find something on it. Well, they did. They found a tiny bloodstain . . . which generated a rush DNA profile . . . which triggered a CODIS near hit . . . which produced a change of heart on the part of Mr. Ballston. Or at least it produced a change in his legal strategy. He and his attorney are now in full-cooperation-to-avoid-lethal-injection mode."

"Back up a second," said Gurney. "The CODIS near hit—whose name popped up?"

"Worked the same way it worked with Melanie Strum—a first-degree family relationship, in this case a convicted child molester by the name of Wayne Dawker. Same last name as a Mapleshade girl, Kim Dawker, who went missing three months before Melanie. Turns out Wayne is Kim's older brother. Ballston's lawyers might be good enough to wiggle around one dead girl on his hands, but not two."

"How'd they get the CODIS response so fast?"

"The phrase 'serial murder conspiracy' could be a motivator. Or maybe somebody in Palm Beach just happens to have the right phone number." Kline sounded envious.

"Either way is fine with me," said Gurney. "What's next?"

"This afternoon Becker will be conducting a formal interrogation of Ballston, which Ballston has agreed to. We've been invited to participate through a computer-conferencing process. We witness the interrogation on a computer monitor and transmit any questions we want asked. I've insisted you be included."

"What's my role?"

"Submit the right question at the right time? Figure out how forthcoming he's being? You're the one who knows this creep best. Hey—speaking of creeps—I heard you had a little unauthorized-entry incident at your house."

"You could call it that. Kind of unnerving at first, but . . . I'm sure we'll get to the bottom of it."

"Looks like someone doesn't want you on the case—you figure that's what it is?"

"I don't know what else it could be."

"Well, we can talk about it when you get here."

"Right." In fact, Gurney had no desire whatever to talk about it. As long as he could remember, he'd recoiled from the discussion of anything remotely connected to his own vulnerability. It was the same dysfunctional form of damage control that was keeping him from being less than forthcoming with Madeleine about his Rohypnol fears.

The police academy's computer-video equipment had been updated more recently than BCI's, so it was in the academy's teleconferencing center that everyone gathered shortly before two that afternoon. The "center" was a conference room whose main feature was a flat-screen monitor mounted on the front wall. A semicircular table with a dozen chairs faced the screen. The attendees were all familiar to Gurney. Some, like Rebecca Holdenfield, he was happier to see than others.

He was relieved to note that they all seemed absorbed in their anticipation of what was about to occur—too absorbed to start asking about the doll and its implications.

Sergeant Robin Wigg was sitting at a small separate table in a corner of the room with two open laptops, a cell phone, and a keyboard with which she seemed to be controlling the monitor on the wall. As she tapped at the keys, the screen displayed a series of digital artifacts and numerical codes, then sprang to high-definition life—and quickly became the focus of everyone's attention.

It showed a standard interrogation room with concrete-block walls. In the center of the room was a gray metal table. On one side of it sat Detective Darryl Becker. Facing him on the other side were two men. One looked like he'd stepped out of a *GQ* article on America's best-dressed attorneys. The other was Jordan Ballston, in whom a devastating transformation had taken place. He looked sweaty and rumpled. His body sagged, his mouth was slightly open, and his hollow gaze was fixed on the table.

Becker turned crisply to the camera. "We're about ready to get started. Hope we're loud and clear at the remote location. Please confirm that." He stared at the screen of a laptop facing him on the table.

Gurney heard Wigg tapping on her keyboard.

A few moments later, Becker smiled at his screen and gave a happy thumbs-up sign.

Rodriguez, who'd been conferring in whispers with Kline, stepped to the front of the room. "Listen up, people. We're here to witness an interrogation, to which we've been invited to contribute. As the result of the discovery of new evidence on his property—"

"Bloodstains on his boat, found as the result of Gurney's nudging," interrupted Kline. He loved to stir the pot, keep the animosities boiling.

Rodriguez blinked and continued. "As a result of this evidence, the defendant has changed his story. In an effort to escape the certainty of the Florida death penalty, he's offering not only to confess to the Melanie Strum murder but to provide details regarding a larger criminal conspiracy—a conspiracy that may relate to the apparent disappearances of other Mapleshade graduates. You should note that the defendant is making this statement to save his life and may be motivated to say more than he actually knows about this so-called conspiracy."

As if to discount the captain's caution, Hardwick called across the room to Gurney, who was seated at the opposite end of the half-moon table. "Congratulations, Sherlock! You ought to consider a career in law enforcement. We need brains like yours."

A voice from the monitor on the wall redirected everyone's attention.

Chapter 66

The monstrous truth, according to Ballston

"It's now 2:03 P.M., September twentieth. This is Detective Lieutenant Darryl Becker of the Palm Beach Police Department. With me in Interrogation Room Number One are Jordan Ballston and his attorney Stanford Mull. This interrogation is being recorded." Becker looked from the camera to Ballston. "Are you Jordan Ballston of South Ocean Boulevard, Palm Beach?"

Ballston answered without raising his eyes from the table. "Yes, I am."

"Have you agreed after consultation with your attorney to make a complete and truthful statement regarding the murder of Melanie Strum?"

Stanford Mull put his hand on Ballston's forearm. "Jordan, I must—"

"Yes, I have," said Ballston.

Becker went on. "Do you agree to answer fully and truthfully all questions put to you in regard to this matter?"

"Yes, I do."

"Please describe in detail how you came into contact with Melanie Strum and everything that occurred thereafter, including how and why you killed her."

Mull looked agonized. "For Godsake, Jordan—"

Ballston looked up for the first time. "Enough, Stan, enough! I've made my decision. You're not here to get in my way. I just want you to be fully aware of everything I say."

Mull shook his head.

Ballston seemed relieved by his attorney's silence. He looked up at the camera. "How large an audience do I have?"

Becker looked disgusted. "Does it matter?"

"The damnedest things end up on YouTube."

"This won't."

"Too bad." Ballston smiled horribly. "Where should I begin?"

"At the beginning."

"You mean when I saw my uncle fucking my mother when I was six years old?"

Becker hesitated. "Why don't you start by telling us how you met Melanie Strum?"

Ballston leaned back in his chair, addressing his answer in an almost dreamy tone to a point somewhere high on the wall behind Becker. "I acquired Melanie through the special Karnala process. The process involves a branching journey through a sequence of portals. Now, each of these portals—"

"Hold on. You need to describe this in plain English. What the hell is a portal?"

Gurney wanted to tell Becker to relax, let the man speak, ask the questions later. But telling Becker what to do at this point could derail him completely.

"I'm talking about website links and passages. Internet sites offering choices of other sites, chat rooms leading to other chat rooms, always in the direction of exploring narrower and more intense interests, and finally leading to a direct one-on-one e-mail or text-message correspondence between customer and provider." In light of the underlying subject matter, Ballston's professorial tone struck Gurney as surreal.

"You mean you tell them what kind of girl you want and they deliver her?"

"No, no, nothing as abrupt or crude as that. As I said, the Karnala process is *special*. The price is high, but the methodology is elegant. Once the direct correspondence has proven satisfactory on both sides—"

"Satisfactory? In what way?"

"In the way of credibility. The people at Karnala become

convinced of the seriousness of the customer's intentions, and the customer becomes convinced of Karnala's legitimacy."

"*Legitimacy?*"

"What? Oh, I see your problem. I mean *legitimacy* in the sense of being who you claim to be and not, for example, the agent of some pathetic sting operation."

Gurney was fascinated by the dynamics of the interrogation. Ballston, who was implicating himself in a capital crime for which he was bargaining to receive a less-than-capital sentence, seemed to be drawing a sense of control from his own calm narrative. Becker, nominally in charge, was the rattled one.

"Okay," said Becker, "assuming that everyone ends up satisfied with everyone else's legitimacy, what then?"

"Then," said Ballston, pausing dramatically and looking Becker in the eye for the first time, "the elegant touch: the Karnala ads in the Sunday *Times.*"

"Say that again?"

"Karnala Fashion. Featuring the highest clothing prices on the planet: one-of-a-kind outfits, custom-designed for you, at a hundred thousand dollars and up. Lovely ads. Lovely girls. Girls wearing nothing but a couple of diaphanous scarves. Very stimulating."

"What's the relevance of these ads?"

"Think about it."

Ballston's creepy gentility was getting to Becker. "Shit, Ballston, I don't have time for games."

Ballston sighed. "I'd have thought it was obvious, Lieutenant. The ads aren't for the clothes. They're for the girls."

"You're telling me the girls in the ads are for sale?"

"Correct."

Becker blinked, looked incredulous. "For a hundred thousand dollars?"

"And up."

"So then what? You send off a check for a hundred grand, and they FedEx you the world's highest-priced hooker?"

"Hardly, Lieutenant. You don't order a Rolls-Royce from a magazine ad."

"So you . . . what? Visit the Karnala showroom?"

"In a manner of speaking, yes. The showroom is actually a screening room. Each of the currently available girls, including the girl featured in the advertisement, introduces herself in her own intimate video."

"You talking about individual porno movies?"

"Something much better than that. Karnala operates at the most sophisticated end of the business. These girls and their video presentations are remarkably intelligent, wonderfully subtle, and carefully preselected to meet the customer's emotional needs." The tip of Ballston's tongue ran idly across his upper lip. Becker looked like he might explode out of his chair. "I think what you're failing to grasp, Lieutenant, is that these are girls with *very* interesting sexual histories, girls with *intense* sexual appetites of their own. These are not hookers, Lieutenant, these are very special girls."

"That's what makes them worth a hundred grand?"

Ballston sighed indulgently. "And up."

Becker nodded blankly. The man appeared to Gurney to be lost. "A hundred grand . . . for nymphomania . . . sophistication . . . ?"

Ballston smiled softly. "For being exactly what one wants. For being the glove that fits the hand."

"Tell me more."

"There are some very good wines available for fifty dollars a bottle, wines that achieve ninety percent of perfection. A far smaller number, available for five hundred dollars a bottle, achieve ninety-nine percent of perfection. But for that final one percent of absolute perfection—for that you'll pay five thousand dollars a bottle. Some people can't tell the difference. Some can."

"Damn! Here's ordinary little me, thinking that a pricey hooker is just a pricey hooker."

"For you, Lieutenant, I'm sure that's the ultimate truth."

Becker went rigid in his chair, his face expressionless. Gurney had seen that look too many times in his career. What followed it was usually unfortunate, occasionally career-ending. He hoped the camera and the presence of Stanford Mull, Esquire, would be effective deterrents.

Apparently they were. Becker slowly relaxed, looking around the room for a long minute, looking everywhere except at Ballston.

Gurney wondered what Ballston's game was. Was he calculatedly trying to ignite a violent reaction in exchange for a legal advantage? Or was his laid-back condescension an effort to demonstrate his superiority as his life collapsed?

When Becker spoke, his voice was unnaturally casual. "So tell me about that screening room, *Jordan*." He articulated the name in a way that sounded oddly insulting.

If Ballston heard it that way, he ignored it. "Small, comfortable, lovely carpet."

"Where is it?"

"I don't know. When I was picked up at Newark Airport, I was given a blindfold—one of those sleeping masks you see in old black-and-white movies. I was told by the driver to put it on and not take it off until I was informed that I was in the screening room."

"And you didn't cheat?"

"Karnala is not an organization that encourages cheating."

Becker nodded, smiled. "Do you think they might consider what you're telling us today a form of cheating?"

"I'm afraid they might," said Ballston.

"So you look at these . . . videos and . . . you see something you like. What then?"

"You verbally accept the terms of the purchase, you replace your blindfold, and you are driven back to the airport. You arrange for a wire transfer of the purchase price to a bank-account number in the Cayman Islands, and a few days later the girl of your dreams rings your doorbell."

"And then?"

"And then . . . whatever one wishes to happen . . . happens."

"And the girl of your dreams ends up dead."

Ballston smiled. "Of course."

"Of course?"

"That's what the transaction is all about. Didn't you know that?"

"All about . . . killing them?"

"The girls Karnala provides are very bad girls. They've done terrible things. In their videos they describe in detail what they've done. Unbelievably terrible things."

Becker moved back slightly in his chair. He was clearly in over his head. Even Stanford Mull's poker face had assumed a certain rigidity. Their reactions seemed to energize Ballston. Life seemed to be flowing back into him. His eyes brightened.

"Terrible things that require terrible punishments."

There was a kind of universal pause, maybe two or three seconds, in which it seemed that no one in the Palm Beach interrogation room or the BCI teleconferencing room was breathing.

Darryl Becker broke the spell with a practical question in a routine tone of voice. "Let's be perfectly clear on this. You killed Melanie Strum?"

"That's correct."

"And Karnala had sent other girls to you?"

"Correct."

"How many others?"

"Two prior to Melanie."

"How much did you know about them?"

"About the boring details of their day-to-day existences, nothing. About their passions and their transgressions, everything."

"Did you know where they came from?"

"No."

"How Karnala recruited them?"

"No."

"Did you ever try to find out?"

"That was specifically discouraged."

Becker leaned back from the table and studied Ballston's face.

As Gurney watched Becker on the screen, it looked to him as if the man was stalling, overwhelmed by his introduction to a level of sickness he hadn't anticipated, trying to figure out where to go next with the interrogation.

Gurney turned to Rodriguez. The captain looked every bit as nonplussed as Darryl Becker by Ballston's revelations and nonchalance.

"Sir?" At first Rodriguez seemed not to hear him. "Sir, I'd like to send a request down to Palm Beach."

"What kind of request?"

"I want Becker to ask Ballston why he cut off Melanie's head."

The captain's faced twitched in revulsion. "Obviously because he's a sick, sadistic, murdering creep."

"I think it could be useful to ask the question."

Rodriguez looked pained. "What else could it be, other than part of his disgusting ritual?"

"Like cutting off Jillian's head was part of Hector's ritual?"

"What's your point?"

Gurney's tone hardened. "It's a simple question, *and it has to be asked.* We're running out of time." He knew that Rodriguez's horrendous difficulties with his crack-addict daughter were compromising the man's ability to deal directly with a case so close to home, but that was not Gurney's largest concern.

Rodriguez's face reddened, an effect heightened by the contrast with his starched white collar and dyed black hair. After a moment he turned toward Wigg with an air of surrender. "Man has a question. 'Why did Ballston cut off her head?' Send it."

Wigg's fingers tapped rapidly on her keyboard.

On the teleconferencing monitor, Becker was pressing Ballston about where Karnala got the girls, and Ballston was reiterating his total lack of knowledge in that area.

Becker looked like he was considering yet another way to pursue this when his attention was drawn to his laptop, apparently to the question Wigg had just transmitted. He looked up at the camera and nodded before switching subjects.

"So, Jordan, tell me . . . why did you do it?"

"Do what?"

"Kill Melanie Strum in that particular way."

"I'm afraid that's a private matter."

"Private, hell. The deal was we ask questions, you answer them."

"Well . . ." Ballston's bravado was fading. "I would say it was partly a matter of personal preference, and . . ." He looked for the first time in the interrogation mildly anxious. "I have to ask you something, Lieutenant. Are you referring to . . . the whole process . . . or simply the removal of the head?"

Becker hesitated. The banal tone of the conversation seemed to be twisting his grip on reality. "For now . . . let's say we're mainly concerned about the removal."

"I see. Well, the removal was, shall we say, a courtesy."

"It was a *what?*"

"A courtesy. A gentlemen's agreement."

"An agreement . . . to do what?"

Ballston shook his head in despair, like the sophisticated tutor of a dull student. "I think I've explained the basic arrangement, and Karnala's expertise in catering to the psychological dimension, their ability to provide a unique product. You did understand all that, Lieutenant?"

"Yeah, I understood it fine."

"They're the ultimate source of the ultimate product."

"Yeah, I got that."

"As a condition for an ongoing business relationship, they did have that one small stipulation."

"The stipulation being that you cut off the victim's head?"

"After the process. An addendum, if you will."

"And the purpose of this 'addendum' was . . . what?"

"Who knows? We all have our preferences."

"Preferences?"

"It was suggested that it was important to someone at Karnala."

"Jesus. Did you ever ask them to explain that?"

"Oh, my, Lieutenant, you really don't know the first thing about Karnala, do you?" Ballston's weird serenity level was rising in direct proportion to Becker's consternation.

Chapter 67

A mother's love

At the conclusion of Jordan Ballston's initial interrogation—the first of three that had been scheduled so that questions raised by the first could be revisited, questions that had been omitted could be asked, and the full scope of Ballston's dealings with Karnala could be probed and documented—the teleconferencing transmission was terminated.

When the monitor went blank, Blatt was the first to speak. "What an evil scumbag!"

Rodriguez took a spotless handkerchief from his pocket, removed his wire-rimmed glasses, and began polishing them distractedly. It was the first time Gurney had seen him with his glasses off. Without them his eyes looked smaller and weaker, the skin around them older.

Kline slid his chair back from the table. "Damn! Don't believe I've ever witnessed an interrogation quite like that. What'd you think, Becca?"

Holdenfield arched her eyebrows. "Care to be more specific?"

"Do you buy that incredible story?"

"If you're asking me do I think he was telling the truth as he sees it, the answer is yes."

"Evil scumbag like that has no regard for the truth," said Blatt.

Holdenfield smiled, addressed Blatt as she might a well-meaning child. "An accurate observation, Arlo. Telling the truth would not rank high among Mr. Ballston's values. Unless he thought it would save his life."

Blatt persevered. "I wouldn't trust him to take out the garbage."

"I'll tell you what my reaction is," announced Kline. He waited for all of them to give him their attention. "Assuming that his state-ments are accurate, Karnala may be one of the most depraved crimi-nal enterprises ever uncovered. The Ballston piece of it, horrendous as it may be, is likely just the tip of an iceberg—an iceberg from hell."

The harsh, single-syllable laugh that erupted from Hardwick was only partially concealed as a cough, but Kline's dramatic mo-mentum carried him on. "Karnala sounds like a large, disciplined, ruthless operation. The authorities in Florida have grabbed one small appendage: one customer. But we have the opportunity to ex-pose and destroy the whole enterprise. Our success could make the difference between life and death for Lord only knows how many young women. Speaking of which, Rod, this might be a good time for a progress report on the calls to the graduates."

The captain put his glasses on, then took them off again. It was as though the twists of the case and its personal echoes were chal-lenging his ability to function. "Bill," he said with some effort, "give us the data from the interviews."

Anderson swallowed a chunk of doughnut and washed it down with a mouthful of coffee. "Of the hundred and fifty-two names on our list, calls have now been completed to or returned by at least one household member in a hundred and twelve cases." He shuffled through the papers in his folder. "Of those hundred and twelve, we've broken out the responses into a number of categories. For example—"

Kline looked restless. "Can we cut to the chase here? Just the number of girls who are not locatable, especially if they had the car argument before leaving home?"

Anderson did some more shuffling, went through half a dozen sheets of paper half a dozen times. He finally announced that twenty-one girls' whereabouts were unknown to their families, and seventeen of them had had the car argument—including those mentioned by Ashton and by Savannah Liston.

"So it seems that the pattern is holding up," said Kline. He switched his attention to Hardwick. "Anything new on the Karnala connection?"

"Nothing new—just that the Skards definitely run it and Inter-pol thinks the Skards these days are mainly into sex slavery."

Blatt looked interested. "How about being a little more explicit about this 'sex slavery' thing?"

Surprisingly, Rodriguez spoke up immediately, his voice full of anger. "I think we all know exactly what it is—the most revolting business on earth. The scum of the earth as sellers, the scum of the earth as buyers. Think about it, Arlo. You'll know you have the right picture when it makes you want to vomit." His intensity created an uneasy silence in the room.

Kline cleared his throat, his face screwed up in a kind of exaggerated disgust. "My own concept of sex trafficking involves Thai peasant girls being shipped to fat Arabs. Are we imagining something like that is happening with Mapleshade girls? I'm having a hard time seeing that. Can someone please enlighten me? Dave, you have any comment?"

"No comment on the Thai-Arab observation, but I do have two questions. First, do we believe that Flores is connected to the Skards? And if so, what does that suggest? I mean, since the Skard operation is a family affair, is it possible that Flores—"

"Might be a Skard himself?" Kline slapped his hand on the table. "Damn, why not?"

Blatt scratched his head in an unconscious parody of confusion. "What are you saying? That Hector Flores is actually one of those boys whose mother was screwing all the coke dealers?"

"Wow!" said Kline. "That would give the whole affair a new center of gravity."

"More like two centers of gravity," said Gurney.

"Two?"

"Money and sexual pathology. I mean, if this were simply a financial venture, why the weird Edward Vallory stuff?"

"Hmm. Good question. Becca?"

She looked at Gurney. "Are you suggesting there's a contradiction?"

"Not a contradiction, just a question about which is the dog and which is the tail."

Her interest seemed to increase. "And your conclusion?"

He shrugged. "I've learned never to underestimate the power of pathology."

Her lips moved in a slight smile of agreement. "The Interpol background summary I was given indicated Giotto Skard had three sons: Tiziano, Raffaello, Leonardo. If Hector Flores is one of them, the question is, which one?"

Kline stared at her. "You have an opinion about that?"

"It's more of a guess than a professional opinion, but if we assign a high value to sexual pathology as a motive in the case, then I'd probably lean toward Leonardo."

"Why?"

"He's the one the mother took with her when Giotto finally kicked her out. He's the one who was with her the longest."

"You saying that could turn you into a homicidal maniac?" asked Blatt. "Being close to your mother?"

Holdenfield shrugged. "That depends on who your mother is. Being close to a normal female parent is very different from being the object of prolonged abuse by a sociopathic drug addict and sexual predator like Tirana Zog."

"I get that," interjected Kline. "But how would the crazy effects of that kind of upbringing—the lunacy, rage, instability—how would that fit into what appears to be a highly organized criminal enterprise?"

Holdenfield smiled. "Insanity is not always an obstacle to the achievement of one's goals. Joseph Stalin isn't the only paranoid schizophrenic who made his way to the top. Sometimes there's a malignant synergy between pathology and the pursuit of practical objectives. Especially in brutal enterprises like the sex trade."

Blatt looked intrigued. "So you're saying nutcases make the best gangsters?"

"Not always. But let's assume for a moment that your Hector Flores is really Leonardo Skard. And that being raised by a psychotic, promiscuous, incestuous mother made him more than a little bit crazy. Let's also assume that the Skard organization, through Karnala, is as involved in high-end prostitution and sex slavery as BCI's contacts at Interpol claim and as Jordan Ballston's confession confirms."

"Lot of assumptions," said Anderson, trying to extract another doughnut crumb from the fibers of his napkin.

"Good assumptions, in my opinion," said Kline.

"And if those assumptions are true," said Gurney, "then Leonardo seems to have found himself the perfect job."

"What perfect job?" asked Blatt.

"A job that neatly combines the family business with his personal hatred of women."

Kline's initial expression of puzzlement gave way to amazement. "The job of a recruiter!"

"Exactly," said Gurney. "Suppose Skard—aka Flores—came to Mapleshade specifically to identify and recruit young women who might be persuaded to satisfy the sexual needs of wealthy men. Of course, he'd describe the arrangement in a way that would appeal to their own needs and fantasies. They'd never know, until it was too late, that they were being delivered into the hands of sexual sadists who intended to kill them—men like Jordan Ballston."

Blatt's eyes widened. "That is some extremely sick shit."

"Profit and pathology, hand in hand," said Gurney. "I knew more than one hit man who thought of himself as a businessman who just happened to be in a business most people didn't have the stomach for. Like embalming. He talked about it as though it were primarily a source of income and only secondarily about killing people. Of course, the truth is the opposite. Killing is about killing. It's about an icy kind of hatred—which the hit man converts into a business. Maybe that's what we're seeing here."

Anderson crumpled his napkin into a ball. "We're getting kind of theoretical, aren't we?"

"I think Dave is right on point," said Holdenfield. "Pathology and practicality. Leonardo Skard, in the guise of Hector Flores, may be making his living by arranging for the torture and beheading of women who remind him of his mother."

Rodriguez rose slowly from his chair. "I think this might be a good time to take a break here. Okay? Ten minutes. Restrooms. Coffee. Et cetera."

"Just one final point," said Holdenfield. "With all the talk about Jillian Perry being killed on her wedding day, has it occurred to anyone that it was also Mother's Day?"

Chapter 68

Buena Vista Trail

Kline, Rodriguez, Anderson, Blatt, Hardwick, and Wigg left the room. Gurney was about to follow when he saw Holdenfield, still in her chair, removing a set of photocopies from her briefcase—photocopies of several Karnala ads. She spread them out in front of her. He walked around to her side of the table and gazed down at them. They had a different impact on him now—presenting a harsher image of disorder and deception—since Ballston had revealed their purpose.

"I don't get it," he said. "Mapleshade supposedly provides some sort of remediation for unhealthy sexual fixations. Christ, if what I'm seeing in the faces of these young women reflects the benefit of therapy, what the hell were they like before?"

"Worse."

"Jesus."

"I've read some of Ashton's journal articles. His goals are modest. Minimal, really. His critics say his approach borders on the immoral. The faith-based therapists can't stand him. He believes in aiming not for major reorientations but for the smallest possible changes. One comment he made at a professional seminar became famous, or infamous. Ashton enjoys shocking his peers. He said if he could persuade a ten-year-old girl to perform fellatio on her twelve-year-old boyfriend instead of her eight-year-old cousin, he would consider the therapy a complete success. In some circles that approach is a tad controversial."

"Progress, not perfection, eh?"

"Right."

"Still, when I look at these expressions . . ."

"One thing you have to remember—the success rate in the field is not high. I'm sure that even Ashton fails more often than he succeeds. That's just a fact of life. When you're dealing with sex offenders . . ."

But Gurney had stopped listening to her.

Good God, why hadn't it registered before?

Holdenfield was staring at him. "What is it?"

He didn't answer immediately. There were implications to be considered, decisions to be made regarding how much to say. Crucial decisions. But making any decision at that moment was beyond his ability. He was nearly paralyzed by the realization that *the bedroom in the photo was the room he'd stepped into to hide from the cleaning people the night he retrieved the little absinthe glass.* He'd seen it for only a fraction of a second when he'd switched the light on and off to get his bearings. At the time it had triggered a strange sense of déjà vu—because he'd already seen the layout of the room in the photo of Jillian on Ashton's wall, but that night in the brownstone he hadn't been able to put the two images together.

"What is it?" Holdenfield repeated.

"It's hard to explain," he said, which was largely true. His voice was strained. He couldn't take his eyes off the ad closest to him. The girl was crouched on a rumpled bed, appearing both exhausted and inexhaustible—inviting, threatening, daring. He was jarred by a flashback from a religious retreat in his freshman year at St. Genesius: a wild-eyed priest ranting about hellfire. *A fire that burns for all eternity, that eats at your screaming flesh like a beast whose hunger grows with every bite.*

Hardwick was the first to return to the conference room. He glanced at Gurney, the ad photo, and Holdenfield, and he seemed to sense immediately the tension in the air. Wigg returned next and took up her station in front of her laptop, followed by a glum Anderson and an antsy Blatt. Kline came in speaking on his cell, trailed by Rodriguez. Hardwick sat across from Gurney, watching him curiously.

"All right," said Kline, again with the air of a man accomplishing a great deal. "Back on track. Following up on the question of the true identity of Hector Flores: Rod, I believe there was a plan to conduct some reinterviews of Ashton's neighbors to make sure no details about Flores had slipped through the cracks first time around. How's that going?"

Rodriguez looked for a moment like he was going to excoriate the whole exercise as a waste of time. Instead he turned to Anderson. "Anything new on that?"

Anderson folded his arms across his chest. "Not a single significant new fact."

Kline shot Gurney a challenging glance—since the reinterviewing idea had been his.

Gurney wrenched his mind back to the discussion and turned to Anderson. "Did you manage to sort out the actual eyewitness stuff, which is scarce, from the hearsay stuff, which is endless?"

"Yeah, we did that."

"And?"

"There's kind of a problem with the eyewitness data."

"What's that?" interjected Kline.

"The eyewitnesses are mostly dead."

Kline blinked. "Say that again?"

"The eyewitnesses are mostly dead."

"Christ, I heard you. Tell me what you mean."

"I mean, who actually spoke to Hector Flores? Or to Leonardo Skard, or whatever the hell we're calling him now? Who had face-to-face contact? Jillian Perry, and she's dead. Kiki Muller, and she's dead. The girls who Savannah Liston saw talking to him when he was working on Ashton's flower bed at Mapleshade, and they're all missing—possibly dead, if they ended up with guys like Ballston."

Kline looked skeptical. "I thought people saw him in the car with Ashton, or in town."

"What they saw was somebody in a cowboy hat and sunglasses," said Anderson. "None of them can provide a physical description worth a shit, excuse my language. We got a boatload of colorful anecdotes, but that's about it. Seems like everybody is telling us stories that somebody else told them."

Kline nodded. "That dovetails perfectly with the Skard reputation."

Anderson gave him a sideways look.

"The Skards are supposedly ruthless about eliminating real witnesses. Seems like anyone who could finger one of the Skard boys ends up dead. What do you think, Dave?"

"I'm sorry, what?"

Kline gave him an odd look. "I'm asking if you think that the diminishing number of people who could ID Flores reinforces the idea that he might be one of the Skard boys."

"To tell you the truth, Sheridan, at this point I'm not sure what I think. I keep wondering if anything that occurs to me about this case is true. My fear is that I'm missing something big that would explain everything. I've worked a hell of a lot of homicide cases over the years, and I've never worked one that felt as wrong as this one. It's like there's a definite elephant in the room that none of us is seeing."

Kline sat back thoughtfully. "This may not be the elephant in the room, but I do have a question that keeps bothering me about the missing girls. I understand the car thing, that the girls are all legally adults, that they told their parents not to try to find them, but . . . don't any of you find it peculiar that not a single parent notified the police?"

"I'm afraid there's a sad, simple answer to your question," said Holdenfield slowly, after a long silence. The oddly softened tone of her voice drew everyone's attention. "Given a plausible explanation for their daughters' departures and a request for no further contact, I suspect that the parents were secretly pleased. Many parents of aggressively troublesome children have a terrible fear they're ashamed to admit: that they'll be saddled with their little monsters forever. When the monsters finally leave, for whatever reason, I think the parents feel *relief.*"

Rodriguez looked sick. He stood quietly and headed for the door, his sallow skin ashen. Gurney guessed that Holdenfield had just hit the man's most sensitive nerve dead-on, a nerve that had been exposed, prodded, needled, and battered from the moment the case had veered from his hunt for a Mexican gardener to a probe of disordered family relationships and sick young women. That nerve had been rubbed so raw over the past week it perhaps wasn't surprising that a man of already limited flexibility was turning into a basket case.

The door opened before Rodriguez got to it. Gerson stepped in with a tinge of alarm on her lean face, effectively blocking his way. "Excuse me, sir, an urgent call."

"Not now," he muttered vaguely. "Maybe Anderson . . . or someone . . ."

"Sir, it's an emergency. Another Mapleshade-related homicide."

Rodriguez stared at her. "What?"

"A homicide—"

"Who?"

"A girl by the name of Savannah Liston."

It seemed to take a few seconds for the news to register—as though he were listening to a translation. "Right," he said finally, and followed her out of the room.

When he returned five minutes later, the vague speculations that had been drifting around the table in his absence were replaced by an eager attentiveness.

"Okay. Everyone is here who needs to be here," he announced. "I'm only going to go through this once, so I suggest you take notes."

Anderson and Blatt pulled out small identical notebooks and pens. Wigg's fingers were poised over her laptop keys.

"That was Tambury police chief Burt Luntz. He called from his present location, a bungalow rented by Savannah Liston, an employee of Mapleshade." There was strength and purpose in the captain's voice, as though the task of passing along information had put him, at least temporarily, on solid ground. "At approximately five o'clock this morning, Chief Luntz received a phone call at his home. In what sounded to Luntz like a Spanish accent, all the caller said was, 'Seventy-eight Buena Vista, for all the reasons I have written.' When Luntz asked the caller for his name, his response was 'Edward Vallory calls me the Spanish Gardener.' At that point the caller hung up."

Anderson frowned at his watch. "This was at five A.M.—ten hours ago—and we're just hearing about it now?"

"Unfortunately, the call didn't set off an alarm with Luntz. He just assumed it was a wrong number or the guy was drunk or maybe both. He's not privy to the details of our investigation, so the Edward Vallory references meant nothing to him. Then, about half an hour ago, he got a call from a Dr. Lazarus at Mapleshade saying that they had an employee, normally responsible, who didn't show up for work today, wasn't answering her phone, and—considering all the crazy things going on—could Luntz send one of his local patrol cars by her house to make sure everything was all right? Then he gives the address as Seventy-eight Buena Vista Trail, which rings a bell, so Luntz drives over there himself."

Kline was leaning forward in his chair like a sprinter on his mark. "And finds Savannah Liston dead?"

"He finds the back door unlocked, with Liston at the kitchen table. Same configuration as Jillian Perry."

"Exactly the same?" asked Gurney.

"Apparently."

"Where is Luntz now?" asked Kline.

"In the kitchen, with some Tambury uniforms on the way to set up a perimeter and secure the scene. He's already gone through the house—lightly, just to verify that no one else is present. Hasn't touched anything."

"Did he say if he noticed anything odd?" asked Gurney.

"One thing. A pair of boots by the door. The kind you slip on over your shoes. Sound familiar?"

"The boots again. Jesus. There's something about the boots." Gurney's tone held Rodriguez's attention. "Captain, I know it's not my place to . . . to try to influence your allocation of resources, but . . . may I make a suggestion?"

"Go ahead."

"I would recommend that you get those boots to your lab people immediately, keep them here all night if you have to, and have them run every goddamn chemical-recognition test they can."

"Looking for what?"

"I don't know."

Rodriguez made a face, but not as bad a one as Gurney had feared. "Based on nothing, that's a hell of a shot in the dark, Gurney."

"The boots have shown up twice. Before they show up again, I'd like to know why."

Chapter 69

Blind alleys

Anderson, Hardwick, and Blatt were dispatched to the Buena Vista scene, along with an evidence team selected by Sergeant Wigg, and a K-9 team. The ME's office was notified. Gurney asked if he could accompany the BCI people to the scene. Rodriguez predictably refused. But he did give Wigg the assignment of coordinating and expediting lab work on the boots. Kline said something about agreeing on a damage-control strategy for a scheduled press conference, and he and the captain went off to confer privately, leaving Gurney and Holdenfield alone in the conference room.

"So?" she said. It was half a question, half an amused observation.

"So?" he repeated.

She shrugged, glanced at her briefcase, in which she had replaced her copies of the Karnala ads.

He guessed she wanted to know more about his earlier disturbed reaction. He'd already told her it was hard to explain. And he still wasn't ready to talk about it, still hadn't figured out the implications of full disclosure, still hadn't figured out the damage-control options.

"It's a long story," he said.

"I'd love to hear it."

"I'd love to tell you about it, but . . . it's complicated." The first part was less true than the second part. "Maybe another time."

"Okay." She smiled back. "Another time."

With no chance of direct access to the lab techs and no other compelling reason to hang around the state police campus, Gurney headed home to Walnut Crossing, with the day's wild bits and pieces swirling through his head.

Ballston's surreal confession, the genteel voice emanating from a hellish mind, describing his compliance with Karnala's beheading request as a *courtesy*, the beheading of Savannah Liston echoing the beheaded doll on the bed echoing the beheaded bride at the table. And the rubber boots. Once again, the boots. Did he really think the lab tests would produce a revelation? He was too worn out from the day to know what he really thought.

The call he got from Sheridan Kline as he was finishing a bowl of leftover spaghetti added facts without adding progress. In addition to repeating everything Rodriguez had passed along from Luntz, Kline revealed that a bloodstained machete had been discovered by the K-9 team in a wooded area behind the bungalow and that the ME estimated the time of death to be roughly within a three-hour window of the cryptic predawn call Luntz had received.

There were many times in his career when Gurney had felt challenged. There were occasionally cases, such as the recent Mellery horror, in which he believed that the challenger might win. But never had he felt so broadly outmaneuvered. Sure, he had a general theory for what might be going on and who might be behind it— the whole Skard operation, with "Hector Flores" recruiting "bad girls" for the murderous pleasure of the sickest men on earth—but it was just a theory. And even if it were valid, it still didn't come close to explaining the twisty mechanics of the murders themselves. It didn't explain the impossible placement of the machete behind Ashton's cottage. It didn't explain the function of the boots. It didn't explain the choice of the local victims.

Why, exactly, did Jillian Perry, Kiki Muller, and Savannah Liston all have to die?

Worst of all, without knowing why those three were killed, how would it be possible to protect whoever else might be in danger?

After exhausting himself by exploring the same blind alleys over and over, Gurney fell asleep around midnight.

When he awoke seven hours later, a gusty wind was heaving waves of gray rain against the bedroom windows. The window next to his bed—the only one in the house he'd left unlocked—was open two inches at the top, not enough to let the rain blow in but more than enough to admit a damp draft that made his sheets and pillow feel clammy.

The dismal atmosphere, the lack of light and color in the world, tempted him to stay in bed, uncomfortable as it was, but he knew that would be an emotional mistake, so he forced himself up and into the bathroom. His feet were cold. He turned on the shower.

Thank God, he thought once again, for the primal magic of water.

Cleanser, restorer, simplifier. As the tingling hot spray massaged his back, the muscles in his neck and shoulders relaxed. His knotted, hyperactive thoughts began to dissolve in the water's soothing rush. Like surf hissing over sand . . . like a benign opiate . . . the pelting of the water on his skin made life seem simple and good.

Chapter 70

In plain sight

After a modest breakfast of two eggs and two slices of plain toast, Gurney decided to reground himself, as tedious as that might be, in the original facts of the case.

He spread out the segments of the file on the dining table and, with a spark of contrariness, reached for the document he'd had the most difficulty concentrating on when he'd gone through everything originally. It was a fifty-seven-page printout listing all the hundreds of sites Jillian had visited on the Internet and the hundreds of search terms she had entered in the browsers on her cell phone and her laptop during the last six months of her life—mostly related to chic travel destinations, super-expensive hotels, cars, jewelry.

After this personal computer and Web-usage data had been acquired by BCI, however, no analysis had been performed. Gurney suspected that it was just another piece of the investigation that had disappeared into the crevasse separating Hardwick's stewardship from Blatt's. The only indication that anyone other than himself had even seen it was a handwritten comment on a sticky note affixed to the first page: *"Complete waste of time and resources."*

Perversely, Gurney's suspicion that the comment was the captain's had intensified his attention to every line of those fifty-seven pages. And without that attention boost, he might very well have missed one little five-letter word halfway down page thirty-seven.

Skard.

It appeared again on the following page, and twice more a few pages later.

The discovery propelled Gurney through the rest of the

document, then back through all fifty-seven pages one more time. It was during this second pass that he made his second discovery.

The car makes that were scattered among the search terms—makes that at first had blended in his mind with the names of resorts, boutiques, and jewelers into a general image of material comfort—now formed a special pattern of their own.

He realized that they were the very same makes that had been the subjects of the missing girls' arguments with their parents.

Could that be a coincidence?

What the hell had Jillian been up to?

What was it she needed to know about those cars? And why?

More important, what was she trying to find out about the Skard family?

How had she come to know they existed?

And what kind of relationship did she have with the man she'd known as Hector Flores?

Was it business? Or pleasure? Or something much sicker?

A closer look at the automobile URLs revealed that they were the proprietary advertising websites maintained by the companies to provide model, feature, and pricing information.

The search term *"Skard"* led to a site with information about a small town in Norway, as well as to a number of other sites with no connection to the Sardinia-based crime family. Which meant that Jillian had already learned in some other way about the family's existence, or at least the existence of that name, and her Internet search was an attempt to find out more.

Gurney went back to the master list and noted the dates of her car and Skard searches. He discovered that she'd visited the car sites months before searching the Skard name. In fact, the car searches went back to the beginning of the six-month time window that had been documented, and he wondered how long she'd been pursuing that kind of data. He made a note to suggest to BCI that they get an expanded warrant for her search records going back at least two years.

Gurney stared out at the wet landscape. An intriguing, if highly speculative, scenario was beginning to take shape—a scenario in which Jillian may have played a much more active . . .

A low rumble from the road below the barn interrupted his train of thought. He went to the kitchen window, which offered the longest view in that direction, and noticed that the police cruiser was gone. He looked at the clock and realized that the promised forty-eight-hour protection window had expired. However, another vehicle, the source of the throaty engine rumble, now distinctly louder, came into view down at the point where the town road blended into the Gurney driveway.

It was a red Pontiac GTO, a seventies classic, and Gurney knew only one person who owned one—Jack Hardwick. The fact that he was driving the GTO instead of a black Crown Victoria meant he was off duty.

Gurney went to the side door and waited. Hardwick emerged from the car in old blue jeans and a white T-shirt under a well-worn motorcycle jacket—a retro tough guy stepping out of a time machine.

"This is quite a surprise," said Gurney.

"Just thought I'd drop by, make sure you weren't getting any more doll gifts."

"Very thoughtful. Come on in."

Inside, Hardwick said nothing, just let his gaze wander around the room.

"You drove a long way in the rain," said Gurney.

"Rain stopped an hour ago."

"No kidding. Guess I didn't notice."

"You look like your brain's on another planet."

"Then I guess it must be," said Gurney with a sharper edge than he'd intended.

Hardwick showed no reaction. "That woodstove save you money?"

"What?"

"That woodstove, does it save you money on oil?"

"How the hell should I know? What are you here for, Jack?"

"Can't a guy drop in on a buddy? Just to shoot the shit?"

"Neither one of us is the kind of guy who ever drops in on anyone. And neither of us has any interest in shooting the shit. So what are you here for?"

"Man wants to get to the point. Okay, I can respect that. No wasted time. How about you make some coffee and offer me a seat?"

"Right," said Gurney. "I'll make coffee. You sit wherever you want."

Hardwick ambled to the far end of the big room and studied the stonework of the old fireplace. Gurney plugged in the coffeemaker and started the brewing process.

A few minutes later, they were facing each other in the pair of armchairs by the hearth.

"Not bad," said Hardwick after a sip of his coffee.

"No, it's actually pretty good. What the hell do you want, Jack?"

He took another sip before answering. "I thought maybe we could trade some information."

"I don't think I have anything worth trading."

"Oh, yeah you do. No doubt about that. So what do you say? I tell you stuff, you tell me stuff."

Gurney felt a surprising surge of anger. "Okay, Jack, why the hell not? You go first."

"I spoke to my friend at Interpol again. Pushed him a bit on that 'Sandy's Den' thing. And guess what? It was also called 'Alessandro's Den.' Sometimes one, sometimes the other. That come as a big shock to you?"

"How could it be a shock?"

"Last time we talked about it, you seemed pretty sure it was all a coincidence. You don't still think that, do you?"

"I guess not. There can't be that many Alessandros in the sexy-photo business."

"Right. So you got your little absinthe glass from Saul Steck, who happens to work under the name Alessandro for Karnala Fashion taking pictures of Mapleshade girls who shortly thereafter disappear. So tell me, ace, what the fuck are you up to? And by the way, while you're explaining that, how about you explain the look on your face yesterday afternoon when you were staring over Holdenfield's shoulder at that Karnala ad."

Gurney leaned back in his chair, closed his eyes, and raised his coffee cup slowly to his lips. He took a few leisurely sips before opening his eyes. Still holding the cup in front of his mouth, he looked over at Hardwick. The man was in the identical position, his cup raised, watching Gurney. They traded small ironic smiles and low-ered their cups to the arms of their chairs.

"Well," began Gurney, "when all else fails, even the wicked sometimes need to fall back on honesty as the only way out." El-bowing the potential consequences from his mind, he went on to tell Hardwick the whole Sonya–Mug Shot Art–Jykynstyl–amnesia story, including the ensuing text messages and his belated recogni-tion of the brownstone bedroom in the Karnala ads. When he came to the end, he discovered that his coffee had gotten cold, but he fin-ished it anyway.

"Jesus fucking Christ," said Hardwick. "You realize what you've done to me?"

"Done to you?"

"By telling me all that shit, you've put me in the same fucking position you're in."

Gurney felt a huge sense of relief but didn't think it would be a good idea to say so. Instead he said, "So what do you think we ought to do?"

"What do *I* think? You're the fucking genius who failed to dis-close significant new evidence in a felony investigation, which in itself is a felony. And telling me these things, you have now put me in the position of—guess what?—concealing significant new evi-dence in a felony investigation, which in itself is a felony. Unless, of course, I go immediately to Rodriguez and hang your ass out to dry. Jesus, Gurney! Now you ask me, what do *I* think we ought to do? And don't think I didn't pick up on that 'we' shit you dropped into the discussion. You're the fucking genius who created this mess. What do *you* think needs to be done?"

The more agitated Hardwick got, the more relieved Gurney felt—because, perversely, it meant that Hardwick was committed to keeping his confession in confidence for the duration.

"I think if we solve the case," said Gurney calmly, "the mess will take care of itself."

"Oh, shit, yeah, sure. Why didn't I think of that? Just solve the case! What a neat idea!"

"Let's at least talk it through, Jack, see what we agree on, what we don't agree on, get all the possibilities on the table. We may be closer to a solution than we think." As soon as he said that, he realized he didn't believe it, but to backtrack at this point would make him sound like he was losing it. Maybe he was.

Hardwick gave him a doubtful look. "Go ahead, Sherlock. I'm all ears, lay it out. I just hope that whatever the hell drug they gave you didn't fry your brain."

He wished Hardwick hadn't said that. He got another cup of coffee and settled back in his chair.

"Okay, this is the way I picture it. It sort of looks like an H."

"What looks like an H?"

"The structure of what's happening. I just tend to see things geometrically. One of the verticals of the H is the established Skard family business—basically the worldwide sale of illegal, expensive forms of sexual gratification. According to your Interpol people, the Skards are a uniquely vicious and predatory crime family. Through Karnala, according to Jordan Ballston, they operate at the ugliest and most lethal S&M extremes of the sex business—selling carefully selected young women to wealthy sexual psychopaths."

Hardwick was nodding in agreement.

Gurney went on. "The other vertical in the H is the Mapleshade Residential Academy. You already know most of this, but let me talk it through. Mapleshade treats girls with intensely disordered sexual obsessions, obsessions that lead to reckless predatory behavior. In recent years they've been focusing exclusively on that clientele and have become well known in the field—due to Scott Ashton's huge academic reputation. He's quite a star in that corner of psychopathology. Suppose the Skards became aware of Mapleshade and saw its potential."

"Its potential for them?"

"Right. Mapleshade provided a concentrated population of intensely sexualized victims and perpetrators of sexual abuse. To the Skards it would look like—forgive my choice of words—the ultimate gourmet meat market."

Hardwick's pale blue eyes seemed to be searching for possible cracks in Gurney's logic. After a few seconds, he said, "I can see that. What's the crossbar on your H?"

"The crossbar connecting the Skards to Mapleshade is the man who called himself Hector Flores. It would seem that his way into Mapleshade was to make himself useful to Ashton, gain his trust, offer to do little jobs around the school."

"But remember, none of the girls disappeared while they were still students."

"No. That would have set off an instant alarm. There's a vast difference between a 'child' disappearing from boarding school and an 'adult' choosing to leave home. I imagine he approached girls who were about to graduate, felt them out in a general way, proceeded cautiously, made specific offers only to the ones he knew would accept, then instructed them how to leave home without arousing suspicion, maybe even arranged for their transportation. Or that might have been handled by someone else in the organization, maybe by the same person who made the videos of the young women talking about their sexual obsessions."

"That would be your buddy, Saul Steck—aka Alessandro, aka Jay Jykynstyl."

"Entirely possible," said Gurney.

"How would Flores have explained the need for the car argument?"

"He could have told them it was a necessary precaution, to make sure no one launched a mis-per hunt and located them with their new benefactor, creating embarrassment all around, ruining the deal."

Hardwick nodded. "So Flores lays the big con on these wacko babes like he's running a hot dating service—matches made in hell. Of course, once the young lady enters the gentleman's home—without leaving any trace of where she's gone—she discovers that the arrangement is not what she'd imagined. But at that point it's too late to back out. Because the sick piece of shit who bought her has no intention of ever letting her see the light of day again. Which is fine with the Skards. More than fine, if we believe Ballston's story about the icing on the cake, the 'gentlemen's agreement' to top off the process with a tasteful beheading."

"That about sums it up," said Gurney. "The theory is that Hector Flores, or Leonardo Skard, if that's his true identity, was the prime facilitator of a kind of homicidal matchmaking service for dangerous sex maniacs—some more dangerous than others. Of course, it's still just a theory."

"Not a bad one," said Hardwick, "as far as it goes. But it doesn't explain Jillian Perry getting whacked on her wedding day."

"I think that Jillian may have gotten involved with Hector Flores and that she may have learned at some point who he really was—maybe that his real name was Skard."

"Involved with him how? Why?"

"Maybe Hector needed a helper. Maybe Jillian was his first con job when he arrived at Mapleshade three years ago, when she was still a student there. Maybe he made some promises to her. Maybe she was his little mole among the other students, helping him select likely candidates. And maybe she finally outlived her usefulness, or maybe she was even crazy enough to try to blackmail him after finding out who he was. Her mother told me she loved living on the edge—and you can't get any closer to the edge than threatening a member of the Skard family."

Hardwick looked incredulous. "So he cut off her head on her wedding day?"

"Or Mother's Day, as Becca pointed out."

"*Becca?*" Hardwick raised a leering eyebrow.

"Don't be an asshole," said Gurney.

"And what about Savannah Liston? Another Flores mole who outlived her usefulness?"

"It's a workable hypothesis."

"I thought she was the one who told you last week about a couple of girls she couldn't get in touch with. If she was working with Flores, why would she do that?"

"Maybe he told her to. Maybe to give me the idea that I could trust her, confide in her. He might have realized that the investigation was going into high gear, and of course that would mean that we'd be talking to Mapleshade graduates. So it would only be a matter of time—and not much time at that—before we found out that a significant number of those graduates were unreachable. He might have been letting Savannah give me that fact a couple of days before we would have found out anyway—to create the impression that she was one of the good guys."

"Do you think she knew . . . that she and Jillian both knew . . . ?"

"Knew what was happening to the girls they were helping

Flores recruit? I doubt it. They probably swallowed the basic sales pitch Hector was serving up—just introducing girls with special interests to men with special interests and earning a nice commission for their efforts. Of course, I don't know any of that for sure. It's possible that this whole case is one big trapdoor to hell, and I don't have the faintest idea what's going on."

"Shit, Gurney. Your total lack of faith in your own theories is really encouraging. What do you suggest for our next move?"

Gurney was saved from the discomfort of having no answer by the ring of his cell phone.

It was Robin Wigg. She began, as usual, without any preamble. "I have preliminary results from the lab tests on the boots found in the Liston residence. Captain Rodriguez has authorized me to discuss them with you, since they were performed at your suggestion. Is this a convenient time?"

"Absolutely. What have you got?"

"A lot of what you might expect, plus something you wouldn't expect. Shall I start with that?" There was something about Wigg's calm, businesslike contralto that Gurney had always liked. Regardless of the content of the words, the tone said that order could prevail over chaos.

"Please. The solutions are usually in the surprises."

"Yes, I find that to be true. The surprise was the presence on the boots of a particular pheromone: methyl p-hydroxybenzoate. How knowledgeable are you in this area?"

"I skipped chemistry in high school. You'd better start at the beginning."

"Actually, it's pretty simple. Pheromones are glandular secretions meant to transmit information from one animal to another. Specific pheromones secreted by an individual animal may attract, warn, calm, or excite another individual. Methyl p-hydroxybenzoate is a powerful canine-attractant pheromone, and it was identified in high concentrations on both boots."

"And the effect of that would be . . . ?"

"Any dog, but especially a tracking dog, would easily and eagerly follow a trail created by a person wearing those boots."

"How would someone get access to this stuff?"

"Some canine pheromones are available commercially for use in animal shelters and behavior-modification regimens. It could have been acquired that way or from direct contact with a bitch in estrus."

"Interesting. Is there any unintentional way you can think of for a chemical like that to get on someone's boots?"

"In the concentrations in which it was found? Short of an explosion in a pheromone-bottling facility, no."

"Very interesting. Thank you, Sergeant. I'm going to put Jack Hardwick on the phone. I'd appreciate your repeating to him what you told me—in case he has questions I can't answer."

Hardwick had one question. "When you call it an attractant pheromone secreted by a bitch in estrus, what you mean is a female sex scent no male dog could ignore, right?"

He listened to her brief answer, ended the call, and handed the phone back to Gurney, looking excited. "Holy shit. The irresistible scent of a bitch in heat. What do you make of that, Sherlock?"

"It's obvious that Flores wanted to be absolutely sure that the K-9 dog would follow that trail like an arrow. He may even have done some Internet research and discovered that the state tracking dogs are all males."

"Which obviously means that he wanted us to find the machete."

"No doubt about it," said Gurney. "And he wanted us to find it fast. Both times."

"So what's the scenario? He lops off their heads, puts on his doctored boots, scurries out into the woods, ditches the machete, comes back into the crime scene, takes off the boots, and . . . then what?"

"In the case of Savannah, he just walks away, drives away, whatever," said Gurney. "The Jillian situation is the impossible one."

"Because of the video problem?"

"That, plus the question of where could he have gone after he came back to the cottage?"

"Plus the more basic question: Why would he bother to come back at all?"

Gurney smiled. "That's the one little piece of it I think I understand. He came back to leave the boots in plain sight so the tracking dog would be excited by that scent in the cottage and immediately follow it out to the murder weapon. He wanted us to find it fast."

"Which brings us back to the big *why?*"

"It also brings us back one more time to the machete itself. I'm telling you, Jack, figure out how it got to where you found it without anyone being caught on camera and everything else will fall in place."

"You really think so?"

"You don't?"

Hardwick shrugged. "Some people say follow the money. You, on the other hand, are big on what you call 'discrepancies.' So you say follow the piece that makes no sense."

"And what do you say?"

"I say follow the thing that keeps coming up again and again. In this case the thing that keeps coming up again and again is sex. In fact, as far as I can see, everything in this weird-ass case, one way or another, is about sex. Edward Vallory. Tirana Zog. Jordan Ballston. Saul Steck. The whole Skard criminal enterprise. Scott Ashton's psychiatric specialty. The possible photographs that have you scared shitless. Even the fucking trail to the machete turns out to be about sex—the overwhelming sexual power of a bitch in heat. You know what I think, ace? I think it's time you and I visited the epicenter of this sexual earthquake—the Mapleshade Residential Academy."

Chapter 71

For all the reasons
I have written

*He was unhappy with the details of the final solution, its crude de-
parture from the elegant simplicity of a razor-sharp blade, a carefully
discriminating blade. But he could see no clearer way to the end of
the road. He was appalled by the imprecision of it all, the abandon-
ment of the fine distinctions that were his forte, but had come to view
it as unavoidable. The collateral casualties would simply be a necessary evil. He took what solace he could in reminding himself that his
planned action was the very definition—the very heart and soul—of
a just war. What he was about to do was undeniably necessary, and if
an action was necessary, then its unavoidable consequences were justified. The deaths of innocent children could be regarded as regrettable.
But who was to say they were innocent? No one at Mapleshade was
truly innocent. One could argue that they weren't even children. They
might not be adults legally, but they weren't children, either. Not in
any normal sense of the term.*

*So the day had arrived; the event was upon him; the opportunity,
not taken, would not come again. Discipline and objectivity must be
his watchwords. It was no time for flinching. He must hang on to the
reality of the thing.*

Edward Vallory had seen that reality with perfect clarity.

The hero of The Spanish Gardener *didn't flinch.*

*Now it was his turn to deliver the final blow to the whores and
liars, the bits and pieces of the devil.*

*"She's a nice little piece." A revealing phrase. Think of the ques-
tion it raises. A piece of what?*

Voice of the snake. Slithering mouth. Sweat on the lips.

"*Onto the heads of these serpents I shall bring down my sword of fire, and not one will slither away.*

"*Into the slime of their hearts I shall drive my stake of fire, and not one will continue to beat.*

"*Thus shall the sickening offspring of Eve be slain, and their abominations put to an end.*

"*For all the reasons I have written.*"

Chapter 72

One more layer

"What about that Zen thing you're always saying about how the problem isn't coming up with the wrong answers, it's coming up with the wrong questions?"

Gurney and Hardwick were driving through the northern Catskill foothills toward Tambury, and Hardwick had been quiet for a while. But now there was something in his tone that implied he had more to say. "Maybe we shouldn't be asking how Hector got the murder weapon from the cottage into the woods. Because, according to the video, he didn't. So maybe that's, like, Fact Number One that we need to accept."

Gurney felt an odd tingle of anticipation on the back of his neck. "What do you think the right question is?"

"Suppose we just asked, how could the machete have gotten to where it was found?"

"Okay. That's a more open-minded version of it, but I don't see—"

"And how did her blood get on it?"

"What?"

Hardwick paused to blow his nose with his customary enthusiasm. He didn't speak until he'd replaced his handkerchief in his pocket. "We're assuming it's the murder weapon because Jillian's blood is on it. Is that a safe assumption? If there was some other way . . ."

"I went down that road already with you, and we got nowhere."

Hardwick shrugged, unconvinced.

Gurney looked across at him. "How else could her blood get on it? And if the machete didn't come from the cottage, where did it come from?"

"And when?"

"*When?*"

Hardwick sniffled, pulled out his handkerchief again, and wiped his nose. "Do you trust the video?"

"I spoke to the video company, and I spoke to the lab people who analyzed it. They tell me the video is accurate."

"If that's true, the machete couldn't have come from the cottage between the murder and the time it was found. Period. So it wasn't the murder weapon. Period. And the goddamn blood must have gotten on it another way."

Gurney could feel an almost physical rearrangement of his thoughts taking place. He knew that Hardwick was right. "If the killer went to the trouble of *putting* the blood on it," he said, half to himself, "that would create a new set of questions—not just how and when, but more important, *why?*"

Why indeed would the killer bother to construct so complex a deception? Theoretically, the purpose of any past action, if it proceeded according to plan, can be deciphered from its results. So what exactly, Gurney asked himself, were the results of the machete being placed where it was with Jillian's blood on it?

He answered his own question aloud. "To begin with, it was found quickly and easily. And everyone jumped to the immediate conclusion that it was the murder weapon. Which aborted any further search for a possible weapon. The scent trail connecting the cottage to the machete seemed conclusive and seemed to prove that Flores had escaped by that route. The disappearance of Kiki Muller reinforced the idea that Flores had left the area, presumably in her company."

"And now . . . ?" asked Hardwick.

"And now there's no reason to believe any of it. In fact, the whole crime scenario adopted by BCI seems to have been crafted by Flores." He paused, thinking through a final implication. "Jesus."

"What is it?"

"The reason Flores murdered Kiki and buried her in her own backyard . . ."

"So it would look like she'd run off with him?"

2

"Yes. And in that light it makes Kiki's murder look like the coldest, most pragmatic execution imaginable."

Hardwick appeared troubled. "If it was so fucking pragmatic, why such a grizzly method?"

"Maybe it's another example of the killer's dual motivation: practical advantage plus raging pathology."

"Plus a talent for creating bullshit for people to spread around the neighborhood."

"What kind of bullshit?"

Hardwick was obviously excited. "Think about it. This whole case has been full of juicy stories, from the very beginning. You remember the old-lady neighbor—Miriam, Marian, whatever, with the Airedale?"

"Marian Eliot."

"Right, Marian Eliot, with all her Hector stories—Hector the star of the Cinderella story, Hector the star of the Frankenstein story. And if you read the neighborhood interview transcripts, you saw the Hector the Latin Lover story and Hector the Jealous Fag story. Along the way you even added your own: Hector the Avenger of Past Wrongs story."

"What are you saying?"

"I'm not saying. I'm asking."

"Asking what?"

"Where the fuck are all these stories coming from? They're fascinating stories, but . . ."

"But what?"

"But zero solid evidence for any of them."

Hardwick fell silent, but Gurney sensed that the man had more to say.

"And . . . ?" he prompted.

Hardwick shook his head, as if unwilling to say more, then spoke anyway. "I used to believe that my first wife was a fucking saint." He fell into a distant silence for a long minute or two, staring out at the passing landscape of wet fields and old farmhouses. "We tell ourselves stories. We miss the real evidence. That's the problem. That's the way our minds work. We love stories way too much. We need to believe them. And you know what? The need to believe can suck you right down the fucking drain."

Chapter 73

Gate of Heaven

O nce they'd passed the exit for Higgles Road, Gurney's GPS
indicated that they'd be arriving at Mapleshade in another
fourteen minutes. They'd taken Gurney's conservative
green Outback, which seemed more appropriate than Hardwick's
red GTO with its rumbling exhaust and hot-rod attitude. The mist
had increased to a heavier drizzle, and Gurney upped the wiper
speed. Weeks earlier an irritating squeak had developed in one of
the wiper blades, which was overdue for replacement.

"How do you picture this guy we've been calling Hector Flores?"
asked Hardwick.

"You mean his face?"

"All of him. What do you picture him doing?"

"I picture him standing naked in a yoga pose in Scott Ashton's
garden pavilion."

"See what I mean?" said Hardwick. "You read about that in the
interview summaries, right? But now you're picturing it as vividly
as if you saw it."

Gurney shrugged. "We do that all the time. Not only do our
minds connect the dots, they create dots where there aren't any
to begin with. Like you said, Jack, we're wired to love stories—
coherence." A moment later he had a sudden, seemingly unrelated
thought. "Was the blood still wet?"

Hardwick blinked. "What blood?"

"The blood on the machete. The blood you told me a minute
ago couldn't have come directly from the murder scene, because the
machete wasn't the murder weapon."

"Of course it was wet. I mean . . . it looked wet. Let me think a second. What I saw of it looked wet, but it had dirt and leaves stuck to it."

"Christ!" interrupted Gurney. "That could be the reason . . ."

"The reason for what?"

"The reason Flores half buried it. Buried the blade. Under a coating of damp leaves and earth."

"So the blood on it wouldn't dry?"

"Or wouldn't oxidize in a way noticeably different from the blood around the body in the cottage. The point is, if the blood on the machete appeared to be in a more advanced state of oxidation than the blood on Jillian's wedding dress, that's something you or the techs would have noticed. If the blood on the machete was older than the blood on the victim . . ."

"We'd have known that it wasn't the murder weapon."

"Exactly. But the wet soil on the blade would have slowed the drying of the blood, plus it would have obscured any oxidation, any observable difference from the color of the blood found in the cottage."

"And that's not something the lab would have picked up, either," said Hardwick.

"Of course not. The blood analysis wouldn't have been done until the following day at the soonest, and at that point a difference of an hour or two in the origination time of the two samples would have been undetectable—unless they were running a sophisticated test to examine that specific factor. But unless you or the ME had flagged it, they wouldn't have had any reason to do it."

Hardwick was nodding slowly, his eyes sharp and thoughtful. "It kicks the foundation out from under some basic assumptions we've been making, but where does it take us?"

"Hah. Good question," said Gurney. "Maybe it's just one more indication that *all* the initial assumptions in this case were wrong."

The efficient female voice of Gurney's GPS directed him to proceed another half mile, then turn left.

The turn was marked by a simple black-and-white sign on a black wooden post: PRIVATE DRIVEWAY. The narrow, smoothly paved drive passed through a pine copse with branches overhanging from both sides, creating the feeling of a sculpted horticultural tunnel. Half a mile into this extended evergreen arbor they drove through an open gate in a tall chain-link fence and came to a stop at a raisable bar that was in its down position. Next to the bar was a handsome cedar-shingled security booth. On the wall facing Gurney, an elegant blue-and-gold sign read MAPLESHADE RESIDENTIAL ACADEMY. VISITS BY APPOINTMENT ONLY. A thickly built man with thinning gray hair emerged from the booth. His black pants and gray shirt gave the impression of an informal uniform, and he had the neutral, appraising eyes of a retired cop. His mouth smiled politely. "Can I help you?"

"Dave Gurney and Senior Investigator Jack Hardwick, New York State Police, here to see Dr. Ashton."

Hardwick pulled out his wallet, extended his BCI ID toward Gurney's window.

The guard eyed it carefully and made a sour face. "Okay, just stay right here while I call Dr. Ashton." While keeping his gaze on the visitors, the man keyed in a code on his phone and began talking. "Sir, a Detective Hardwick and a Mr. Gurney here to see you." A pause. "Yes, sir, they're right here." The guard shot them a nervous glance, then spoke into the phone. "No, sir, no one else with them . . . Yes, sir, of course." The guard handed the phone to Gurney, who put the receiver to his ear.

It was Ashton. "I'm afraid you've caught me in the midst of something. I'm not sure I can see—"

"We only need to ask you a few questions, Doctor. And maybe someone on your staff could show us around the grounds afterward? We'd just like to get a feel for things."

Ashton sighed. "Very well. I'll make a few minutes for you. Someone will come to pick you up shortly. Please put the security man back on."

After confirming Ashton's authorization, the guard pointed to a small gravel area extending off the side of the pavement just past the booth. "Park over there. No cars beyond that point. Wait for your escort." A moment later the bar across the driveway rose and Gurney drove through to the small designated parking area. From that position he could see a longer stretch of the fence than was visible as he was approaching it. He was surprised to see that apart from the portion adjoining the road and the booth, the fence was topped with spiral coils of razor wire.

Hardwick had noticed it, too. "You think it's to keep the girls in or the local boys out?"

"I hadn't thought about the boys," said Gurney, "but you may be right. A boarding school full of sex-obsessed young women, even if their obsessions are hellish, could be quite a magnet."

"You mean *especially* if they're hellish. Hotter the better," said Hardwick, getting out of the car. "Let's go shoot the shit with the man at the gate."

The guard, still standing in front of his booth, gave them a curious look—friendlier now that they'd been approved for entry. "This about the Liston girl who worked here?"

"You knew her?" asked Hardwick.

"Didn't *know* her, just knew who she was. Worked for Dr. Ashton."

"You know him?"

"Again, more to see him than to talk to him. He's a little—what would you say? *Distant?*"

"Standoffish?"

"Yeah, I would say he was standoffish."

"So he's not the guy you report to?"

"Nah. Ashton doesn't really have anything to do with anybody. A little too important, you know what I mean? Most of the staff here report to Dr. Lazarus."

Gurney detected a not-quite-hidden distaste in the guard's voice, waited for Hardwick to follow it up. When he didn't, Gurney asked, "What kind of a guy is Lazarus?"

The guard hesitated, seemed to be looking for a way to say something without saying something that could get him in trouble.

"I hear he's not a smiley-face kind of guy," said Gurney, recalling Simon Kale's unflattering description.

Gurney's mild encouragement was enough to put a crack in the wall.

"Smiley-face? Jeez no. I mean, he's okay, I guess, but . . ."

"But not too pleasant?" Gurney prompted.

"It's just, I don't know, like he's kind of in his own world. Like sometimes you'll be talking to him and you get the feeling that ninety percent of him is somewhere else. I remember once—" He broke off the sentence at the sound of tires rolling slowly on gravel.

They all looked toward the little parking area—and the dark blue minivan that was coming to a stop next to Gurney's car.

"The man himself," said the guard under his breath.

The man who emerged from the van was ageless but far from young, with even features that made his face look more artificial than handsome. His hair was as black as only dye could make it, and the contrast with his pale skin was striking. He pointed to the back door of the van.

"Please get in, Officers," he said as he slipped back into the driver's seat and waited. His attempted smile, if that's what it was, resembled the strained expression of a man who found daylight unpleasant.

Gurney and Hardwick got in behind him.

Lazarus drove slowly, gazing intently at the road ahead. After a few hundred yards, they rounded a bend and the dark pine woods yielded to a parklike area of mowed grass and widely spaced maples. The driveway straightened into a classical allée, at the end of which stood a neo-Gothic Victorian mansion with several smaller structures of similar design on either side of it. In front of the mansion, the road split. Lazarus took the right fork, which brought them around beds of ornamental shrubs to the rear of the building. There the split road came back together in a second allée that proceeded on, surprisingly, to a large chapel of dark granite. Its narrow stained-glass windows might on a cheerier day have given the impression of ten-foot-high red pencils, but at that moment they looked to Gurney like bloody gashes in the stone.

"The school has its own church?" asked Hardwick.

"No. Not a church anymore. Deconsecrated a long time ago. Too bad, in a sense," he added, with a touch of that disconnection the guard had described.

"How so?" asked Hardwick.

Lazarus answered slowly. "Churches are about good and evil. About guilt and punishment." He shrugged, pulling up in front of the chapel and switching off the ignition. "But church or no church, we all pay for our sins one way or another, don't we?"

"Where is everyone?" asked Hardwick.

"Inside."

Gurney looked up at the imposing edifice, its stone face the color of dark shadows.

"Is Dr. Ashton in there?" Gurney pointed at the arched chapel door.

"I'll show you." Lazarus got out of the van.

They followed him up the granite steps and through the door into a wide, dimly lit vestibule that smelled to Gurney like the parish church of his Bronx childhood: a combination of masonry, old wood, the age-old soot of burned candle wicks. It was a scent with a strangely dislocating power, making him feel a need to whisper, to step quietly. From beyond a pair of heavy oak doors that would lead presumably into the main space of the chapel came the low murmur of many voices.

Above the doors, carved boldly into a wide stone lintel, were the words GATE OF HEAVEN.

Gurney gestured toward the doors. "Dr. Ashton is in there?"

"No. The girls are in there. Settling down. All a bit volatile today—shaken up by the news about the Liston girl. Dr. Ashton's in the organ loft."

"Organ loft?"

"That's what it used to be. Converted now, of course. Converted into an office." He pointed to a narrow doorway at the far end of the vestibule, leading to the foot of a dark staircase. "It's the door at the top of those stairs."

Gurney felt a chill. He wasn't sure whether it was the natural temperature of the granite or something in Lazarus's eyes, which he was sure were fixed on them as they climbed the shadowy stone steps.

Chapter 74

Beyond all reason

At the top of the cramped stairwell was a small landing, weirdly illuminated by one of the building's narrow scarlet windows. Gurney knocked on the landing's only door. Like the doors off the vestibule, it looked heavy, gloomy, uninviting.

"Come in." Ashton's mellifluous voice was strained.

Despite its weight and promise of creakiness, the door swung open fluidly, silently, into a comfortably proportioned room that might have passed for a bishop's private study. Chestnut brown bookcases lined two of the windowless walls. There was a small fireplace of sooty fieldstone with old brass andirons. An ancient Persian rug covered the floor, except for a satin-polished border of cherrywood two feet wide all the way around the room. A few large lamps, set atop occasional tables, gave the dark, woody tones of the room an amber glow.

Scott Ashton sat wearing a troubled frown at an ornate black-oak desk, placed at a ninety-degree angle to the door. Behind him, on an oak sideboard with carved lion-head legs, was the room's major concession to the current century—a large flat-screen computer monitor. He motioned Gurney and Hardwick vaguely to a pair of red velvet high-backed chairs across from him—the sort of chairs one might find in the sacristy of a cathedral.

"It just keeps getting worse and worse," Ashton said.

Gurney assumed he was referring to the murder the previous evening of Savannah Liston and was about to offer some vague words of agreement and condolence.

"Frankly," Ashton went on, turning away, "I find this organized-

crime angle almost incomprehensible." At that point the sight of his
Bluetooth earpiece, along with the oddness of his comments, told
Gurney that the man was in fact in the middle of a phone call. "Yes,
I understand . . . I understand . . . My point is simply that every step
forward makes the case more bizarre . . . Yes, Lieutenant. Tomorrow morning . . . Yes . . . Yes, I understand. Thank you for letting me
know."

Ashton turned toward his guests but seemed for a moment to be
lost in contemplation of the conversation just ended.

"News?" asked Gurney.

"Are you aware of this . . . criminal-conspiracy theory? This . . .
grand scheme that may involve Sardinian gangsters?" Ashton's expression seemed strained by a combination of anxiety and disbelief.

"I've heard it discussed," said Gurney.

"Do you think there's any chance of it being true?"

"A chance, yes."

Ashton shook his head, stared confusedly at his desk, then back
up at the two detectives. "May I ask why you're here?"

"Just a gut feeling," said Hardwick.

"Gut feeling? What do you mean?"

"In every case there's some common point where everything
converges. So the place itself becomes a key. It could be a big help
for us just to take a walk around, see what we can see."

"I'm not sure that I—"

"Everything that's happened seems to have some link back to
Mapleshade. Would you agree with that?"

"I suppose. Perhaps. I don't know."

"You telling me you haven't thought about it?" There was an
edge in Hardwick's voice.

"Of course I've thought about it." Ashton looked perplexed. "I
just can't . . . see it that clearly. Maybe I'm too close to everything."

"Does the name Skard mean anything to you?" asked Gurney.

"The detective on the phone just asked me the same question—
something about some horrible Sardinian gang family. The answer
is no."

"You're sure Jillian never mentioned it?"

"Jillian? No. Why would she?"

Gurney shrugged. "It's possible that Skard may be Hector Flores's real name."

"Skard? How would Jillian know that?"

"I don't know, but she apparently did an Internet search to find out more about it."

Ashton shook his head again, the gesture resembling an involuntary shudder. "How awful does this have to get before it ends?" It was more a wail of protest than a question.

"You said something on the phone just now about tomorrow morning?"

"What? Oh, yes. Another twist. Your lieutenant feels that this conspiracy angle makes everything more urgent, so he's pushing up the schedule for interviewing our students to tomorrow morning."

"So where are they all?"

"What?"

"Your students. Where are they?"

"Oh. Forgive my distractedness, but that's part of the reason for it. They're downstairs in the main area of the chapel. It's a calming environment. It's been a wild day. Officially, Mapleshade students have no communication with the outside world. No TV, radio, computers, iPods, cell phones, nothing. But there are always leaks, always someone who's managed to sneak in some device or other, and so of course they've heard about Savannah's death, and . . . well, you can imagine. So we went into what a sterner facility might call 'lockdown mode.' Of course, we don't call it that. Everything here is designed to have a softer edge."

"Except for the razor wire," said Hardwick.

"The fence is aimed at keeping problems out, not people in."

"We were wondering about that."

"I can assure you it's for security, not captivity."

"So right now they're all downstairs in the chapel?" asked Hardwick.

"Correct. As I said, they find it calming."

"I wouldn't have thought they'd be religious," said Gurney.

"Religious?" Ashton smiled humorlessly. "Hardly. There's just something about stone churches, Gothic windows, the muted light. They calm the soul in a way that has nothing to do with theology."

. "The students don't feel like they're being punished?" asked Hardwick. "What about the ones who weren't acting out?"

"The agitated ones settle down, feel better. The ones who were okay to begin with are given to understand that they are the main source of peace for the others. Bottom line, the agitated don't feel singled out and the calm feel valuable."

Gurney smiled. "You must have put a lot of thought and effort into engineering that view of the experience."

"That's part of my job."

"You give them a framework for understanding what's happening?"

"You could put it like that."

"Like what a magician does," said Gurney. "Or a politician."

"Or any competent preacher or teacher or doctor," said Ashton mildly.

"Incidentally," said Gurney, deciding to test the effect of a hairpin turn in the conversation, "was Jillian injured in any way in the days leading up to the wedding—anything that would have caused bleeding?"

"Bleeding? Not that I know of. Why do you ask?"

"There's a question about how the blood got on the bloody machete."

"Question? How could that be a question? What do you mean?"

"I mean the machete might not have been the murder weapon after all."

"I don't understand."

"It might have been placed in the woods prior to your wife's murder, not after it."

"But . . . I was told . . . her blood . . ."

"Some conclusions could have been premature. But here's the thing: If the machete was put in the woods before the murder, then the blood on it must have come from Jillian before the murder. The question is, do you have any idea how that could have happened?"

Ashton looked stunned. His mouth opened. He seemed about to speak, didn't, then finally did. "Well . . . yes, I do . . . at least theoretically. As you may know, Jillian was being treated for a bipolar disorder. She took a medication that required periodic blood tests to assure that it remained within the therapeutic range. Her blood was drawn once a month."

"Who drew the blood?"

"A local phlebotomist. I believe she worked for a medical-services provider out of Cooperstown."

"And what did she do with the blood sample?"

"She transported it to the lab where the lithium-level test was performed and the report was generated."

"She transported it immediately?"

"I imagine she made a number of stops, her assigned client route, whatever that might be, and at the end of each day she'd deliver her samples to the lab."

"You have her name and the names of the provider and the lab?"

"Yes, I do. I review—reviewed, I should say—a copy of the lab report every month."

"Would you have a record of when the last blood sample was drawn?"

"No specific record, but it was always the second Friday of the month."

Gurney thought for a moment. "That would have been two days before Jillian was killed."

"You're thinking that Flores somehow intervened at some point in that process and got hold of her blood? But why? I'm afraid I'm not really understanding what you're saying about the machete. What would be the point of it?"

"I'm not sure, Doctor. But I have a feeling that the answer to that question is the missing piece at the center of the case."

Ashton raised his eyebrows in a way that looked more baffled than skeptical. His eyes seemed to be moving across the disturbing points of some inner landscape. Eventually he closed them and sat back in his tall chair, his hands clasped over the ends of the elaborately carved armrests, his breathing deep and deliberate, as though he might be engaged in some tranquilizing mental exercise. But when he opened them again, he only looked worse.

"What a nightmare," he said. He cleared his throat, but it sounded more like a whimper than a cough. "Tell me something, gentlemen. Have you ever felt like a complete failure? That's how I feel right now. Every new horror . . . every death . . . every discovery about Flores or Skard or whatever his name is . . . every bizarre revelation about what's really been happening here at the school—everything proves my total failure. What a brainless idiot I've been!" He shook his head—or rather moved it back and forth in slow motion, as if it were caught in some oscillating underwater current. "Such foolish, fatal pride. To think that I could cure a plague of such incredible, primitive power."

"Plague?"

"Not the term my profession commonly applies to incest and the damage it does, but I think it's quite accurate. The longer I've worked in this field, the more I've come to believe that of all the crimes human beings commit against one another, the most destructive by far is the sexual abuse of a child by an adult— especially a parent."

"Why do you say that?"

"Why? It's simple. The two primal human relationship modes are parenting and mating. Incest destroys the distinct patterns of these two relationships by smashing them together, essentially polluting them both. I believe that there is traumatic damage to the neural structures that support the behaviors natural to each of these relationship modes and that keep them separate. Do you understand what I'm saying?"

"I think so," said Gurney.

"A bit over my head," said Hardwick, who'd been quietly observing the exchange between Ashton and Gurney.

Ashton shot him a glance of disbelief. "An effective therapy for that kind of trauma needs to rebuild boundaries between the parent-child repertoire of responses and the mating repertoire of responses. The tragedy is that no therapy can match in force—in sheer megatonnage of impact—the violation it seeks to repair. It's like rebuilding with a teaspoon a wall smashed by a bulldozer."

"But . . . wasn't that the problem you chose to focus your career on?" asked Gurney.

"Yes. And now it's perfectly clear that I've failed. Totally, miserably failed."

"You don't know that."

"You mean not *every* graduate of Mapleshade has chosen to disappear into some sick sexual underworld? Not *every* one has been slaughtered for pleasure? Not *every* one has gone on to have children and rape them? Not *every* one has emerged as sick and deranged as when she entered? How can I *know* that? All I know at this point is that Mapleshade under my control, guided by my instincts and decisions, has turned into a magnet for horror and murder, a hunting preserve for a monster. Under my leadership Mapleshade has been utterly destroyed. That much I know."

"So . . . what now?" asked Hardwick sharply.

"What now? Ah. The voice of a practical mind." Ashton closed his eyes and said nothing for at least a full minute. When he spoke again, it was with a strained ordinariness. "What now? The next step? The next step for me is to go downstairs to the chapel, show my face, do what I can to calm their nerves. What your next step is . . . I have no idea. You say you came here because of a gut feeling. You'd better ask your gut what to do next."

He got up from his massive velvet chair, taking something resembling a remote garage-door opener from the desk drawer. "The downstairs lights and locks are operated electronically," he said, explaining the device. He started to leave, got as far as the door, came back, and switched on the large computer monitor behind his desk. A picture appeared: the main interior chapel space, with a stone floor and high stone walls whose colorless austerity was broken by intermittent burgundy drapes and indecipherable tapestries. The dark wood pews were not set in the rows typical of churches but had been rearranged into half a dozen seating areas, each made up of three pews formed into a loose triangle, evidently to facilitate discussion. These areas were filled with teenage girls. From the monitor speakers came a hubbub of female voices.

"There's a high-definition camera and a mike down there, transmitting to this computer," said Ashton. "Watch and listen, and you'll get some sense of the situation." Then he turned and left the room.

Chapter 75

. Shut your eyes tight

The computer screen showed Scott Ashton coming in through the chapel's rear door behind the groupings of pews and closing it behind him with a heavy thump, the small remote unit still in one hand. The girls filled most of the space in the pews—some sitting normally, some sideways, some in cross-legged yoga positions, some kneeling. Some seemed lost in their own thoughts, but most were engaged in conversations, some more audible than others.

The surprise for Gurney was the ordinariness of these girls. They looked at first glance like most self-absorbed female teenagers, hardly like the inmates of an institution ringed by razor wire. At this distance from the camera, the malignancy of the behavior that had brought them here was invisible. Gurney assumed that only face-to-face, with their expressions in sharper focus, would it become obvious that these creatures were more than ordinarily self-centered, reckless, cruel, and sex-driven. Ultimately, as it was with his murderer mug shots, the sign of danger, the ice, would be in the eyes.

Then he noticed that the students were not alone. In each of the pew triangles, there were one or two older individuals—probably teachers or counselors or whatever Mapleshade called their providers of guidance and therapy. In a rear corner of the room, almost invisible in the shadows, stood Dr. Lazarus, his arms folded, his expression unreadable.

Moments after Ashton entered, the girls began to notice him, and the conversational din began to diminish. One of the older-looking, more striking girls approached Ashton as he stood at the back of the center aisle. She was tall, blond, almond-eyed.

Gurney glanced over at Hardwick, who was leaning forward in his chair, studying the screen.

"Could you tell if he called her over?" Gurney asked.

"He may have gestured," he said. "Sort of a wave. Why?"

"Just curious."

On the super-sharp screen, the profiles of Ashton and the tall blonde were clear to the point that their lip movements were visible, but their voices were indistinct—words and phrases merging with the voices of a group of students near them.

Gurney leaned toward the monitor. "Do you have any idea what they're saying?"

Hardwick focused intently on their faces, tilting his head as though that might heighten the discrimination of his hearing.

On the screen, the girl said something and smiled, Ashton said something and gestured. Then he walked purposefully down the center aisle and stepped up onto a raised portion of the floor, presumably the area the altar had occupied in the time of the building's liturgical use. He turned to face the assembly of students, his back to the camera. The murmur melted away, and soon there was silence.

Gurney looked inquiringly at Hardwick. "Did you catch anything?"

He shook his head. "He could have said absolutely anything to her. I couldn't pick the words out of the background noise. Maybe a lip-reader could tell. Not me."

On the screen, Ashton began speaking with a natural-sounding authority, his chocolate baritone composed and satiny—and deeper than usual in the resonant Gothic nave.

"Ladies," he began, inflecting the word with an almost reverential gentility, "terrible things have happened, frightening things, and everyone is upset. Angry, frightened, confused, and upset. Some of you are having trouble sleeping. Anxiety. Bad dreams. Just not knowing what's really happening may be the worst part of it. We want to know what we're facing, and no one is telling us." Ashton radiated the angst of the mental states he was referring to. He had turned himself into a depiction of emotion and understanding, and yet at the same time, perhaps through the steady richness of his voice, its almost cellolike timbre, he was managing to communicate at some unconscious level a profound reassurance.

"Man, that's good shit," said Hardwick, in the tone of one admiring the legerdemain of a superior pickpocket.

"Definitely a pro," agreed Gurney.

"Not as good as you, ace."

Gurney screwed up his face into an uncomprehending question mark.

"I bet he could learn a thing or two from your academy gig."

"What do you know about my acad—"

Hardwick pointed at the screen. "Shhh. Let's not miss anything."

Ashton's words were moving like clear water over polished rocks. "Some of you have asked me about the progress of the criminal investigation. How much do the police know, what are they doing, how close are they to catching the guilty person? Logical questions, questions a lot of us are wondering about. I think it would help if we knew more, if we each had the opportunity to share our concerns, to ask what we want to ask, to get some answers. That's why I've invited the key detectives working on the case to come here to Mapleshade tomorrow morning—to talk to us, let us know what's happening, what's likely to happen next. They'll have questions, we'll have questions. I believe that it will be a very useful conversation for all of us."

Hardwick grinned. "What do you think of that?"

"I think he's—"

"Smooth as a greased pig?"

Gurney shrugged. "I'd say he's good at managing the way people see things."

Hardwick pointed at the screen.

Ashton was taking a cell phone from a clip on his belt. He looked at it, frowned, pressed a button on it, and put it to his ear. He said something, but the girls in the pews had resumed talking to one another, and his words were again lost in the background chatter.

"Are you catching any of that?" asked Gurney.

Hardwick watched Ashton's lips, then shook his head. "Same

as before, when he was talking to the blonde. He could have said anything."

The call ended, and Ashton replaced the phone in his pocket. A girl far in the back was raising her hand. Unseen or ignored by Ashton, she stood and waved it side to side, and that seemed to get his attention.

"Yes? Ladies . . . I think someone has a question, or a comment?"

The girl—who happened to be the almond-eyed blonde to whom Hardwick had just referred—asked her question. "I heard a rumor that Hector Flores was seen here today, right here in the chapel. Is that true?"

Ashton appeared uncharacteristically flustered. "What . . . Who told you that?"

"I don't know. People were talking in the stairwell in the main house. I'm not sure who it was. I couldn't see them from where I was standing. But one of them said she saw him—that she saw Hector. If that's true, that's scary."

"If it were true, it would be," said Ashton. "Maybe the person who said she saw him can tell us more about it. We're all here. Whoever said it must be here, too." He looked out at the assembly in an expectant silence, letting a protracted five seconds pass before adding with an avuncular tolerance, "Maybe some people just like to spread scary rumors." But he didn't sound entirely at ease. "Are there any more questions?"

One of the younger-looking girls raised her hand and asked, "How much longer do we have to stay in here?"

Ashton smiled like a loving father. "As long as the process is helpful and not a minute longer. I would hope that in each of your groups you're sharing your thoughts, concerns, feelings—especially the fears that have naturally been triggered by Savannah's death. I want you to express everything that comes to mind, to take advantage of the help your group facilitators can provide, the help you each can offer one another. The process works. We all know it works. Trust it."

Ashton stepped down from the raised platform and began circulating around the room, appearing to offer a word of encouragement here and there but mainly observing the group discussions in progress in the pews. Sometimes he would appear to be listening carefully, other times withdrawing into his own thoughts.

As Gurney watched, his attention was drawn again to the fundamental weirdness of the scene. Deconsecrated though it might be, the building still looked, sounded, smelled, and felt very much like a church. Combining that with the wild and twisted energies of Mapleshade's current residents was disconcerting.

In the chapel scene on the screen, Ashton was continuing his leisurely stroll among the students and their "facilitators," but Gurney had stopped paying attention.

He closed his eyes and rested his head against the velvet back cushion of his chair. He concentrated as best he could on the simple feeling of his breath passing in and out through his nostrils. He was trying to clear his mind of what felt like an incoherent tangle of debris. He almost succeeded, but one little item refused to be swept away.

One little item.

It was a comment by Hardwick that had been gnawing at the edge of his consciousness—the comment he'd made when Gurney had asked him if he could tell what Ashton was saying to the girl who'd walked over to him when he entered the chapel.

Hardwick had replied that Ashton's voice, amid all the others in the chapel, was indistinct, the words indecipherable.

He could have said absolutely anything to her.

That notion had been bothering Gurney.

And now he knew why.

It had triggered a memory, at first below the level of consciousness.

But now it came vividly to mind.

Another time. Another place. Scott Ashton in earnest conversation with a young blonde on the broad sweep of a manicured lawn. A conversation that could not be overheard. A conversation whose words were lost in the undertone of two hundred other voices. A conversation in which Scott Ashton could have said anything to Jillian Perry.

He could have said anything. And that single fact could change everything.

Hardwick was watching him. "You all right?"

Gurney nodded slightly, as if any greater movement might jar apart the infinitely delicate chain of possibilities he was considering.

He could have said anything. There really was no way of knowing what he said, because the actual voices couldn't be heard. So what might he have said?

Suppose what he said was, "No matter what happens, don't say a word."

Suppose what he said was, "No matter what happens, don't open the door."

Suppose what he said was, "I have a surprise for you. Shut your eyes tight."

Good God, suppose that's exactly what he said! "For the biggest surprise of your life, shut your eyes tight."

Chapter 76

Another layer .

"The hell's the matter?" demanded Hardwick.

Gurney just shook his head, not ready to answer, as he followed the logical chain of possibilities in his mind with an animal excitement that brought him to his feet. He began to pace, slowly at first, across the antique carpet in front of Ashton's desk. The large porcelain lamp on the near corner cast a soft circle of light, illuminating the intricate garden design in the carpet's fine weave.

If he was right—and it was at least possible that he was right—what would follow from that?

On the screen, Ashton could be seen standing next to one of the dark red drapes that covered portions of the chapel walls, his gaze drifting benignly over the assembly.

"What is it?" demanded Hardwick. "The hell's on your mind?"

Gurney stopped his pacing long enough to lower the sound slightly on the computer monitor in order to better focus on his own train of thought. "That comment you made a minute ago? That Ashton could have said *anything*?"

"Yeah? What about it?"

"You may have demolished one of the key assumptions we've been making about Jillian's murder."

"What assumption?"

"The biggest one of all. The assumption that we know why she went into the cottage."

"Well, we know why she *said* she went in. On the video she told Ashton she wanted to persuade Flores to come out for the wedding toast. And Ashton argued with her. Told her not to bother with Flores. But she went right the fuck in, anyway."

Gurney's eyes gleamed. "Suppose that conversation never happened."

"It was on the video." Hardwick looked as annoyed by Gurney's excitement as he was confused by what Gurney was saying.

Gurney spoke slowly, as if each word were precious. "That conversation isn't actually *on* the reception video."

"Of course it is."

"No. What's recorded on the video is a meeting between Scott Ashton and Jillian Perry on the lawn, at the reception, in the background of the scene—too far in the background for the camera to record their voices. The 'conversation' you're recalling—and that everyone who's seen that video has been recalling—is Scott Ashton's *description* of the conversation to Burt Luntz and his wife, after it occurred. The fact is, we have no way of knowing what Jillian actually said to him or what he said to Jillian. And until now we've had no reason to question it. All we really have is what Ashton *claims* was said. And as you commented a minute ago on his inaudible conversation with that blonde in the chapel, *he could have said anything.*"

"Okay," said Hardwick uncertainly. "Ashton could have said anything. I get that. But what do you think he *actually* said to her? I mean, what's the point of this? Why would he lie about Jillian's reason for going into the cottage?"

"I can think of at least one horrible reason. My point is—once again—we don't know what we thought we knew. All we really *know* is that they spoke to each other and she went into the cottage."

Hardwick began tapping impatiently on the carved arm of his thronelike chair. "That's not *all* we know. Don't I remember someone going to get her? Knocking at the cottage door? One of the catering people? And wasn't she already dead—or at least not able to answer the door? I'm not getting where the hell you're going with this."

"Let's start at the beginning. If you look at the actual visual evidence and forget the narrative we've been given, the question is, is there *another* credible narrative that's consistent with what we see happening on the screen?"

"Like what?"

"On the video it looks like Jillian gets Ashton's attention and points at her watch. Okay. Suppose he'd asked her to remind him when it was time for the wedding toast. And suppose when he went over to her, he told her that he had a huge surprise for her and he wanted her to go into the cottage, because that's where he was going to give it to her—just before the toast. She should go into the cottage, lock the door, and be completely quiet. No matter who came to the door, she shouldn't open it or say a word. It was all part of the big surprise, and she'd understand it all later."

Hardwick was paying serious attention now. "So you're saying that she may have been perfectly fine when the catering person knocked on the door?"

"And then when Ashton himself opened the door with his key, suppose he said something like, 'Shut your eyes tight. Shut your eyes tight—for the biggest surprise of your life.' "

"And then what?"

Gurney paused. "You remember Jason Strunk?"

Hardwick frowned. "The serial killer? What's he got to do with this?"

"Remember how he killed his victims?"

"Wasn't he the one who chopped them up, then mailed the pieces to the local cops?"

"Right. But it's the weapon he used that I was thinking about."

"Meat cleaver, wasn't it? Razor-sharp Japanese thing."

"And he carried it in a simple plastic sheath under his jacket."

"So . . . what are you saying? Oh, no, come on! You're not saying that . . . that Scott Ashton went into the cottage, told his brand-new wife to close her eyes, and then chopped her head off?"

"Based on the visual evidence, it's just as possible as the story we've been given."

"God, lots of things are *possible*, but . . ." Hardwick shook his head. "Then what? After he chops off his bride's head, he lays it neatly on the table, starts screaming, slips his bloody cleaver back into his plastic-lined pocket, comes stumbling out of the cottage, and collapses?"

Gurney went on. "Exactly. That last bit is recorded on the

video—him screaming, stumbling out, collapsing in the flower bed. Everyone comes rushing over, everyone looks in the cottage, and everyone reaches what under the circumstances is the obvious conclusion. Exactly the conclusion Ashton would want them to reach. So there was no reason for anyone to search him. If he did have a cleaver or a similar weapon hidden inside his jacket, no one would ever have known. And as soon as the K-9 team found the bloody machete in the woods, everything seemed perfectly clear. The Hector Flores narrative was set in stone, just waiting for Rod Rodriguez to put his stamp of approval on it."

"The machete . . . with Jillian's blood . . . but how . . . ?"

"That blood could easily have come from the sample taken for her lithium-level blood test two days earlier. Ashton could have canceled the regular phlebotomy appointment and drawn that sample himself. Or he could have gotten it some other way, pulled some kind of switch—just like we were starting to think Flores might have done. And he could have planted the machete in the woods that morning, before the reception. Could have smeared the blood on it, carried it out through the back window of the cottage, left a drop or two on the back windowsill, left that sex-pheromone trail with the boots for the dogs to follow, then came back in through the cottage. At that point, there wouldn't have been any cameras running, which would explain how the machete got from the cottage to where it was found with no video record of anyone passing that goddamn tree."

"Wait a second, you forgot something. How the hell did he swing a cleaver through her neck—through the carotids—without getting sprayed with blood? I mean, I know about that thing in the ME's report about the blood all running down the far side of her body and my own idea of how the killer could have used the head itself to deflect the flow. But there'd still be some splatter, wouldn't there?"

"Maybe there was."

"And nobody noticed?"

"Think about it, Jack—the scene on the video. Ashton was wearing a dark suit. He falls in a muddy flower bed. A bed of rosebushes. With thorns. He was a muddy mess. And as I recall, some helpful guests took him into the house. I'd bet my pension he went to a bathroom. Which would offer an easy opportunity to ditch the cleaver, maybe even switch into a matching suit with some mud already on it. So when he came out, he'd still be a muddy mess, but a mess with no trace of the victim's blood."

"Fuck," murmured Hardwick thoughtfully. "You really believe all that?"

"To be honest, Jack, I have no reason to believe *any* of it. But I do think it's *possible.*"

"There are some problems with it, don't you think?"

"Like the credibility problem of a famous psychiatrist being a stone-cold assassin?"

"Actually, that's the part I like best," said Hardwick.

Gurney grinned for the first time that day. "Any other problems?" he asked.

"Yeah. If Flores wasn't in the cottage when Jillian was killed, where the hell was he?"

"Maybe he was already dead," said Gurney. "Maybe Ashton killed him to make it look like he was guilty and ran away. Or maybe the whole scenario I just cooked up is as full of holes as every other theory of this case."

"So this guy is either a world-class criminal or the innocent victim of one." Hardwick glanced over at the monitor behind Ashton's desk. "For a man whose whole world is supposedly collapsing, he looks pretty damn calm. Where did all the despair and hopelessness go?"

"They seem to have evaporated."

"I don't get it."

"Emotional resilience? Putting up a good front?"

Hardwick looked increasingly baffled. "Why did he want us to watch this?"

Ashton was making his way slowly around the chapel, almost imperiously, like a guru among his disciples. Proprietary. Confident. Imperturbable. Radiating more pleasure and satisfaction by the minute. A man of power and respect. A Renaissance cardinal. An American president. A rock star.

"Scott Ashton seems to be a jewel of many facets," said Gurney, fascinated.

"Or a murdering bastard," countered Hardwick.

"We need to decide which."

"How?"

"By reducing the equation to its bare essentials."

"Which are?"

"Suppose that Ashton did in fact kill Jillian."

"And that Hector wasn't involved?"

"Right," said Gurney. "What would follow from that starting point?"

"That Ashton is a very good liar."

"So maybe he's been telling a lot of other lies, and we haven't noticed."

"Lies about Hector Flores?"

"Right," said Gurney again, frowning thoughtfully. "About . . . Hector . . . Flores."

"What is it?"

"Just . . . thinking."

"What?"

"Is it . . . possible that . . . ?"

"What is it?" asked Hardwick.

"Just a minute. I just want to . . ." Gurney's voice trailed off into the electricity of his racing thoughts.

"What?"

"Just . . . reducing . . . the equation. Reducing it to the simplest . . . possible . . ."

"God, don't keep stopping in the middle of sentences! Spit it out!"

Christ it couldn't be that simple, could it?

But maybe it was! Maybe it was perfectly, ridiculously simple!

Why hadn't he seen it sooner?

He laughed.

"For Godsake, Gurney . . ."

He hadn't seen it sooner because he'd been searching for a missing piece. And he hadn't been able to find it. Of course he hadn't been able to find it. Because there was no missing piece. There never was a MISSING piece. There was an EXTRA piece. The piece that kept getting in the way of everything else. The piece that had been getting in the way of the truth from the beginning. The piece that had been designed specifically to get in the way of the truth.

Hardwick was glaring at him in frustration.

Gurney turned toward him with a wild smile. "Do you know why no one could find Hector Flores after the murder?"

"Because he was dead?"

"I don't think so. There are three possible explanations. One, he escaped from the area like everyone thought he did. Two, he's dead, killed by the real murderer of Jillian Perry. Or three... *he was never alive to begin with.*"

"The fuck are you talking about?"

"It's possible that Hector Flores never existed, that there never was any such person as Hector Flores, that Hector Flores was a myth created by Scott Ashton."

"But all the stories . . ."

"They could all have come from Ashton himself."

"What!?"

"Why not? Stories get started, they spread, take on a life of their own—a point you've made many times. Why couldn't the stories all have had the same starting point?"

"But people saw Flores in Ashton's car."

"They saw a Mexican day laborer in a straw cowboy hat with sunglasses. The man they saw could have been anyone Ashton might have hired on that particular day."

"But I don't get how . . ."

"Don't you see? Ashton could have created all the stories himself, all the rumors. Perfect food for gossip. The special new gardener. The wonderfully industrious Mexican. The man who learned everything amazingly quickly. The man of tremendous potential. The Cinderella man. The protégé. The trusted personal assistant. The genius who began to develop little quirks. The man who stood naked on one foot in the garden pavilion. So many stories, so interesting, so colorful, so shocking, so delicious, so *repeatable*. The perfect food for gossip. God, don't you see? He fed his neighbors an irresistible saga, and they ran with it, told it to one another, embellished it, told it to strangers. He created Hector Flores out of nothing and turned him into a legend, one chapter after another. A legend that Tambury couldn't stop talking about. The man became bigger than life, realer than real."

"What about the bullet in the teacup?"

"Easiest thing in the world. Ashton could have fired the bullet himself, hid the gun, reported it stolen. Perfectly believable that the crazy, ungrateful Mexican would have stolen the doctor's expensive rifle."

"Hold on a second. On that videotape, at the very beginning, before the reception starts, Ashton went to the cottage to talk to Flores. When he knocked on the door, the audio picked up a very low *'Esta abierto.'* If there was no Hector Flores in there, who said that?"

"Obviously Ashton could have said it himself in a muffled voice. His back was to the camera."

"But the girls Hector spoke to at Mapleshade . . ."

"The girls he *supposedly* spoke to are all conveniently dead or missing. So how do we know he ever spoke to anyone? There's no one available who can actually say she saw him face-to-face. Isn't that a pretty goddamn strange thing all by itself?"

They looked at each other, then at the computer screen, where Ashton could be seen speaking briefly to two of the girls, pointing instructively to various parts of the chapel area. He looked as relaxed and commanding as the winning general on the day the enemy surrendered.

Hardwick shook his head. "You really believe that Ashton came up with this incredibly elaborate scheme—that he invented this mythical person and managed to nurture the fiction for three years—just so he'd have someone to blame in case he decided someday to get married and murder his wife? Doesn't that sound a little ridiculous?"

"Put that way, it sounds totally ridiculous. But suppose he had another reason for inventing Hector?"

"What reason?"

"I don't know. A bigger reason. A more practical reason."

"Seems awfully shaky. And what about the Skard business? Wasn't that all based on the theory that one of the Skard brothers, probably Leonardo, was masquerading as Hector and talking unrepentant Mapleshade girls into leaving home for money and thrills after graduation? If there was no Hector, what happens to that whole sex-slavery scenario?"

"I don't know." It was a crucial question, thought Gurney. What sense did any of their theories make if they depended on the idea that Leonardo Skard was operating in the guise of Hector Flores— if no one called Hector Flores had ever existed?

Chapter 77

The final episode

"By the way," said Gurney, "you happen to have your weapon on you?"

"Always," said Hardwick. "My ankle would feel naked without its little holster. In my humble opinion, bullets sometimes rank right up there with brains as problem solvers. Why do you ask? You intend to make a dramatic move?"

"No dramatic move just yet. We need to be a lot surer about what's going on."

"You sounded damn sure of yourself a minute ago."

Gurney made a face. "All I'm *sure* of is that my version of the Perry murder is *possible*. Or that it's not *im*possible. Scott Ashton could have killed Jillian Perry. *Could have*. But it needs more digging, more facts. Right now there's zero evidence and zero motive. We've got nothing but speculation on my part, a logical exercise."

"But what if——"

Hardwick's question was cut short by the sound of the heavy chapel door on the floor below opening and shutting, followed by a sharp metallic click. They both leaned reflexively toward the shadowy stairs beyond the doorway of the office and listened for footsteps.

A minute later Scott Ashton emerged from the top of the stone stairwell and entered the office, moving with the same air of power and control they'd witnessed on the screen. He sank into the plushly upholstered chair behind his desk and removed his Bluetooth earpiece and dropped it in the top drawer. He brought his hands together on the massive black desktop, slowly interlocking the fingers—except for the thumbs which he held parallel to each other as if to facilitate a close comparison between them. It was a comparison that seemed to interest him. After smiling for some time at his private thoughts, he separated his hands, turning up the palms with the fingers loosely splayed in a queerly insouciant gesture.

Then he reached into his jacket pocket and withdrew a small-caliber pistol. The action was casual—so similar to taking out a pack of cigarettes that, for a second, Gurney thought that that was what Ashton had done.

With an almost sleepy motion, he pointed the little semiautomatic, a .25-caliber Beretta, at a point somewhere between Gurney and Hardwick, but his eyes were fixed on Hardwick.

"Do me a favor, please. Put your hands on the arms of your chair. Right now, please. Thank you. Now, remaining seated just as you are, raise your feet slowly off the floor. Thank you. I really appreciate your cooperation. Raise them higher. Thank you. Now please extend your legs forward, toward my desk. Keep extending them until you can rest your feet on the desktop. Thank you. That's very good, very accommodating."

Hardwick followed all these instructions with the relaxed seriousness of a man listening to a yoga instructor. Once his feet were propped up on the desk, Ashton leaned across from his side of it, reached under Hardwick's right cuff, and removed a Kel-Tec P-32 from its holster. He looked it over, hefted it in his hand, then placed it in the top desk drawer.

He sat again and smiled. "Ah, yes. Much better. Too many armed people in one room is a tragedy waiting to happen. Please, Detective, feel free to put your feet down. I think we can all relax, now that the order of things is clear."

Ashton looked at one of them and then at the other in an idle, amused way. "I must say it's turning into an absolutely fascinating day. So many . . . developments. And you, Detective Gurney, you've really had that little mind of yours in overdrive." Ashton's voice was purring with honeyed sarcasm. "Quite a lurid plot you've described. Sounds like a movie pitch. Scott Ashton, famous psychiatrist, murdered his wife in the presence of two hundred wedding guests. And all he had to tell her was, *'Shut your eyes tight.'* There never was a

Hector Flores. The bloody machete was a clever ruse. There was a cleaver in his pocket. A pseudo-accidental dive into the roses. A clever switch of suits in the bathroom. And so forth and so on. An ingenious conspiracy uncovered. A sensational murder case solved. Merchants of perversion exposed. The dead get their day of justice. The living live happily ever after. Is that about the size and shape of it?"

If he expected a reaction of shock or fear at his ability to summarize Gurney's conversation with Hardwick, he was disappointed. One of Gurney's strengths when blindsided was to react mildly but in a tone that was slightly off, a tone that might be appropriate to more secure circumstances. That's what he did now.

"That pretty much sums it up," he said simply. He showed no surprise that while Ashton was downstairs, he'd been listening in on their conversation—probably via a transmission to his earpiece from a hidden microphone. No—it was *definitely* a transmission to the earpiece. Gurney secretly kicked himself for not having noted the anomaly of Ashton's speaking on a handheld cell phone earlier on the chapel floor—indicating that his earpiece at that moment was being used for something else. It was painful that something so obvious had escaped his notice, but that kind of pain he would never show.

Gurney found the effect of his blasé response hard to measure. He hoped it had the jarring effect intended. Any speck of doubt he could toss into Ashton's grasp of the situation would be a plus.

Ashton shifted his gaze to Hardwick, whose eyes were on the pistol. Ashton shook his head as though admonishing a naughty child. "As they say in the movies, Detective, *don't even think about it.* I'd have three bullets in your chest before you got out of your chair."

Then he addressed Gurney in the same tone. "And you, Detective, you're like a fly that's found its way into the house.. You buzz around, you walk on the ceiling. Bzzzz. You see what you can see. Bzzzz. But you have no grasp of what you see. Bzzzz. Then SWAT! All that buzzing around—for nothing. All that searching and looking—all of it for nothing. Because you can't possibly understand what you see. How could you? You're nothing but a fly." He began to laugh, soundlessly.

Gurney knew that the strategic imperative was to create delay, to slow things down. If Ashton was the killer he appeared to be, the mind game would be what it usually was in such cases: a contest for the high ground of emotional control. So the practical agenda for Gurney now was to prolong it—to engage his opponent in the game and make it go on until a game-ending opportunity presented itself. He sat back in his chair and smiled. "But in this case, Ashton, the fly got it right, didn't he? You wouldn't have that gun in your hand if I hadn't gotten it right."

Ashton stopped laughing. *"Gotten it right?* The deductive mastermind is taking credit for having *gotten it right?* After I fed you all those little facts? The fact that some of our graduates were missing, the fact of the car arguments, the fact that the young ladies in question had all appeared in Karnala ads? If I hadn't been tempted to tease you—to make the contest interesting—you wouldn't have gotten any further than your moronic colleagues."

Now Gurney laughed. "Making the contest interesting had nothing to do with it. You knew that our next step would be to talk to former students, and all those facts would come to light immediately. So you weren't giving us a damn thing we wouldn't have gotten in another day or two ourselves. It was a pathetic effort to buy our trust with information you couldn't keep hidden." Gurney's reading of Ashton's expression—a frozen attempt at the appearance of equanimity—convinced him that he'd hit the target dead center. But sometimes in the management of a confrontation like this, there was such a thing as being *too* right, of scoring *too* direct a hit.

Ashton's next words gave him the awful feeling that this was one of those cases.

"There's no point in wasting any more time. I want you to see something. I want you to see how the story ends." He stood up and with his free hand dragged his heavy chair to a point near the open office door that formed a triangle with the large flat-screen monitor on the table behind his desk and the pair of chairs opposite the desk that were occupied by Gurney and Hardwick—a position with his back to the door from which he could observe the screen and them at the same time.

"Don't look at *me,"* said Ashton, pointing at the computer.

"Look at the screen. Reality TV. *Mapleshade: The Final Episode*. It's not the finale I'd intended to write, but in reality television one has to be flexible. Okay. We're all in our seats. The camera is running, the action is in progress, but I think we could use a little more light down there." He took the small lights-and-locks electronic remote from his pocket and pressed a button.

The chapel nave grew brighter, as rows of wall-sconce lamps were illuminated. There was a brief hiatus in the conversational hum as the girls in the discussion groups looked around at the lamps.

"That's better," said Ashton, smiling with satisfaction at the screen. "Considering your contribution, Detective, I want to be sure you can see everything clearly."

What contribution? Gurney wanted to ask. Instead he put his hand over his mouth and stifled a yawn. Then he glanced at his watch.

Ashton gave him a long, cool stare. "You won't be bored much longer." A swarm of minuscule tics migrated across his face. "You're an educated man, Detective. Tell me something: The medieval term *condign reparation*—do you know what it means?"

Strangely, he did. From a college philosophy class. Condign reparation: Punishment in perfect balance with the offense. Punishment of an ideally appropriate nature.

"Yes, I do," he answered, triggering a hint of surprise in Ashton's eyes.

And then, at the edge of his field of vision, he detected something else—a quickly moving shadow. Or was it the edge of a dark piece of clothing, a sleeve perhaps? Whatever it was, it had disappeared in the recess of the landing, where there would be barely enough room for a man to stand, just outside the office doorway.

"Then you may be able to appreciate the damage your ignorance has done."

"Tell me about it," said Gurney, with a look of increasing interest that he hoped would hide—better than his feigned yawn—the fear he was feeling.

"You have exceptional mental wiring, Detective. Quite an efficient brain. A remarkable calculator of vectors and probabilities."

This characterization was precisely the opposite of Gurney's current estimate of his capabilities. He wondered, with a nauseating chill, if Ashton's perception of his state of mind could be so keen that the observation was intended as a joke.

Gurney's own sense was that the brain that was responsible for his great professional victories was sliding sideways in the mud, losing traction and direction, as it strained to fit together so many things at once: The unreal Hector. The unreal Jykynstyl. The decapitated Jillian Perry. The decapitated Kiki Muller. The decapitated Melanie Strum. The decapitated Savannah Liston. The decapitated doll in Madeleine's sewing room.

Where was the center of gravity in all this—the place at which the lines of force converged? Was it here at Mapleshade? Or at the brownstone, tended by Steck's "daughters"? Or in some obscure Sardinian café where Giotto Skard might at that very moment be sipping bitter espresso—lurking like a wizened spider at the center of his web, where all the threads of his enterprises converged?

Unanswered questions were piling up fast.

And now a very personal one: Why had he, Gurney, failed to consider the possibility that the room might be bugged?

He'd always felt that the "death wish" concept was a grossly facile and overused paradigm, but now he wondered if it might not be the best explanation of his own behavior.

Or was his mental hard drive just too damn full of undigested details?

Undigested details, wobbly theories, and murders.

When all else fails, return to the present.

Madeleine's persistent advice: Be here, in the here and now. Pay attention.

Awareness of the moment: the holy grail of consciousness.

Ashton was in the middle of a sentence. ". . . tragicomic clumsiness of the criminal-justice system—which is neither just nor systematic, but surely criminal. When it comes to dealing with sex offenders, the system is inanely political and ludicrously inept. Of the offenders it catches, it helps none and makes the majority worse. It frees all those clever enough to fool the so-called professionals who evaluate them. It publishes public lists of sex offenders that are incomplete and useless. Under cover of this PR scam, *it turns snakes loose to devour children!"* He glared at Gurney, at Hardwick, at Gurney again. "This is the wretched system all your fine mental wiring, all your logic, all your investigative skill, all your intelligence ultimately serves."

It was a strange speech, thought Gurney, an elegant diatribe with the practiced ring of one delivered before, perhaps at conferences of his peers, yet it was animated by a palpable fury that was far from artificial. As he gazed into Ashton's eyes, he recognized this fury as an emotion he had seen before. He had seen it in the eyes of victims of sexual abuse. Most memorably, most vividly, he had seen it in the eyes of a fifty-year-old woman who was confessing to the ax murder of her seventy-five-year-old stepfather who had raped her when she was five.

Her defense in court was that she wanted to be sure her own granddaughter would have nothing to fear from him, that no one's granddaughter would have anything to fear from him. Her eyes were full of a wild, protective rage, and despite the efforts of her attorney to silence her, she went on to swear that the only desire she had left was to kill them all, every monster, every abuser, kill them all, chop them to pieces. As she was removed from the court, she was shouting, screaming, that she would wait at the doors of prisons and kill every offender who was released, every single one of them who was turned loose on the world. She'd use every last ounce of strength God gave her to "chop them to pieces!"

That's when Gurney caught a glimpse of the possible connection—the simple equation that might explain everything.

He spoke matter-of-factly, as if they'd been discussing the subject all evening. "There's no chance of Tirana ever being turned loose on anyone."

At first the man showed no reaction, seeming not to have heard the words Gurney had uttered, much less the accusations of murder they implied.

Behind Ashton on the dusky landing, however, Gurney detected another movement—more identifiably this time as a brown-clad arm and at the end of it a small reflective glint of something metallic. Then, as before, it was withdrawn into the shallow nook beyond the doorway.

Ashton's head until then had been tilted a little to the left. Now it pivoted, in the slowest-motion arc imaginable, to the right. He switched the pistol from his right hand to his left, which rested in his lap. He elevated his right hand tentatively to the side of his head, so that his fingertips lightly touched his ear and his temple, remaining there in a gesture that was both delicate and disconcerting. Combined with the angle of his head, it created the peculiar impression of a man listening for some elusive melody.

Eventually his eyes met Gurney's and he lowered his hand to the arm of his chair, at the same time raising the hand that held the pistol. A smile bloomed and faded on his face like some grotesque, short-lived flower. "You're such a clever, clever man."

The background murmur of voices emanating from the speakers in the monitor behind him grew louder, sharper.

Ashton seemed not to notice. "So clever, so perceptive, so eager to impress. Impress whom?, I wonder."

"Something's burning," Hardwick said in a loud, urgent voice.

"You're a child," Ashton went on, following his own train of thought. "A child who's learned a card trick and keeps showing it to the same people over and over, trying to re-create the reaction they had to it the first time."

"Something's goddamn burning!" Hardwick repeated, pointing at the screen.

Gurney was alternately watching the gun and the deceptively calm eyes of the man who held it. Whatever was happening on the screen would have to wait. He wanted Ashton to keep talking.

There was another movement on the landing, and a small man in a brown cardigan stepped slowly and quietly into the office doorway. It took Gurney's mind an extra second to register that it was Hobart Ashton.

Gurney purposely kept his eyes on Scott Ashton's gun. He wondered how much of what was happening, if anything, the father understood. What, if anything, did he intend to do? What accounted for the stealth of his approach? What knowledge or suspicion accounted for the caution with which he'd climbed the stairs and concealed himself on the landing? More urgently, could he see his son's gun from where he stood? Would he even understand what it meant?

How delusional was he? And perhaps *most* urgently, if the old man were to create, purposely or inadvertently, some momentary distraction, would it afford an opportunity for Gurney to launch himself across the room and get to the gun before Ashton could use it on him?

These desperate musings were interrupted by a sudden outburst.

"Shit! The chapel is on fire!" shouted Hardwick.

Gurney looked at the screen while staying peripherally aware of the positions of Scott Ashton and his father. On the screen, the video transmission clearly showed smoke coming from the sconce lamps on the chapel walls. The girls had either exited their seating areas or were in a hasty scramble to do so, congregating in the center aisle and on the raised platform nearest the camera position.

Gurney rose reflexively to his feet, followed by Hardwick.

"Careful, Detective," said Ashton, switching the pistol to his right hand and pointing it at Gurney's chest.

"Unlock the doors," commanded Gurney.

"Not right now."

"What the hell do you think you're doing?"

From the monitor came an eruption of screams. Gurney glanced back at it just in time to see one of the girls operating a fire extinguisher that had turned into a flame thrower, laying a stream of burning liquid along the length of one of the wooden pews. Another girl came running to the spot with another extinguisher—with the same result, a stream of liquid that ignited the moment it touched the existing fire. It was clear that the extinguishers had been tampered with to reverse their effect. It reminded Gurney of an arson murder in the Bronx twenty years earlier, where it was discovered later that one of the fire extinguishers in a small hardware store had been emptied and recharged with jellied gasoline—homemade napalm.

The chapel was now in a state of panic.

"Unlock those fucking doors, you fucking asshole!" Hardwick shouted at Ashton.

Ashton's father reached into the pocket of his sweater and withdrew something with a shiny end. As he unfolded a small blade from its handle, Gurney realized what it was—a simple pocketknife, the kind a Boy Scout might whittle a stick with. He held it at his side and stood, expressionlessly, his eyes on the high back of his son's chair.

Scott Ashton's gaze was fixed on Gurney. "This is not the finale I would have preferred, but it's the one your brilliant interference requires. It's the second-best solution."

"God, let them out of that room, you fucking maniac!" shouted Hardwick.

"I did my best," said Ashton calmly. "I had hopes. Each year a few were helped, but after a time I had to admit that most were not. Most left here as poisonous as the day they arrived, left us to go out into the world, poisoning and destroying others."

"There was nothing you could do about that," said Gurney.

"I didn't think so, either . . . until I was given my Mission and my Method. If someone chose to lead a poisonous life, then at least I could limit her exposure, limit the period of her toxicity to others."

The shouts and shrieks from the monitor speakers were growing more chaotic. Hardwick started moving toward Ashton with a black look on his face. Gurney put out his hand to hold him back, as Ashton raised his gun calmly, centering his aim on Hardwick's chest.

"For Christ's sake, Jack," said Gurney, "let's not provoke the bullet solution when we don't have any."

Hardwick stopped, his jaw muscles bulging.

Gurney offered Ashton an admiring smile. "Hence the 'gentlemen's agreement'?"

"Ah. Mr. Ballston has been talking."

"About Karnala, yes. I'd like to know more."

"You already know so much."

"Tell me the rest."

"It's a simple story, Detective. I came from a *dysfunctional family.*" He grinned hideously, managing to convey the nightmares buried in that most overused of all pop-psych terms. Tics moved through his lips like insects under the skin. "I was finally extricated, adopted, given an education. I was drawn to a certain kind of work. Mostly I failed. My patients continued to rape children. I didn't know what to do—until it occurred to me that my family connections provided a way to funnel the worst girls in the world

to the worst men in the world." He grinned again. "Condign reparation. A perfect solution." The grin faded. "Clever young woman
that she was, Jillian found out just a hair more than she should
have, overheard a few words of a phone conversation she shouldn't
have, pursued her unfortunate curiosity, became a possible threat to
the entire process. Of course, she never grasped the whole picture.
But she imagined she could leverage her morsel of knowledge into
some personal advantage. Marriage was her first demand. I knew it
wouldn't be her last. I addressed the situation in a way that I found
particularly satisfying. *Condignly* satisfying. For a time all was well.
Then you came along." He aimed the pistol at Gurney's face.

On the screen, two pews were in flames, flames were rising from
half the lamps, some of the drapes were smoldering. Most of the
girls were on the floor, some covering their faces, some trying to
breathe through torn pieces of their clothing, some crying, some
coughing, a few vomiting.

Hardwick appeared to be on the verge of an explosion.

"Then you came along," Ashton repeated. "Clever, clever David
Gurney. And this is the result." He waved his gun at the screen.
"Why didn't your cleverness tell you that this is the way it would
end? How else *could* it end? Did you really think I'd let them go? Is
clever, clever David Gurney really that stupid?"

Hobart Ashton took a few short steps to the back of his son's
chair.

Hardwick screamed, "This is your solution, Ashton? This is it,
you crazy fucker? Burn a hundred and twenty teenage girls to death?
This is your fucking solution?"

"Oh, yes, yes, yes, it is! You really thought when I was finally
trapped, I'd let them go?" Ashton's voice was rising now, out of control, hurtling at Gurney and Hardwick like a wild thing with a life
of its own. "You thought I'd turn a nest of snakes loose on all the
little babies of the world? These toxic things, these slimy, venomous
things! Demented, rotten, sucking, slimy things! These slither—"

It happened so quickly that Gurney almost thought he hadn't
seen it. The sudden flash of an arm around from the back of the
chair, a quick curving movement, and that was all—Ashton's rant
cut off in the middle of a word. Then the old man stepping quickly,

athletically to the side of the chair, grasping the barrel of Ashton's gun, pulling it away with a twisting yank and the disturbingly sharp crack of a finger bone. Ashton's head lolled forward on his chest, and his body began to tilt forward, curling downward, toppling onto the floor, collapsing sideways into a fetal position. It was then that the actual method of killing was made obvious by all the blood that began to pool around his throat.

Hardwick's jaw muscles bulged.

The little man in the brown cardigan wiped his pocketknife on the back cushion of the chair in which Ashton had been sitting, folded it deftly with one hand, and replaced it in his pocket.

Then he looked down at Ashton and, as if in benediction to his son's passing soul, said softly, "You're a piece of shit."

Chapter 78

All he had left

The intense revulsion Gurney had felt toward violence and blood as a rookie cop, especially the blood from a fatal wound, was something he had learned to contain and conceal during his twenty years in homicide. When he had to, he was able to cloak pretty effectively what he felt—or at least to wrap his horror in the semblance of mere distaste. Which is what he did now.

Commenting on the blood spreading out in a slow oval, being absorbed into the delicate intricacies of the Persian rug, he said, as if he were describing nothing more tragic than bird shit on a windshield, "What a fucking mess."

Hardwick blinked. He stared first at Gurney, then at the body on the floor, then at the fiery bedlam on the screen. He looked uncomprehendingly at Ashton's father. "The doors. Why don't you unlock the fucking doors?"

Gurney and the old man gazed at each other with an eerie lack of any visible concern. In past difficulties the ability to project an attitude of perfect calm had served Gurney well, given him an advantage. But that didn't seem to be the case now. The old man was radiating a quiet, brutal confidence. It was as though killing Ashton had brought him a deep peace and strength—as though an imbalance had finally been righted.

This was not a man with whom one could win a simple staring contest. Gurney decided to up the ante and change the rules. And he knew that he needed to do it quickly if anyone was going to get out of that building alive. It was time to take a wild swing.

"Reminds me of Tel Aviv," said Gurney, gesturing toward the screen.

The little man blinked and stretched his lips in a meaningless smile.

Gurney sensed that the wild swing had produced a solid hit. But now what?

Hardwick was staring at them with a bewildered fury.

Gurney continued to focus on the man with the gun. "Too bad you didn't come a little sooner."

"What?"

"Too bad you didn't come sooner. Like five months ago instead of three."

The little man looked honestly curious. "What's that to you?"

"You could've stopped that crazy shit with Jillian."

"Ah." He nodded slowly, almost appreciatively.

"Of course, if you'd intervened even sooner, back when you should have, everything would be different now. Better, I think, don't you?"

The little man continued nodding, but vaguely, without any apparent meaning. Then he frowned. "I don't know what you're talking about."

Gurney was seized by the sickening possibility that he was on the wrong track. But there was nowhere left to go except forward, no time left for thinking twice. So, then, forward with a vengeance. "Maybe you should've killed him a long time ago. Maybe you should've strangled him when he was born, before Tirana really sank her teeth into him. Little fucker was nuts from the beginning, like his mother, not a businessman like you."

Gurney searched the man's face for the slightest reaction, but his expression was no more communicative—or human—than the pistol in his hand. So once again there was nowhere to go but forward. "That's why you showed up here after the Jillian drama, right? Leonardo killing her was one thing, that could just be good business, but cutting her fucking head off at the wedding, that was . . . more than business. My guess is you came to keep an eye on things. Make sure that things were conducted in a more businesslike fashion. You didn't want the crazy little fucker fucking it all up. But, to be fair, Leonardo had some strong points. Smart. Imaginative. Right?"

Still no reaction beyond a dead stare.

Gurney went on. "You have to admit that the Hector idea was pretty good. Inventing the perfect fall guy in case anyone caught on to all those Mapleshade graduates being unlocatable. So the mythical Hector 'appeared on the scene' just before the girls started disappearing. That shows forward thinking on Leonardo's part. Real initiative. Good planning. But it came with a price. He was just too fucking crazy, wasn't he? That's why you finally had to do it. Backed into a corner. Crisis management." Gurney shook his head, looked with dismay at the huge bloodstain on the rug between them. "Too fucking little, Giotto. Too fucking late."

"The fuck did you call me?"

Gurney returned the man's granite stare for a long moment before answering, "Don't waste my time. I have a deal for you. You have five minutes to take it or leave it." He thought he saw a tiny crack in the stone. For maybe a quarter of a second.

"The fuck did you call me?"

"Giotto, get it through your head. It's over. The Skards are done. The Skards are fucking done. You get it? Clock's ticking. Here's the deal. You hand me the names and addresses of all Karnala's customers, all the Jordan Ballston creeps you do business with. I especially want the addresses where some Mapleshade girls might still be alive. You give me all that and I give you a guarantee that you will live through the process of being arrested."

The little man laughed, a sound like gravel being crushed under a blanket. "You got amazing balls, Gurney. You're in the wrong fucking business."

"Yeah, I know. You're down to four and a half minutes. Time fucking flies. So if you choose not to give me the addresses I want, here's what's going to happen: There will be a careful, by-the-book attempt to take you into custody. You, however, will foolishly try to escape. In doing so you will endanger the life of a police officer, making it necessary to shoot you. You will be shot twice. The first bullet, a nine-millimeter hollow-point, will blow your balls off. The second will sever your spinal cord between the first and second cervical vertebrae, resulting in irreversible paralysis. This combination of wounds will convert you into a soprano in a wheelchair in a prison hospital for the rest of your fucking life. It will also give your fellow inmates an opportunity to piss in your face whenever they feel the urge. Okay? You understand the deal?"

Again came the laugh. A laugh that would make Hardwick's nasty rasp sound sweet. "You know why you're still alive, Gurney? Because I can't fucking wait to hear what you're going to say next."

Gurney looked at his watch. "Three minutes and twenty seconds to go."

There were no voices coming from the monitor now—just moans, hacking coughs, a sharp little scream, crying.

"What the fuck?" said Hardwick. "Jesus, what the fuck?"

Gurney looked at the screen, listened to the piteous sounds, turned to Hardwick, spoke with deliberate clarity and evenness. "In case I forget, remember that the door opener is in Ashton's pocket."

Hardwick looked strangely at him, seeming to register the implication of his statement.

"Time is running out," Gurney added, turning toward Giotto Skard.

Again the old man laughed. He could not be bluffed. There would be no deal.

A girl's face appeared on the screen, half obscured by a tumble of blond hair, full of fear and fury, larger than life, distorted into ugliness by its closeness to the camera.

"You fuck!" the girl screamed, her voice cracking. "You fuck! You fuck! You fuck!" She began to cough violently, wheezing, hacking.

The cadaverous Dr. Lazarus appeared from behind an upended pew, crawling like a giant black beetle across the smoky floor.

Giotto Skard was watching the screen. Worse than emotionless, he seemed amused.

This minor distraction, Gurney concluded, was as good as it was going to get. This one last chance was all he had left.

There was no one to blame. No one to save him. His own decisions had brought him to this place. This most dangerous place in all his life. This narrow place, teetering on the edge of hell.

Gate of Heaven.

There was only one thing he could do.

He hoped it would be enough.

If it wasn't, he hoped that perhaps one day Madeleine would be able to forgive him.

Chapter 79

The last bullet

There was no course at the academy that adequately prepared you for being shot. Hearing it described by those who'd been through it gave you some idea, and seeing it happen added a certain disturbing dimension, but like most powerful experiences, the idea of it and the reality of it existed in two different worlds.

His plan, such as it was, conceived as it was in a second or two, was, like jumping out a window, simplicity itself. The plan was to launch himself directly at the little man with the gun, who was standing ten or twelve feet from him next to Ashton's empty chair just inside the open door. The hope was to smash into him with sufficient force to drive him backward through the doorway—the momentum carrying them both over the small landing and down the stone stairs. The price was getting shot, probably more than once.

As Giotto Skard watched the blond girl shrieking "Fuck!" Gurney hurled himself forward with a guttural roar, placing one arm across the heart area of his chest and the other across his forehead. Skard's .25-caliber pistol would not have great stopping power, except to those two areas, and Gurney was resigned to absorbing elsewhere whatever damage was necessary.

It was crazy, probably suicidal, but he saw no alternative.

The deafening report of the first shot in the small room came almost immediately. With a shocking impact, the bullet shattered Gurney's right wrist, which was pressed against the heart side of his breastbone.

The second bullet was a spike of fire through his stomach. The third was the bad one.

Neither here nor there.

An explosion of electricity. A blinding green spark, a spark like an exploding star. Screaming. A scream of terror and shock, screaming into a rage. The light is the scream, the scream is the light.

There is nothing. And there is something. At first it's hard to tell which is which.

A white expanse. Could be nothing. Could be a ceiling.

Somewhere below the white expanse, somewhere above him, a black hook. A small black hook extended like a beckoning finger. A gesture of vast meaning. Too vast for words. Everything now is too vast for words. He can't think of any words. Not a single one. Forgets what they are. Words. Small bumpy objects. Black plastic insects. Designs. Pieces of something. Alphabet soup.

From the hook hangs a colorless transparent bag. The bag is bulging with colorless transparent liquid. From the bag a transparent tube descends toward him. Like the neoprene gas tube on a model airplane in the park. He can smell the airplane fuel. He watches as the practiced flick of a deft forefinger on the propeller brings the little engine sputtering to life. The volume and pitch of the sound rises, the engine screaming, the scream building to a constant shriek. On the way home from the park, trailing his father, his taciturn father, he falls on a pile of stones. His knee is cut and bloody. The blood trickles down his shin onto his sock. He doesn't cry. His father looks happy, looks proud of him, later tells his mother about his great achievement, that he's reached an age where he doesn't have to cry anymore. It's a rare thing for his father to look at him with pride. His mother says, "For Godsake, he's only four, he's allowed to cry." His father says nothing.

He sees himself driving his car. A familiar Catskill road. A deer crossing ahead of him, a doe passing into the opposite field. And then her fawn following her, unexpectedly. The thump. Image of the twisted body, mother looking back, waiting in the field.

Danny in the gutter, the red BMW speeding away. The pigeon he was following into the street flying away. He was only four.

Nino Rota music. Poignant, ironic, giddy. Like a sad circus. Sonya Reynolds slowly dancing. The autumn leaves falling.

Voices.

"Can he hear us now?"
      "It's possible. The brain scans yesterday showed significant activity in all the sensory centers."
   "Significant? But . . . ?"
   "The patterns remain erratic."
   "Meaning?"
   "His brain shows evidence of normal function, but it comes and goes, and there's some evidence of sensory switching, which may be temporary. It's a bit like certain drug experiences, hallucinogenics, where sounds are seen and colors are heard."

"And the prognosis for that is . . . ?"

"Mrs. Gurney, with traumatic brain injuries . . ."

"I know you don't *know*. But what do you *think*?"

"I wouldn't be surprised if he recovered fully. I've seen cases in which a sudden spontaneous remission—"

"And you wouldn't be surprised if he didn't?"

"Your husband was shot in the head. It's remarkable that he's alive."

"Yes. Thank you. I understand. He may get better. Or he may get worse. And you really don't have a clue, do you?"

"We're doing as much as we can. When the brain swelling goes down, the situation may be clearer."

"You're sure he's not in pain?"

"He's not in pain."

Heaven.

Warmth and coolness bathed him like the inflow and ebbing of a wave or a shifting summer breeze.

Now the coolness had the scent of dewy grass and the warmth carried the subtle scent of tulips in the sun.

The coolness was the coolness of his sheet, and the warmth was the warmth of women's voices.

Warmth and coolness were combined in the soft pressure of lips against his forehead. A wonderful sweetness and gentleness.

Judgment.

New York County Criminal Court. A crappy courtroom, bleak, colorless. The judge a cartoon of exhaustion, cynicism, and faulty hearing.

"Detective Gurney, the accusations are voluminous. How do you plead?"

He can't speak, can't respond, can't even move.

"Is the defendant present?"

"No!" cries a chorus of voices in unison.

A pigeon rises from the floor, disappears in the smoky air.

He wants, tries, to speak, to prove he is there, but he can't speak, can't utter a word or move a finger. He strains to force even a syllable, even a gagging cry from his throat.

The room is on fire. The judge's robe is smoldering. He announces, wheezing, "The defendant is remanded for an indefinite period to the place where he is, which shall be reduced in size, until such time as the defendant is dead or insane."

H*ell.*

He's standing in a windowless room, a cramped room with stale air and an unmade bed. He looks for the door, but the only door opens into a closet, a closet just inches deep, a closet backed by a concrete wall. He's having trouble breathing. He bangs on the walls, but the bang isn't a bang; it's a flash of fire and smoke. Then, by the side of the bed, he sees a slit in the wall and in the slit a pair of eyes watching him.

Then he's in the space behind the wall, the space from which the eyes were watching, but the slit is gone and the space is totally dark. He tries to calm himself. Tries to breathe slowly, evenly. He tries to move, but the space is too small. He can't raise his arms, can't bend his knees. And he topples sideways, crashing to the floor, but the crash isn't a crash; it's a scream. He can't move the arm beneath his body, can't raise himself. The space is narrower there, nothing will move. An accelerating terror makes it almost impossible to breathe. If only he could make a sound, speak, cry out.

Far away the coyotes begin to howl.

. . .

L *ife.*

"Are you sure he can hear me?" Her voice was pure hope.
"What I can tell you for sure is that the activity pattern I'm seeing on the scan is consistent with the neural activity of hearing." His voice was as cool as a sheet of paper.

"Is it possible that he's paralyzed?" Her voice was at the edge of darkness.

"The motor center wasn't directly affected, so far as we can see. However, with injuries of this sort . . ."

"Yes, I know."

"All right, Mrs. Gurney. I'll leave you with him."

"David," she said softly.
He still couldn't move, but the panic was evaporating, somehow diluted and dispersed by the sound of the woman's voice. The enclosure that held him, whatever it was, no longer crushed him.

He knew the woman's voice.

With her voice came the image of her face.

He opened his eyes. At first he saw nothing but light.

Then he saw her.

She was looking at him, smiling.

He tried to move, but nothing moved.

"You're in a cast," she said, "Relax."

Suddenly he remembered the mad dash across the room at Giotto Skard, the first deafening shot.

"Is Jack all right?" he asked in a hoarse whisper.

"Yes."

"Are you all right?"

"Yes."

Tears filled his eyes, blurring her face.

After a while his memory expanded backward. "The fire . . . ?"

"Everyone got out."

"Ah. Good. Good. Jack found the . . . ?" He couldn't remember the word.

"The remote lock thing, yes. You reminded him to look in Ashton's pocket." She made an odd little laughing, choking, sobbing sound.

"What was that all about?"

"It just flashed through my mind that 'Look in Ashton's pocket' might have been your last words."

He started to laugh but immediately cried out from the pain in his chest, then started to laugh again and cried out again. "Oh, God, no, no, don't make me laugh." Tears were streaming down his cheeks. His chest ached dreadfully. He was becoming exhausted.

She leaned toward him and wiped his eyes with a crumpled tissue.

"What about Skard?" he asked, his voice hardly audible now.

"Giotto? You made as big a mess of him as he made of you."

"Stairs?"

"Oh, yes. Probably the first time he'd ever been thrown down a flight of stairs by a man he'd already shot three times."

There was so much in her voice, so many vying emotions, but he detected in that rich mixture an element of innocent pride. It made him laugh. The tears came again.

"Rest now," she said. "People are going to be lining up to talk to you. Hardwick told everyone at BCI everything that happened, and everything you discovered about who was who and what was what, and he told them what an incredible hero you were and how many lives you saved, but they're eager to hear it all from you personally."

He said nothing for a while, trying to reach out as far as his memory would take him. "When did you talk to them?"

"Exactly two weeks ago today."

"No, I mean about the . . . the Skard business, and the fire."

"Two weeks ago today. The day it happened, the day I got back from New Jersey."

"Jesus. You mean . . . ?"

"You've been a little out of it." She paused, her eyes filling suddenly with tears, her breath coming in shaky gasps. "I almost lost you," she said, and as she said it, something wild and desperate swept across her face, something he'd never seen before.

Chapter 80

The light of the world

"Is he asleep?"

"Not really asleep. Just sort of dazed and dozing. They put him on a temporary Dilaudid drip to reduce the pain. If you talk to him, he'll hear you."

It was true. He smiled at the truth of it. But the drug did more than reduce the pain. It obliterated it in a wave of . . . of what? A wave of . . . okayness. He smiled at the okayness of it.

"I don't want to disturb him."

"Just say what you have to say. He'll hear you perfectly well, and it won't disturb him."

He knew the voices. The voices of Val Perry and Madeleine. Beautiful voices.

Val Perry's beautiful voice: "David? I came to thank you." There was a long silence. The silence of a distant sailboat crossing a blue horizon. "I guess that's all I really have to say. I'm leaving an envelope for you. I hope it's enough. It's ten times the amount we agreed on. If it's not enough, let me know." Another silence. A small sigh. The sigh of a breeze over a field of orange poppies. "Thank you."

He couldn't tell where his body ended and the bed began. He couldn't even tell if he was breathing.

Then he was awake, looking up at Madeleine.

"It's Jack," she was saying. "Jack Hardwick from BCI. Can you talk to him? Or shall I tell him to come back tomorrow?"

He looked past her at the figure in the doorway, saw the gray crew cut, the ruddy face, the ice-blue malamute eyes.

"Now is good." Something about the need to make sense with Hardwick, to focus, began to clear his thought process.

She nodded, stepped aside, as Hardwick came to the bed. "I'm going downstairs for some horrible coffee," she said. "I'll be back in a little while."

"You know," Hardwick rasped after she left the room, raising a bandaged hand, "one of those fucking bullets went right through you and hit me."

Gurney looked at the hand, didn't see much damage. He remembered how Marian Eliot had referred to Hardwick: *a smart rhinoceros*. He started to laugh. Apparently the Dilaudid drip had been reduced enough that the laugh hurt. "You have any news that I might care about?"

"You're cold, Gurney, very cold." Hardwick shook his head in mock distress. "You aware that you broke Giotto Skard's back?"

"When I pushed him down the stairs?"

"You didn't *push* him down the stairs. You *rode* him down the stairs like he was a fucking sled. Result being that he ended up in that paraplegic wheelchair you'd been threatening him with. And I guess then he started thinking about that other little unpleasantness you mentioned—the possibility of his fellow inmates taking the occasional piss in his face. So, bottom line, cut to the chase, he made a deal with the DA for life without parole with guaranteed medical separation from the general prison population."

"What kind of deal?"

"He gave us the addresses of Karnala's *special* customers. The ones who liked to go all the way."

"And?"

"And some of the girls we found at those addresses were . . . still alive."

"That was the deal?"

"Plus, he had to turn in the rest of the organization. Immediately."

"He turned in his other two sons?"

"Without a second thought. Giotto Skard is not a sentimental man."

Gurney smiled at the understatement.

Hardwick went on. "But I got a question for you. Given how . . . practical . . . he is about his business affairs, and how crazy Leonardo was, why didn't Giotto do away with him the first time he heard about those peculiar little beheading requests that Leonardo was inserting into Karnala's customer transactions?"

"Easy. *Don't kill the goose that lays the golden eggs.*"

"The goose being Leonardo, aka Dr. Scott Ashton?"

"Ashton was big in his field . . . drawing card at Mapleshade. Kill him, the school might close . . . cut off a ready supply of sick young women." Gurney's eyes drifted shut momentarily. "Not something . . . not something Giotto would want to happen."

"Then why kill him at the end?"

"All unraveling . . . going up in smoke, you might say. No more . . . golden eggs."

"You okay, hotshot? You sound a little fuzzy."

"Never better. Without the golden eggs . . . the crazy goose . . . becomes a liability. Risk-reward thing. In the chapel Giotto finally saw Leonardo as all risk, no reward. Scale tipped . . . Greater benefit in killing him than keeping him alive."

Hardwick emitted a thoughtful grunt. "A very practical madman."

"Yes." After a long silence, Gurney asked, "Giotto turn in anyone else?"

"Saul Steck. We went in with some NYPD boys, found him in that Manhattan brownstone. Unfortunately, he shot himself before we could get to him. Interesting thing about Steck, by the way. Remember I told you about his stint in a psychiatric hospital after his arrest years ago on multiple rape charges? Guess who the consulting psychiatrist was in the hospital's sex-offender rehabilitation program?"

"Ashton?"

"The very same. Guess he got to know Saul pretty well— decided he had enough potential to make an exception to the Skard family-only rule. When you think about it, the man was a damn good judge of character. Could spot a useful psychopathic scumbag a mile away."

"You find out who Saul's 'daughters' were?"

"Maybe new Mapleshade grads doing an internship? Who knows? They were gone when we got there, and I'd be damn surprised if they reappeared."

This sounded to Gurney like some form of reassurance, but even in his gentle Dilaudid haze it didn't entirely reassure him. The feeling created an awkward silence. Finally Gurney asked, "You find anything of interest on the premises?"

"Of interest? Oh, yeah, definitely. Lots of interesting videos. Young ladies describing their favorite activities in detail. Some sick shit. *Very* sick shit."

Gurney nodded. "Anything else?"

Hardwick raised his arms in an exaggerated shrug. "Might have been. Who knows? You do your best to keep track of everything. But sometimes stuff just disappears. Never gets inventoried. Gets accidentally destroyed. You know how it is."

Neither of them said anything for a few seconds.

Hardwick looked thoughtful, then amused. "You know, Gurney, you're a more fucked-up guy than most people realize."

"Aren't we all?"

"Hell no! Take me, for example. I *appear* totally fucked up. But inside I'm a rock. A finely tuned, well-balanced machine."

"If you're well balanced..." Normally Gurney could have ended the sentence with a smart rebuttal, but the Dilaudid was getting in the way, and his voice just trailed off.

The two men held each other's gaze for a moment longer, and then Hardwick took a step toward the door. "Well, I'll be seeing you around, okay?"

"Sure."

He started to leave, then turned back for a moment. "Relax, Sherlock. Everything's cool."

"Thanks, Jack."

. . .

Sometime after Hardwick left, Madeleine returned to the room, carrying a small container of coffee. Wrinkling her nose at it, she laid it on a metal table in the corner.

Gurney smiled. "Not very good?"

She didn't answer. Instead she came to the side of the bed and took both of his hands in hers and held them tightly.

She stood there next to him, just like that, holding his hands, for a long while.

It could have been a minute or an hour. He couldn't tell.

All he was truly aware of was her steady, perceptive, loving smile—the smile that was hers alone.

It enveloped him, warmed him, delighted him like nothing else on earth.

He was amazed that anyone who saw everything so clearly, who had all the light of the world in her eyes, saw in him something worthy of such a smile.

It was a smile that could make a man believe that life was good.

Acknowledgments

When I finished my first novel, *Think of a Number*, I had the extraordinary good fortune to be represented by a remarkable agent, Molly Friedrich—along with her wonderful associates, Paul Cirone and Lucy Carson.

My good fortune was confirmed when the book was acquired by Crown's Rick Horgan, a marvelous editor.

Today I continue to be blessed by the guidance and support of these honest, smart, and talented people. Their ideal combination of perceptive criticism and heartening enthusiasm made my new novel, *Shut Your Eyes Tight,* better in every way.

Rick, Molly, Paul, Lucy—thank you!

About the Author

After a successful career in the advertising industry, John Verdon retired with his wife, Naomi, to the rural mountains of upstate New York—an ironically tranquil environment for creating the Dave Gurney series of thrillers.